THE
TWELFTH
STONE

SAMUEL BAVLI

TAMBORA BOOKS

PROLOGUE

As the sun set in the western sky, the prophet sat upon a rock a hundred paces outside the city gate. The richness of his priestly garments and the pure whiteness of his well-groomed beard contrasted with the wretchedness of his demeanor. Resting his left cheek on his palm, he sat with eyes cast downward as he probed the great abyss of sorrow that welled up in his bosom. In the mists of his prophetic vision, the city was in flames. The walls and battlements were toppling in the fury of the fire; the smoke was rising up to heaven, darkening the sky; and in the distance, a lone figure with a golden crown upon his head was fleeing from the burning city, covering his eyes.

Belying the physical reality of the city walls that stood intact not far behind him, the old man could feel the heat radiating from the conflagration of his prophetic vision. He smelled the smoke; he heard the screams of dying men and women; he heard the exultant cheering of the enemy and the cries of captives being led away in chains. He saw the image of the king of Babylon standing amidst the burning city, his blood-drenched sword outstretched in victory.

"Is this Jerusalem that I see burning?" the prophet asked with quivering voice. Slowly he raised his eyes, gazing into the emptiness of space. There was nobody within earshot, and the wind carried the prophet's words away.

"You have seen well, Jeremiah," said the voice, enveloping the prophet in its majesty. "Jerusalem has failed to heed my many warnings, and for her iniquity she must fall."

"My Lord, when will this be?" cried the prophet.

The voice thundered in the prophet's mind. "Before this year is out, the city will be in ruins, and my Holy Temple will be no more upon the earth. My people and their king will be led away in chains, captives of the king of Babylon. Long will they sit in a foreign land, weeping for their grandeur that was lost."

"Is there, then, no hope?"

"Despair not, Jeremiah," said the voice. "For I will still be with them in their exile. I will not abandon them through all their suffering, and some day they shall return again in joy to their own land.

"But now I have a mission for you, Jeremiah. Go you to the Temple, and tell the high priest what you have seen in prophecy. Bid him give you his breastplate with the twelve precious stones set within it. The power of the breastplate is great, and it must not fall into the hands of enemies. I will show you where to hide it, and there it will remain until the distant future, when, in another time of suffering, my people will need its power to avert disaster. Go now, Jeremiah, and do my bidding quickly, for there is much that you must do."

PART I

CHAPTER 1

A s night fell and the stars came out, the full moon rising in the eastern sky glowed an orange-red: an evil portent, some would say. But few were there who saw that sight, for the streets of Camryn were deserted, but for one lone figure, a black-garbed friar, his visage hidden in his cowl to protect him from the wind. As he walked through the narrow, dirt-paved streets, he slowed his pace, looking at the numerous Jewish homes. He paused in front of one home, and his gaze fixed on a small crack in the shuttered window, through which he saw the house aglow with the light of Sabbath candles and heard the sounds of fervent, radiant song. Then quickly he turned the corner, speeding up, heading towards the church where his eager audience waited.

Camryn was home to twenty Jewish families, all of whom lived in the southwest corner of the village, adjoining Sherwood Forest. Near the center of the Jewish community was the synagogue, and just a short distance southward down the street was the home of Isaac the merchant.

Isaac, dressed in a white robe, sat in a tall wooden armchair at the head of a large table covered with a white tablecloth and adorned with beautifully-wrought silver utensils, while Isaac's wife and three children sat on benches on either side. In the center of the table stood a silver candelabra, the flames of its four candles dancing to the cadence of Isaac's melodious voice. For tonight was not just the Sabbath but the start of Passover, the Jewish holiday of redemption, a night on which Jews throughout the world recounted the Biblical story of the Exodus from Egypt more than twenty centuries ago.

Holding the silver wine cup in his right hand, Isaac recited: "In every generation, our foes rise up against us seeking to destroy us, but the Lord God saves us from their hands." There was a tremor in Isaac's voice, and some wine spilled as he put down his cup. Joseph, his oldest son, was staring at him intently.

"What is it, Joseph?"

"Nothing, Father."

"What is on your mind? What were you about to say?"

"Where was God at York?" Joseph asked in an undertone, biting his lip. "Why did he not save us from the murderers?"

Joseph's mother appeared as though she had been struck. "Joseph!" she said. "You mustn't talk that way."

Joseph's eyes shifted to his mother. "Why not?" he asked, gaining courage. "They are all dead, aren't they? All the Jews of York: all two hundred of them, murdered, massacred! And it was just one week ago."

Isaac was about to say something, but Joseph turned on him again. "God doesn't always save us, does he?"

Isaac looked at Joseph. A tear trickled down the corner of Isaac's eye. "Yes," he said softly; "it pains me also." And, in a voice almost inaudible, he added: "You know, my father's brother lived in York."

No one spoke as Isaac slowly uncovered the unleavened bread and took his wine cup in his hand again. "Tonight is a holiday, a day of celebration. So let us, then, continue."

But Isaac did not continue. For as he finished speaking, a shout was heard from somewhere in the distance, a shriek of terror that pierced the night. Joseph froze, his gaze fixed on the front door; Joseph's mother gasped and gathered her two younger children in her arms; and Isaac's hand again began to tremble, though he uttered not a sound.

Outside in the street, a voice rose up, deep and sonorous: "My fellow Christians, cast the demons from your midst. Root out the vile contamination that mars the sanctity of your village. Whilst you prepare for Easter Sunday two days hence, Satan walks among you in your very streets, and Satan's agents mock you as they celebrate their vile holiday. Do you not hear their laughter? Do you not feel their hatred? Do you not know with what contempt they hold our Lord Jesus Christ and all who follow him? Rise up, good people; avenge your lord who died upon the cross; and purge your village of the evil that dwells amongst you. Christ commands it!"

Isaac rose from his chair, quickly whispering a prayer under his breath. Joseph's mother jumped up, toppling her bench. "Come quickly, Joseph," she commanded as she hustled her two younger children from the table.

To the loud crashing sound of splintering wood, the door burst open, revealing a large man brandishing a sword, and a large black cross emblazoned on his chest. As he advanced towards Isaac, four other men scrambled over the fallen door, each armed with sword or spear or dagger. And behind them strode a friar dressed in black, his hooded face serene, his chiseled features shimmering eerily in the light of the guttering torch he carried in his hand.

Joseph was under the table now, watching helplessly from beneath the long white table cloth. He wanted to rush forth and help his father. But he knew he was just a boy, unarmed, defenseless. What could he do against a seasoned warrior? And so, he watched, paralyzed by terror.

The burly man who wore the cross held Isaac in a steel-like grip. He held his sword aloft. "Jew, accept the cross or die."

"It is too late for that," the friar said. "He is Satan's minion. His soul is damned already."

Isaac spat at the man who held him, and the spittle landed on the man's tunic, in the center of the cross. The man drew back his sword-arm, prepared to thrust.

"Not yet," the friar shouted, shifting his gaze, and the man stayed his hand.

One of the other men dragged Joseph's mother forward by her hair. Pushing her with his body against the armchair at the head of the table, the man jerked her head backwards, exposing her throat.

Joseph almost screamed, but only a muffled whimper escaped his lips. For a second, he feared the sound had given him away. But simultaneously with Joseph's whimper, Isaac had shouted, "No!" And Joseph's voice appeared to go unnoticed.

The man pulled harder on Joseph's mother's hair, jerking her head still farther backwards. Joseph cringed at his mother's pain, and in his heart he heard her scream, a scream that resonated through his very being. And yet, he knew, his mother hadn't screamed at all, except within his mind.

His mother closed her eyes. She opened her mouth. Her lips moved. "The Lord is one," he heard her whisper as a blade was drawn across her throat. Her body slumped in the man's arms, and Joseph could no longer see his mother's face; but briefly he heard a gurgling sound escape her throat, and he saw a dark red stain spread rapidly over her beautiful white Sabbath dress.

Tears trickled down Joseph's cheek, and yet he watched, transfixed. The man released his hold on Joseph's mother and let her limp body fall to the floor. The man turned, and for the first time Joseph saw his features. Joseph recognized the man: it was his next-door neighbor, Alfred the blacksmith.

Joseph reeled. A wave of nausea almost overcame him. He wanted to strike at the blacksmith, to avenge his mother's murder. But what could he do against this great brute of a man? He wanted to run, but he was too scared to move. He could only watch, in horror.

Isaac squirmed as a sword pierced his side, but he made no sound.

The friar made the sign of the cross while holding his torch in front of Isaac's face. The friar's voice was calm and yet compelling. "With your swords and spears you must release the devil from his body. Five times. That's right. Do not kill him outright, but pierce his body deeply. Five times you must stab him, in commemoration of the wounds inflicted on our Lord. Five times only: no more, no less. Then leave him. Let him bleed to death."

Each of the men took his turn stabbing Isaac, and Alfred delivered the final blow while another man held Isaac tightly in his grip. Alfred pulled his sword out of Isaac's flank, waved the bloody tip tauntingly before Isaac's eyes, and spat in Isaac's face. Alfred laughed and turned away. The other man let go, and Isaac slumped to the floor, blood flowing from his wounds.

Alfred seized the chair against which he had pinioned Joseph's mother. Raising the chair above his head, he brought it smashing down upon the table. The sound reverberated through the room, shaking Joseph out of his reverie. He knew he must not wait one moment longer, lest he be discovered. Alfred no doubt soon would notice Joseph's absence.

Joseph began to crawl away from the light. As he emerged from underneath the table, he noticed that the Sabbath candles on the table were now extinguished, and there was no other light besides the friar's torch.

"Brother Peter!" a voice called from the adjoining room. "Over here. They almost got away." Then a scream – a girl's voice – Joseph's sister.

The light of the torch receded, and darkness enveloped Joseph.

"No. Please, no!" his sister screamed. Joseph froze. His sister's sobbing tore at his heart. He began to turn, following the light of the friar's torch.

The friar's voice resonated from the next room: "That's only two of them. Where is the oldest one? You mustn't let him get away."

Listening intently, Joseph no longer heard his sister's voice, and he knew he hadn't heard his little brother's voice at all. He broke out in a cold sweat, and he felt his heart beating wildly in his chest. He wanted to help his sister and his brother, but he restrained himself.

Suddenly, he heard his mother's voice resounding in his head: "Run, my Joseph, run. Do not look back. Run, and save yourself."

Joseph ran to the fallen front door. Momentarily he hesitated. He heard his father's labored breathing in the room behind him, but he did not look back. With a heavy heart, he ran into the street.

"Joseph!" called a whispered voice.

Joseph froze. He was disoriented. Frightened. No, that was not his mother's voice this time. It was a male voice. An enemy. He must run away. But he could not. He felt dizzy, faint.

"Joseph, over here. Quickly. Come."

Joseph turned to his left. It was Matthew, the blacksmith's son. Joseph turned his head away and tried to run from Matthew. He tripped and almost fell. Matthew caught him in his arms.

"Hurry, Joseph. You cannot stay here in the moonlight. You will be discovered."

Joseph struggled with Matthew. "I must run. Let me go. They will kill me."

But Matthew would not let go. Though not yet eighteen years of age, and only a few months older than Joseph, Matthew was big and muscular like his father, and Joseph felt his own strength ebbing as Matthew dragged him up the street.

Joseph tried to speak again, but Matthew cut him off. "There are people all around. You will not escape. You've got to trust me, Joseph. We're still friends, aren't we?"

They were now in front of Matthew's home. Matthew led Joseph around the house to the stable. He opened the stable door and shoved Joseph inside. "Stay here," he commanded. "And do not leave until I come for you."

The door closed, leaving him in darkness, sprawled on the floor where Matthew had pushed him. Not far from him in the darkness, Joseph heard a horse stirring. He held his breath and hoped the horse would not make noise.

He felt something brush by his leg – something small and furry. He nearly screamed. Sweat poured down his face. He tried to rise, but a wave of nausea and dizziness overcame him, and he remained where he was, waiting in silent dread.

*   *   *

Matthew ran back to Joseph's house and arrived just as Alfred was coming out the door, his sword bloody.

Matthew stopped short a few feet from Alfred. "Father, what is happening? What have you done in there?"

Alfred raised his sword and looked at it with pride. "I stabbed that devil's-spawn. I and the others, we stabbed him. Five times we stabbed him, just as Friar Peter told us to. Released the demons from his body. He's still alive, but not for long, I reckon. I killed his bitch, slit her throat I did. The Devil take 'em both."

Matthew crossed himself.

"It's well you do that, son. Guard against the Evil Eye. You know those Jews cast the Evil Eye on us Christians. Their souls be damned."

The black-cloaked friar now emerged from Joseph's house, followed by the other men. The friar's face was drawn. "One has gotten away – the eldest. He's nowhere to be found inside. It's most important that we find him."

Matthew's face brightened. "Do you mean Joseph? I thought I saw him run by, but I'm not quite sure. He didn't see me. He was running north past our house, up the street to the synagogue."

Alfred quickly wiped his sword and sheathed it. He gave Matthew a fond clap on his shoulder, turned northwards, and began to run. The friar, walking briskly, followed Alfred.

*　　*　　*

Joseph heard shouting outside, and the jarring sound of splintering wood. He crept to the stable door and opened it a crack. He saw torchlight flickering in the street. He saw a neighbor dragged from his home and beaten to unconsciousness. He heard the sound of running feet and saw the lights receding. Farther up the street, he saw the synagogue in flames. He smelled the smoke and saw it billowing to heaven from the burning house of worship. As he watched, the flames rose even higher. He heard the roaring of the conflagration. He heard the cheering of the crowd that had gathered around the synagogue to watch. And above the din he heard one voice that would forever be engraved upon his heart: the voice of the man who had inflamed the people with his words and brought about this night of terror for the Jews of Camryn. It was the strident voice of the black-cloaked friar, who was known to his votaries as Peter the Pious.

Joseph closed the stable door again. For a long time, he lay in the darkness, listening. The shouting in the streets was distant now, and Joseph could no longer hear the friar's voice. Joseph slowly rose to his feet. He took a step forward, and then another step. The nausea had abated, and he no longer felt faint.

Suddenly the door flew open, and a large figure stood in the moonlight. Joseph felt his heart skip a beat before he recognized Matthew's face. Signaling Joseph to be silent, Matthew pulled Joseph outside. He closed the stable door and beckoned Joseph to follow him. Then he turned right and began to run southwards down the street.

Joseph followed, running as quickly as he could, just barely keeping up with Matthew. As he passed his own home, he looked through the open doorway, and all was dark inside. Lifeless. Beyond his house, there were bodies lying in the street: bodies of friends, acquaintances, people he had seen alive just yesterday or earlier today. He wanted to cry, but he could not. He wanted

to scream, to rail at God for allowing this to happen. But he had
no strength to scream. All he could do was run and save himself,
following Matthew: first south, then west, to the edge of town.

At the border of the forest, Matthew stopped. He took the
package that he had been carrying and thrust it into Joseph's
hands. "Take it," he said. "It's food."

Joseph began to say something, but Matthew interrupted:

"Yes, I know, it's Passover, and you can't eat our food. I tried
not to pack anything that's really forbidden for you. I hope I got
it right. But this is life-or-death. So eat when you are hungry,
and live. For my sake. So I can atone for my father's sin, and
for my own."

Joseph put his arms around Matthew. Joseph's tears now ran
freely as he released his embrace. "Thank you, Matthew," he said.

"Fare thee well, my friend. Now go, and God be with you."

*　　*　　*

Isaac lay on the floor, trying to cling to consciousness, to life.
He knew he had very little time. Through excruciating pain and
waning strength, he tried to pray. Each breath was labored, raspy.

He looked around the room. It seemed brighter now. Perhaps,
he thought, the moonlight was shining through the doorway.
How he would like to see the moon in its full splendor! The
moon – symbol of King David's reign. Slowly, Isaac moved his
lips, pronouncing the Blessing of the Moon: "David, King of
Israel, is alive and enduring."

Slowly Isaac turned his head, and, framed in the doorpost by
the moonlight, he caught a glimpse of a man in a hooded cloak.
For a moment he thought it was the friar, and he shuddered. But
no, this man was taller; his cloak was tattered, and light in color.

The man approached. In his hand he held a weathered cane,
but he seemed to move with ease despite the walking stick. He
stood in the moonlight and bent down toward Isaac. His face
was hidden in his hood.

Isaac tried to raise his head. "Are you the angel of death?" he asked. "Have you come for me?"

"No, Isaac, I am not he."

"But he is here with you."

The man nodded. "Yes, he is here indeed. I feel his presence, and I hear his wings. But he will wait a while until I finish."

The man pulled back his hood, and the moonlight shone on him. His face was long; his eyes were green and penetrating; his hoary beard was long but neatly trimmed.

Surprisingly, Isaac felt a small degree of strength returning, and he could speak with greater ease. "I know you," Isaac said. "You are Enoch."

The man smiled. "Yes," he said.

Through a mist of memory, Isaac recalled this man's previous visits. Twice before, Isaac had encountered him, the first time many years ago. And yet, Enoch seemed no older after all those many years. Indeed, apart from his white beard, Enoch's facial features appeared surprisingly youthful.

Isaac coughed. He drew a labored breath and spoke in gasps. "Has any of my family survived?"

"One. Joseph has escaped."

"Then, Enoch, swear to me that you will keep him safe. This I ask of you before I die."

"That is my purpose here, and I will do whatever is in my power to guard your son. This I swear to you."

Isaac closed his eyes. He tried to think, but his mind was numb. Something, some forgotten matter of great import, nudged at him. He struggled to remember it but couldn't.

He opened his eyes again. "That is your purpose here, you said."

"Yes."

"But you have another purpose also." He clutched Enoch's sleeve.

Enoch nodded. "Yes."

All at once, the memory returned, and Isaac knew what he must do. He dropped his hand from Enoch's sleeve and undid the sash around his waist. He placed his hand inside his robe. He felt the leather pouch hanging from a cord. It comforted him to know the murderers had not taken it. But, of course, he reasoned, they would not have known to search for it or even known of its existence. He held it in his hand a moment and then undid the clasp that fastened it to his robe.

"See. I have not forgotten what you told me when I saw you last. Tonight at midnight I would have shown it to my son." Trembling, he held it out to Enoch.

Enoch took the pouch. "I will guard it well," he said. "Now, Isaac, be at peace."

Enoch stood, put on his hood, and turned to go. Isaac's vision dimmed; his breathing slowed; and he remembered nothing more.

CHAPTER 2

Joseph stopped to catch his breath. He had been running for several minutes, and he was now deep in the forest. The underbrush was thick, making it difficult to run. He leaned against a tree, exhausted.

An owl hooted in the distance. Joseph listened to the sounds of the forest, which were simultaneously both comforting and frightening. He heard the sound of flowing water before he saw the stream wending its way among the trees just several paces from where he stood. Cautiously, furtively, he approached the stream. He looked around in all directions, bent down, and drank.

Having drunk his fill, he moved back into the thicket, found a large rock, and sat down on the ground, his back against the rock. He knew he should be moving on, but some inner need prevented him. He felt numb, in limbo. In one brief moment his entire world had been snuffed out, and he was homeless, orphaned, friendless. Abandoned.

Again the owl hooted, closer than before. But in the distance Joseph still could hear the sounds of Camryn echoing through the forest: the din of the mob and the screaming of the hapless victims. And those sounds told him that he was not yet safe, not yet far enough away.

He began to rise, steeling himself for what lay ahead. He paused to get his bearings, looking at the stars that flickered in and out amidst the leaves and branches of the trees.

A shriek of terror reverberated through the forest. It was a female voice, somewhere in the distance. And the forest answered, with the flapping of wings and the rustling of trees.

A large animal, perhaps a deer, scuttled through the bushes far away.

Joseph crouched in the thicket, on his guard. Silence, unnerving silence filled the air. He waited, listened. And again the screaming rent the silence of the night. It was closer now, much closer, approaching rapidly.

*   *   *

Rachel ran as fast as she could, but she knew it was not fast enough. Nimbly she jumped over fallen tree limbs. She made sharp turns, first left, then right. But the man was gaining ground. Her legs were tiring. She had lost her shoes. Her chest was heaving, and it hurt to breathe.

Rachel stumbled, almost fell. The man caught her by the wrist. Terror welled up from her very core. She grasped with her free hand at a hanging branch, and, as the man advanced, she let it go. The branch snapped back and hit him in the face. Startled, the man released his grip.

She bounded forward, gaining ground, but the man recovered quickly and resumed pursuing her. Soon she felt his presence close behind her. She heard him grunt. He swiped at her, but she dodged his hand. She continued running, but a boulder and a fallen tree stood in her path. She tried to change direction, but suddenly he was in front of her. The large white cross emblazoned on his chest assaulted her consciousness, and she cringed at the sight of it. She spun around, away from him, and tried to run again.

She felt her head jerk backwards. He had her by the hair. She shook her head. She tried to hit the man. To no avail.

She felt herself falling, with the man on top of her. She landed on her side, and he turned her on her back. She squirmed and struggled to get free. He held her by the neck. He ripped her clothes. She smelled his foul breath and felt its heat against her face. She tried not to think of what he had in mind to do to her. She closed her eyes, hoping her soul would leave her body and escape.

She tried to will her mind away from here, tried to numb her senses to the pain she knew the man was going to inflict on her.

He kissed her on the lips and tore away the tatters of her clothes. He raised his head and gazed upon her nakedness. He smiled. His right hand stroked her face while his left still held her by the neck.

She looked into his cold eyes and cried.

*   *   *

Joseph heard the sound of a struggle and the frantic crying of the girl. He overcame his shock and fear. He crept forward. His knee scraped against a rock. He pried the rock loose from the damp ground and hefted it. It was heavy but manageable.

Joseph heard a sound of ripping clothes, and a man's voice exclaimed, "Ah, you're a feisty one. But now I've got you." Again, the sound of ripping clothes, and an anguished female cry.

Joseph recognized the voice: it was Rachel, his best friend Aaron's younger sister. He jumped up and ran forward, the rock cradled in his arm. Emerging from the thicket, Joseph saw the man. He was on his hands and knees, pinning Rachel's naked body under him.

Rachel tried to squirm, in vain. The man held her with an iron grip. He laughed, and pulled his trousers down. Rachel screamed a blood-curdling scream. The man just laughed again and slapped her face hard. He stroked her naked breasts, and bending low, he whispered something in her ear.

The man rose slightly, pulling Rachel's thighs apart. Joseph sneaked up behind the man, taking care not to make any noise. Joseph's heart was pounding. His throat constricted. Sweat trickled down his brow.

An unmistakable sign of recognition crossed Rachel's face, and Joseph's heart sank. He was sure that Rachel's look had given him away. But Rachel quickly looked aside, and the man seemed not to notice.

The man again kissed Rachel on her lips. She screamed. She shook her head. He seized her by the throat and laughed again loudly.

Joseph now was close enough. With both his hands, he heaved the rock above his head. Momentarily he froze as he realized he was about to kill a man. The horror of that thought overwhelmed him, and he almost lost his nerve; but just then Rachel's pleading eyes caught his, and with all his might he smashed the heavy rock down on the man's skull. Silently the man pitched forward, his bloody, ruined skull hanging at an awkward angle to his left.

Rachel was pinned under the corpse, screaming and crying frantically. Joseph rolled the body off so that it lay beside her, face up, the wound no longer visible. Rachel rolled away, began to rise, and vomited on the ground. She was shaking uncontrollably.

Again she tried to rise and almost fell. "Joseph, help me!" she cried.

He caught her in his arms, and she clung to him, sobbing. He held her, putting one arm around her back. She was completely naked, and he felt awkward holding her. He felt embarrassed for her. He wanted to let go of her and turn away, but she was still trembling, crying, clinging to him. He put his other arm around her and held her close.

"Are you alright?" he asked. "Did he hurt you?"

"Just my face. Nothing else."

She had her arms around him. Her face was pressed against his shoulder. Soon he felt her shaking beginning to diminish, and her crying became less frantic. Suddenly she pushed away from him. She turned her back.

"Go, Joseph. Turn away," she said. "I'm naked."

"Oh, I didn't mean to —" he mumbled awkwardly, and, leaving his words unfinished, he turned away from her. He heard Rachel bending down, gathering her torn garments.

"My dress is ruined," she said, sobbing softly.

"Rachel, take the man's clothing. I will remove it from his body, if you want."

"No!" she screamed. Even without seeing her, Joseph sensed her shudder, felt her deep revulsion.

"You have no choice. You cannot wear your own clothes; they are in tatters, and there is nothing else to wear."

At first she did not answer, but her sobbing stopped. "What about the blood?" she asked.

"It's only on his shirt. I'll wash it off for you – there, in the stream."

At first she hesitated, but finally she agreed. Joseph stripped the man of his clothes.

There was a dagger in its sheath strapped to the man's body. Joseph took it. He went to the stream to wash the bloody shirt, while Rachel took the man's other garments and put them on.

Joseph returned with the wet shirt, and Rachel hid behind a tree.

He put the shirt on a rock and turned away. "There," he said. "Put it on."

"But the shirt is wet."

"I know. I'm sorry. But we can't stay here. There will be others coming soon. We have to go."

She took the shirt. She put it on. He heard her shiver.

He turned and looked at her. The clothes were baggy, but they would do. He noticed she had rolled up the trousers so they wouldn't drag on the ground. She was barefoot.

"His shoes were too big. But maybe I can find mine."

"Do you remember where you lost them?"

She pointed. "Over there. Not far away." She began to cry again. "I lost them when Aaron fell. He hit Aaron on the head. I think he's dead. They're all dead – father, mother, sister, brother. I'm the only one who's left. Where will I go? What will I do? Help me, Joseph. Help me."

Holding the shreds of her once-beautiful dress in both her hands, she hid her face in it, crying frantically again. Joseph put one arm around her shoulder. She was shaking.

He kissed her on the head and led her forward gently. "Let's go find Aaron. Perhaps he is alive."

The full moon illuminated the forest floor, and it wasn't long before they found Rachel's shoes. But Aaron was nowhere to be seen.

In the distance, Joseph heard the shouting of the mob, perhaps less strident than before, but closer. He imagined townsfolk and sword-wielding warriors of Christ thrashing through the forest searching for survivors, their blood lust not yet sated. In his mind he saw the image of the black-robed friar walking calmly amidst the raging mob, exhorting them to further acts of violence. Deep in the marrow of his bones Joseph felt the friar's hatred, sensed the friar's wrath.

From far away, Joseph heard the friar's voice. It pierced the air and sped unerringly to Joseph's heart. Fear gripped at Joseph's throat. His instincts told him he must flee. And yet, he knew he couldn't just abandon Aaron to the mob. Aaron was alive. He knew it. He felt it in his heart.

He looked at Rachel. "Listen. Do you hear them? We must hurry. We must find Aaron quickly and be gone from here before they come."

Joseph turned. He heard a sound. Something moving in the bushes. An animal. Or an enemy. Joseph signaled to Rachel to stand still. He drew the dagger from its sheath, and slowly, soundlessly he advanced.

In the bushes something stirred again. He braced himself. He took a breath.

Beyond the bushes he saw something lurking. A dog with yellow eyes. No, not a dog. It looked evil, threatening. A wolf! Again, his first thought was to flee, but something on the ground got his attention. The wolf pawed and sniffed at it.

Joseph advanced a step, to get a better look. The wolf, guarding its prize, looked up at Joseph, baring its teeth, and a low-pitched growl emanated from between its jaws.

For a moment, Joseph froze in fear, but quickly his gaze shifted to the ground. He saw a person lying face down. He advanced another step, and the wolf did likewise, crouching low, its yellow eyes following Joseph's movement.

Joseph momentarily took his eyes off the wolf and stole another look at the motionless body. It was Aaron. He advanced a little, shifting somewhat to his left, trying to draw the wolf away from Aaron.

The moon illuminated the lupine form poised for the attack. Joseph raised his blade, keeping his eyes fixed on the predator before him. He signaled Rachel to run, and he hoped she understood. In his heart he said a prayer. He waited.

The wolf advanced, stalking Joseph, holding him with its cold, malevolent gaze. Its sharp teeth glistened in the moonlight. Joseph shuddered.

Joseph moved sideways. The wolf moved closer still. Joseph's hand tightened around the dagger's hilt. He knew he had only seconds before the wolf would charge at him.

He thought he saw the animal's muscles tighten, and somehow its gaze seemed more intense. The time had come. The wolf was about to pounce. Joseph took a breath – perhaps his last.

An arrow whizzed through the air. Even before it hit its mark, Joseph heard it coming. He flinched, taking his eyes momentarily off the wolf. He looked up and saw a luminous object – a bright ray of light – tear through the air and strike the animal's neck. He heard a thud and then a gurgling sound. On the ground before him, the wolf lay dead, an arrow through its neck.

Joseph looked in the direction from which the arrow had been shot. The undergrowth was thicker there, and his vision was obscured. Crouching down, he started walking cautiously in that direction. He heard Rachel following.

In the distance, Joseph thought he saw a human form receding, a longbow slung about his shoulder. Joseph ran, hoping to overtake the stranger. But the man had disappeared without a trace.

Rachel came up behind him. "Did you see the bowman? Where did he go?" Her voice was strained.

"He vanished. He saved our lives, but who was he?"

He took her by the hand and led her back to where the wolf lay dead, blood oozing from the arrow wound.

Nearby in the undergrowth, something stirred. At first, Joseph thought it might be another wolf, but quickly he realized it must be Aaron.

He heard a moan, and Rachel ran forward. She recognized the voice.

It was Aaron! He was alive!

Rachel reached him first. "What happened? Are you badly hurt?"

Aaron raised his head. A rivulet of blood trickled down his scalp. "My head hurts. He hit me. I can't remember anything after that." He blinked and looked at Rachel, then at Joseph. "Is he gone?"

Gently Rachel helped her brother rise. He was unsteady on his feet, but he seemed to have no serious injuries. Aaron tried to walk. He stumbled, almost fell.

Again the sounds of angry men echoed among the trees. They were not far away at all, and they were getting closer.

Joseph took Aaron by the arm. "Hurry, Aaron. We must leave immediately. Rachel and I will help you walk."

And so they started out, slowly at first, just barely succeeding in maintaining their distance from the mob. After a few minutes, when Aaron had regained his strength somewhat, they increased their speed. Deeper into the forest they went, where the trees were thicker and the moonlight dimmer. Clouds began to gather in the sky. They felt moisture in the air. A cold wind began to blow. They could not stop. They heard thunder. They must find shelter, but there was no shelter to be seen. They kept on going: walking, running, fleeing from the ghosts and shadows of their former life.

When Joseph, Aaron, and Rachel were out of sight, a man emerged from the thicket and approached the dead wolf. The man wore a tattered robe, and a cowl was drawn over his head. A longbow was slung over one shoulder, a quiver of arrows hung at his back, and in one hand he held a walking stick. He bent down, pulled the arrow out of the animal's neck, and smoothed the fur around the wound. He spoke some words under his breath, and, rising to his full height, he turned away and vanished into the forest.

CHAPTER 3

Friar Peter bent down and ran his fingers over the wet ground. He picked up two broken branches, held them in front of his eyes, and turned them this way and that. He ran his gaunt fingers over the broken edge of one of the branches. Then he put the branch to his nose and drew in a long breath. Alfred watched the friar with curiosity. Surely last night's rain would have washed away all traces of their quarry, but Alfred did not doubt that Peter could see things no one else could see.

Alfred shivered in the early morning air. He didn't understand why Friar Peter had insisted on taking twenty men and going into the forest even before the sun rose. Why was Peter so intent on catching that good-for-nothing Joseph? If Joseph got away, so be it. Good riddance, Alfred thought. And what did Joseph have to do with Harald's disappearance? Most likely, Harald was just lying in a drunken stupor somewhere in town.

Peter rose and strode forward, deeper into the forest. He pointed to the ground before him. "There was a chase here. They went this way." Friar Peter kept on walking; Alfred and the others followed Peter's lead.

Abruptly, Peter stopped again. A dead wolf lay on the ground before him in a pool of dried blood. Peter nudged the wolf's carcass with his booted foot, turning it over. He bent down and inspected the neck. He probed the carcass with his fingers, then ran his hands over the ground. He looked up at the sky. He looked among the trees in all directions. He waved his right hand in a circular motion, a ward against the Devil. He made the sign of the cross.

He stood. "This animal died of sorcery, I surmise."

A gasp was heard among the men, and some of the men turned pale.

Peter raised his hand. "This wolf seems to have been shot. See the blood around the neck. And yet, there is no arrow here."

"Maybe the bowman took his arrow back," somebody offered.

"Not likely," said the Friar. "We just saw evidence of pursuit: one person pursuing another. Do you think the bowman was the pursuer or the one pursued? In either case, there was no time to take the arrow back. No, I rather think that sorcery killed this wolf."

They went on, a bit unnerved. Alfred wasn't sure he believed the friar's explanation, but he was unwilling to dismiss it either. He spat on the ground over his left shoulder, against the evil eye.

They passed a stream. Again the friar stopped. There were many broken branches, and even Alfred could tell there had been a struggle here. The friar bent down and examined the ground with his fingers. After a few moments, he stood up and looked around. "This way," he said.

"A body!" someone shouted, and they all gathered round to see.

Sure enough, a man's body lay on the cold ground face up, completely naked but for the undergarment covering his nether parts. Even from a distance, Alfred could see the skull had been smashed in. Someone turned the body over. "It's him."

Alfred pushed through the crowd and looked down at the body on the ground. It was Harald. *By the rood! Harald wasn't drunk. The holy man was right after all.*

Peter raised his hand for silence. "As all of you can plainly see, this man was murdered. But ask yourselves, my friends, why has he been stripped almost naked? Remember who he was: a man who pledged his soul to serve his Lord, a man who took the cross, a man who would go to the ends of the earth, even to the Holy Land, for the honor and the glory of the Christ. In short, he was an enemy of Satan, an enemy of those who mock our church and all it stands for, an enemy of the legions of the infidel. And who are Satan's children here on earth? Who are they who do his bidding? Who are Satan's minions? Must we travel to the Holy Land to find them? Are the Saracens Satan's only agents here on earth? No, I say to you. Satan's children dwell amongst us and walk our very streets. They greet us courteously; they pretend to be our friends and wish us well, while deep within their souls the venom of the Evil One is burning, and they curse us in their hearts. They cast the Evil Eye upon us and try to thwart our every holy act. And who are these sons of Satan? By what name are they called?"

He paused and looked around him. His eyes caught the morning sunlight, and his gaze was terrible to look upon. His voice was soft but penetrating. "They are called the Jews."

Peter moved closer to the body and pointed at the bloody head. "Mark this murder well. The murderer stripped his victim and left him lying naked but for his braies. Why? To mock him. The murderer took the victim's clothes. What purpose could he have in that foul act? To strip the victim of humanity, to rob him of his dignity. I say, my friends, mark this murder well. It is no ordinary act of violence. It is a ritual murder, a sacrifice to Satan, perpetrated by the Jews. Good friends of Harald: his soul cries out to you for justice. His lifeless body cries to you for vengeance. His murderer has fled into the forest. My friends, I call upon you: avenge Harald's death! Eradicate this plague of infidels upon the land."

They marched deeper into the forest, their anger rising as they went. Alfred thought again about his former neighbor Joseph. He felt ashamed that he had ever doubted the friar's judgement. Surely, Joseph was the murderer. The friar said so, but Alfred should have known it even without the friar's telling him. He should have known it in his heart. Joseph's father Isaac had been the leader of the Jews in Camryn, the chief representative of Satan. And Alfred remembered Peter's words last night at Isaac's home as vividly as though the friar had just now spoken them: "He is Satan's minion. His soul is damned already."

* * *

Joseph shook Aaron and Rachel awake, signaling them to be quiet. Joseph's face was drawn. His eyes darted to and fro. "I hear voices. They are not far away."

The spot where Joseph and his friends had spent the night was on high ground, ending in a steep drop to the forest floor below. Joseph crept cautiously towards the edge of the precipice. Aaron and Rachel followed.

Far below them on the forest floor, a large group of men were moving quickly among the trees, led by a man in a long black robe. Friar Peter. Joseph muttered the name under his breath.

Joseph lay on his belly, straining to hear the friar's words. Voices drifted upwards, but the words were mostly indistinct. Once or twice, Joseph was sure he heard "Jews" and "murderers," but it was not the friar's voice speaking. How long he lay there listening, Joseph couldn't say. Probably it was just a minute, maybe two, but it seemed to him like hours as he lay transfixed, watching the friar and his grisly retinue.

And then the friar spoke. His voice was penetrating, his words distinct. "They came this way. They are not far."

The friar's voice wrenched at Joseph's heart, evoking images of horror in his mind. He saw his father lying bleeding on the floor. He heard his mother's anguished final cry to God; felt the cruel blade that slid across her throat; he saw the image of the black-cowled friar standing in the midst of darkness, directing the wanton slaughter of Joseph's family. And the horror of the friar's words reverberated in his mind: "Five times you must stab him. Five times only: no more, no less. Then leave him. Let him bleed to death."

A chill wind blew, and Joseph shivered. He turned, a solitary tear running down the corner of his eye. He wiped the tear away. He slid away from the precipice and rose to his feet. "Hurry. We must leave immediately," he said.

They ran, entering the thickness of the forest once again. Soon the underbrush grew up around them, and they were forced to slow their pace. Their path twisted and turned as they tried to evade their pursuers. Half an hour passed; an hour; maybe more. And yet they dared not stop to rest. Behind them they could hear the voices of the men of Camryn, still distant but relentlessly overtaking them.

Joseph looked at his two friends. It was but yesterday that Aaron had been knocked unconscious, and Joseph eyed him with concern. Aaron was visibly tiring and probably could not go on much longer without a rest.

To their left, the ground inclined steeply downwards, and the undergrowth was thicker there below. Joseph pointed. "Hide there. I will lead them onwards and then return to you."

Aaron began to scramble down, but Rachel stopped him with her hand. She turned to Joseph. "What if you can't return? What if you try but cannot find us?"

Joseph's voice was firm. He tried his best to project an air of confidence. He looked deep into Rachel's eyes and said, "Do not worry, Rachel. I will find you. Wait for me."

Joseph began to run as best he could among the underbrush and fallen branches. The voices of the men of Camryn echoed in his ears. They were close now, very close.

"There they are. There must be three of them, but I can't be sure."

"Quick. Don't let them get away."

"I'm onto one of them. Don't worry: he won't escape."

Joseph ran. His heart was pounding hard against his chest. It hurt to breathe, and his lungs felt as though they would burst. But fear, and grim determination to survive, spurred him on.

He sensed the presence of his pursuer. He felt the distance narrowing. His hope began to dim. And yet, a smile dawned upon his face as he realized that he had led the men of Camryn far afield, far away from where his friends were hiding.

Joseph heard the man's heavy breathing just behind him. The dread of being caught surged through Joseph's veins, giving him the strength to keep on running. But he knew his strength was running out. Another minute, maybe two, and the man would be on top of him. He knew he must act fast. He glanced to his left and saw the forest floor sloping gently downward to where a stream cut through the valley.

Something moved below. He heard it, and he saw the stirring of the bushes near the stream. It was probably a deer. His pursuer must have heard it also, because Joseph felt the man's gaze shift away from him.

Joseph dropped to the ground and rolled down the hill. The man ran after him. Joseph came to rest alongside the stream at the bottom of the hill. He rose slowly, a bit unsteady on his feet. He turned, facing upstream toward where the deer had been. He drew a breath, and once again began to run.

His feet raced along the rocky ground. To his left, the stream gurgled past. Behind him, he heard his pursuer's footfalls thrashing through the undergrowth. A fallen tree lay in Joseph's path. Nimbly he jumped over it, but his pursuer was still faster, clearing the hurdle just seconds behind Joseph.

Joseph pretended to snag his foot on a vine protruding from the ground. He fell and rolled. He thrust his right hand inside his garment just as the man fell on top of him. The man pinned Joseph's shoulders to the ground. He yelled, "I've got him."

Joseph spat in the man's face. The man's head drew back, and his grip on Joseph's shoulders momentarily relaxed. Joseph quickly swung his right hand around and plunged a dagger in his assailant's ribs. He pulled the dagger out and rolled the man over. The man was still alive but badly injured, struggling to breathe. Joseph raised the dagger high but then thought better of it. He wiped the dagger clean, re-sheathed it, and continued running upstream.

When he thought he was far enough away that he had eluded the friar's search party, Joseph bent down and took a long drink from the stream. He crossed to the other bank, went deeper into the forest so that the stream was no longer visible, and stopped to rest. He sat facing downstream, listening for men's voices in the distance. When he heard no human sounds, after several minutes he started back to find his friends, remaining constantly alert for the sounds of pursuit.

*   *   *

It was a long time since the friar and his men had passed, and Aaron no longer heard even the faintest sounds of their voices echoing through the forest. And yet, he and his sister remained crouched amidst the undergrowth. He glanced at Rachel and squeezed her hand. It was not yet safe to rise.

In the distance, Aaron heard a sound. He tensed, and his heart began to race. *Could it be the friar's men returning?* He pressed himself against the ground and listened. But the sound was coming from the wrong direction, from deep within the forest, off the beaten path. And, Aaron realized suddenly, it was the voice of a woman, and she was singing:

> Go not to the forest, dearie.
> Go not to the forest, child.
> There evil spirits, ghosts, and goblins,
> And animals roam wild.
>
> Follow not the song of angels,
> Though angels you may hear.
> For though an angel lead you on,
> The devil, too, is near.
>
> Go not to the forest, loved one,
> Where Fear and Darkness hold their sway.
> Peace, my child; let old Mab guide you
> Back into the light of day.

Aaron pushed Rachel down against the ground, signaling her to remain quiet. He held Rachel's hand, watching nervously as the woman approached. She was old, very old, judging by her wrinkled facial features. In her gnarled hand she held a walking stick, but she seemed to walk with ease among the undergrowth. Not far from Aaron, she came to a halt.

"You can come out now. I know you are there." Her eyes scanned the forest.

Aaron did not move.

"Come on. Old Mab won't hurt you, child. And the friar's men are far away by now. I know you are there, you and your sister, so there's no use hiding." She turned to face their hiding place. She put her left hand on her hip and waited.

Slowly Aaron stood up, holding a large stick in his right hand. He moved forward, while he eyed the woman suspiciously.

"You won't be needing that. I'm not a cutpurse or a vagabond, you know. Surely you've heard of me: Old Mab. Oh yes, I see you have. Well, don't believe the things they say about me there in Camryn. I'm not a bad sort, really now. I'm not a sorceress or anything like that, but just a simple sort who makes her home here in the woods. I've come to help you."

Aaron lowered the stick but did not drop it. He stood agape.

"Come on. Both of you. Old Mab won't hurt you. And you've got me outnumbered anyway, haven't you?"

Rachel stood up and came to Aaron's side.

Old Mab smiled but did not look at Rachel. She kept her eyes on Aaron. "Yes, that's much better. Now come with me."

But Aaron stood his ground. "Not yet, Old Mab. Not yet. I have heard of you, and what I've heard does not encourage me to trust you. What do you know about us? How did you know we were hiding here? And why should we trust a woman such as you?"

The old woman put her hands on her hips and looked into Aaron's eyes. "Stubborn are you, son? And lacking trust. Well, I don't think you have much choice in your position, do you?

But I'll answer you. You are Jews from Camryn, escaping last night's massacre. I see surprise written on your face."

She paused and drew a long breath. "Old Mab knows everything that happens in this forest. I have seen you fleeing, and I have seen the friar chasing after you. I know your friend has killed a man defending the honor and the life of your sister. Old Mab sees all."

"Are you not a sorceress as people say?"

Mab turned her head to her left and spat on the ground. "Hah! Old Mab doesn't deal with Satan and his kind." She looked into Aaron's eyes again and jabbed a finger at his chest. "Don't you believe such nonsense, son."

Putting a trembling hand to his chest where Mab had just touched him, Aaron drew back a step. "If you are not a sorceress, how do you know these things?"

Mab turned to her right and looked up at the treetops. Slowly she raised her hand and pointed to the forest. "Mab sees everything. Most people see only with their eyes and hear only with their ears. But Mab sees all, with eyes and ears and heart. The forest speaks to me: the trees, the birds, the beasts, they all speak to Mab, each in his own way and in his own tongue. They tell me all that happens in the forest and all that happens in the towns nearby – yes, even in Camryn. This is not sorcery, but a gift the Lord has given me, to see and hear and know what others are unable to perceive."

Aaron took a step towards Mab. With trembling voice, he said, "In that case, can you tell us where the friar is right now?"

"Yes, I can," said Mab. "Your friend has stabbed a man in self-defense, and Friar Peter is tending to the injured man. It will soon be dark in Sherwood Forest, and the friar will not continue his pursuit tonight. He will return to Camryn along this path, and he will find you here if you remain. So do not tarry. Come. My cottage is that way, off the road, farther in the woods a bit. Your friend is coming back to find you now, and we will meet him on our way. Do not fear. You will be safe with me."

CHAPTER 4

Joseph turned. He thought he had heard something moving in the bushes behind him.

Nothing.

Warily, he started walking again. The wind rustled through the trees. In the distance, a bird called. Joseph continued walking.

Again he heard movement behind him. It was the time of day when shadows lengthen and when, it was said, evil things arouse. He must be on his guard.

He turned around and walked a few steps towards the sound. He looked to his right and to his left, trying to discern a human shape that might be hiding in the shadows.

Now he thought he heard a sound coming from his right, and he moved warily in that direction. Just then, he again remembered the dagger that he had taken from the dead attacker, and he began to reach for it under his cloak. But suddenly, the forest was alive with human forms, running at him from all directions, and before he realized what was happening, he was seized in a vice-like grip. He felt a fist plunge into his stomach, sending a wave of pain and nausea through his body. He tried to double over to allay his pain, but the four brawny arms that held him in their grip kept him standing upright as the fist rammed into him again, robbing him of all his breath and sending bolts of pain coursing through his entire being. His vision dimmed, and the sounds of his captors' voices became distant echoes in the darkness. At the edge of consciousness, he heard the hateful friar's voice, and it jolted him awake:

"Do not strike again. I need to question him. Then we will take him back to Camryn, where he will be tried for murder and for sorcery."

The friar stood before Joseph. He smiled a beatific smile and said, "What is your name, my son?"

Joseph cringed. "I am not your son! And it is you who are the murderer. You killed my father. You killed my mother. You killed my friends and neighbors. Where you go, death follows. I curse you in the name of Heaven."

The smile faded from the friar's face, but otherwise he seemed unruffled by Joseph's outburst. He moved a step closer. "What is your name?" he asked in a soft, soothing voice.

Joseph looked at the friar's retinue, and his eyes fixed on Alfred. Alfred the blacksmith, Alfred his neighbor. Alfred, the father of his good friend Matthew. His mind flashed back to his parents' murder, and with difficulty he held back tears. His gaze bored into Alfred as he answered Friar Peter's question. "I am Joseph, son of Isaac, may God avenge his blood!"

Alfred looked somewhat shaken at Joseph's words, and he lowered his eyes; but Friar Peter, unperturbed, advanced another step. "What are the names of your two friends, and where are they hiding?"

Joseph did not answer.

The friar made the sign of the cross in front of Joseph's face.

"I will repeat my question, son of Satan, and you will answer me. What are the names of your two friends who fled with you from Camryn, and where are they hiding?"

Joseph looked at Friar Peter. Hatred and deep revulsion welled up inside him. He resolved to remain silent, no matter what the consequences. Unwaveringly, he held the friar's gaze, trying to see into the darkness of the friar's soul.

The friar opened his mouth to speak again, but before he managed to say a word, a commanding female voice echoed from the shadows of the forest.

"His friends are not in hiding, friar. They are under my protection, and so is Joseph. You will release your prisoner and leave."

All eyes turned in the direction of the voice. An ancient woman with a walking stick emerged from among the trees. Two dark figures loped out of the shadows behind her, and she signaled them to stay.

She held the walking stick in her clenched fist and raised it in front of her. Her dark eyes burning with intensity, she looked at Friar Peter and, in a commanding tone, she said, "You are trespassing on my domain. You will release your prisoner, and you will leave immediately."

A few of the friar's men began to laugh, but others had a look of terror in their eyes, and the few who laughed soon stopped laughing. Some made the sign of the cross and drew away from the woman. The two men who held Joseph relaxed their grip a little, but not enough for Joseph to break free.

"Who are you, woman?" Friar Peter asked, drawing back a step.

The woman advanced a step towards Peter. "My name is Mab. And you are Friar Peter, I presume. Your fame precedes you, friar. I have heard that you have certain extraordinary powers; but know that I am also someone to be reckoned with, and you are in my territory. You are not from these parts, so perhaps you've never heard of me. But look around you, Friar Peter. See the fear written upon the faces of the men who follow you. They know of me, and they know my power. I am one with Sherwood Forest, and the creatures of the forest do my bidding. Even the trees, the rocks, and flowing brooks obey my will. I can make the brooks and streams flow backwards and the very ground on which you walk rise up against you. So do not test me, Friar Peter. For the final time, I warn you: release your prisoner, and return to Camryn."

Joseph again felt his captors' grip relax, and this time he almost was able to free himself. But Friar Peter gave the men a stern look, and they held Joseph fast.

The friar turned again to face Mab. He moved forward several paces, holding a crucifix before him. "Do not threaten me, sorceress. I do not take orders from your kind. How dare you threaten a man of the cloth." Turning to his men, he commanded, "Seize her!"

But instead of seizing Mab, the friar's men receded, their attention drawn to the shadowy forms emerging from the trees to Old Mab's right. They looked like specters in the fading light, slowly advancing towards the friar's men, their jowls parted, displaying their sharp teeth. Soft growls emanated from their throats.

One of the men screamed and began to run, but he abruptly halted as other specters approached from that direction also. Wolves. Twelve of them, surrounding the friar and his men from all directions.

The two men holding Joseph released him and ran to join their friends. Joseph, trying to appear calm and unshaken, turned his eyes away from the wolves and took a step in Mab's direction. The friar, apparently unperturbed, turned toward Joseph, advancing, his crucifix held up before him.

Mab raised her walking stick again and pointed it at Friar Peter. "Do not touch him. Move away."

But Friar Peter did not obey. While keeping his gaze fixed on Mab, he took one more step towards Joseph. He paused, defiance in his eyes.

After several seconds, Friar Peter took another step towards Joseph.

Joseph looked at the friar, trying to read the friar's face, but Peter's face was like a mask, emotionless, inscrutable.

The friar seemed about to advance yet another step towards Joseph. But, in a burst of unnatural speed, one of the wolves bounded towards the friar and landed at his feet. The wolf bared his teeth and growled.

Friar Peter stood his ground, staring the wolf down.

Old Mab advanced, her walking stick still pointed at Friar Peter. "Do not think it is your puny will that keeps the wolf at bay. No, Friar Peter. It is my will alone that restrains that wolf," she said. "One more step, and he will attack."

Mab lowered her stick and waved her other hand in a sweeping motion.

The other eleven wolves moved closer together. A gap opened at one point in the circle of wolves. Gradually, the gap widened, as the wolves tightened their lines on either side of the gap.

Old Mab pointed at the gap. "There," she said. "Go, all of you, whilst you have the chance. I will not warn you again."

The men began to run, not waiting for the friar's permission. Friar Peter stood motionless until all his men had left. Then, giving Mab a hate-filled look, he turned his back and walked briskly away, following his men.

CHAPTER 5

Joseph, Aaron, and Rachel sat around the hearth warming themselves by the fire, while Mab bustled about the cottage, rummaging among her pots and pans that were haphazardly strewn about, and adding ingredients to a cauldron from which exotic aromas wafted through the common room. Joseph inhaled the soothing fragrance and tried to relax, but his eyes kept straying to the window, seeking to penetrate the growing darkness of the forest.

Momentarily, he marveled at the glass of Mab's window, a rare luxury that very few could afford. But that thought did not hold his attention for long. It was not the window but what lay beyond that occupied his mind.

"What do you expect to see out there?" Mab stood by her cauldron, looking at Joseph, one hand on her hip, the other holding a wooden stirring rod.

Joseph turned toward Mab but said nothing.

Mab continued stirring the cauldron. Without looking up, she said, "It's dark out there, you know, and things are lurking in the darkness. Birds. Wolves. All manner of beast. You can't see them. You can't hear them. Not unless I want you to. But as for Friar Peter and his men – they are gone, returned to Camryn. Oh, they'll come back again, but not until tomorrow they won't, and by then you will be gone too. But you are safe in Mab's cottage, and nought can harm you here. So quit fretting about what's out there in the darkness. We've got plans to make and words to speak, so let Old Mab guide you, and put your mind to the task at hand."

"How will you save us? You took Friar Peter by surprise today, and you won a victory, but that is only temporary. We cannot stay with you forever, and it is quite apparent that Peter will not give up the chase. Where will we go? How will we escape?" Joseph's gaze turned downwards as he added, "It is only a matter of time."

"Time?" Old Mab put her wooden stirring rod on the counter with an emphatic thump. She shook her head. "Is it time that you fear? Why, time is on your side; and distance too. Tomorrow's Easter Sunday. The friar is supposed to deliver a sermon at the church. He won't be starting out so early. Not until his sermon's done. And you are not alone: you have friends to help you. The friar's retreated for the night. In the morning, you'll be gone, and he will know not where you go."

"Then that makes two of us. I also have no idea where we are going."

Mab lowered her voice, as though telling a secret. "But I do. You will listen, and do as I say. In the morning, before the sun comes up, I shall point the way out of Sherwood Forest. If you follow my directions, you'll come to a road going south. A few miles farther down the road, you'll reach an inn, the Black Horse Inn it's called, and there you'll stay the night. You'll be safe there."

"How can you be sure? What if the friar catches up to us?"

"Do not fear, Joseph. Even if the friar comes there, you will be safe."

Joseph looked at Mab suspiciously. "How can you be so sure of that? What do you know that you are not telling me? And how do I know I can trust you?"

Mab turned from Joseph and went back to her cauldron. She threw in another herb and stirred slowly. "You don't. But your options are limited, and if you don't listen to me, then, as you said, it is only a matter of time."

Mab threw in another herb and stirred the cauldron again. "Old Mab sees many things. Some of what she sees is in this world, and some is in the other world."

Joseph turned pale. "What other world?"

A wry smile crossed Mab's lips. She shook her head and said, "No, not the world of Satan. Mab will have no truck with Satan and his kind. I mean the world of spirit: the world of angels and departed souls, a world that borders on our world but is hidden from our eyes. The path to reach that world is difficult, and only very few can find it; and Mab has entered that world fully only once or twice. More often, Mab can only peer into that mysterious world from the outside, as through a lattice window. Sometimes she sees some things there faintly glimmering in the distance. Sometimes she hears a whisper of what is said up there. Sometimes she sees the future, or the past, but only in brief glimpses, and it's not for Mab to tell. That is something you will have to discover on your own."

Joseph opened his mouth as if to speak, but he said nothing.

Mab turned from her cooking and looked directly at Joseph. "I see you doubt me now, but remember what I say. Do not forget. Someday you will have to enter that world. Otherwise you will not defeat your enemy. But I have said enough already. Let us turn to other matters."

Joseph shook his head. "No. Wait. You said we have friends to help us. Who?"

"Old Mab's your friend, whether you know it or not."

"You and who else? You said 'friends,' didn't you?"

Mab went back to her cooking. A moment passed before she answered. "So I did. 'Twas a slip of the tongue. I meant myself. That's all I meant."

"Maybe it was a slip of your tongue, or maybe not. But you did have someone else in mind. I see it on your face. I hear it in your voice. And if you don't tell me the truth about what you meant, how can I believe the other things you said?"

Mab stirred her pot again. She looked at Joseph. She looked at Aaron and at Rachel. With her wooden stirring rod she pointed at Rachel, who was still dressed in the tunic of the man who had attacked her the previous day. "She can't go around dressed like that. She'll have to change into something decent."

Mab spun around, and, moving faster than Joseph had ever seen her move before, she went to the corner of the common room, opened a large wooden chest, and extracted an undergarment, a man's brown tunic, a pair of dark breeches, a brown hooded cloak, a pair of gloves, a reddish-brown round cap with rolled brim, and a pair of boots. She strode across the room, let the boots fall to the floor at Rachel's feet, and dropped the other garments in Rachel's lap.

Rachel looked at her questioningly.

Mab looked Rachel up and down. "Yes, that will do, I think. You can't go dressed in your attacker's clothing, but you cannot dress in a maiden's kirtle either. On the road, you must appear to be a boy. It's safer that way. Before you leave me in the morning, shorten your hair a bit, and wear it under the hood or pulled up and bound under the hat. You may change in the other room."

Rachel began to rise.

Joseph got up from his seat and moved a step towards Mab, while motioning to Rachel to stay where she was. "Wait. You didn't answer me. What other friend or friends do we have to help us?"

Mab returned to her cooking. She stirred her pot again. She looked out the window. She turned to Joseph. "I have offered you my help, and I could leave it at that. But, if you don't believe me and fail to follow my instructions, you will be captured, and I will have failed my mission. 'Twas indeed a slip I made. And now I'll have to tell you more. Sit down, and I'll answer you as best I may."

When Joseph was seated again, Mab said: "Friar Peter is a man of influence, and of great power. When he speaks, people follow him, and he is not easily thwarted. You saw what happened in Camryn yesterday. Do you know that you three are the only Jews who survived?"

She paused to let her words penetrate. Rachel began to cry, and Aaron held Rachel's hand. Joseph was expressionless, but his hand trembled.

Mab continued: "Do you think it coincidence that you survived? Do you think you could have done it without assistance?"

Joseph looked at her. Defiance burned in his eyes. "Matthew helped me. But who helped them?" He pointed at Aaron and Rachel.

Mab raised her voice. "You did. You rescued them in the forest. But think again. How did the three of you escape the friar? Do you remember the wolf that pawed at Aaron as he lay fallen in the forest? Who shot the arrow that pierced its neck? Surely not one of the friar's men."

"You?"

"No, not I. I would not kill a wolf. There's another. He came to me last night to ask my help, but I may not tell you more. He will reveal himself to you when time is right."

"I thought you said no other Jews survived. Then who is this man?"

Mab stood in the middle of the common room. She looked at Joseph intently. "The man is not from Camryn, but he was there last night. Like the friar, he is someone of great power, but he could not prevent or stop the massacre. He did what he could in saving you."

She turned away, and, in a lower voice she added: "Old Mab has said more than she should have. You must believe me and follow my instructions."

CHAPTER 6

Easter Sunday, 25ᵗʰ March 1190

They rose at dawn. Mab packed provisions for the way, and they were off by sunrise, following Mab's directions out of Sherwood forest and southwards on a road that skirted the forest. The road forked three times before they reached their destination, and, as instructed, they took first the left fork, then the right, and then the left again. Shortly before nightfall they reached the Black Horse Inn.

Joseph, Aaron, and Rachel sat at a table in a dark corner of the inn, making a meal of codfish, cheese, and elderberry wine. It was not very filling, but they could not have bread, cake, or beer, since those foods were forbidden during the Passover holiday. The second day of Passover had just ended at nightfall, and there were still six days left to go.

Joseph ate slowly, trying to savor his food. He looked at his two friends. They appeared exhausted, both physically and emotionally, and he wondered whether his own appearance was as bad. He ate slowly, saying nothing. He looked at Rachel, dressed in masculine garb. For a moment, their encounter in the forest flickered through his mind: the man attacking Rachel, his own actions saving her from the attacker, and her reluctance to don the clothes of her attacker to cover up her nakedness. With an effort, he dismissed the image from his mind and looked into Rachel's eyes.

He knew she still felt ill-at-ease dressed in a man's clothes, and he worried whether her disguise would be sufficient. Even in the dim light, he could see the blueness of her eyes. Unspeaking, with just a look, he tried to reassure her, and he felt her eyes reply to him, as it were: *Thank you, Joseph, for your concern. Yes, I will be alright.*

Joseph turned his gaze from Rachel's eyes and looked down at her garments, trying to assess her masculine disguise. It was somewhat chilly where they sat, far from the hearth, and thus her heavy cloak did not seem out of place. The curve of Rachel's breasts was well concealed under the cloak, and her hair was hidden under the hood. From any distance, she would appear to be a boy.

Neither Aaron nor Rachel spoke. So much had occurred. Joseph found it hard to believe that just two days had passed since the first night of Passover, since Friar Peter had transformed the joyous feast into a night of terror, and since Peter's followers had murdered his father and his mother, his sister and his brother, and almost all the Jews of Camryn – all save the three of them alone.

He felt a void inside himself, a strange numbness of the soul. He tried to think of his murdered family: his father's kind face and the twinkle of his father's eyes, his mother's loving smile, his brother's and his sister's mischievous antics. But he could not think of them, could not bring the image of their faces to his mind, nor hear the echo of their voices. He knew he should be overwhelmed by sorrow. He knew he should be weeping, at least internally. And yet, he could not do so, even in his heart. It was as though his heart had turned to stone.

He looked at Aaron and at Rachel, and he wondered whether their souls were also numb. For a moment, he thought to ask them, but guilt overcame him, and he was afraid to ask.

He took a bite of cheese. He raised his cup and took a sip of elderberry wine. The image of Matthew thrusting a package of food into his hands flashed through his mind, and he thought of Matthew's words as they parted at the edge of Sherwood Forest: "Eat when you are hungry, and live. For my sake. So I can atone for my father's sin, and for my own." He wondered what

Matthew could have meant by that. What sin did Matthew have? Joseph could not imagine. How different Matthew was from his father and all the other men of Camryn. *May God bless Matthew.*

All around them, people came and went. Men sat about, eating and drinking, laughing and carousing, telling tales and trading news from near and far. Nobody paid them any attention.

A nearby table was briefly vacant. Soon, four men approached. One had a white cross painted on his dark cloak, and a sword hung at his left hip. Removing his cloak, he took a seat at the vacant table, and his three friends followed suit. A waitress quickly brought them tankards of beer. As she was about to leave them, she turned to the man with the cross and said, "There's no charge for your beer. Compliments of the house for one who takes the cross."

The man with the white cross raised his tankard to her and smiled. The man to his right also raised his tankard of beer and said, "Your health, Wilbur. May the good Lord protect you and bring you back alive and unharmed from the Holy Land."

"Aye," said the man to Wilbur's left, raising his cup as well.

"Amen," echoed the fourth man. "And may you slay a thousand infidels."

All four men took a gulp of the frothy liquid, thumped their tankards on the table – causing the beer to slosh over the sides – and cried out in unison, "Amen!"

The man to Wilbur's right raised his cup again. "I admire you, Wilbur. Doing God's work you are, fighting against those cursed Saracens. It's three years now since they conquered the Holy Land and drove all the Christians from the city of Jerusalem. By the rood, ye'll take the Holy Land back from those Saracen infidels. Indeed ye will."

"Amen," said the other two again, and they all took a long swig from their cups.

"Y'know, Wilbur, they say the leader of the Saracens is the devil's own son, straight out of hell he is. Demons follow him into battle, each more horrible than the other. And ye have to kill 'em three times before they're really dead. Even after ye cut their heads off, they still ride into battle, just as fearsome as before. Until ye kill 'em two more times. That's how Saladin and his army conquered Jerusalem three years ago. But wi' brave and God-fearing men like you, we'll take the Holy City back for certain."

Now the man opposite Wilbur spoke. "Have ye ever killed one, Wilbur? An infidel, I mean. Any infidel – Jew or Saracen – no matter which. An infidel's an infidel. They're all the same, ye know – devils in human form."

"Never have," said Wilbur. "But I soon will. How'd ye like to come with me, Thomas? There's enough infidels for both of us to kill."

"No," answered Thomas. "There's plenty o' infidels around in England. No need for me to go to the Holy Land to find 'em. Have ye heard of the doings at Camryn just two nights ago?"

"Yeah," said Wilbur. "York last week; Camryn this week. Maybe another nearby town next week. Those Jews got what was coming to 'em. They're Satan's servants, and they can join him in hell as they deserve."

"Amen," they all said in unison. They drained their tankards and thumped them on the table loudly.

"Amen!" they cried out again, raising their empty tankards and bursting into raucus laughter.

Rachel looked at Joseph. "Let's leave this place."

"We can't. Mab told us to stay the night."

"Do you hear what they are saying?" Rachel's voice trembled, and she was on the verge of tears.

Joseph thought a moment and said in a whisper, "Perhaps you're right. But first, calm down. We mustn't attract attention. We'll get up slowly. Take the leftover cheese. We'll need it."

Slowly they rose from their seats. But just as they left their table, the front door of the inn burst open, and five armed men entered. Two of the newcomers stood at the entrance – one at either side of the door – while the other three spread out. A cold wind blew through the open door.

All conversation stopped abruptly, and all the people stared into the darkness outside. Approaching slowly through the darkness was a hooded figure. He held something in his right hand. People sat with bated breath and mouths agape. Some crossed themselves. But no one spoke.

Joseph turned away from the door, signaling Aaron and Rachel to follow him, sliding slowly along the wall away from the front door.

The hooded figure entered the inn. His right hand held a walking stick in the shape of a cross. He stood between the two armed men at the door. He drew back his cowl. It was Friar Peter.

"We seek a fugitive," Peter said, his voice cutting through the stillness of the inn. "A murderer is here among you."

Gasps and murmurs erupted at Peter's pronouncement, and Peter pounded his staff on the floor for silence.

"Yes, a murderer I say. He is a youth, but a murderer nonetheless. A Jew from Camryn, who, with the Devil's help, has escaped retribution."

Again murmurs filled the room, and Peter again pounded his staff on the floor for silence.

"This Jewish youth brutally murdered a soldier of Christ, a man of God bound for the Holy Land. It was a ritual murder, and the murderer is now among you, perhaps in the company of two friends. They are enemies of Christ, and if you see them here, you are duty-bound to hand them over to us so that justice may be done."

A man not far from Joseph rose and shouted, "There he is." He lunged at Joseph and caught him by the arm. Joseph tried to squirm away, but the man held him tightly. Aaron emerged from the shadows and struck the man in the face with a metal salt cellar, spraying salt in the man's eyes. Startled, the man lost his grip on Joseph's arm. "'Sblood!" he screamed; "I'm blinded. Don't let the fiend get away!"

Two men bounded at Joseph from the next table, their daggers drawn, and yet another man came up from behind Aaron. Rachel crouched in the darkness, apparently still unnoticed. Joseph's eyes darted from side to side, assessing his chances, and he could see his chances weren't good. There was no place to run. He was cornered.

The two men with their drawn daggers stood before him, their daggers raised, barring his way. "Surrender, murderer," one of them shouted, sending a shiver up Joseph's spine. He knew he could not escape; and yet, somehow he had to stay alive, if only to perpetuate his parents' memory, if only to deprive Peter of his total victory over Camryn's Jews, if only to save his two friends. Joseph tensed his muscles, preparing to attempt an evasive maneuver.

But the men saw what Joseph was about to do. "Surrender now," they shouted at him. "There's no escape."

Without warning, suddenly another man appeared. He was old, with a long, white beard. He wore a light-gray hooded cloak, the hood resting between his shoulder blades. In his hand he held a weathered cane, and, with amazing speed, his cane shot out and smashed the two men's hands, causing their daggers to clatter to the floor. As they turned to face their attacker, the old man seized one man by the throat. He did not squeeze hard, but the man immediately slumped to the floor, unconscious, while the other turned and fled.

The old man spun around, his cane raised above him like a club, advancing on the man threatening Aaron. The man feinted to the side, recovered, and lunged at the old man. But the old man was quicker, easily dodging the attack. He spun around and brought his cane down hard, but it wasn't his attacker at whom he struck. Instead, his cane struck an adjacent table covered with a tablecloth. Quickly, the old man seized the tablecloth, pulled it off the table, and with his cane he flung the cloth at a nearby table upon which a candle burned.

"Fire!" yelled the people as the tablecloth erupted in flames. People scurried frantically about the inn, getting pitchers and basins of water to douse the flames. In the tumult, Joseph and his companions were forgotten. Friar Peter's men tried to get across the room to where Joseph was, but they could make no headway against the press of the terrified crowd.

The old man took Joseph by the arm and signaled Aaron and Rachel to follow. He led them to a short corridor at the far end of which was a wooden door. The old man took a torch from a sconce near the door. He opened the door and led them down a staircase to the cellar, which was stocked with row upon row of wine barrels. At the far wall of the cellar, he stopped in front of a barrel of somewhat different texture from the others. He balled up his fist and rapped on the barrel. It was empty. He moved the barrel aside, revealing an opening in the wall.

Joseph looked at the opening but did not enter. He looked at the old man. "Do you expect us to go in there?" he asked.

"Yes," said the man, "if you want to live. I am the man about whom Old Mab spoke to you. My name is Enoch. Now go. This tunnel is your escape route. There is no other way."

Joseph hesitated for a second. He turned to his friends and nodded. Then they all plunged into the darkness. Enoch, the torch in his hand, followed them into the tunnel and pulled the empty wine barrel back against the cellar wall, blocking the tunnel entrance. Joseph gazed into Enoch's green eyes twinkling in the firelight and at their own shadows dancing on the tunnel wall by the light of the flickering torch. He looked at Enoch and tried to read him, to see into his soul and gauge whether he could trust him. But Enoch's eyes were like deep wells, unknowable, impenetrable.

Enoch waved his torch forward, beckoning. "We must not tarry here. You are not yet safe. Hurry. We must be near the tunnel's end before they realize that you are gone."

CHAPTER 7

When Enoch and the three youths emerged from the tunnel, they were on a rocky hillside quite far from the road by which they had come. Enoch had doused the torch's flame just before leaving the tunnel, and, once outside, they stood a moment to get their bearings and allow their eyes to adjust to the darkness. It was misty out, and somewhat colder than before they had entered the inn. Joseph shivered. In the misty moonlight, he could still see the Black Horse Inn in the distance. He saw the flickering light of torches on the road, moving both north and south of the inn, but there seemed to be no torches approaching their position.

Enoch whispered, "Come this way. We must stay off the road and go southeast among the hills. There's a fog coming in, and that will help to hide us. We must go quickly, though. We have a lot of ground to cover before we rest."

"Where are we going?" Joseph asked.

"There is a cave, deep in the hills. Now hurry. Say no more until we get there."

Silently they made their way among the hills, walking on the rocky terrain, running whenever there were fewer rocks. Enoch led them. Joseph marveled at how surefooted and agile he was, not at all like the old man he appeared to be. A few times, they had to stop to catch their breaths, but Enoch wasn't winded in the least.

After more than an hour, Enoch stopped and pointed to a nearby hill. "Up there. On the far side of the hill there is a cave. That is our destination."

When finally they reached the cave about fifteen minutes later, the hillside below them was engulfed in a thick fog, and they were unable to see the valley. Where they were, the fog was not as dense, however, and moonlight illuminated the outermost portion of the cave. Just within, a wooden chest stood against the wall. Enoch opened it and removed an embroidered white tablecloth, food, and drink. He spread the tablecloth on the ground and placed the food upon it. Joseph wondered about the presence of the wooden chest and its contents in this cave. Apparently, Enoch had prepared for this contingency. But how? And why? Joseph wondered about this but said nothing.

"Eat," said Enoch, and the three youths sat down around the tablecloth.

"You may rest here until morning," Enoch said as he sat down across from Joseph. Enoch watched the three youths as they began to eat, but Enoch did not eat. "You will be safe," he said.

Joseph eyed him suspiciously. "That's exactly what Old Mab said about the Black Horse Inn. But we were not safe there."

"Yes, I know, but I am not Old Mab. I am Enoch. Her powers do not reach far beyond the borders of Sherwood Forest. She could not help you at the inn. But she knew that I would be there, and she knew I would protect you. That is why she was so certain that no harm would come to you."

Joseph rose. "What powers do you have? I know nothing more than your name. That, and Mab's assurance that you are here to help us. But who are you? Why are you helping us? And what reason do I have to trust you?"

Enoch motioned for Joseph to sit. When Joseph had done so, Enoch said, "I see you are not very trusting. That is good, under the circumstances. But at the moment, you will have to trust me if you want to live."

Joseph almost rose again, but Enoch's sharp look arrested him, and he sat back down. Nevertheless, impatience and frustration were written on his face, and his voice seethed with anger. "You talk as if I have no will of my own. I will not be manipulated. Not by Mab, and not by you. If you want me to follow your directions, you will have to win my confidence and give me some explanations. You can start by telling me who you really are, where you came from, and why you are helping us."

Unperturbed by Joseph's outburst, Enoch answered calmly: "As I told you, my name is Enoch. My home is all the world. I am from nowhere and from everywhere. I go wherever the Good Lord guides me, wherever I am needed. I am a long-time friend of your father's, and your father trusted me, but I had not seen him for many years. When I arrived in Camryn two nights ago, your father was on the verge of death from wounds inflicted by Friar Peter's men. Unfortunately, it was not in my power to save him. But before he died, he made me promise that I would watch over you and protect you."

"Then where were you these past two days, until now?"

Enoch paused and looked from Joseph to Aaron to Rachel. He looked into Joseph's eyes and answered: "Do you think you could have escaped without my help? Initially, Matthew helped you get away, and that was not my doing; but from the moment that you entered Sherwood Forest, you were again in mortal danger. Who do you think asked Mab to help you? And who shot the wolf with an arrow through the neck? It was I who did those things, and it was I who rescued you at the inn. It was I who brought you to this cave, where I had this food prepared for you. If by these actions I have not earned your trust, then nothing will convince you."

Joseph thought a moment. He took a bite of his food and said: "Alright. You are not my enemy. But you say I have no choice but to follow your instructions, and I still wonder why you are helping us. What is your purpose? And where are you leading us?"

"Your questions are reasonable enough. Of course you have free will, as do all people. But so do your enemies have free will. So did Friar Peter, and so do all the men who follow him, as indeed does every person in the world. God gives everyone a choice: good and evil, life and death. It is only through a person's choosing that he becomes an evil man. Even Peter was not born to evil, but he has chosen the path of evil; and you, Joseph, stand in his way. You want to live a life of peace and quiet, in a dream-world where hatred does not exist, in a Camryn of the past, where your parents and your family and friends are still alive. But stark reality has imposed itself upon you and shattered your dream. You are caught up now in a great war of Peter's making, and you must make the best of it. You still have free will, but the stakes are higher now, and if you do not choose correctly, you will die: you and everything that you hold dear will die with you."

"What war are you talking about? The Jews of one small village are killed, and you call it a war?"

Enoch shook his head. "It is not just one small village, Joseph. Think. Last week it was York; this week it is Camryn. York is no small village, and Camryn is but a way-station on Friar Peter's route. These are the opening salvos of a long campaign to follow, and it is not the Jews alone whom Peter's actions threaten. There is much at stake. Peter is no ordinary friar. He is a man of extraordinary influence and force of spirit; and powerful forces have rallied to his cause. Friar Peter intends to incite massacres of Jews in every Christian land and eventually to annihilate all the Jews in Christendom. This is the enemy whom you face, and you cannot defeat him without my help."

Rachel stopped eating. She looked at Enoch and said: "You talk as though Friar Peter were Joseph's personal enemy and as though it were Joseph's singular task to defeat him. But the friar had never heard of Joseph or of Aaron and myself until two nights ago, and I am sure he will forget about us soon. Once we have escaped, with your assistance, he will never find us again."

Enoch stood up and paced. At length, he sat down again and said: "So you would like to believe. But that is not to be. I told you Peter is no ordinary friar, but you do not believe me, because you have not yet seen his powers. You saw Old Mab's powers in the forest. The friar's powers are much greater, beyond anything you imagine. But in the forest, Mab was in her element, and Peter was out of his. Even so, Peter may well have succeeded in defeating her, but he didn't want to take the risk. Withdrawing made Friar Peter lose face, but that is only temporary, with no long-term consequences. Old Mab holds no importance for Friar Peter." He looked at Joseph. "You, however, are a different matter. He will pursue you to the ends of the earth, and you will find no peace until you have defeated him."

"But why?" Joseph asked. Now he was completely confused. "What am I to him? And if he is so powerful, how can I defeat him?"

Enoch sat down again opposite Joseph. "You really do not know," he said. It was a statement, not a question.

"No. What are you talking about?" Joseph's voice was tremulous.

"You, Joseph, are a descendant of King David, a descendant of the Judean royal family, and as such, you have the power to thwart the friar's plans."

Joseph shook his head. "No, that explains nothing. Father told me long ago that we are descendants of King David. But there are hundreds of David's descendants in the world today. Why is Friar Peter interested particularly in me? And how can I hope to defeat the friar if he has such extraordinary powers as you say he has?"

Instead of answering, Enoch reached into his robe and extracted a pouch. "Your father gave me this before he died. He had it on his person, and I think he had intended to show it to you or perhaps to give it to you later that evening. Do you wish to see it?"

Joseph nodded. In a faint voice, he answered, "Yes."

Enoch stood up and walked to the mouth of the cave. He beckoned Joseph and his companions to follow. "Come here in the moonlight," he said.

Slowly, carefully, Enoch untied the rope that held the pouch shut. He inverted the pouch and shook the contents into his palm. A smile crept over Enoch's face as the three youths stared at the beautiful, large emerald in his hand. The stone seemed to absorb the moonlight, giving off a faint green glow, which seemed to increase in intensity as they watched.

Joseph stood agape. After a few moments, he recovered his composure and said, "How is it glowing? I've never seen a stone do that."

"Yes," said Enoch. "This stone is unique. It glows in the moonlight, but only when the moon is full."

"Tonight is not the full moon," Aaron interjected. "That was two nights ago, on the first night of Passover."

"Ah," said Enoch. "That is true. And indeed the emerald would not glow tonight, except that I have willed it to do so."

Joseph looked at Enoch defiantly. "Then let's see you make it stop."

Slowly the glow faded away.

"Now make it glow again."

Enoch said, "You are a hard man to convince, Joseph. But I will do as you say."

The emerald glowed again with a faint green glow. Enoch smiled at Joseph. He closed his fist around the stone and walked back into the cave.

"It belonged to my father?" Joseph asked, following Enoch into the cave. He still had his doubts about Enoch, but there was no doubt the man had Powers.

"Yes," said Enoch. "It is a perfect stone."

He placed the emerald back into its pouch and tied the rope around it. He took Joseph's hand and thrust the pouch into it. "And now, the stone is yours," he said.

Joseph's hand was trembling. "But how? Where did he get such a stone? And what does this stone have to do with what happened two nights ago in Camryn?"

Enoch returned to the spot where he had been sitting before. "Sit," he said, "and I will explain."

When they were all seated on the ground again around the tablecloth, Enoch continued. "About one thousand six hundred years ago, shortly before the exile of the Jewish people from the Holy Land, God appeared to the prophet Jeremiah in a vision and told him of the tragedy that was to come. He revealed to Jeremiah how the Babylonians would soon conquer Jerusalem, burn the holy temple to the ground, and exile the remnant of the Jewish people to a distant land. But, the Lord told Jeremiah, certain objects, among them the high priest's breastplate, must not fall into Babylonian hands. He instructed the prophet to take the breastplate and hide it away in a secret place, there to remain until the latter days, when it will reappear in time of need, in a period of great suffering, and its power will be used to save the Jewish people and the world."

"Is this one of the stones of the breastplate?" Aaron asked.

"Yes," said Enoch. "As you may know, the breastplate was made of a fabric of woven gold thread intertwined with blue, purple, and crimson linen and silk threads, upon which were inlaid twelve precious stones in a rectangular pattern of three by four. Each stone represented one of the twelve tribes of Israel. In time of national emergency and at certain other times, the high priest could ask the Lord for guidance, and the Lord would answer by making certain stones light up successively, according to a code known only to the high priest and one other designated priest. The emerald was the stone of the tribe of Judah, the tribe of King David and his descendants."

"Where is the rest of the breastplate?" Aaron asked. "And how did this emerald get to England?"

"Be patient, Aaron, and I will tell you all that is within my power to tell." Enoch paused a moment and looked at Joseph. Then he continued:

"Jeremiah hid the high priest's breastplate as instructed. But before hiding it away, he removed one stone – the emerald. You see, the power of the breastplate is great, but all twelve stones must be in place before its power can be used. Jeremiah wanted to ensure that if the breastplate fell into the wrong hands, its power could not be used without the missing stone.

"The breastplate was a priestly garment, and only the high priest was allowed to wear it, but the emerald was the stone of Judah, the stone of royalty; and therefore Jeremiah gave it to your distant ancestor, a member of the royal family, to be passed down through the generations until the appointed time."

Joseph said, "Do you mean to tell me that this stone has been passed from father to son for centuries in my family?"

Enoch nodded.

"Then why can I not hold it for many years, as my father did, and pass it on to my son? Nobody can use the breastplate without this stone, and what makes you think that now is the appointed time?"

"I don't know that it is," said Enoch. "But this you need to understand: the world exists in constant tension of opposing forces – love and hatred, water and fire, light and darkness, good and evil. Right now, the world is in equilibrium between good and evil, but Peter has brought the world to the verge of crisis, threatening to tip the balance to the side of evil. Peter is not what he seems. He is not a man of God. If Peter can control the power of the breastplate, he will not only annihilate the Jews from Christendom and massacre the Saracens, but he will eventually rule the world, or what remains of it. It is true that Friar Peter has a special loathing for the Jews, but rousing the masses to kill the Jews is also a convenient first step to raise a coterie of followers in his quest for worldly power. When he has achieved that goal, he will trample justice even among the Christians, and he will unravel the entire fabric of humanity. Peter knows about the breastplate, and he is seeking it. He does not know you have the missing stone; perhaps he doesn't even know that one stone is missing; but he sensed your presence as

soon as he arrived in Camryn, and somehow, when your father
expired, Peter sensed that you hold the key to the object that he
seeks. And this he also knows: in all the world, only you have
the power to thwart his plans. Joseph, you too have powers of
which you have no knowledge yet, but you will discover them in
time. Peter does not know your powers either, but as soon as
he entered your home, he sensed a threat. He fears you, Joseph,
and yet he knows he also needs you somehow if he is to find the
breastplate. He will pursue you relentlessly to the ends of the
earth. He will not rest until one of you defeats the other."

"How do you know these things? Can you read the friar's
mind?"

"I told you, I have powers. I am sorry; I can tell you no more.
I see you still are skeptical. You will have to find out for yourself
that there is no escape from your appointed role. I just pray that
when you do, it will not be too late." Enoch turned and drew his
cowl over his head.

Rachel asked, "Are you leaving us? How will we escape?"

Enoch turned to Rachel. "Do not fear. I have given my word
to Joseph's father, and I will keep my oath. Mind you, it is not
my role to defeat Friar Peter. That is Joseph's task. But I will
protect Joseph to the best of my ability. And I will protect
you too – you and your brother – until Friar Peter's defeat has
been assured. It is not coincidence that brought the three of
you together. As you well know, you and your brother are of
the priestly class, but there is also something more about your
lineage: you are descendants of Seraya, the last high priest of
the holy temple in Jerusalem at the time of the prophet Jeremiah.
Your destinies are intertwined with Joseph's. But now I must
depart, for there are other pressing matters to which I must
attend immediately."

"How will we survive?"

"Sleep now. No one will disturb you here. In the morning,
go east two miles, away from Sherwood forest. You will come to

a road. Follow it southwards. There is more food in the chest there by the wall. Take it with you on your journey."

Joseph asked: "How far south must we go?"

"To Dover, where you will meet a ferryman named Cuthbert. He will transport you across the English Channel to Calais. You must not rest there, however. Your destination is the Rhone Valley, in the south of France. There you will be safe, at least for a while. But do not think to hide from Peter forever. He is seeking you, and he will find you."

"What will happen then?" Rachel asked.

"When Joseph is ready to accept his role, I will be there."

He reached into his cloak and pulled out a large leather purse. He threw the purse to Joseph. "There is plenty of money in that purse," he said. "You won't starve. May God be with you."

Joseph asked, "How long will it be before he finds us?"

Enoch did not answer. He turned away and exited the cave.

Joseph ran to the mouth of the cave. He looked down the hillside, to his left, and to his right. But there was no sign of Enoch. He had disappeared.

CHAPTER 8

Monday, 26ᵗʰ March 1190

Monday, 26ᵗʰ March 1190

Joseph, Aaron, and Rachel set out before sunrise.

In his mind, Joseph re-played last night's events. The emerald glowed in the moonlight, and its glow seemed to wax and wane at Enoch's will. There was no doubt that Enoch had powers. And yet ... . Joseph was not completely sure he should trust the man. Nevertheless, as Mab had said, his options were limited. For now, he would suspend his doubts.

Last night's fog still lingered in the valley, and Joseph was thankful for the protection it afforded them. After about an hour, they reached the southward road that Enoch had indicated. At first they stayed off the road and walked among the trees parallel to the road, but the rough terrain slowed them down. By mid-afternoon, they were exhausted, and they had finished the last of their food.

"Someone's coming," Joseph said, motioning to his friends to lie on the ground.

A mule-drawn cart passed by on the road, its wooden wheels creaking loudly. A large pile of hay occupied the back of the cart. The driver, a tall man wearing a black cloak, was humming softly to himself. Joseph did not see any passenger in the cart.

"Whoa, Timothy," said the driver, pulling on the reins. "Time to rest. The cart halted about thirty paces down the road from Joseph, and the driver dismounted. He led the mule to a tree and tied him up. "That's a good boy, Timothy," he said, caressing the mule's neck. He took a pitchfork from the cart and pitched some hay onto the ground in front of Timothy.

"There you are," he said, walking away. "Now eat. I won't be long."

As the driver disappeared from view, Aaron whispered, "Where's he going?"

"To relieve himself, I think," said Joseph.

After a few minutes, the man returned to his cart. Now Joseph was able to see him more clearly. He appeared to be about forty years old, with a pleasant face and an easy-going manner. He was unarmed, and under his cloak he wore a long purple gown.

"A priest," Joseph whispered, and Aaron nodded.

The priest reached up to the cart and found some cheese and a loaf of bread. He sat down on a rock by the roadside and began to eat.

"I'm hungry," Rachel whispered, "and we have no more food. Do you think we can trust him? Maybe he can give us something to eat."

"But maybe he's in league with Friar Peter," Joseph said.

Aaron put his hand on Joseph's shoulder and said, "We can't stay hidden forever, or we'll starve. This priest has a kind face, and I have a good feeling about him. I think we should chance it."

"Wait a few more minutes," Joseph said. "I want to observe him a while longer."

"A few more minutes, and he may be gone," said Aaron. "What more will you know about him in a few minutes? I think we should approach him now."

Joseph thought a few seconds and said, "Alright, Aaron. I will put my trust in your intuition. Let's go."

Slowly they approached the priest, still walking cautiously among the trees. His gaze was on the road, and he apparently was not yet aware of their presence. He was still eating, but between each bite of food, he looked up at the sky and spoke some words in a melodious voice. "Quis ascendet in montem Domini? Aut quis stabit in loco sancto ejus?"

He took another bite of cheese, looked upwards, and continued: "Innocens manibus et mundo corde, qui non accepit in vano animam suam."

A branch snapped under Joseph's foot. The priest interrupted his recitation and shifted his gaze. His face turned pale. He crossed himself and stood up. "I am but a poor priest," he said. "Please have mercy on your Christian brother, and I will bless you if you will."

"We are not here to rob you," said Joseph. "We are tired and hungry. It is we who ask your mercy. Can you spare some food?"

The priest breathed a sigh of relief. "Of course, of course. I was just reciting a psalm of David, and God must have sent you to me. My name is Father John. Pray, what are your names?"

Joseph hesitated.

"Oh, I see," said Father John. "You may remain nameless. I understand. If you are not brigands, then you must be fugitives. Yes, I see that by your appearance. Terror is written on your young faces. You have been through much. Are you come from Camryn?"

After a momentary pause, Joseph nodded, but he did not speak.

"Yes, I thought so. Jews from Camryn. I know what happened there. It is the talk of the countryside, and news travels fast." He looked at each of them in turn, studying their faces. "Do not fear," he said. "I have no doubt that God has sent you to me, and I will help you."

He reached into his cart and extracted a large cheese. "Here. Take this. Go back off the road and eat, but you must eat quickly. Then return, and I will take you as far as you want to go. I can hide you under the haystack."

Hidden behind a large rock among the trees, they ate their cheese. Joseph whispered: "Maybe we should run away. I don't know if it is wise to trust this priest. The whole Christian world seems to be against us, and didn't we experience their wrath just three nights past? Why should he be different?"

"Because he is," said Aaron. "They aren't all against us. There is goodness and kindness also among the Christians. Didn't Matthew save your life? I think the priest may be right: God sent us to him. And I think we have to trust him, because on our own we'll soon be caught."

Joseph remained unconvinced. He looked at Rachel questioningly. "I'm not sure," she said.

Joseph looked up. "I hear something," he said.

In the distance, on the road, he saw a cloud of dust, and he heard the thunder of horses' hooves. His first thought was to run, but he quickly realized it was too late for that. If the horsemen were seeking him, he could not run far before they caught him. He would be better off staying in hiding and hope that Aaron was right, and the priest would not give them away.

Soon two horses came to a halt near Father John's cart. Mounted on the horses were two men in chain mail. A long sword hung at each one's side. One man dismounted and saluted the priest. "Good day, Father," he said.

Father John nodded. "Good day to you, and God speed."

"Thank you, Father. We are in pursuit of a murderer, a Jewish youth escaped from Camryn. He may be in the company of two others. Have you seen anyone of that description?"

Father John thought a moment and answered, "This road is not much traveled. I have not encountered any travelers on this road for at least an hour, and those were grown men on horseback. And before that, nobody fitting your description either."

"Thank you, Father. I am sorry to disturb you. May God be with you," he said, mounting his horse. The two riders spurred their horses, and they sped away southwards.

"I suppose we will have to trust him now," said Joseph. He rose and ran to Father John. Aaron and Rachel followed close behind.

When they reached the road, Father John had already untied the mule, and he was sitting on his cart, in the driver's seat.

Father John smiled. "Well, it's about time. So, you've decided to throw your lot in with me after all. Where can I take you? I am going south, to Canterbury."

"We are bound for Dover, but if you will take us to Canterbury, it will not be far from there."

"Very well," said Father John. "Climb in, and get under the hay. We have many miles to travel."

*   *   *

In Camryn, the mood was one of rejoicing and merriment. That evening, the Camryn Inn was filled to capacity. In Friar Peter's wake, several men had taken up the cross, and they were at the inn to celebrate their expected battles and victories on behalf of God and Church. Alfred sat at a table with Matthew and with the four friends who had been with him on the night of the massacre.

"Cheer up, Matthew," Alfred said. "Today's a great day, a day for celebration. No need to be so serious, son. Easter's over, and today we celebrate our town's rebirth – free from Jews, free from evil, free from Satan's influence. The holy friar was right. You can feel the difference in the air already." He raised his cup in a toast. "Here's to Friar Peter. God bless Peter the Pious."

Alfred's four friends raised their cups. "God bless Friar Peter," they cried out in unison. Matthew was the last to lift his cup. He raised it to his lips and took a sip of beer but didn't join the toast.

"What's ailing Matthew?" one of the men at the table asked Alfred. "He doesn't seem himself today."

"Oh, I don't know," Alfred said. "He was friends with that Jewish lad. Mayhap the Jews cast an evil spell on him. But we broke their spell, didn't we? When Christians come together, even the Jews' most powerful hexes are no match for us. Yes, surely Matthew was under a spell. But he'll get over it. Give him time."

Another of Alfred's friends looked Matthew in the eyes and said, "Y'know, Matthew, ye're lucky we rid you of yer Jewish friend. Saved you from the Lord's wrath we did. He'd 'ave dragged you down to Hell, he would. Hell and eternal damnation. Someday ye'll realize that, and then ye'll thank us for it."

"I'll never thank you for it. What you did was murder. Jews or Christians, it makes no difference. It was murder."

The man shook his head in obvious dismay.

Matthew rose and turned to go.

Alfred said sternly, "Come back here, Matthew. Where's your manners? You haven't been excused."

But Matthew ignored his father and walked away. As he left, he heard his father say, "Don't mind the boy. He's just misguided, but he'll come around."

Matthew walked down the street slowly. Soon he turned a corner and found himself in the former Jewish part of town. He passed the site where the synagogue had stood but three days ago, now a burnt-out heap of rubble. Walking southwards, he passed the many vacant homes that lined the street. The pall of death hung over the neighborhood. Matthew looked up at the moon, no longer full as it had been three nights previously. It was beginning to wane, as Camryn itself was also waning, Matthew thought.

He passed Joseph's former home. The house was empty, dead. A tear trickled down Matthew's cheek, and he quickly wiped it away.

"I can't stay here anymore," Matthew said to no one in particular. He looked toward Sherwood Forest. "May God be with you, Joseph," he whispered.

He continued wandering the streets, walking aimlessly, for how long he did not know. Eventually he found himself before his own front door. Slowly he opened the door and entered, looking all around. A tunic was lying on a chair. He picked it up and looked at it. Somehow, it did not look familiar, although it probably was his. His home seemed alien to him now. He no longer belonged here.

"Is that you, Matthew?" It was his mother's voice.

"Yes, mother," Matthew said, before he realized it couldn't possibly be his mother after all. She had died in childbirth when he was nine years old, nor had the child survived long after her. Matthew was alone in the house, and, he quickly realized, the voice he had heard, his mother's voice, was only in his mind.

He smiled, and his eyes looked up to heaven. "Yes, mother," he said; "I am glad you are with me now."

He gathered his belongings and stuffed them in a bag. As he left the house, he said, "Farewell, mother. Please tell father that I have left. I won't be back. No longer can I stay in this sinful place; and if father will not recognize that he has sinned, then I must atone for him, and indeed for all of Camryn. I don't know yet how, but I will find a way. I must, because I am as guilty as the rest of them. You are not like father, and I know I have your blessing, mother. May your soul be blessed."

He closed the door and left. He did not look back.

CHAPTER 9

"**S**o you want to atone for your father," said Abbot Geoffrey. The abbot, an elderly man with a bald pate, dressed in an immaculate dark, almost black, tunic and matching dark woolen cowl, sat behind his desk, his bright blue eyes scrutinizing Matthew.

"Yes, Father Abbot," said Matthew. "For my father and for all of Camryn." *And for my own part in this atrocity.* But of his own role he dared not speak aloud to Abbot Geoffrey. That would remain hidden in his soul, and revealed to God alone.

"That is commendable, and I greatly admire your spirit, but do you understand what you wish to undertake?"

"Yes, Father, indeed I think I do."

"How did you choose this abbey? There are, after all, so many abbeys in England."

Matthew thought a moment. On leaving Camryn three nights ago, he had not yet made up his mind where he would go or what he meant to do. He had taken the road north, skirting Sherwood Forest, and later, on a whim, veering eastward. He soon realized his feet were taking him in the direction of this abbey, whose abbot was known as far away as Camryn for his wisdom and compassion. It was a long, hard walk, and in his three days on the road, Matthew passed by several other abbeys, but none of them seemed right to him.

"I see you hesitate to answer. Am I, then, to infer that this abbey was a random selection?" Abbot Geoffrey smiled. "No, I did not think so. Do not be afraid. Speak up. I need to understand your reason."

"Permit me to say, Father, the monks of St. Dunstan's Abbey are known far and wide for their kindness and generosity of spirit. And it was not only the abbey that attracted me, but the Right Reverend Abbot himself. All the world knows of Abbot Geoffrey. I seek your blessing and your guidance."

Geoffrey smiled again. "That is very kind of you to say. My blessing I can give you, and my guidance also, for you are most deserving. But the other matter that you ask of me is much more difficult."

"Why, Father? I do not understand. Does this abbey no longer accept novice monks?"

"Oh, no; of course we do. And I fully understand your desire to do something beyond the ordinary to serve the Lord. But I see your soul is restless, and I do not think your restlessness of spirit results purely from your recent circumstances. My heart tells me that you are not suited to monastic life."

"But aren't prayer and self-deprivation the surest way to penance?"

Abbot Geoffrey leaned forward and whispered: "It is our way, but surely not the only way. There are many paths to holiness. There are many ways to God."

Matthew turned his gaze away. He twisted in his seat. Certainly he had not expected this turn of events. He looked up again and said, "What, then, would Father Abbot suggest I do?"

Abbot Geoffrey leaned back in his chair. "What do restless souls do to expiate their sins? Have you thought of taking up the cross and going to the Holy Land to fight the battles of the Lord?"

Matthew didn't think even a second. "No," he said emphatically. "I mean, I have thought of it, but I will not do it."

The abbot said nothing, but his look encouraged Matthew to continue.

"Surely, fighting the battles of the Lord is a very worthy cause, and the pope himself has given it his blessing and his imprimatur. But, as Father Abbot said, there are many paths to holiness. I am a blacksmith, not a warrior. I have seen the men who took the cross when Friar Peter preached in Camryn. They were ruffians mostly, thirsting for blood. I am not one of them."

The abbot looked into Matthew's eyes. "Yes," he said, "St. Dunstan was a blacksmith too, like you. I will grant you that. And yet, perhaps a pilgrimage would suit you better, an unarmed pilgrim to Rome or to the Holy Land."

"Please, Father Abbot," Matthew said; "I have witnessed friends and neighbors being slaughtered. I have seen blood flowing in the streets. I have no desire to witness more horrors. As a blacksmith, my arms are strong, and I could wield a weapon as well as anybody if I had to do so. But I am not like other blacksmiths. My mother, God rest her soul, taught me the value of words. Since her untimely death, I have taught myself to read. I train myself to speak like a man of learning and not like an ordinary lout. I have taught myself Latin. I read the Bible. I try to make myself worthy in the eyes of God. It is my wish to join your abbey and devote myself to works of kindness. I ask your blessing, Father Abbot."

Geoffrey thought for a long while. He looked again into Matthew's eyes. Finally, he said, "I see you are sincere, but in my heart I know this path is not for you. And yet, you have suffered greatly. You need time to mend. I will not accept you as a postulant in this abbey, but you may stay here as a guest."

Geoffrey paused a moment, and Matthew interjected: "But Father Abbot … ."

Abbot Geoffrey held his hand up. "I haven't finished yet, my son. When your soul has mended somewhat, you must undertake a pilgrimage to Rome, to the tombs of St. Peter and St. Paul. You may travel alone or with companions, but you must go on foot. The journey is long and difficult, and it will do much to heal you. Do not wait too long, however, to begin your pilgrimage, for there is some urgency about it."

"Thank you, Father Abbot. I am very grateful for your insight and your understanding. But I ask you humbly, why is it urgent?"

Abbot Geoffrey shook his head. "I cannot say for certain. It is just a feeling, a premonition that I have."

He paused a moment and scrutinized Matthew's face. "I see you have doubts," he said; "doubts that a pilgrimage to Rome will be sufficient to expiate your feelings of guilt, doubts about my assessment of your nature, doubts about my premonition and the urgency that I feel is needed. And yet, my son, you came to me initially to seek my guidance. It seems you put your trust in me and in my judgement. I am truly sorry that I cannot explain my reasons further, but it is my strong belief that you must go to Rome, and also that there is some urgency about your journey.

"While in Rome, even before visiting the tombs of St. Peter and St. Paul, there is one more thing I will require you to do. First you must go to see a friend of mine, a man of great erudition, Cardinal Giacinto Bobone. Many years ago, in my youth, I journeyed to Rome to enhance my learning, and there I met Giacinto. We became fast friends, and to this day we correspond. You must go to him and report what you have seen in Camryn. By then, he will have heard about it, but I think it important that he hear it told to him by someone who experienced it first-hand. Before you leave for Rome, I shall give you a letter of introduction to Cardinal Bobone. The cardinal will tell you what more you must do, and he will give you his blessing."

CHAPTER 10

Joseph stood on the pier looking out at the water. The day was very windy, and great white waves thrashed across the surface. The ferryboat moored to the pier lurched back and forth with the waves.

"Get in, get in," the ferryman said. "Just waiting for two more passengers. Then we cast off."

Rachel looked at the hull of the ferry and asked, "Are you sure this boat can make it across the channel?"

"Aye," said the ferryman sternly. "This ferry's crossed the channel an 'undred times without a scratch. She's sturdy as they come."

Rachel looked out to sea.

"Don't mind the waves," said the ferryman, smiling. "They'll beat agin' the boat and rock us to and fro, and if ye're not accustomed to it, ye may get sick. But I'll get ye safe across, or my name's not Cuthbert. I've been ferrying folks across the channel now for many years. Never lost a passenger yet."

Aaron helped Rachel into the boat. Joseph followed them and was about to sit down. But cutting through the thunder of the waves against the boat, Joseph heard the clatter of horses' hooves. He turned around and saw three men approach on horseback. The men were covered head to toe in chain mail. They came to an abrupt stop next to the pier. The lead man wore an orange badge on his upper arm, and his sword was drawn.

"Halt!" said the man with the drawn sword. "The three of you, get out of the boat. Now!"

Joseph hesitated, but Cuthbert said, "I think ye'd better do as he says and go with him. That's the constable. I'll wait for ye if I can."

As the three youths started to leave the boat, the constable turned to Cuthbert. "Are these youths known to you?" he asked.

"Aye," said Cuthbert. "What seems to be the problem, Constable?"

"They may be wanted for some unrest up north some days ago. You say you know them?"

"They're friends."

The constable dismounted and motioned to Joseph to follow him. His men, still mounted, moved closer.

The constable pointed his sword at Joseph and motioned him and his two friends forward. When they were out of earshot of the ferry, the constable asked, "Where are you from?"

"Most recently from Canterbury."

"Most recently?"

"Yes, Constable. I am orphaned. My family lived in York – an uncle, but he died too. So I left."

"York, eh?" said the constable. He thought a moment. "With whom did you live in Canterbury, and how long were you there?"

"We were guests of a priest, Father John by name. We were with him in Canterbury for several months, I reckon."

"Father John is it? I know a Father John, but he doesn't live in Canterbury."

"Perhaps it is a different Father John," said Joseph. "It is a common name. Our Father John is in Canterbury now. We just left him yesterday."

"I see," said the constable. "And who are these?" He pointed to Aaron and Rachel with his sword.

"Friends of mine. I am going on pilgrimage, and they are traveling with me."

"Friends from York?"

Joseph nodded.

"Speak up so I can hear you."

"Yes, Constable."

"That's better." He turned to Aaron and asked, "Are you also on pilgrimage?"

"No, Constable. But for now, we are traveling together."

"What is your destination?"

"For now, Calais. I have kinsfolk I want to visit there."

"And then?"

"I have not decided. Perhaps I and my sister will continue with my friend."

The constable motioned to Joseph to go back to the pier. He turned to Cuthbert and called out: "You say you vouch for them?"

"Aye," said Cuthbert. "They're friends."

"Friends from where, Cuthbert?"

"From Canterbury, Constable. They're good friends o' mine from Canterbury. Is anything amiss?"

The constable sheathed his sword and mounted his horse. He looked at Joseph for a long while. He shook his head.

"I don't know," he said. "But Cuthbert vouches for you, and I have no cause to hold you. You may go."

As the constable and his men departed, Joseph said to Cuthbert, "Please, can we leave now? I will pay you extra."

"No need," said Cuthbert, but Joseph thrust a coin into his hand, and Cuthbert pocketed the coin.

"Thank you," Joseph said as the ferry pulled away from the pier.

"For what?"

"You told the constable that we are your friends."

"Aren't ye? Ye're friends o' Enoch," said Cuthbert. "Enoch's done good by me. I wouldn't be alive now if not fer him. 'Twas many years ago. A band o' cutthroats attacked me on the road. Enoch appeared out o' nowhere and single-handedly beat 'em back. He said I was a good man and didn't deserve to die just yet. He said there still was something I had to do before I die. He saved my life, and Cuthbert don't forget. Any friend o' Enoch's is a friend o' mine."

As the ferry pulled away from shore, Enoch stood on a cliff overlooking the English Channel. From afar, he watched the boat as it tossed about, pummeled by the waves and wind. They had escaped, for now.

Enoch raised his face to heaven. "Thank you, Lord," he said. "Protect these innocents from evil. May Your presence and your blessings go with them. Shine your face upon them, and give them peace."

Enoch waited a moment, but he heard no answer to his prayer. He looked out over the channel covered with fog.

He looked again to heaven and raised his arms, palms upwards. "Protect them, Lord," he said again.

"It is out of your hands, Enoch," said a whispered voice resounding in his head. "I will still send you on several missions to facilitate Joseph's way, but you will not intervene again directly on his behalf unless his life is threatened and if only by your actions can he be saved. Friar Peter's ultimate defeat must come about through Joseph's actions, not through yours. Therefore, if need be, you may do what is necessary to save his life, but you may do so one time only. The rest is up to him and his two friends."

"But they are defenseless, unaware of the great dangers that they face; and the power of their enemy is great."

"Nevertheless, Enoch, you will not intervene except as I have said. Joseph must find his way himself."

"Yes, my Lord," said Enoch. "I am your faithful servant. I will obey."

PART II

Enoch walked with God, and then he was no more,
for God had taken him.

Genesis 5:24

CHAPTER 11

Lyon, Rhone District (France)
Thursday, 30ᵗʰ August 1190

"Be careful, Joseph," said the older man. "That barrel contains our best wine, and I wouldn't want to disappoint the innkeeper."

"Don't worry, Daniel," said Joseph as he and three other men unloaded the heavy barrel from Daniel's wagon. "I am always careful. And this is the last barrel."

Daniel went inside the inn and emerged a few minutes later with another man, a tall, burly fellow with flowing hair and a large mustache. The man handed Daniel a purse.

"Thank you, Paul my friend," said Daniel, attaching the purse to his belt and closing his tunic over it. "I shall return next week."

"Yes," said Paul; "And that is good. My guests are always thirsty." He smiled at Daniel.

"By the way," said Daniel. "Did you know that Antoine is very ill?"

"I knew he was indisposed, but very ill?" He shook his head.

"I think the family doesn't want people to know how ill he is, so please don't publicize it. But I know you buy a lot of wine from him also, so I thought you should know. He's a good man. Go and visit him today. I just came from there. He does not look good at all. He may not last long, I think."

Daniel turned to mount his wagon, but Paul held his arm. "Be careful, Daniel. I have heard bad rumors lately."

Daniel waved his hand in a gesture of dismissal. "Oh, there are always rumors, but we are safe here."

"No, Daniel. I think you Jews may be in danger, even here. For months, I've heard of riots against the Jews up north. But now they're getting closer. Much closer. I hear people talking. An innkeeper hears many things, and I do not like what I hear lately."

"You worry too much, Paul," said Daniel, mounting his wagon.

"I sincerely hope so," said Paul. He shook his head and slowly walked back towards the inn, apparently deep in thought.

Joseph looked from Paul to Daniel, and he felt his heart racing in his chest. He closed his eyes, but Friar Peter's menacing visage flashed before his vision, and the dying screams of men and women in the streets of Camryn rang in his ears. He saw the image of his mother, blood flowing from her severed throat as she gasped her last breath. He saw his father lying on the floor, dying of his wounds as Friar Peter stood and watched, directing his men to violence and murder. In the distance, he heard the whispered echo of Enoch's parting words spoken months ago: "Do not think to hide from Peter forever. He is seeking you, and he will find you."

He opened his eyes again and looked down. His hands were shaking. As the wagon pulled away from the inn, Joseph turned to Daniel. "Are the riots really getting close?" he asked.

Daniel didn't look at Joseph. He kept his eyes on the road. "Don't worry, Joseph. We are not in danger here." But Daniel's face was solemn, and his voice was shaking ever so slightly. Joseph didn't ask him any more.

Several minutes passed in silence. Joseph tried to divert his attention to more happy thoughts. He listened to the creaking of the wagon's wheels and the rhythmic beat of the horses' hooves upon the road. In his mind's eye, the image of Sarah, the wine-merchant's daughter, came to him unbidden.

He reflected on the last three months since his arrival here. His chance meeting with Daniel the wine-merchant and his introduction to Sarah seemed so right, so pre-destined. Perhaps Daniel had also realized that when he hired Joseph to be his assistant. And very soon thereafter, love blossomed between Joseph and Sarah.

He thought of his many walks with Sarah through her father's vineyards and the throbbing of his heart whenever he caught sight of her. Propriety limited their physical closeness, and yet with words and caressing tone of voice, and the occasional stolen, secret, physical caress, they managed to communicate their feelings for each other.

He thought of Sarah's eyes and hair and lips. He smiled.

Suddenly he felt a need to share with Aaron his feelings about Sarah. Over the course of the summer, he had occasioned to meet with Aaron several times, and he had mentioned her to him. But he had not shared with Aaron the depth of his feelings for Sarah.

At length, Joseph asked, "May I stop off and visit my friends Aaron and Rachel before we leave Lyon? It is on our way."

"Yes, of course, of course," said Daniel. "We've made some good sales today, and the day is still young. But don't be too long. We must be back home in Chateau Blanc before evening."

*   *   *

In the city of Troyes, in the north of France, Friar Peter sat behind a large wooden desk in an ornately furnished room that was reserved for visiting ecclesiastic dignitaries. On the wall behind Peter, a large tapestry depicted a scene from the Book of Revelation, the breaking of the Sixth Seal: the sun was darkened, the moon was red as blood, the stars fell from heaven, the earth's crust was rent by a great earthquake, and the kings of the earth and the mighty men hid in dens and rocks among the fallen mountains.

Standing across the desk from Peter were two men. They appeared somewhat disheveled, and clods of dirt clung to their boots. A flash of metal gleamed beneath each of their cloaks.

Friar Peter eyed them sternly, looking them up and down. "So you had no success, you say."

"Yes, Reverend Brother," said one of the men.

"Yes, Reverend Brother," Peter repeated in a mocking, high-pitched tone. "The two of you are a disgrace!" he shouted, slamming his hand on the desk and standing up.

The men startled, and quickly looked down at the floor.

"You are silent. Are you ashamed of yourselves? Indeed you should be. There is no excuse for your failure, is there?" His voice was no longer loud, but it seethed with pent-up fury.

"No, Brother Peter," they answered in a small voice.

Peter glared at them. Still standing behind his desk, he rested both his fists on the desk and leaned forward toward the men. "Do not answer me like women. Speak up, with a full voice, like the men you claim to be, like the men you ought to be. Now let me hear you give a proper answer to my question."

"No, Brother Peter," they said in unison, somewhat louder than before. They looked up at Peter, and at the terrifying scene of the apocalypse on the tapestry behind him.

Peter sat down again behind the desk. "The boy Joseph whom you seek is of utmost importance to me. I have pursued him now these many months, from Camryn southwards and across the Channel. He must be caught; he must not get away. He is a murderer. He is a purveyor of evil. He is a son of Satan, a demon in the flesh. And you, through your stupidity and incompetence, have allowed him to slip away again." His voice rose to a crescendo.

"We have searched for him far and wide, but there was no sign of him. No one has seen him."

"You agree there is no excuse for failing to bring the boy to me, but still you make excuses. You say that no one saw him. But surely, he did not vanish off the face of the earth. I know for certain that he crossed the Channel. If you haven't found him yet, then you must search for him farther south. Do you not have minds of your own? Must I tell you everything that you must do?"

"Yes, Brother Peter, we will search farther south. We will find him this time, with God's help."

"With God's help. With God's help, you say. Do not fail me again. And do not think to blame God for your failures. It is you whom I hold responsible, not God."

"Yes, Brother Peter," they answered in unison.

"That is better." Peter's tone was more mellow now. He sat back in his chair. He motioned toward two chairs facing his desk. "Please sit down," he said.

When the two men were seated, Peter continued: "Much as I am eager for you to resume your search, there is something that I wish you to witness first. Tomorrow in the town square, I will preach to the good people of Troyes. Of course, you have heard me preach before, but tomorrow you will see a sight such as you have never seen in all your lives. For tomorrow I will show you what powers I command, and you will know what forces I can turn against you if you do not bring this boy to me."

*   *   *

The following day, a large crowd gathered in the town square. Standing on a podium elevated several steps above the crowd, Peter spoke to the hearts of the assembled throng, his voice rising and falling with the content and the cadence of his words. No one spoke. Their eyes were fixed on Friar Peter, and he felt their spirit flowing through him, inspiring his speech as his words inspired the religious fervor of his audience. He was their heart, their source of energy, animating their desire and their will.

"My friends, my fellow Christians," Peter said. "All I have said to you today is true, and all I have described for you will come to pass, unless you act with conviction and resolve. You must act to save the Church, to save the world, to save your souls from Hell. Evil is all around us, the gates of Hell are open wide, and the forces of Satan mingle among us every day, tempting good Christian folk to sin. The Saracens have taken Jerusalem. They have banished Christ from the Holy City, and their accursed prophet Mohammed usurps the rightful place of Christ. They have desecrated our holy shrines and repeatedly killed our pilgrims in their wrath. Their armies fight against us, against the holy Church, spreading Satan's power in the world. To those of you who can, I urge you to join the pilgrims in the Holy Land. Take up the cross, and take up your sword and axe and mace. Swear an oath. Ride into battle against the accursed Saracens, and help redeem Jerusalem from the infidel."

One large man in the crowd raised his sword above his head and called out: "Yes, Friar Peter. To God I pledge my sword."

"And I," shouted another man, raising his sword.

"And I," a third man cried.

Several others also pledged themselves. At length, Peter raised his hands. His voice rose above the jostling crowd. "That is well, my friends. We need spirit such as yours. God will grant His blessings to all who pledge themselves to fight His battles. And yet, I know that not all of you can fight the Saracens. Not all of you can leave your home, your family and friends. To you I say, God's battles are not fought only in the Holy Land. It is not the Saracens alone who fight in Satan's army. Not all of Satan's forces are armed with scimitar and dagger, fighting our armies on the field of battle. No, my fellow Christians: Satan's forces are everywhere, even here among you. Yes, in this very city of Troyes. They are demons in the guise of men, in the guise of women, and even in the guise of children. Their mission is to tempt your souls, to taint your purity, to lead you into sin."

"Who are these demons? Where can we find them? Tell us, Friar Peter," people shouted.

"They are here among you, this demonic army, disguised as ordinary people. Forced to wander the earth in punishment of their sins, condemned forever for their blasphemy against our Lord, despised and rejected from humankind, we must not show them any mercy; we must not let them live and walk among us, lest they bring us down to Hell along with them."

"Who are they, Friar Peter?"

"They greet you in the streets and wish you well. They buy your produce, but they will not eat with you. They converse with you, and yet they live apart, so you may never hear the dark secrets they communicate among themselves. They pretend to be good citizens of your cities and your towns. But all the while, within their hearts they mean you ill. Deceit and trickery are in their hearts. Make no mistake about it; do not be deceived: they are your deepest, darkest enemies."

"Who are they, Friar Peter?"

"My friends, you know them as well as I do. You know their evil, yet you shrink from purging it. You know very well who they are. You know this in your hearts: they are the Jews."

No sooner had Peter spoken those words than the crowd erupted in shouts and curses. A great wave of people flowed from the square, running, screaming, carried on the frenzied fury of their hatred. They reached the Jewish part of town. They broke down doors of Jewish shops and homes, taking and vandalizing property, dragging Jewish men and women into the streets and beating them. One man tried to fight back, and they clubbed him to death.

With a loud crash, they entered a home near the synagogue and soon emerged with a struggling woman. She had a pretty face, but her lower lip was bleeding, and her cheeks were red and swollen. Two men held her arms splayed outwards, and a third man held her legs, while a fourth man slapped her face repeatedly. "Where is your husband?" the fourth man shouted in her face.

"I do not know."

"Where is he?" He slapped her face again.

"Please stop hurting me. I don't know where he is."

The man pulled a dagger from his belt and held it up before her eyes.

The woman screamed. "Don't kill me. Please, don't kill me. I don't know where he is." She broke out in tears and loud sobs.

He seized her dress in his left hand, and with his right hand he slashed it down the middle to her waist, exposing her breasts. "You're a good-looking woman," he said, grabbing both her breasts. "The rabbi must enjoy you, eh?"

He released her breasts. Still holding his dagger, he took her face in both his hands and kissed her on the lips, a long, lascivious kiss. He withdrew his mouth from hers. "How old are you?" he asked.

"Thirty years old," she said through her tears.

He squeezed her breasts again, hard.

She screamed. "Please stop. Please don't do this to me. Please, I beg you."

"You beg me? Ha. I'll show you how to beg." He took the torn dress in his hand and, drawing his dagger again, he slashed the dress down to the ground and ripped it off her, along with her undergarment.

Somebody handed him a rope, and he tied it around her neck. "Get down on your hands and knees, and beg," he said. The three men holding the woman relaxed their grip, and the man with the rope pushed her down to the ground.

"On your hands and knees," he bellowed. "And kiss my feet."

A tear trickled down her cheek, but she uttered not a sound. Completely naked and trembling, she lowered herself slowly to her hands and knees. She bent her head. Her lips touched the man's leather boot.

One man got behind her and slapped her hard on her bare bottom. The crowd laughed, and many cheered.

"Hit her again!" somebody called out nearby.

She tried to rise, but somebody pushed her down again.

Somebody slapped her buttocks, harder than before. She tried to scramble away on hands and knees, but other men came forward, slapping her again, laughing and cheering in delight.

A man with a long black beard ran down the street. He was shouting frantically. "What have you done to my wife? My Rosa, what have they done to you?"

Three men seized him and brought him closer. "No, no!" he screamed. "How could you do this? Tell me what you want, and I will do it. But please release my wife."

"Be quiet, Rabbi, you son of Satan," one man shouted as he rammed his fist into the pit of the rabbi's stomach.

As the rabbi doubled over gasping for breath, Friar Peter appeared. "Enough!" he shouted. "Release the woman. Bring me the rabbi, and let him stand before me."

"This is Rabbi Abraham," said one of the bearded man's captors. "He is the rabbi of Troyes. We went to his home to arrest him, as you had ordered, but he was not at home."

"So we questioned the wife," another man interjected.

From the corner of his eye, Friar Peter glanced at the naked woman trying to gather up the tatters of her dress. "Yes," said Peter; "I see."

Friar Peter turned to the rabbi and took a step closer. "Rabbi, I charge you with sorcery and with the worship of the Lord of Darkness. I charge you with being Satan's minion and conspiring to lead the good people of Troyes into sin. I charge you with public immorality and with blasphemy. How do you plead?"

"Murderer!" the rabbi shouted. "You killed a man for defending himself. His body is still warm, lying on his back, his face upturned to heaven, bearing witness against you. You shamed and hurt my wife. You beat my people in the streets. May God curse you, Friar Peter, with the most horrible of punishments and the most terrible of deaths."

Friar Peter stood before the rabbi, apparently unperturbed by the rabbi's outburst. In a voice devoid of all emotion, he said, "You have not answered my question, Rabbi. How do you plead?"

Instead of answering, Rabbi Abraham spat a great wad of phlegm at the friar, splattering him in the face.

"Very well," said Peter, wiping the phlegm away and flinging it back at the rabbi. "You have condemned yourself."

"Death to the rabbi," shouted the rabble. "Kill the demon. Kill the son of Satan."

Peter smiled. "Do you hear that, rabbi? Do you hear them calling for your death?"

"It is you who are the devil. You may kill me, but you will not escape God's vengeance. I curse you, Friar Peter. I curse you in the name of God most high, the Lord of Hosts."

As the din of the mob rose higher, Peter turned his face upwards. In a booming voice, he shouted: "You heavens, I summon you. Obey me. May the darkness gather. Pour out your wrath at my command."

At once, the crowd was silent. Ominous clouds gathered in the sky where no clouds had been before. The sky turned dark, and a rumble of thunder echoed in the distance.

"Release the rabbi," Peter said. "Let him stand and face me. Rabbi, for the third time I ask you: you are charged with sorcery; how do you plead?"

Friar Peter's men released their captive. The rabbi stood erect. His face shouted defiance. "I accuse you of murder, Friar Peter, of murder, of violence, and of lechery. How do you plead?"

Peter's face turned white. His lips trembled slightly. He opened his mouth as if to speak, but there was only silence.

"How do you plead?" the rabbi said again.

"You will not defend yourself against the charge?" said Peter, regaining his composure. "Very well. Your silence condemns you and sentences you to death."

Peter paused. He looked at the crowd gathered around him. He looked at his own men, and his eyes met theirs.

His men drew their swords, but Peter held up his hand, palm outward, and the men stayed where they were.

Again he turned his face towards the rabbi. "I call upon the force of life." He pointed a finger at the rabbi's chest and shouted, "I call upon the forces of life and death. Blasphemer! Murderer! Demon! Jew! I sentence you to death. I command your wicked heart to stop."

The rabbi's face turned pale. He tried to speak, but no words came. He raised his hand and gripped his chest. Then, heavily he fell to the ground, dead.

*   *   *

In Rome, Cardinal Giacinto Bobone paced the floor. Despite his advanced age, he moved with ease, and his eyes sparkled with innate intelligence. He was a big man, well-built but not corpulent. He had a full face, a ruddy complexion. a sculptured nose, and a neatly-trimmed beard. He hardly seemed like a man of eighty-four years. "You do not understand," he said. "None of you do. Despite all my efforts, even His Holiness will not take it seriously."

"Of course not," said Cardinal Albino sitting behind his desk. "What matters it to you that there are riots against the Jews? Why do you seek to defend them? Are they not blasphemers? Are they not condemned to eternal punishment for their sins?"

Cardinal Bobone stopped pacing. "Are we, then, to be the agent of God's punishment? Judge not, lest ye be judged. If God chooses to punish, He is perfectly capable of doing so himself. Crimes have been committed in the name of God: vandalism, violence, and even murder. The Church must not contaminate itself with such deeds."

"Now, now. Do not exaggerate. It is not the Church. The Church does not preach violence against the Jews. It is the local populace who do these things. You know as well as I do that a deep-seated antipathy towards Jews is commonplace among the masses."

"Indeed. But we condone it. And through our preaching, often we reinforce their hatred and incite men to riot."

"We?" said Cardinal Albino. "No, not we. A few wayward preachers have incited men to riot and to mayhem."

Cardinal Bobone's voice rose. "But they are men of God. Some of them are friars; a few of them are priests. They represent the Church. This is not the way the Church should act. Have you not read St. Augustine?"

"I think," said Cardinal Albino, "your words are more inspired by Abelard than by Augustine. If it were anyone but you, my friend, who spoke these words, I would give your argument no credence at all. Among all the College of Cardinals, it is you whom we hold in the highest esteem. And yet, despite your standing in the College, I must reject your argument; and so, I think, will all the cardinals reject it. As your friend, I caution you against continuing to raise this issue."

Cardinal Bobone paced the floor again, more slowly this time. His hands were clasped before him. His eyes looked out into the distance.

At length, in a soft tone, he said, "Yes, my friend. I thank you for your advice, and I shall consider it. Good day."

On returning to his own chambers, Cardinal Bobone sat down heavily behind his desk. He sighed and turned his face to heaven. "O Lord," he said, "guide me, and show me the way that I must go. May the words of my mouth be pleasing to You. May my heart be steadfast in Your mission, and through me may great evil be averted."

No sooner had he finished his prayer than a knock on his door jolted him out of his reverie.

"Who is it?"

"Marco," said a voice.

"Come in, Marco."

The door opened a crack, and the cardinal's secretary appeared in the doorway. "Your Eminence," he said; "Father John has returned from his travels and requests an urgent audience with you."

"Yes, yes, of course. Bring him in at once."

The door opened, and in walked a clean-shaven man of about forty years, clad in a long purple robe and holding a black cloak over his arm. It was the same man who had helped Joseph and his friends in their escape from Friar Peter months before. He now approached the cardinal, genuflected, and kissed the ring on the cardinal's outstretched hand.

Cardinal Bobone motioned Father John to sit. "Is it as bad as they say?"

"Worse," Father John answered. "As you requested, I went to England. I arrived there just before the massacre at Camryn. I have been following Friar Peter for months, Your Eminence, ever since the massacre."

The cardinal shook his head, and his face turned grave. "Yes, Camryn. Such cruelty. Such inhumanity. Such Godlessness. And all in the name of God. It is hard to believe. I have heard reports of Camryn many times, but none from an eyewitness. Did you witness the massacre, my son?"

"No, Your Eminence, I did not. I reached Camryn too late. But I was close by, and I met some refugees whose families had been murdered and who themselves had escaped death by the skin of their teeth. Later, I heard Friar Peter preach several times in England and in France. In each town that he visits, he stirs up the people to take the cross and fight for God in the Holy Land. He is a great orator, a demagogue; and when he has lit the hearts of men on fire with his rhetoric, he turns his wrath against the Jews, calling them sons of Satan and purveyors of evil. I have witnessed this myself in Bedford, Winchester, and Canterbury, and again across the Channel in Rouen and Chartres. From there, he was headed to Paris when we parted ways. I thought it best to return to Rome and report to you."

"My God! Were there massacres of Jews in all those cities? I have not heard of this."

"No, Your Eminence. In some there were riots in which Jews were humiliated, beaten, and many of their homes and shops destroyed or vandalized. In some towns, isolated deaths occurred. In Camryn, Stamford, Norwich, Lynn, and York, wholesale massacres of Jews took place, but Friar Peter was responsible only for those in Camryn and in Stamford, and perhaps in York as well, although of York I am not certain."

"Yes," said the cardinal. "News of some of those events have reached my ears. But I waited to hear of this from you, my trusted messenger. I thank God that you continued on your course and did not see fit to return to me earlier. But today I was expecting you, having been informed of your approach in a dream I had last night. Tell me, Father, what is your impression of the friar?"

"Well, I thought … ."

"I know, I know. You have told me already about the facts. What I want is your impression of Friar Peter's motives. What sort of man is he? What motivates him? What animates his soul? Is he impelled by hatred or by religious zeal?"

The priest thought a moment and said, "In truth, Your Eminence, I do not know for certain. I have seen both hatred and religious fervor in his speech. Surely, Friar Peter's agitation against the Jews is not unique in content. It is commonplace in the sermons of friars throughout Christendom. And yet, Friar Peter's demeanor, and his power over the masses somehow give me pause. His words convey true virtue and Christian spirit. But in his voice I feel the sound of hatred, of malice, and of other feelings that I can't identify for certain. Truly, Your Eminence, Friar Peter is an enigma."

"Yes, Father John; I see," said the cardinal. "It is indeed a difficult problem, and I must think a moment. Please excuse me while I meditate on it." Cardinal Bobone lowered his gaze. He clasped his hands together. He closed his eyes.

After about two minutes of silence, the cardinal opened his eyes, but his eyes were still turned downwards. His lips began to move, and whispered words escaped his lips:

"Venite, et videte opera Domini, quae posuit prodigia super terram, auferens bella usque ad finem terrae. Arcum conteret, et confringet arma, et scuta comburet igni."

The cardinal looked up. "These are terrible times," he said. "Good and evil are clouded over, and we discern with difficulty wherein lies the path of righteousness. I have heard reports of Friar Peter's actions, and they have disturbed me greatly. By all accounts, he is a holy man, fervent and devout."

The cardinal paused, and Father John asked, "Does His Eminence, then, not believe the friar is sincere?"

"Oh, no. I did not say that. In truth, I do not know for sure. And yet, although the friar may indeed be holy and sincere, and although his intentions may be for the sake of heaven, neither he nor we can know what other forces his venom-filled words may unwittingly unleash. The friar stirs men to attack the Jews, but it is not the Jews alone that his words attack. In my long years, I have trained myself to see and feel God's presence in the world. Some might call this mysticism, but I prefer to call it sensitivity to the divine will. For months I have felt the stirring of evil forces in the world. No, not in the Holy Land where our brave warriors fight the infidel, but here within the body of Christendom itself. It is only something vague, a portentous ripple in the air, a diaphanous veil of darkness prodding at the soul. But I have no doubt. I have felt this, and I know that it is real. I have tried to warn my colleagues of the danger, but none believe me, not even my closest friends, not even the Holy Father himself. And so it is my task alone to fight against this evil as best I can."

Cardinal Bobone rose and walked slowly across the room. He went to a chest of drawers against the wall, and, opening one of the drawers, he extracted five scrolls sealed with red wax bearing the cardinal's seal. He handed the scrolls to Father John.

"These scrolls contain an urgent message, which must be delivered before Friar Peter arrives. He may be still in France, but

I surmise that he intends to come to Rome before the year is out; perhaps much sooner. He will probably arrive by ship in Naples or in Genoa. Father John, you will go first to Naples, then to Florence, Lucca, Genoa, and finally to Pisa, and you will deliver the scrolls to the prelates of those cities. Go quickly, before Friar Peter arrives. There is not much time."

CHAPTER 12

Chateau Blanc, Rhone District (France)
Thursday, 13ᵗʰ September 1190

The sun was high in the sky, bathing the vineyard in yellow light. The vines were rich with plump red grapes. Soon the harvest would begin, and there would be no time for leisure. But today, Joseph strolled through the vineyard with Sarah, the wine merchant's daughter.

Joseph stopped and looked into Sarah's eyes. "I love your eyes in the midday sun."

Sarah laughed. "Is it because you see a reflection of your own face?"

Joseph took both of Sarah's hands in his. "No, no, not myself. I see into your soul. I see your heart. I see the world. I see our future."

Sarah smiled whimsically. "And what is in our future?" she asked.

Joseph hesitated.

Sarah's face turned serious. "What is it, Joseph? Do you see nothing in my eyes?"

Joseph brushed a golden hair out of Sarah's eye. His hand gently caressed her cheek. "I love you, Sarah, and I want to marry you. But how can I ask your father for your hand? I have no land. I have little money. I have no reputation in your community, and I have been here for so short a time. I just arrived in the early summer, an orphan, unknown. Your father likes me well enough,

I think. But he likes me only as his employee. I doubt he would accept me as his son-in-law."

Sarah put her forefinger on Joseph's lips. "Enough," she said, and kissed him.

Joseph drew away slightly. He looked around furtively.

"What is it, Joseph?" She asked with a smile and a twinkle in her eye. "Has your love evaporated so quickly?"

He clasped both her hands in his. Again, he looked deep into her eyes. "You know that is not so," he said seriously. "It is just that I was afraid someone may have seen that kiss and will think ill of us."

She laughed merrily and playfully kissed him on his lips again.

"No one sees us here," she said. "You worry too much. You are very well regarded by those who know you, especially by my father. And he's the only one who counts."

"But ... ."

"No buts. My father will say yes. You will see. Just ask him."

It was late afternoon when Joseph and Sarah emerged from the vineyard. A man in a horsedrawn wagon passed by. He gave them a cursory nod but didn't say a word. Two minutes later, another man rode by on horseback, followed shortly by yet another rider. Neither rider seemed to notice Joseph and Sarah at all.

"That is very strange," said Sarah. "I know those men. They are friends of my father. Something is not right."

Three more men passed them before they reached the house. As they approached, Sarah's mother ran out towards them.

"Thank God you are safe," she said in a tremulous voice, taking Sarah's hand. She embraced Sarah and kissed her head.

Sarah's face turned pale. "What happened? Is father ... ?"

"Your father is fine," she said. "Just go in quickly."

Inside, a large number of men were assembled, talking loudly and arguing with each other. Sarah's mother motioned to Joseph to join the men, while she took Sarah to another room.

Daniel the wine merchant entered and called the men to order. Joseph took a seat in the back of the room, feeling very much out of place among the leaders of the Jewish community.

"My friends," said Daniel. "Thank you for coming in this time of crisis. By now you have all heard the news. Our community may be in grave danger, and we must plan a strategy to defend ourselves."

"That is ridiculous," one man called out. "We are not in danger here in Chateau Blanc. Even though there have been occasional hateful sentiments expressed toward Jews, such incidents are uncommon. Unlike many other communities, we have generally good relations with the Christians here. And please remember, our businesses are important to the local populace. They wouldn't harm us."

There were several murmurs of agreement, but Daniel raised his hand. "Yes, our businesses are important to our Christian neighbors, but Jewish businesses were also prominent in Rouen and Chartres. They also thought themselves safe from harm. And yet, Jews were murdered there. You have all heard the reports."

"Yes," another man called out. "A hateful friar who preaches to the masses."

"A demagogue," said another man.

"A messenger of death."

"Yes," said Daniel. "He is all those things, and more. Much more. The last I heard, he had left Paris and was nearing Troyes. Everywhere he goes, death follows him. Everywhere, he stirs up hatred against the Jews. I fear he is heading in our direction. We must prepare to meet this threat."

Joseph felt his mind drifting, hearing the proceedings as though from a great distance. His mind was elsewhere – back in Camryn. He heard the screams of friends. He smelled the stench of blood. He heard his mother's voice in her final anguished moments. He heard the friar's voice saying, "Where is the oldest one? You mustn't let him get away." A tear trickled down Joseph's cheek, and then another.

His mother was dead, and yet, through his tears, Joseph heard his mother's voice again: "Run, my Joseph, run. Do not look back. Run, and save yourself."

"What is the friar's name?" Joseph heard the question asked. It echoed through him as through a fog, and all at once it stirred him back to consciousness. He blinked. He looked around him, trying to see who had asked the question.

Everybody turned around. They looked at Joseph. Only then did he realize that it was he who had asked the question.

"Who is this young man?" one person asked.

"He has no right to speak," said another. "He's a stranger here."

Daniel held up his hand. "Do not be harsh, my friends. It is true he is a stranger, but he has every right to speak. He is a guest in my house, come to me from England, where he lost his family in just such a riot as you have heard described. Better than any of you, he knows the cruelty that stirs men's hearts and the evil that they can commit. With his own eyes he has witnessed what we must here prevent."

He paused a moment, and, almost in a whisper, he said, "The friar's name is Peter. 'Peter the Pious' he is called."

*　*　*

In the guest house of a monastery north of Lyon, Friar Peter paced the floor. There was a knock at the door, and Friar Peter stopped his pacing. He took a seat behind the bare wooden desk. "Come in," he called out.

The door opened, and a tall man in riding boots entered. A sword hung at his side. "Reverend Brother," he said. "I've brought news."

The friar cocked his head but said nothing.

"I found them, Brother Peter. First I located the friends, the brother and sister who escaped with him from Camryn. They are now living in Lyon." He paused and looked at the friar.

The friar waved his hand in the air dismissively. "Yes, I know. That is old news. I was informed of it a few days ago already. That is exactly why we are now traveling towards Lyon. Have you nothing else to report?"

The man smiled. "Indeed I have. After locating his friends, it was easy to find the youth you seek. He's living in a village near Lyon, by the name of Chateau Blanc."

Friar Peter's expression did not change in the least, nor did his tone of voice display any emotion. "How far from here?" he asked.

"Only a short distance, Reverend Brother. About twenty five miles. And, Reverend Brother, he has a love interest there."

"That is very good. We should be able to make use of that. We will make our plans, and then we leave for Chateau Blanc."

"One more thing, Reverend Brother. Rumors have circulated about your coming. I fear the Jews may already be alerted."

Friar Peter's lips curled. "I have anticipated that. The bishop of Lyon has been called away urgently. The Jews therefore will not be able to request his protection. Call the men together. We will meet here in one hour."

CHAPTER 13

On a platform raised two steps above the floor of the village meeting hall, Friar Peter sat behind a large, ornate desk. A pair of priests sat at the desk with Friar Peter, one on either side of him. A guard stood at either side of the desk, each armed with a long spear held in his right hand, its haft resting on the floor. At the foot of the platform, two more armed guards stood, one on either side, each armed with a spear in hand and a sword hanging at the left hip. The hall was large, and four wooden columns stood on each side, supporting the high, arched ceiling. The village elders sat in high-backed wooden armchairs arranged along the sides of the meeting hall, twenty on each side. In the center of the floor there was a single vacant chair. An armed guard stood at each side of the chair. At a signal from the friar, two guards escorted a prisoner into the hall, his wrists bound behind him. The guards positioned the prisoner in front of the chair and pushed him down forcefully into the chair.

"State your name," said Friar Peter.

"My name is Daniel."

"Daniel the Jew?"

"Yes, I am Jewish."

"State your profession, Daniel the Jew."

"I am a wine merchant."

"Are there any other wine merchants in the vicinity of Chateau Blanc?"

"Most certainly, yes."

"How many are there, Daniel the Jew?"

"I do not know for sure. Several."

"And they are your competitors, are they not?"

"Yes, they are."

"Did you know a wine merchant named Antoine?"

Daniel lowered his eyes and took a deep breath. "Yes," he said. "I did."

"Why did you hesitate, Daniel the Jew?"

"I hesitated because Antoine died two weeks ago. He was a friend of mine, and a good man."

"A friend, you say? I thought he was your competitor."

"Yes, he was. But also a friend. A good friend."

"Antoine was a Christian, was he not?"

"Yes."

"And a competitor in business?"

"Yes."

"And yet, Daniel the Jew, it is interesting that you have the gall to call him a friend."

"I — "

Friar Peter rose, and his voice thundered through the meeting hall. "You are out of order! You will be silent until you are directly asked a question. My last sentence was a statement, not a question."

Friar Peter sat down again, and in a normal voice, he asked, "For how long was Antoine ill before he died?"

"Two weeks, I think. Perhaps a little more."

"And did you visit him when he was ill?"

"Yes. Twice."

"And before his illness also?"

"Yes. I saw him perhaps a week before his illness."

"Did anyone come with you on your visits?"

"Yes. An employee came with me."

"What is the employee's name?"

"His name is Joseph."

"Is Joseph a Jew?"

"Yes."

"And is not Joseph your daughter's lover?"

Daniel began to rise from his seat, but the guards pushed him down again.

"You will answer the question," said the friar.

"They have been seeing each other for several weeks."

"I see. Just one more question, Daniel the Jew. Is not Antoine's death most fortunate for you? Does not Antoine's death accrue to your advantage? Financially, I mean."

"What?" Daniel began to rise again, but a guard slammed his fist into Daniel's face, and Daniel fell back down, his lip bleeding.

"You will answer the question, Daniel the Jew."

"You cannot be serious."

Peter's voice rose a notch. "Answer the question, Daniel the Jew."

"No. He was my friend."

"Then you are a liar, Daniel the Jew. It is quite apparent to everybody that Antoine's death accrues to your advantage. This court therefore finds you guilty of perjury." He waved his hand in the air. "Take him away," he said. "And bring in the accused."

When the guards had removed Daniel from the meeting hall, another pair of guards entered, escorting a female prisoner. Her hair was tied behind her head. Her wrists were bound behind her back. She wore a long, loosely-fitting dress that reached down to her ankles.

When she had sat down in the chair, Friar Peter said, "The prisoner will state her name."

"My name is Sarah."

"And what is your father's name, Sarah?"

"My father's name is Daniel."

"Daniel the wine merchant?"

"Yes."

"Sarah the Jewess, daughter of Daniel the wine merchant. This court has been convened under ecclesiastical authority in consideration of a charge of sorcery. Sarah the Jewess, how long have you practiced sorcery?"

A murmur went through the audience like a wave. But Sarah sat unmoving. "I do not practice sorcery," she said.

"You deny you are a sorceress?"

"I am not a sorceress."

"Do you know the symptoms of Antoine's illness?"

"No, I do not," she said.

Friar Peter looked at Sarah. Their eyes met. For a second, the friar hesitated. He took a breath. "Prior to interrogating your father, the court has heard testimony about Antoine's symptoms. The doctor who had treated Antoine described his findings in detail; and in the expert opinion of the doctor and of one other witness, Antoine's illness was brought about by sorcery. Yes, by sorcery, not by natural causes. I ask you one more time, Sarah the Jewess, how long have you practiced sorcery?"

"I have never practiced sorcery." she answered.

"Sarah, Sarah. Sweet Sarah." His tone was condescending, as though speaking to a little child. "Earlier this morning, this court heard testimony from two witnesses who swore they saw you fly. Do you still deny you are a sorceress?"

Sarah looked at Peter coolly, her face expressionless. In a soft but steady voice, she said, "Your witnesses are liars. Let them say it to my face, and I will tell them that they lie. I am no such thing, nor am I capable of flying."

"My dear Sarah, in addition to the witnesses who saw you fly, other incontrovertible evidence of your nefarious activities has been presented. Therefore, despite your protestation, this court has already established that you practice black magic. It is only the object of your sorcery that we now seek to establish. Did you cast a spell on poor Antoine?"

"No. That is preposterous."

"Did you murder Antoine?"

"No!" she said. "Most definitely not."

"Did you, then, recite an incantation or employ some other form of sorcery that resulted in Antoine's death?"

"No. No. A thousand times, no."

Peter whispered to the two priests by his sides, and they nodded. He rose from his seat, and the two priests rose also. "It is the decision of this court that the witness is obstinate, and nothing further will be gained by continuing to question her in this manner. As stated, the court has already established beyond reasonable doubt that the accused is guilty of sorcery. However, we have not yet been able to ascertain whether the accused sorceress used her powers to effect Antoine's death. The ecclesiastical court will therefore adjourn until four hours hence, while we interrogate the witness *in camera*."

*   *   *

"No," said Joseph. "I cannot just stand by while they sentence Sarah to death." He struggled with the bonds that confined him to the chair, to no avail.

"Be calm, Joseph. We are your friends. We are Daniel's friends. We mean you no harm."

"Then release me. What permits you to tie me to this chair? You are Jews. What Jewish law allows you to do this? I have committed no crime. I demand you let me go immediately."

"We are sorry, Joseph. It is a ruling of necessity. We cannot permit you to disrupt the court. It would then go badly for Sarah."

Joseph tugged at his restraints. His voice grew louder and more shrill. "Go badly? How much worse can it be? You know as well as I that her trial is a sham. They have condemned her already. The verdict is pre-determined. They will kill her if you don't act. Just as they killed my mother and my father. They killed my brother and my sister. They killed everyone in Camryn. And they will kill you too if you do nothing."

"No, Joseph. You do not know that. This is not Camryn. And they will surely kill Sarah if you do anything rash."

*　　*　　*

The men led Sarah into a small room. Along one wall she saw two tables. Some metal instruments were on the small square table, while the larger, long rectangular table was empty. Lined up along another wall were three high-backed armchairs. Two pairs of ropes were suspended from pulleys on the ceiling in the middle of the room, and a pair of vertical metal poles protruded from the floor. Along each wall were sconces in which were placed burning torches that illuminated the room. Sarah's eyes darted from the ropes to the two tables, to the sharp instruments on the smaller table. Her legs felt weak, her head felt faint, and fear overwhelmed her.

I must be strong. I must not show fear. That is what they want of me, and I must not give them satisfaction.

The two priests sat down on two of the chairs along the wall. The middle seat stood empty.

Sarah forced herself to walk forward and not to fall. She felt her entire body trembling. She clenched her fists. She took deep breaths and tried to calm herself.

Peter stood in front of Sarah. His breath was rancid, and Sarah almost recoiled, but she stood her ground. He stroked her cheek gently. "You have a very pretty face," he said.

Sarah's eyes were fixed on Peter's. Gently he stroked her cheek again, but her eyes looked into the darkness of his pupils, and she saw only malice in his gaze.

"I give you one last chance, Sarah the Jewess. Confess to sorcery now, or we must interrogate you. It will be very painful, and in the end you will confess."

"I am not a sorceress," she said.

Peter stood aside. "Very well," he said. "Prepare her."

Four guards came forward and held her by her wrists and ankles. They fastened her wrists and knees to the ropes suspended from the pulleys in the middle of the room. They hoisted her up by her arms and knees, they removed her shoes, and they tied her ankles to the vertical metal poles. She was suspended horizontally high above the floor, her shoulders and hips at the level of a man's chest, her knees slightly raised, and her feet below the level of her body. The hem of her dress was gathered up above her knees and fastened in place.

Peter stood at Sarah's right side, looking at her. She closed her eyes, but still she felt his eyes on her.

She opened her eyes. Peter was still looking at her. He smiled and gently cupped her right breast through her dress. "I think we are ready to begin," he said.

Fear almost overcame her, but she braced herself for the pain that she knew would be coming soon. "You are a fraud, Friar Peter. I see the lust in your eyes."

Peter did not answer. He nodded to the guards. Two of the guards brought a brazier of burning coals. She glimpsed at the coals, and her knees began to quake. She closed her eyes. A sudden pain shot through her as the heat of the coals licked the soles of both her feet. She screamed. But the pain wouldn't stop. She tried to convince herself that this was not happening to her but to someone else. She thought of Joseph and tried to imagine herself walking with him again through her father's vineyards. But the pain again intruded itself upon her consciousness. She heard the friar ask her something, although she could not make out his words. A searing pain tore again through the soles of both her feet, her heels, her toes. She squirmed. She gasped for breath. She smelled the odor of burning flesh – her own flesh. She screamed again. And again. She urinated.

The pain diminished somewhat. Her feet still hurt terribly, a boring, throbbing pain that coursed through her veins to her very soul, but she knew the heat of the coals no longer touched her feet, and she felt somewhat relieved.

A cold hand touched her cheek. She opened her eyes. It was Peter.

"Confess, Sarah the Jewess. Confess to sorcery. Will you confess to Antoine's murder by your sorcery?"

She shook her head.

Peter stood aside, and Sarah saw the two guards who had just burned her feet approaching once more with the brazier.

"No. No. Please. Not again!"

A man walked up to the two guards at her feet and handed them sharp instruments. They stabbed at the soles of her burnt feet, and she screamed.

"That's good," said Peter. "She still feels pain. Continue."

Again they raised the brazier to her feet, this time closer than before; and her pain was still more terrible than previously. She screamed from the depths of her existence. Again. And yet again. She couldn't stop. The pain enveloped her like a shroud. She cried. She wept uncontrollably.

She tried to disconnect herself from the pain. Her mind drifted, but the pain kept jolting her back. Time stood still. She was suspended in an eternity of agony. She heard herself screaming. "Stop. Please stop. No more! I can't stand the pain."

"Confess, Sarah, and the pain will stop."

"No. Please stop. Please don't do this to me. Don't burn me any more."

"Confess."

She heard the friar's voice as through a fog. It grated at her soul. It prodded at her heart. It called to her again, and again, and yet again: "Confess."

And through her pain, the friar's voice sorely tempted her. She wanted to confess. She almost did confess, but something deep within her soul prevented her. How could she admit to the heinous crime of sorcery, when she in fact was innocent? How could she say she practiced black magic? How could she say she called upon the power of the Other Side? The very thought of it repulsed her. She closed her eyes again, trying to shut out the pain. She smelled her burning flesh and screamed: "No, no, no! I am not a sorceress. I am not a sorceress. I am not a sorceress. It is you, Friar Peter, who are the sorcerer. It is you!"

Sarah opened her eyes. She was lying on the long table, but her wrists, knees, and ankles were still tied. Peter was standing at her side, and the two priests were standing on the other side of her.

"Hello, Sarah," Peter said. "It is good to see you awake again. I hope you had a good rest before embarking on the next part of your journey."

She turned to face him. "What do you mean? What are you going to do to me now?"

Peter smiled. He had a long needle in his hand, and he held it up for her to see. "You are very obstinate, Sarah. Confess to sorcery, and the next step will not be necessary."

She turned her eyes away. "No! I will never confess. I am not a sorceress."

"You leave us no choice. We will now look for the Mark of Satan."

"The Mark of Satan?"

"Yes, Sarah," Peter said as the guards hoisted her body in the air and took the table out from under her. "The Mark of Satan is a mole, a wart, or some other imperfection or discoloration of the skin. It can be anywhere on the body of a sorceress. Anywhere at all. It is the indelible mark of Satan's kiss on his devoted servant's body."

"I have no such mark."

"We shall see," he said.

* * *

Sarah opened her eyes and looked around the room. She was sitting in the same chair in which she had sat before her ordeal. She was wearing the loosely-fitting dress again, and on her feet she was wearing shoes. She looked around the room. The village elders were sitting in their seats; two guards were standing at her sides; Peter and the two priests were sitting on the podium behind their desk. Peter spoke:

"The ecclesiastical court is again in session. The accused has been interrogated, but she did not confess to sorcery. The court then conducted an examination, searching for the Mark of Satan, and on careful examination, the Mark was found."

"No!" Sarah screamed. "That is a lie."

A guard struck Sarah across her face, and she lurched backwards, stunned.

"The accused will keep silent unless she is addressed," Peter said matter-of-factly. He paused a moment, and continued: "No visible mark was found upon her body. And yet, hidden from the eye, we found the evidence of Satan's kiss – a spot immune to pain. Satan has condemned her."

Sarah shook her head. She opened her mouth. "No," she screamed. "It is lie. It cannot be."

Peter stood, and the two priests stood with him. Peter looked at Sarah. "Sarah the Jewess, daughter of Daniel the wine merchant, this court finds you guilty of sorcery and conspiracy to commit murder by means of sorcery. You are condemned to be burned at the stake until you are dead. The sentence will be carried out in one hour hence."

*   *   *

The fire rose with fury in the village square, enveloping the pyre in its shimmering embrace. At a safe distance, the crowd stood transfixed, watching the solitary figure in the center of the pyre. Her screams rose to a crescendo, as she desperately squirmed and struggled to free herself, to no avail. Then her screams grew weaker, her struggling stopped, her body slumped, and soon the only sound was the roaring of the flames and the crackling of the pyre upon which she stood.

Joseph, now released from his restraints, tried to push himself through the crush of people. Sarah's lifeless form stood in the midst of the conflagration, and there was nothing he could do to help her. But he must see; he must bear witness. He stood among the crowd. A shriek of horror welled up inside him, but no sound escaped his lips. He thought of running to the pyre and throwing himself upon it, but the press of the crowd was too great, and he could hardly move. He stood among the crowd, and cried.

He scanned the crowd, looking for Friar Peter, but he saw no sign of him.

He turned to a man standing beside him. "Where is Friar Peter?" he asked.

"He just left." The man pointed toward the judgement hall. "He went back there."

Joseph pushed his way outwards through the crowd. A sturdy branch lay in the street, probably originally meant for the pyre. Joseph picked up the branch and burst into the judgement hall.

"Peter!" he shouted.

Peter sat behind the desk on the podium at the far end of the hall. He smiled. "I have been expecting you," he said, slowly rising from his seat.

Joseph ran forward, the branch clutched in his right hand. "Murderer!"

Peter raised his hand. "Halt, Jew! Do not come even one step closer." His voice reverberated through the hall, seeming to emanate not from Peter's mouth but from all directions at once. The walls seemed to shake from the power of Friar Peter's voice. And Joseph stood in the center of the hall, momentarily stunned.

He looked down and saw that he was standing beside the witness's seat. In his mind's eye, he envisioned Sarah sitting in the chair as Peter questioned her.

"Yes, Joseph, that is the seat where Sarah sat just a short while ago. Come. Let me show you the room where we interrogated her *in camera*." His voice was mellow. He smiled again. He walked slowly to a door, beckoning Joseph to follow him in.

Joseph followed, dazed. He still held the branch in his hand. It would make a good weapon to use against Peter – a good club. But his arm felt limp, and he walked as though in a dense fog.

He looked around the room. He saw the ropes hanging from the ceiling. He saw the two tables and the long, sharp instruments. An acrid odor lingered in the room – the odor of burnt flesh. Sarah's flesh.

The image of Sarah standing on the pyre flashed through his mind. He saw her dress catch fire. He heard her screaming, saw her suffering.

The acrid odor in the room assaulted his senses; his vision blurred; his head felt light. He screamed a wordless scream. He raised his right arm, holding his club aloft. His eyes began again to focus, and he saw Friar Peter standing before him, smiling. He ran towards Peter, seething with rage.

Peter's voice rose again, engulfing Joseph with its fury and ferocity, intensified by the relatively small dimensions of the interrogation room. "Halt!"

Joseph froze in his tracks, as Peter gracefully moved away from him.

Peter now stood by the door. "You will not escape this time. It is time for you to die, you son of Satan. Die, and join your family in hell."

Joseph tried to move, but Peter's voice fixed him in his place. The voice echoed through the room and reverberated in Joseph's head. His ears hurt. His heart raced. His breathing felt constrained, as though a heavy weight rested on his chest. He looked around. The walls were shaking. Cracks appeared in the ceiling.

Peter raised his voice again. "Die!"

As Peter left the interrogation room, the door and its adjoining wall collapsed, and part of the ceiling fell. Joseph quickly hid under one of the tables, hoping it would protect him from the falling ceiling.

Joseph looked beyond the fallen wall, squinting to see past the dust in the air. Peter stood in the judgement hall, a burning torch in his hand. He had pushed the judges' desk against a wall, and now he held the torch to the desk. The desk burst in flames.

Joseph knew he had little time. He began to rise. But Peter's voice again echoed through the building, and large chunks of ceiling fell down around Joseph.

Joseph lifted the table over his head and started to move forward, but the weight of the table and the falling debris impeded his advance. Beyond the fallen door, he saw the fire in the judgement hall spreading along the wall. He saw Peter walking slowly towards the exit. Peter looked at Joseph and laughed.

The flames were all around, blocking Joseph's way. He coughed. His eyes were tearing. He felt the heat radiating towards him. Fear almost overcame him. He turned around, moving back into the interrogation room, trying to escape the fire.

One wall of the interrogation room had collapsed, and only two walls and part of a third wall now remained standing. Pieces of ceiling continued to rain down, and the room was filled with smoke and dust. In desperation, Joseph went towards the far wall, still carrying the heavy table over his head. His arms ached. His chest hurt. He could hardly breath.

Through the haze, a human figure suddenly appeared among the rubble. Over his head he wore a hood, and in his hand he held a walking stick. As he approached, Joseph recognized him. It was Enoch.

Enoch took Joseph's hand in his, and Joseph felt a warm tranquility spread over him. It was as though he was no longer in the burning building, as though he was far from danger, far from sorrow. His mind drifted, seeing nothing, hearing nothing. He felt Enoch's hand, but nothing more.

He opened his eyes. He was no longer in the interrogation room. He could not understand how he had gotten here, but he was now standing in the judgement hall, his back to the flames. Peter stood before him. Enoch stood a few feet away.

"You will not escape." The voice rose in fury, and the walls quaked. Peter lunged at Joseph. "Fiend!" he shrieked.

Joseph tried to dodge, but his feet were leaden, and his motions slow. To Joseph's amazement, Enoch rose to his full height, and, with a speed beyond anything in Joseph's recollection, he stood in front of Joseph, thrusting his staff at Peter, barring Peter's way.

Peter staggered backwards. He glared at Enoch. "Accursed demon!" he screamed. "Away! You will not take my prize from me."

Peter waved his hand. The outer door of the judgement hall flew open, and a great wind blew through the hall. Chairs were flung across the room, striking the walls with resounding blows. Joseph threw himself down on the floor and put his arms around a column, holding on with all his might against the force of the wind. Flames shot up to the ceiling, engulfing the entire hall in orange light. A crack appeared in the ceiling over Joseph's head. Pieces of the ceiling crumbled and fell to the floor at Joseph's feet. The crack widened, and Joseph cringed in fear.

Joseph looked up and saw Enoch standing by his side. Somehow, seeing Enoch next to him took his fear away. Enoch raised his arms and spread them wide. In his right hand he held his staff, pointed toward the ceiling. The ceiling shook, but the crack no longer widened, and pieces of the ceiling no longer fell. The wind billowed through Enoch's robe. His long hair blew in all directions in the wind. But Enoch stood unmoving, firmly planted with his feet apart.

Enoch's voice filled the hall, rising above the wind and flames: "No, Peter, you will not succeed. You will be defeated in the end."

CHAPTER 14

Friday, 21ˢᵗ September 1190

It was late at night, and Joseph was now many miles from Chateau Blanc, camped at a distance from the main road. The horror of Sarah's execution still coursed through Joseph's being, wrenching at his heartstrings, bringing tears to his eyes. Till now, he had hardly had a chance to mourn her in his hasty departure and his frenzied flight from Friar Peter. Even here, so many miles away, the pungent scent of Sarah's burning flesh still filled his nostrils, and the smoke still burned his eyes. In his mind, he heard the roaring of the conflagration, saw her body struggling to escape, heard her screams that pierced the fire and the shimmering air, sensed her immortal soul flying up to heaven as the flames consumed her flesh. He saw Friar Peter as he sat behind the desk in the judgement hall after Sarah's soul had flown. He saw the hateful friar's smile; he heard the friar's voice. "I have been expecting you," the friar said.

He reached under his tunic and fingered the dagger that he had taken from the man he killed in Sherwood Forest months ago. He wished he could have used the dagger against Friar Peter, but he quickly realized he had never had the opportunity to do so. He felt helpless against the friar's power, a power that had taken his father and his mother, his sister and his brother; and, now Sarah too. He wished he had joined Sarah on the pyre, to die with her. He felt despondent, ready to end it all, to let the friar find him, ready to suffer martyrdom at the friar's hands. He wept uncontrollably.

After several minutes, when he had regained his composure, he looked at the two sleeping forms on the ground nearby. He thought back to his escape from Chateau Blanc, trying to remember, but his memory was a blur. He remembered only that Enoch somehow had whisked him away from Friar Peter, and shortly after, on the road westward, they had met up with Aaron and Rachel, whom Enoch had brought from Lyon to the rendezvous point some hours earlier.

Why had Enoch brought them there that very day? Had he known in advance what was about to happen in Chateau Blanc? Joseph had no answers to those questions. And yet, no matter Enoch's reasons, Joseph was glad to have his friends with him again. Their presence sustained him and gave him purpose. But it was good they had not seen him weep. He must not cry. He was their leader, and they depended on him. If they only knew how much he wavered in his resolve. Nevertheless, because of them, he knew he had to carry on. If only for their sakes, he must never give in. He must not allow Friar Peter to find them.

Joseph woke Aaron to take the second watch. Joseph lay down on the hard ground and was asleep almost immediately. He dreamt of his youth in Camryn.

In his dream, he saw himself as an eleven-year-old boy. It was the second day of Rosh Hashana, the Jewish New Year, and Joseph was in the synagogue with his father. The synagogue service had reached the point when the ram's horn – the Shofar – must be blown, but the rabbi announced that the man who was supposed to blow it had taken ill, and the great ram's horn sat waiting on the cantor's table. As Joseph well knew, a hundred measured blasts of the Shofar must be blown, interspersed among the prayers: a task requiring great skill and stamina. The rabbi was old and frail, and unequal to the task. Who else was there to blow the Shofar? Joseph and all the congregation waited with bated breath for someone to stand up and volunteer. But no one did.

Suddenly the rear door of the synagogue opened, and a stranger in a ragged, hooded robe shuffled down the aisle, supporting himself with a weathered walking stick. As he reached the cantor's desk, he turned to the congregation and drew back his hood. His beard was white and long, and his bright green eyes seemed like unfathomable wells of hidden mysteries and wisdom. It was a face unlike any other that Joseph had ever seen before. The stranger turned to the rabbi and said in Hebrew: "I have come to blow the Shofar."

The stranger took the Shofar from the table, put it to his lips, and, at the rabbi's signal, he began to blow. A hundred blasts he blew, with such precision and such clarity as none among the congregation had ever heard before. Then, at the end of the service, the stranger disappeared. People turned to each other, asking, "Who was that man?" Nobody had ever seen him before. Surely, some said, he must have been none other than the prophet Elijah. But Joseph's father kept silent, and as they walked home from the synagogue, Joseph had the feeling that his father knew the man.

Joseph awakened from his dream. The events of the dream were not fictitious, but they had long ago receded into the far recesses of his memory. Now, in the wake of his dream, he had a vivid recollection of that day six years ago, and he recalled how his suspicions had been confirmed that evening when the holiday ended, and the stranger showed up at his home unannounced. Joseph remembered how his father's face lit up when he opened the front door, and how his father welcomed the man as though he were a long-lost friend. The two of them talked in private for perhaps an hour. At length, the stranger left, and Joseph never saw him again.

Joseph sat up, shivering although the night was warm. Something troubled him about the dream, about the man. He looked up at the sky and tried to think. He lay down again and closed his eyes. He turned over, and the emerald in its pouch suspended from his belt nudged at his flank. He turned again, finding a more comfortable position.

All at once, realization struck him like a deluge pouring over him and sweeping him up. Now he knew the identity of the mysterious stranger who had blown the Shofar in his synagogue six years ago.

He sat up again, and Aaron turned around. "Why are you awake?" he asked.

"I had a dream."

"I know," said Aaron. He placed his hand on Joseph's shoulder. "I understand. It was terrible in Chateau Blanc."

"No, no," Joseph said. "That's not it. I dreamt about something that happened six years ago, in Camryn. Do you remember that time on Rosh Hashana when the Shofar blower got sick and a stranger appeared?"

"Yes, of course; and he blew the Shofar for us. But why should that disturb your sleep?"

"Because I just realized who the stranger was. It was Enoch."

"Are you sure?"

"Yes, I'm absolutely sure. And in the evening, he came to our house. My father knew him. They seemed like old friends, and they talked together for a long time. Don't you see? This changes everything. Do you remember what Enoch told us in the cave? I doubted him then, but now I see that everything he said was true. Peter's presence in Camryn and in Chateau Blanc was no coincidence. He is pursuing me. He is pursuing the emerald, just as Enoch said."

"But why is Enoch's presence in Camryn six years ago so convincing? So what if your father knew him?"

"It is the key that made me realize how it all fits together. When I confronted Peter in the judgement hall, he called me by my name and said he was expecting me. And when Enoch saved me from Peter afterwards, Peter shouted, 'You will not take my prize away.' Don't you see? What Peter did to Sarah was all for the purpose of ensnaring me. If not for Enoch, I would be dead. Enoch is my guardian, as he told us in the cave."

Joseph reached into his garment and extracted the pouch that Enoch had given him. He emptied it into the palm of his hand and stared at the emerald. "What a beautiful stone," he said. "But see how much suffering it has brought."

Aaron put a hand on Joseph's shoulder, and Joseph looked into Aaron's eyes.

Joseph continued: "Do you remember what else Enoch said? He said that if Peter can control the power of the high priest's breastplate, not only will he annihilate all the Jews in Christendom and massacre the Saracens, but he will rule the world. He will unravel the entire fabric of humanity. And in all the world, only I have the power to thwart the friar's plans. He will pursue me relentlessly to the ends of the earth, and he will not rest until one of us defeats the other. I did not want to believe Enoch's words. I tried to run away. I tried to hide from Peter, and from my destiny. But now I see I have no choice. I must search for the high priest's breastplate and thwart the friar's plans."

PART III

CHAPTER 15

October 1190

Matthew, weary from his travels, arrived in Rome as the sun was setting. He made his way through the darkening streets, searching for a place to stay the night, but there seemed to be no inns in this part of the city. Ramshackle houses lined the streets, garbage was strewn in the road, and the few people who passed by appeared unsavory, so that Matthew had no desire to stop anyone to ask directions. He quickened his pace.

Two men stood by the roadside staring at him as he passed. They muttered something to each other. He knew only the little Italian that he had picked up in the last few weeks, but he thought he had heard the men identify him as a stranger. He tried not to look at them, not to attract their attention, not to let them see his fear.

The two men followed Matthew down the street. He looked back over his shoulder, alarmed. He quickly turned a corner. The two men turned also. A third man appeared in front of Matthew. He held a knife in his hand. Matthew glanced back and saw that the other two men now had knives in their hands as well.

The man in front of him approached. "Dami il tuo denaro," he said, pointing his blade at Matthew.

Briefly, Matthew considered whether to fight these men. He was bigger than they, and more muscular. But his long journey had weakened him, and these men were armed. He quickly dismissed any thought of resistance. Matthew reached under his cloak and pulled out a purse. He handed it to the robber.

The robber pointed to a piece of paper protruding from under Matthew's cloak. "Che cos' è quello?"

"It's a letter. It's not something that would interest you."

The two men behind Matthew seized him and held his arms. The man in front advanced, brandishing his blade. His left hand lashed out and snatched the paper from under Matthew's cloak. He unfolded the paper and stared at it blankly. It was a letter written in Latin and addressed to Cardinal Bobone. "È una lettera," he said.

"Please give it back to me. It means nothing to you."

The robber shifted his blade to his left hand and waved it in front of Matthew's face. "Un buco di culo!" he muttered under his breath, as he buried his right fist in Matthew's stomach. The other two men threw Matthew to the ground, and the three robbers kicked him several times.

"Buco di culo!" they repeated.

The robber who had taken Matthew's letter waved the letter in front of Matthew's face. "Ecco la lettera," he said, pocketing it. The three robbers laughed, turned around, and walked briskly down the street, never looking back.

*   *   *

Joseph, Aaron, and Rachel arrived in Lucca in the late afternoon. Their trek across the mountains from France to northern Italy had been long and difficult, and they had lived in constant fear of pursuit. At first, the weather and the rough terrain had impeded their progress; but as the weeks wore on, the landscape changed, the climate mellowed, and they began to feel more confident that they had made good their escape.

It was almost sunset when they reached the Jewish quarter. The streets here were narrower but somewhat more populated than in the Christian part of the city. Women bustled by, carrying groceries; men walked in twos and threes discussing business matters; and children played in front of the shops that lined the street. Joseph looked about, taking in the sights and the aromas of the neighborhood.

They passed a tailor's shop, in front of which the tailor stood displaying the latest in men's fashion. He smiled broadly, beckoning to Joseph, but Joseph merely nodded to him and walked on. They passed a fish monger shouting out the price of fish. They smelled the mouth-watering scent of fresh bread long before they saw the baker's shop. Joseph stopped and looked inside, but the baker was busy serving another customer and didn't notice Joseph.

Joseph was about to enter the baker's shop when an old man approached them, crossing the street. His beard was white and neatly trimmed. His eyes bespoke a keen intelligence. His face was open and inviting. "Stranieri?" he asked.

"Yes, we are strangers here," Joseph answered in Hebrew.

The old man switched to Hebrew and said, "Welcome. Welcome to Lucca. My name is Simone. May I ask where you have come from?"

"We are from England. We just today arrived in Lucca. Could you direct us to a place where we could stay the night?"

"There are no inns in this neighborhood, and none in Lucca where a Jew would be safe today. The sun is setting, and you must not be found in the streets after dark. Come with me. You will be my guests."

"You do not even know our names."

"That is correct," said Simone; "and I do not want to know them. It is better that way. You are Jews in need of lodging, and that is enough for me. Hurry. My home is on the next street, over there."

Joseph, Aaron, and Rachel sat around Simone's table while Simone's wife cleared the remains of their repast. The room was spacious, and the table seemed much too large for just a man and his wife. Along the nearest wall to Joseph were several lecterns, upon which were manuscripts in Hebrew, in Italian, and in Latin. Each manuscript was bound in a leather binding inlaid with colorful, ornate designs and letters written in a flowery hand. Such manuscripts must be very expensive, and Joseph couldn't even imagine how much they must have cost. Joseph looked at the books, trying to discern their titles. He looked at his host, trying to figure him out.

"You like my books?"

"They are very interesting."

"Yes, I have many interests."

Joseph was bursting with questions regarding Simone's cryptic statements when he had first encountered them on the street, but Simone had insisted that they not discuss the matter until after they had eaten. Now, as Simone's wife brought dessert, Joseph said, "May I ask you something now?"

Simone spread some jelly on his cake and put a piece in his mouth. "That is delicious, as always," he said, looking lovingly at his wife, and she smiled back at him.

Simone leaned back in his chair and looked at Joseph. "Yes," he said. "Now I will answer your questions."

Joseph opened his mouth to speak, but Simone held up his hand and said, "Your first question is: why did I not want to know your names? And your second question is: why must you not be seen on the streets after dark? Am I correct so far?"

"Yes."

Simone smiled. "Don't look so surprised. It was not so difficult to figure out."

Simone's face turned serious. He looked from Joseph to Aaron to Rachel, and back again at Joseph. "There are men looking for you," he said.

Rachel turned pale. "For us?" she asked. "How do you know this?"

"Yes, for the three of you. Just yesterday, armed men swept through the Jewish quarter searching for three fugitives of your description. A Christian clergyman rode behind them – a friar. He spoke not a word, but I could see a fire burning in his eyes. His look was terrifying, and filled with hatred. I do not know for certain that you are the ones they seek, but I deem it likely; and the less I know, the better."

Rachel shuddered. "Did they say why they wanted us?"

"Yes. They said they had followed you from France and that one of you was wanted for murder of a Christian and for sorcery."

"And knowing all that, you were not afraid to invite us to your home?" Joseph asked.

Simone laughed. "Of course not. I know a blatant lie when I hear it. No, I am not afraid. But you should be. The three of you may sleep here tonight, but you must depart before dawn, for your own safety."

"Where should we go?"

"That depends upon what your purpose is."

Joseph glanced again at Simone's books. "Do your many interests include the high priest's breastplate?"

Simone thought a moment before answering. "Of course," he said. "The *choshen mishpat* – the breastplate of judgement – is described in the Bible. But that is not what you are asking, I suspect."

Joseph was silent. He looked at Aaron questioningly, and Aaron nodded.

"When the Holy Temple in Jerusalem was destroyed, what happened to the breastplate? And where is it now?"

Simone's expression changed, as though a great mystery had just been revealed to him. "Ah, I see. So that is your purpose. That is a secret known to very few, if any, men. It is the subject of esoteric knowledge and speculation, and I am afraid that neither I nor anyone in Lucca has such knowledge. I suggest you go to Bari, on the southeast coast of Italy. There you must seek out a man named Rabbi Tuviah. He is well versed in the mysteries of the Torah, and if any man in Italy can help you, Rabbi Tuviah is the one. But first, you must elude your pursuers. Until you get to Bari, you must stay away from major cities and especially from cities where there are many Jews, because the friar will expect you in such places. Above all, you must avoid passing even close to Rome. Now sleep. I will wake you before dawn and point out the road that you should take."

*   *   *

Matthew stumbled and almost fell. He was hungry, bleary-eyed, and dizzy, and his stomach and ribs still hurt from the beating he had received hours earlier. He had no idea how long he had been wandering the streets of Rome, but he was sure it was now well past midnight. He was now in a better neighborhood, but he saw no inns here, and anyway he had no money with which to buy food or pay for lodging.

Dejected, Matthew sat down on the cold ground and held his head in his hands. He thought of that terrible night in Camryn and of his wanderings since then. He thought of Abbot Geoffrey and of the abbot's letter to Cardinal Bobone that he no longer had in his possession. Without money, without the letter, he had failed in his mission. He searched his soul. Was this a sign from God that he must turn back? Or was the Lord just testing him to see whether he would be steadfast in his purpose to redeem himself, his father, and the village of Camryn from their sins? But what more could he do? Where was he to turn? Without the abbot's letter, who would help him now?

"Giovane, cosa c'è?"

Startled, Matthew looked up and saw an old man standing beside him. Behind the old man was a donkey harnessed to a cart loaded with produce. The man smiled pleasantly at Matthew.

Pardon me, said Matthew in English; "I know only little Italian, and I didn't understand you."

The old man switched to English. "I said, 'Young man, what is the matter?' Surely the world is not yet coming to an end."

The old man's English was flawless, and without any foreign accent. Matthew looked the man up and down. Matthew's mouth opened, but no words came out.

"Don't look so surprised, young man. I have traveled the world, and I speak many languages. Walk with me, and keep me company. I am eager to hear your story, and any news of the world that you may have to tell. It is lonely walking the streets with only a donkey for companionship."

Matthew eyed the produce in the old man's cart. Hesitantly, he asked, "May I have something to eat?"

"Of course, of course. You see I have plenty here." The old man pointed to his cart.

"I have no money. I was robbed."

"Then you are fortunate to have escaped with your life. I have cheese and fruit. Please help yourself."

For a long time, Matthew walked with the donkey driver, telling him of the massacre at Camryn, of his own quest for penance and salvation, of Abbot Geoffrey's letter, and how the robbers took the letter from him. The donkey driver listened attentively but said nothing.

They were crossing a bridge over the Tiber River. The donkey driver pointed to a distant location across the river. "Your cardinal lives there."

Matthew halted and looked at the man. "Haven't you heard my story? I told you the robbers took my letter of introduction that Abbot Geoffrey gave me. How can I ever hope to see the cardinal without that letter?"

The old man smiled. He put a hand on Matthew's shoulder. He looked deep into Matthew's eyes, and in a calm, soothing voice, he said, "Do not worry, Matthew. As I told you before, the world is not coming to an end. I see that you are intelligent and resourceful. You will find a way."

They walked a while in silence. At length, the donkey driver said, "I must leave you here, Matthew. I wish you well."

"Wait, sir. I do not know where I am going."

The old man pointed. "There. Cardinal Bobone's residence is up ahead of you."

Matthew glanced up the street to where the donkey driver had pointed. But he made no move to go there. He looked at the old man questioningly.

"What is it, Matthew?"

"I never asked you. What's your name?"

"You may call me Enoch."

The old man led his donkey and began to walk away, but after only a few steps, he turned and said, "If all else fails, you must attempt to gain the ear of the cardinal's chamberlain. Be sure to tell him that you come from Camryn."

"Thank you," Matthew said, puzzled by the old man's words. He glanced up momentarily at the cardinal's residence and turned again toward the donkey driver. "What do you mean?" he asked. But the man, the donkey, and the cart were gone, without a trace.

Matthew walked slowly up the hill to the cardinal's residence. A guard stood at the gate and eyed him suspiciously.

Matthew stopped in front of the guard. "My name is Matthew, from England. Please sir, I wish to speak to Cardinal Bobone. It is important"

The guard waved his hand dismissively. "Va! Il cardinale dorme."

"Please sir. I have come here all the way from England. I must speak to the cardinal."

"Va!"

But Matthew didn't leave. He stood and stared the guard down. At length, another man in a guard's uniform approached from within.

The second guard held up his hands. In heavily accented English, he said, "Are you pazzo? It is middle of night. You can't see il cardinale now."

"Please, sir, I can wait here till morning, but I must see the cardinal. I have come a very long way to speak to him."

The second guard turned and went inside. When he returned, he had yet another guard in tow. While the first guard stood watch, the other two guards opened the gate, seized Matthew, and started to march him away.

They had gone only a few paces when Matthew turned abruptly and shook off both guards. The English-speaking guard drew a dagger, and the other drew a sword, but Matthew pivoted and delivered a crushing blow to the sword-wielding guard's shoulder. The guard fell to the ground, his sword clattering on the cobbles of the street. Pivoting again, Matthew's boot collided hard with the other guard's wrist. The dagger dropped out of the guard's hand, and Matthew retrieved it from the ground. He twisted the guard's arm behind his back and marched him back to the cardinal's gate.

Matthew released the guard in front of the gate, and in a loud voice he said, "I must speak to Cardinal Bobone. I will wait, if I must. I ask to see the cardinal's chamberlain."

"Go away!" the guard commanded. "You are nuisance. You will not see il cardinale, even if you wait."

Matthew rattled the gate loudly and shouted, "Then let me speak to the chamberlain. I demand to speak to the chamberlain."

He continued rattling the gate, and soon a man of dour face appeared, dressed in night clothes and carrying a lantern in his hand. The first guard turned to him, pointed to his own head, and said, "È pazzo."

"Are you the cardinal's chamberlain?" Matthew asked.

"Yes, I am, he answered in English. "But do you know what time it is? "

"I am very sorry. I truly am. But I come from Camryn in England, and I must speak to Cardinal Bobone. It is very important."

At the mention of Camryn, the chamberlain's demeanor changed abruptly. He opened the gate. "Come in," he said. "You may see the cardinal, but you will have to wait till morning."

CHAPTER 16

Father John looked out onto the road ahead and saw a group of armed men in the distance. It was early morning, and the sun was still low on the horizon behind him, but Father John had already been traveling for about two hours, on his second day out of Florence. He was expecting to reach Lucca by early afternoon, and he hoped the men up ahead would not delay him. He flicked the reins of his horse, and his cart sped up a little.

As he approached, he saw there were four men on horseback blocking the road. "Good day," Father John said cheerfully, tipping his hat.

The four men said nothing.

Father John smiled, trying not to show the apprehension that he felt. "What can I do for you, gentlemen?"

"State your name and your business here," commanded one of the men.

"I am Father John, and I am going to Lucca on official business for Cardinal Bobone. My mission is most urgent, and I must not be detained."

The man put his hand on his sword hilt. "Your answer is insufficient. What type of official business?"

The priest looked into the man's eyes and said, "I answer only to the cardinal, and to God. I will say no more. And I demand you let me pass."

The men-at-arms nudged their horses sideways, two to the right and two to the left. A black-cowled friar emerged on foot from between the horses. His cowl was pulled up over his head, and Father John could not make out his face. The friar came to a halt and stood in front of Father John's cart but did not look up at the priest. "Get down from your cart," he commanded, "so I can talk to you."

Father John thought the friar's voice sounded familiar, but he couldn't quite remember where he had heard that voice before. He thought it strange that this friar was hiding his face under his cowl; and yet, he found a friar's presence here somewhat reassuring: at least it was unlikely that these armed men meant to rob or kill him. Nevertheless, the friar's gruff demeanor served to keep him on his guard.

Father John made no move to dismount. "If you wish to talk to me, it is customary to introduce yourself, and to let me see your face."

One of the men-at-arms drew his sword. "Get down off your cart, Father. You will make no more demands. When the reverend friar commands, you will obey. And you will answer the friar's questions. Understood?"

Father John dismounted but neither answered nor looked at the man-at-arms. He kept his eyes fixed on the black-cowled friar.

The friar looked up, and his eyes met Father John's. Recognition struck Father John like a hammer blow, but years of training in diplomacy and secret dealings on behalf of the Church had taught him to keep his face expressionless. He held the friar's gaze.

Friar Peter said, "We are searching for three Jewish fugitives. Have you passed any Jews on the road?"

"To my knowledge, I have not."

"Again, Father, you are being evasive. Why do you say, 'To my knowledge'? It is either yes or no."

"What, pray tell, have these Jews done that you are seeking them?"

"It is not your place to ask, Father, but I will answer you this time. One committed murder, and the other two are his accomplices. They are desperate and could be dangerous. Have you encountered them? Now answer, yes or no?"

Father John did not answer immediately. He looked into Friar Peter's face and eyes, trying to assess the friar's character. He looked for signs of holiness and compassion; but all he saw was a burning, raging vehemence, without compassion, without humility, without the slightest trace of the divine spirit that should be evident in a man devoted to the pursuit of holiness.

Father John took a deep breath. "No," he said. "I have not seen them."

"That is much better, Father," Peter said in a sarcastic tone.

"May I go now?"

"Yes, Father, you may go. But if you do encounter any Jews along the way, be sure to send word to me immediately. I or my men will be here on the road."

The priest mounted his cart again and held his horse's reins, but the men-at-arms still blocked his way.

"You have not yet responded," said the friar. "I need your word that you will inform me immediately if you encounter any Jews along the road to Lucca."

"Of course I will do all I can to apprehend a murderer."

"That is what I wanted to hear," said Friar Peter.

As the men-at-arms parted to let the priest pass, Father John flicked the reins and said, "Just remember, Friar Peter: seeking to apprehend a criminal is one thing, but agitation against the Jews and inciting Christian folk to riot does not have the approval of the Holy Father."

Friar Peter laughed. It was not a pleasant laugh. "We shall see about that," he said, as he scornfully waved the priest onward on his journey.

After leaving the friar and his men, Father John was greatly troubled by the friar's demeanor. He reflected on the friar's previous activities in England and in France. He reflected on Cardinal Bobone's reaction to his report about the friar's agitation against the Jews. He recalled that the cardinal, although he

found the friar's actions greatly troubling, considered Friar Peter
to be misguided but still thought the friar's motives may be good.
However, Cardinal Bobone had never met the friar, and Father
John previously had seen the friar only from a distance; he had
never had occasion to look into the friar's eyes and see into his
soul until today.

Today's encounter cast a whole new light on things. Father
John thought about his effort to penetrate Peter's mask and see
into his soul; and what he saw in Peter's face was a spirit wrapped
in darkness, devoid of kindness, devoid of the divine light. He
shuddered at the thought. His instincts told him that the friar
was not at all the holy man that he was said to be.

He stopped his horse and looked back. The men-at-arms were
still visible in the distance, but just barely. He flicked the reins
again, and considered what to do. He knew he should return
to Rome as soon as possible and report his findings to Cardinal
Bobone. And yet, he was loathe to abort the mission on which
the cardinal had sent him. He continued on the road to Lucca
until he was sure he was out of sight of the friar's men. He
stopped his horse and looked up to heaven. Silently he said
a psalm in his mind. He looked back again to where the friar's
men should be, and he made his decision. He flicked the reins
again and continued on the road to Lucca for half a mile more.
Then, at a fork in the road, he took the southward fork, away
from Lucca. He would return to Rome immediately.

CHAPTER 17

A village in Northumbria (England)
Twelve years earlier – Summer, 1178

Peter emerged from the woods and walked along the riverbank. He had already taken his leave hours ago, shortly after giving his sermon that morning, and by now he should have been well on his way. But just after leaving the village, his donkey had needed to be re-shod, and so he had been delayed. Still, he could have left shortly after noon, but he had decided to walk in the woods for a while in peace and serenity, and the time had slipped away. It was now late afternoon.

His sermon this morning had been a great success. He had seen the reaction of the crowd, and he felt that they had taken his message to heart. Although only twenty-nine years old, already he had a reputation for great piety and was known far and wide for his rousing sermons that stirred men's souls. Originally, he had studied for the priesthood and had been ordained, but quickly he came to realize his oratorical skill, and shortly before his ordination he had decided to become an itinerant preacher. Reflecting on the preachers he had encountered in the past, he realized that the greatest of them, those who had spoken most deeply to his soul, were all friars. Therefore, shortly after ordination he had become a friar. He had never regretted that decision, and now more than ever he felt a sense of pride and accomplishment as he looked back over the last four years.

Since his early days of preaching, Peter's sermons had been about piety and devotion to God's will, concluding with a call to action, to extirpate the Satanic influences that have infiltrated the body of Christendom. There were many such influences: greed and avarice, jealousy and hatred, prostitution and carnal lust; but gradually he came to realize that chief among the messengers of Satan were the Jews, and Peter was convinced that Christendom would never be purified, would never be redeemed from the claws of Satan, until the Jewish influence was purged. This morning's sermon had brought that point home in eloquent fashion. He knew that hatred of the Jews was prevalent and that many in his audience were already long convinced of the Jews' Satanic nature, but they needed something more to rouse them into action, to counteract the defilement spread by Jewish influence. He considered it his holy mission to bring about salvation, and his private battle against the Jews was a means to that end.

A girl's voice jolted Peter from his reverie. It was an angelic voice, singing a beautiful tune, but Peter could not make out the words. The girl was on her knees by the riverbank, washing clothes in the clear water. She seemed oblivious of Peter's presence. Slowly he advanced, as silently as possible, being careful to stay out of her line of sight.

She finished her song but continued to hum, while wringing the water from her wash. Peter came still closer.

Suddenly she stopped humming. She turned around and looked at Peter. She did not look to be afraid, and yet she no longer seemed at peace with herself as she had been before. She had dark, flowing hair and dark, exotic eyes. Her face was radiant with an inner beauty such as Peter had rarely seen. The shape of her body was pleasing, and her breasts were round and full. Peter estimated her age to be about fifteen years old.

Peter smiled. "That was a beautiful song," he said. "But you should not be here all alone. My name is Friar Peter. What is your name?"

The girl looked at Peter questioningly but did not answer. She looked Peter up and down. Her eyes darted to the forest beyond, and back again at Peter.

"Why are you here?" she asked.

"I was just walking in the forest. I heard you singing and was curious. Do not fear. I will not harm you."

She turned from Peter and started gathering her laundry in a basket by her side. With her hand, she brushed a lock of hair away from her face. Her every movement was filled with grace and beauty. Peter felt a throbbing in his loins, and his heart was racing in his chest. She looked up again, and Peter hoped she had not noticed anything amiss.

"It is late," said Peter, "and you should be returning home. Soon the sun will set, and it is not safe to be here after dark. Would you like me to walk you home?"

"Thank you, Sir. But the sun will not set for an hour or two, I think, and I can manage by myself."

"I see you can. But really, you should not be alone here."

She stared at Peter for several seconds. At length, her expression softened somewhat, and she said: "My name is Judith. I came here with a friend, but she fell down and hurt herself. She had to return home."

"So you decided to stay and do your wash all by yourself."

"It had to be done."

"And you were not afraid? A beautiful maiden alone and unprotected?"

She shrugged. "It had to be done."

"Let me help you." He took a step closer, but she stopped him with a stern look.

"I said I can manage by myself."

"Alright, but let me walk you home when you are done gathering your wash."

She stood up. "I know what you are doing, Sir. It is unseemly for a man like you. You are a friar, a Christian man of the cloth, who has taken a vow of chastity. And I am Jewish. I do not mean to be rude or disrespectful, but it is unseemly that we should be together like this."

Peter did not move. He opened his mouth, about to protest his innocence, but she cut him off.

"I do not think I mistook your meaning, but if I did, I apologize sincerely. Now please leave."

Peter turned and slowly walked away. Her accusation had hurt him, although of course it was true. He felt ashamed, and yet still drawn to her, perhaps even more than before. As he entered the woods again, he glanced back and saw that she had returned to the water and was washing the last of her laundry.

He walked among the trees, thinking. How could he have succumbed to this maiden's charms? And if it were not bad enough that he had lusted for a maiden, moreover she was Jewish, a daughter of Satan, a demoness. He was Peter the Pious, the man of God who preached devotion to the kingdom of heaven and separation from matters of this world, and above all from Satanic influence. Yet here he was, no better than a churlish knave, flirting with a maiden.

No – he was flirting with a devil in the guise of a maiden. He stopped and slammed the side of his fist into a tree trunk. It hurt, and that was good – punishment for his sin of lust, a reminder of the proper path that he must tread.

He walked onwards, thinking, trying to rationalize his behavior. He tried to put the incident out of his mind. He tried to think of holy matters. But Judith's image kept re-appearing in his mind. He could not let her go.

He struggled to understand. Was he a fraud? Was he no better than a common lout? From deep within his soul, something gnawed at him – some long-forgotten memory. It almost crystallized, almost surfaced into consciousness, but it quickly slipped away again into oblivion. He looked up to heaven. He spread his hands in prayer.

"God, let me not fall into the pit of temptation. Let me not be ensnared by the Devil's wiles. Protect me, Lord. I serve only You."

He lowered his face. He closed his eyes, and there she was again – Judith – invading his thoughts, tempting him with her beauty, taunting him with her body, calling to him silently with her eyes, her lips; enchanting him with her every movement. Again, he felt a throbbing in his loins.

In his mind he saw her dancing, her body undulating to the sound of distant music. Slowly she removed her garments as she danced, looking at him all the while. He knew he shouldn't watch this sight, but he couldn't help himself. He knew he had only to open his eyes, and the vision would dissolve, but he couldn't bring himself to do so. The image of Judith continued to approach. She was now close enough to touch. His breathing became more rapid.

No, I must not do this. I must resist.

He opened his eyes. He shook his head. Again he slammed the side of his fist against a tree trunk. "No!" he cried. "Stop! I am Peter the Pious. You must leave me. Do not taunt me any longer. You must not do this to me!"

He looked around. There was nobody nearby. He started walking. He had to leave this place of temptation.

It is the Devil tempting me. It is an apparition sent by Satan. It is a test. Christ himself was tempted, was he not? But he resisted. He would not worship Satan, nor will I. Avaunt! Plague me no more, Judith, you Devil's spawn. You cannot conquer me.

But the thought of Judith would not leave his mind, and the image of her naked body flitted in and out of his thoughts. He walked faster, trying to escape the Devil's grip. He reached the edge of the woods, and there beyond the woods she was before him once again – the real Judith, not an apparition – still kneeling by the river doing her wash. Her face was turned away from him, and her hair seemed to glow in the sunlight.

Slowly, silently, he approached. She did not seem to be aware of his presence.

He came closer. Still she seemed unaware of him. He looked at her beautiful form and her long, flowing hair. She seemed so angelic. Peter found it hard to believe that she was from the demonic realm. And yet ... .

He hesitated, momentarily uncertain what to do. He felt the throbbing in his loins, the racing of his heart. Quickly, he made his decision.

He lunged at her from behind. His left hand shot out and covered her mouth, while his right arm wrapped around her body below her breasts. She struggled with him and tried to scream, but only a muffled sound emerged from under Peter's hand. He threw her to the ground on her belly. He sat on her back, pinning her to the ground, his left hand still covering her mouth.

His right hand now was free, and he reached into Judith's laundry basket, extracting a soft cloth garment. He jerked her head up and forced the cloth deep into her mouth. He reached into his own robe and pulled out a leather flask.

Quickly he turned her over on her back, pinning her to the ground with his body and holding her head still with his left hand. She tried to squirm, but he held her fast. She tried to scream, but the gag filled her mouth, and only muffled whimpers emerged. Tears trickled down her cheeks.

Peter opened the flask. With one finger, he pushed the gag slightly at the side of her mouth. Judith began to make a sound, but Peter quickly poured some liquid from the flask into her mouth, and she gagged. She coughed, as well as she could against the cloth that filled her mouth.

Peter waited briefly until she finished coughing. "Do not try that again," he said, "or you will choke."

She was breathing rapidly, and her beautiful eyes were wide with fear. Tears were streaming down her cheeks. She looked up at him pleadingly. He looked into her terror-filled eyes, and his excitement mounted.

Still holding her head firmly, he bent down and kissed her gently on the cheek. "You are beautiful," he said. He raised his head and looked at her. He smiled.

Again he pushed the cloth aside very slightly and poured more liquid into her mouth. This time she did not attempt to scream. She swallowed, and he poured more aqua vitae in.

Several minutes later, when the intoxicating liquid had done its work and Judith was barely conscious, he relaxed his grip. Gently he lifted up her dress to reveal her naked body. She was even more beautiful than he had imagined. He removed her dress completely, and softly he caressed her body. He kissed her soft breasts and put her nipple in his mouth. She did not resist. He spread her thighs and kissed her there, inhaling the fragrance of her sex.

He opened up his robe. His member was erect. He lay down, and his flesh tingled as he felt her soft flesh touching his.

When he had finished with her, he stood up and dressed himself. He looked down at her beautiful naked body. He bent down and kissed her again, on her breasts and on her cheeks. She was completely unconscious now, although she did moan a little when he shook her hard.

He removed the gag and dressed her. He looked at her again, admiring her beauty. *What a pity*, he thought. *Such beauty clothing a demonic spirit.* He knew what he must do.

He opened his flask again and poured more aqua vitae into her mouth. He could not take a chance on her waking up.

He stood up and dressed himself quickly. He looked around to make sure he was not seen.

He lifted her up and carried her to the riverbank. He pushed her into the water, straddled her prone body, and held her head down. She struggled feebly, but he held her tightly as the water filled her lungs. When he was sure she had stopped breathing, he left her there, lying face down in the river.

Emerging from the water, he looked back, making sure that Judith had not risen again. But the water was still, and no sign of life was visible. He turned and slowly walked away.

He looked at the ground. It was gravelly and would leave no tracks. He looked around again and saw no witnesses. He surmised that if the signs of sexual molestation were discovered on Judith's corpse, her family would not want the shame, and her death would therefore be attributed to accidental drowning. But even if her death were ascribed to murder, he doubted anyone would think to implicate him. He was thought to have left hours earlier; and besides, who would think Peter the Pious capable of such an act? Casually, he walked away, towards the nearby woods.

He found his donkey fettered in the woods where he had left it. When he emerged from the woods a half hour later, he made sure to stay off the road. The sun was setting, and not many people would still be on the road, but he could not afford to have anyone see him.

After about two hours, he came upon a monastery, where he stayed the night. As he lay in bed, finally he felt at peace again. The specter of Judith had left him. He had conquered temptation. How, he asked himself, had she tempted him so sorely? Surely, he thought, she must have been a sorceress, and she had cast an evil spell upon him. Now he was free, and she had been dispatched to Hell, to join her master. He smiled to himself as sleep overtook him.

CHAPTER 18

Rome

Present time – 1190

It was well past midnight, in the early morning hours, and Cardinal Giacinto Bobone was fast asleep in bed. The previous day had been a difficult one, filled with sensitive diplomatic meetings with foreign dignitaries, a long debate with several other cardinals regarding various doctrinal matters, and, at the end of the day, an inconclusive hour spent meditating on the state of the world and what course the Church should take in these difficult times. Finally, he had gone to bed feeling the full weight of his eighty-four years, and looking forward to a few hours of respite from his labors.

"Giacinto." The voice echoed through his mind, as though coming from a great distance. He tried to ignore the voice. He turned over in bed and tried to get back to sleep.

"Giacinto," the voice called again.

Dreamily, he opened his eyes and looked around. At first he saw nothing unusual; but after a few seconds, his eyes focused, and he noticed a white-bearded man sitting in a chair across the room, dressed in a grey, hooded robe. The room was still dark, but a soft, unnatural light – perhaps moonlight, but the cardinal doubted it – illuminated the man's face, giving him an other-worldly appearance. The man sat immobile, his hands upon the upholstered armrests of the chair in which he sat, his bright eyes glinting from underneath his hood, his gaze fixed on the cardinal's face. The man smiled but said nothing.

Cardinal Bobone propped himself up on his elbow. "Who are you? And how did you get in here?"

"My name is Enoch, and I have come from afar to speak to you. Listen carefully to what I have to say. The fate of the world may depend upon it."

Cardinal Bobone felt a shudder go down his spine. He stared for a long time at Enoch, trying to figure him out. Many questions raced through the cardinal's mind, but somehow he sensed that it would be futile to ask: How had this man gotten past the guards? How, really, had he gotten into this room? Why had he evaded the question? And what was his motive for coming here? The man did not appear to be threatening in the least, and yet the cardinal felt something disquieting in the air.

"What is it that you wish to tell me?" the cardinal asked.

"Things are not always as they seem, nor are people always as they appear to be. You know this in your heart, but be careful not to be misled. Soon you will be tested. Trust your intuition. Only then will you be able to distinguish good from evil."

"I do not understand. Why are you telling me these things?"

"You do not understand, because I speak of things that have not happened to you yet, and of events that have not yet transpired in the world. You were quite correct when you spoke to Father John: evil indeed is brewing in the world; yet, few are those who have the perspicacity to recognize it, and fewer still who have the foresight and the power to take arms against the evil forces and to thwart the spread of Satan's tentacles. One such combatant is now traveling southwards to Bari and thence to the Holy Land. Cardinal Bobone, you have it within your power to provide him aid and thereby to counteract the force of evil. Soon you will be given a sign, and you must act with resolution, lest evil conquer."

Enoch's voice faded, and the cardinal's vision blurred. His head fell back on his pillow, and sleep again overtook him. An hour later, he woke up. He looked around, squinting in the darkness.

Enoch was no longer in the room. Had he really been there, or was it just a dream? The cardinal was not certain.

Cardinal Bobone heard distant noises coming from outside his house. It sounded like somebody rattling the metal gate. Yes, that is the sound that had just awakened him from sleep. Momentarily the noise stopped. Cardinal Bobone closed his eyes and thought to go back to sleep. But soon he heard the sound of angry voices through his window. An unfamiliar voice spoke his name, demanding audience. Then all was silent once more.

CHAPTER 19

About a half hour after dawn, Matthew was admitted into the presence of Cardinal Giacinto Bobone and began to tell of the Camryn massacre and of his own quest to atone for the people of Camryn, but most particularly for his father. The cardinal listened attentively, with only occasional interruption to ask for clarification or additional details. As Matthew reached the end of his tale, there was a knock at the door.

The cardinal looked up. "Come in."

The door opened half-way, and the cardinal's secretary entered cautiously. "Your Eminence, the sun has already risen, and you have a busy day ahead. Your first appointment is in one hour."

"Yes, Marco, I know. I am afraid my first appointment will have to be delayed. The news this young man brings is of utmost importance. All other matters must wait." After a brief pause, he added, "Perhaps some refreshments would be in order while we continue our conversation. Please bring breakfast for me and my guest."

"But —"

"Yes, yes, I know. That is not according to protocol. No matter. My guest will eat with me."

"Yes, Your Eminence." Marco looked perturbed, but he said nothing more. He bowed and closed the door behind him.

The cardinal smiled and looked into Matthew's eyes. Matthew respectfully bowed his head, but quickly he looked up again, holding the cardinal's gaze.

Cardinal Bobone said, "I see you are a very special young man. Few would have reacted as you did to the events in Camryn. Few would have found fault with your father's actions. Few would have felt a need for penance. And rare indeed is the person who would have accepted the burden of the sins of all the village and taken it upon himself to seek atonement for those sins. But tell me, what made you defy your upbringing and your father's teaching to act as you did?"

"I suppose, in part it was my mother's influence. She died many years ago, but she taught me to be kind to all people, including Jews. Also, Joseph was my neighbor, and my friend. How could I abandon him to his fate? How could I not help my friend escape certain death? And how could I condone the massacre of Joseph's family, who did nobody any harm? I cannot believe that it was God's will, no matter Friar Peter's words."

The cardinal looked at Matthew questioningly. "Do you not, then, accept the words of a man of God? Do you, my son, reject the authority of the church and its ordained clerics?"

Without hesitation, Matthew answered. "No, I do not reject the authority of the church, and I do not reject the church's ordained clerics. I reject Friar Peter."

"But is not Friar Peter an ordained cleric? In fact, I am told he was ordained as a priest before he chose to become a friar. And he is reputed far and wide to be a man of piety and great devotion."

"Be that as it may. To me, he is no priest. He is not a man of God. He is not at all like you. He is evil."

"How can you be sure?" Cardinal Bobone asked.

Matthew paused a moment. He looked into the cardinal's eyes again and said, "I do not know exactly how. I saw it in his eyes, I suppose. I saw hatred and malice there, just as I see goodness in your eyes. I also saw goodness and kindness in Joseph's eyes and in his father's and his mother's eyes as well. Friar Peter called them devils and sons of Satan. He called them enemies of God. I know what I see is true, and I know that Friar Peter is a liar. I know that what I have said contradicts the general consensus both in the matter of the Jews and regarding Friar Peter's holiness, and I hope my answer has not been too bold. I hope my words have not offended Your Eminence."

Cardinal Bobone smiled. "You are very bold to speak such words. But no, you have not offended in the least. As I said, you are a very special young man, and I thank you for your observations. Not many would have felt as you have felt, and still fewer would have done as you have done. I give you my blessing, and I admonish you to continue your pilgrimage to the tombs of St. Peter and St. Paul in Rome, and thence to Venice, where you must take a ship to the Holy Land. For the eyes of the Lord are always on the Holy Land, and in that land is His presence most felt, and His hand is outstretched to heal all those who seek him earnestly. In the Holy Land, your soul will finally find peace."

There was a knock at the door, and the cardinal's secretary entered, a tray of food in his hands. Wordlessly, he placed the various dishes on a table near the cardinal. He bowed, and closed the door behind him.

Matthew looked at the cardinal. "What must I do in the Holy Land, Your Eminence? Is there some shrine at which I am to pray? Is there someone there whom I should visit? Are there certain words that I must utter?"

Cardinal Bobone thought a moment. "I do not know for sure," he said. "I have had strange dreams of late, and I feel in my heart that you have a role to play in events that will soon unfold. When you reach the Holy Land, follow the dictates of your heart, and let your intuition guide you. I see you have good sense, and, despite your youth, you have great insight into men's souls. Things are not always as they seem or as the populace believe. May you always listen to your inner voice, and do not be misled by the messages of hate that some reputedly-holy men may preach."

Matthew bowed his head. "I thank you, Your Eminence. You have eased my soul. But one matter still troubles me and will not let me rest. May I request one more thing?"

The cardinal smiled again. "I will try to help you, if it is in my power. Speak, my son."

Matthew's expression turned solemn. In a trembling voice, he said, "I know my friend Joseph made good his escape from Camryn, but I do not know what became of him afterwards. If, by the grace of God, his path should cross yours, I beg Your Eminence to give him your blessing also, and to assist him in whatever way you can."

"You ask me to bless an infidel?"

Matthew looked at Cardinal Bobone. At first, his resolve appeared to waver, but quickly he regained his composure. "No," he said emphatically. "I ask you to bless my friend."

When they had finished breakfast and Matthew had left, Cardinal Bobone paced the floor, deeply troubled. Matthew was the first eye-witness to Friar Peter's actions that he had been able to question, and Matthew's account tended to support the cardinal's suspicion that Friar Peter was not the holy man he was said to be. Matthew had been emphatic that Peter was evil. But how trustworthy was the assessment of one so young and inexperienced?

"Giacinto!" The ethereal voice from last night's dream echoed in his mind. Had not Enoch given Cardinal Bobone exactly the same instruction that the cardinal later gave to Matthew? "Trust your intuition," he had said. And his intuition told him that Matthew, despite his age, could see into men's souls.

As he considered what his best course of action should be, there was a knock at the door, and the cardinal's secretary entered again. "Your Eminence," he said, "Your brother Ursus asks to see you urgently, and Bishop Cataldo – your first appointment – also awaits your pleasure."

"I will see Ursus. Have the bishop wait."

Ursus entered and bent his knee, but as soon as the secretary left, Ursus ran to his brother and embraced him.

Cardinal Bobone sat down and motioned to his brother to do likewise. "What brings you here so early?" he asked.

"I bring news that will interest you. An emissary from the Templar Council in the Holy Land has arrived in Rome, and he is meeting with the pope this morning."

"How did this information come to you?"

"Ah, Giacinto, you are not the only one who has connections. As it happens, the Templar commander who is the council's emissary is Silvio – the same Silvio who used to play with my youngest son in his youth. Silvio was often in my home, and I used to give him treats. Perhaps you remember him."

"Yes, I do remember him. He is originally from Bari, is he not?"

"Indeed he is. I happened to encounter him in the street yesterday evening, and when I asked what brings him here to Rome, he told me he was soon to see the pope. But he would not reveal the purpose of his meeting. It is apparently regarding some secret of the Templar Council, I surmise."

"Yes, I see." Cardinal Bobone rose and paced the floor again. Ursus began to rise, but the cardinal signaled him to remain seated.

"Yes," Cardinal Bobone repeated to himself; "the Templar emissary is from Bari. And the man in my dream said that Friar Peter's adversary is heading now for Bari."

The cardinal sat down. "Ursus my brother, will you help me?"

"Of course, Giacinto. You know I will do anything for you. But what are you saying? Is it Peter the Pious of whom you speak?"

The cardinal nodded.

"Then tell me, who is this adversary, and what must I do to thwart him?"

Cardinal Bobone shook his head. His face became solemn. "No, my brother. It is not Peter who needs my help. It is his adversary whom I wish to help."

Ursus sat forward in his chair. "But Friar Peter is a holy man! I do not understand. Why would you want to help his adversary?"

The cardinal leaned forward. He lowered his voice and said, "No, my brother. Peter is not the holy man that he appears to be. He is a man full of hate and malice. He spreads lies about the Jews and incites crowds to violence and even to murder. These are not the actions of a man of God. The friar has sinned against both God and humankind. This is the work of the Devil."

Ursus's face bespoke great concern. He looked at his brother for a long while. Finally, he said, "Do not say such things, Giacinto. I know that tone of voice only too well. You must not jeopardize your political standing among the cardinals, as you surely will if you attack Friar Peter before the other cardinals or if you defend the Jews too vehemently. Friar Peter is not alone in his views about the Jews, and many in the Church will come to his defense. Who of all the cardinals deserves more than you to be elected pope? But you will alienate too many, and you will never be pope if you persist in speaking as you have spoken now."

"You do not understand, my brother. It is not the Jews alone that Friar Peter threatens, but the whole fabric of the Church as well. Peter has perverted the whole basis of our faith, and what he preaches is pure heresy, though couched in words of seeming piety. Ours is a religion of love and not of hate. Though the Jews have rejected Christ, they are still human and not the sons of Satan, despite the popular belief among the masses. And though the Jews persist in their rejection of Christian faith, it is not our place to mete out punishment for that. Such matters are best left to God."

Ursus made to speak again, but Cardinal Bobone held up his hand. He leaned back in his chair and said, "As for my being elected pope, I am eighty-four years old, and I have been a cardinal for close to forty-seven years. I have long abandoned hope of ever being pope. But even if I still could aspire to that office, I would not allow such thoughts to prevent me from acting in accordance with divine justice."

Ursus sat in thought. He shifted his position. His gaze wandered. After a while, Cardinal Bobone said, "I see you do not approve, my brother."

Ursus looked up. He shook his head. "No, Giacinto. It is not that way at all. I trust your judgement regarding Friar Peter's nature and intentions. It is what you plan to do that gives me pause."

Cardinal Bobone looked surprised. "But Ursus, I have not yet told you what I mean to do."

"I know you well, Giacinto. Headstrong as always. But I will put my trust in you."

"Good. Then once again, Ursus, I ask your help. There are two things that I ask of you. First, I would have you send men to watch Friar Peter and report to me on his activities. And second, this emissary from the Templar Council – Silvio – do you think you can bring him to me after his meeting with the pope?"

Ursus looked perturbed. "Yes, I can try," he said. "But why?"

"You will have to trust me, Ursus, as you said you would. In fact, I do not know quite how to explain it to you, or even to myself. But your news, and the news that I received from two visitors who preceded you this morning, all converge. My intuition tells me that this Silvio may play an important role in great events that will soon unfold. Please, my brother, bring him to me. I must speak with him."

"Yes, Giacinto. I will do my best." Ursus rose from his seat, embraced his brother, then bowed, kissed his brother's ring, and left the room.

CHAPTER 20

Summer, 1178

T hree days had passed since Friar Peter's encounter with Judith.
He had gone many miles since then, and he was now at
a roadside inn, where he had rented a room for the night.
Before going to his room, Peter spent an hour in the common
room, listening to whatever news was circulating among the
patrons. He was pleased to hear no news at all about a recent
murder or even about an accidental death. Yesterday, at a different
inn, someone had very briefly mentioned a recent accidental
drowning, but tonight he was still farther away, and here there was
no mention at all of the drowned girl. Satisfied that the matter
had been put to rest, Peter went up to his room. He smiled to
himself as he got into bed, and sleep overtook him quickly.

In his dream, Friar Peter stood on a podium in a village square,
a great throng surrounding him, eager to hear his words. Many
came forward, bowing before him and asking for his blessing. Friar
Peter made the sign of the cross and blessed each supplicant in
the name of the Father, the Son, and the Holy Spirit, whereupon
the supplicant bowed again and said, "Thank you, Friar Peter."

A hooded man approached the platform upon which Friar
Peter stood. He did not bow. He took Friar Peter's hand in
his two hands, and his hands were cold as death. Friar Peter
shuddered. He wanted to pull his hand away, but he had not
the strength to do so. The man stood silently, and stared deeply
into the friar's eyes. Under the hood, the man's face could not

be seen, but his eyes burned like fire, and Peter could not bear to look upon them.

The man released the friar's hand and lowered his hood, revealing a long face with pointed beard, and two horns protruding from his head. Peter looked down and saw that the man's feet were not human feet at all, but hooves.

"Peter!" the man called loudly, and Peter's body trembled.

Friar Peter took a step away and looked around. The throng had vanished; and only he and the horned man now stood in the village square.

"Peter!" the man cried out again. "I am but a messenger. My lord is calling to you. Come with me." The man held out his left hand to Peter, while his right hand beckoned to him.

"No! Do not tempt me. Away! I will not yield. I am Peter. Peter the Pious. I preach the word of God."

The horned man smiled. His eyes flashed fire. His left hand approached Friar Peter's shoulder, almost touching him. His right hand beckoned once again.

"Avaunt! Be gone!" the friar screamed, backing away. "I will not deal with Satan or his minions. I will not yield."

The horned man disappeared, and Peter was all alone. He looked around again. He was no longer in the village square, but in a forest. The light was dim, and the air was ominously thick with shadows. He looked up, but the branches of the trees seemed to form a canopy above him, and he could not see the sky. He felt there was something sinister about this forest. He knew he must escape the forest lest the shadows engulf him; and yet, he knew not whether he should go right or left, and he feared the evil spirits that may be lurking here, waiting to pounce on him should he move deeper into the forest, waiting for him to let down his guard. Cautiously, he made his way among the trees, his heart pounding in his chest. Slowly he advanced, hoping he was going in the right direction. With a trembling hand, he wiped the sweat from his brow.

He looked around again. He wasn't certain, but the forest seemed to have darkened further. Panic overtook him, and he began to run, but he did not run very far before he was out of breath and panting. He stopped, and looked behind to make sure he was not being followed. For a long time, he stood still, listening to the sounds of the forest, hoping to hear something that would help him find his way. In the distance, he thought he heard the sound of running water, and he hurried towards the sound.

He emerged from the forest, relieved that he had escaped. The sun was shining, and the air was much warmer than it had been in the forest. He squinted in the bright light of day. He looked ahead, toward the sound that he had heard. A girl knelt beside a stream, washing clothes. She looked up, and he recognized her. It was Judith.

He advanced towards Judith. She rose and took him by his hand. She kissed him on his lips.

A thought wafted through his mind, trying to intrude itself upon his dream. *That is not how it happened.* But he pushed the thought aside. Judith of his dream continued kissing him, stroking his cheek. She smiled seductively and led him to the stream. Slowly she removed her clothes, while he watched her, enthralled.

She stood before him completely naked. "Come to me," she said.

Peter advanced a step. He stretched out his hand to touch her breast.

But his hand never touched her flesh. In an instant, the girl, the stream, and the nearby forest vanished, and his vision blurred.

When his eyes again came into focus, he was standing on the podium in the village square once more. As before, a great throng surrounded him. But now the crowd was silent, and no one approached to ask his blessing. Friar Peter looked about, confused. He did not understand why the attitude of the people had changed. He looked into their eyes but found there only coldness and repressed anger.

He opened his mouth. He spread his arms, palms up. "My friends. My brothers in Christ. I bring you God's blessing." He looked up to heaven and made the sign of the cross.

"Liar!" someone called, and a hundred voices repeated after him. "Liar, liar, liar."

"No, I am Peter. I am Peter the Pious. I have come to bless you and to bring you the word of God."

A light appeared in the sky above him, and from the midst of the light emerged an angel, his great white wings spread over the village square, and in his right hand he held a fiery sword. Quickly the angel descended, his sword pointed at Friar Peter.

"Murderer!" the angel called, raising his sword for the kill.

"No!" Peter shouted. He turned and ran from the podium, the crowd parting to let him through.

He ran and ran until he could run no more. He stopped a moment and looked back. The angel was nowhere in sight, but now the crowd was chasing after Peter. "Murderer!" they shouted, running towards him, throwing stones at him.

He began to run again, trying to escape the angry mob. They pelted him with stones. He raised his hood and put his hands above his head to shield himself. He ran as he had never run before, and somehow he was gaining ground, escaping from the mob. But just as it seemed that he was almost safe, the angel appeared again, this time in front of him.

The angel stood before him, and his face was terrible to look upon. "Murderer!" Again, he raised his sword for the kill.

Peter knelt, his right hand raised to fend off the blow. "No! I am no murderer. I am a pious servant of the Lord. I am a friar and an ordained priest. I speak the word of God, and I lead men to serve His will. I am not a murderer."

The angel did not strike, but his sword stood poised above Friar Peter's head. "You are a liar and a murderer," the angel said.

"No, no. As I told you, I am a man of God. I resisted the temptation of the Devil. Judith was not human but a Jewess and a devil's spawn. She tried to tempt me. She tempted me sorely, but I did not yield. Killing a demon is not murder. What I did to her was no crime at all. Everyone knows my piety and my devotion to the Lord, and only a demon could have tempted me as Judith did."

"Murderer!" the angel shouted yet again, and his sword descended in an arc towards Peter's outstretched neck.

Peter screamed and woke up, trembling. The angel was gone, and the angry mob as well, but Peter's heart was racing, his neck was throbbing, and he was drenched in sweat. He sat up. He touched his neck where the angel's sword would have struck. It was very tender to the touch, and very warm. He collapsed on the bed, breathing heavily, listening to the sounds of the night.

CHAPTER 21

Present time – late November 1190

It was shortly after sunrise, and they had been on the road for more than two hours already. Joseph looked at his two friends and tried to smile. They were all very tired, but it would be many hours more before they could stop to rest.

After leaving Lucca well before dawn, at first they had taken the eastward road to Florence, but less than an hour later they had veered off onto a smaller road heading south. Joseph felt much better now that they were no longer on the main road, but he knew they were still too close to Lucca to consider themselves out of immediate danger. Ahead of them, the road curved, and a thicket of trees obscured their view of the road beyond. Joseph held up his hand, and they slowed their pace.

As they came around the bend, four armed men sprang from the thicket. Joseph startled, and his first impulse was to retreat, but quickly he realized that retreating would raise suspicion. He stood his ground.

One of the men drew his sword and confronted Joseph. "Chi siete, giovani?"

Joseph looked at the man questioningly and said, "We don't speak Italian. We are from England."

Another one of the men-at-arms stepped forward, stood by the side of his comrade with the drawn sword, and asked in heavily-accented English, "Who are you? What is your business here, and where are you going?"

"We are three friends, devout in our service to the Lord. We have walked here all the way from England, on a pilgrimage."

The man-at-arms looked skeptical. "A pilgrimage, you say? What kind of pilgrimage? Is it a pilgrimage to atone for some great sin?"

Aaron stepped forward and said, "No, no; it is nothing like that. We are devout servants of the Lord, and I am studying for the priesthood. But I feel I am unworthy and need to purify myself. This is my best friend, and his wife. They, too, wish to serve the Lord in holiness, and thus they agreed to accompany me on my journey."

"I see. Your story almost sounds believable. So tell me, where are you bound for?"

"We are bound for Rome," said Joseph.

The man laughed. "For Rome? If it is Rome you want, you are on the wrong road. Why don't you tell us what you are really up to?"

As Joseph began to search his mind for a plausible reply, out of the corner of his eye another of the men-at arms caught his attention. The man was smiling broadly, and he was advancing towards Rachel. "Bella ragazza! Come ti chiami?"

Rachel drew back. She glanced at Joseph and quickly turned her attention again to the approaching man-at-arms. Joseph noted a slight twitch of Rachel's lips, but otherwise she showed no sign of fear.

The man took another step forward. He held out his hand to Rachel and beckoned. "Your name?" he said in English.

The man with the drawn sword looked approvingly at his comrade who was advancing on Rachel, and he also took a step towards her.

Rachel said nothing. She took another step backwards. Joseph turned in her direction.

Aaron looked alarmed and started to move towards Rachel, but the fourth man-at-arms blocked him. He drew his sword, and Aaron quickly retreated.

The man who was questioning Joseph and Aaron took a step towards Joseph, blocking his path, and said, "Pay no attention to them. It is none of your business. Just answer my question: where are you really going, and what are you three up to?"

Joseph thrust his right hand under his shirt, and his fingers wrapped around the hilt of his dagger. Joseph spun around quickly and caught the man by surprise as he lunged, plunging the dagger into the man's right flank. The man went for his sword, but Joseph was too fast for him. Pulling the dagger out of the wound, Joseph slashed upwards, cutting the man's right wrist and hand. The sword fell to the ground, and Joseph took it.

The injured man fell, holding his bleeding flank. Two of the other men seized Aaron, while the fourth man began to chase after Joseph.

Joseph feinted to his right, keeping the wounded man between himself and his pursuer. He glanced at Rachel and saw that she had already begun to run away, southwards off the road and into the woods. Joseph continued running along the road, northwards, away from Rachel. As the road curved again, a man in a mule-drawn cart passed by, going south. The man, apparently a local peasant, was nobody Joseph had ever seen before, but Joseph waved to him in a friendly gesture and continued running. As soon as Joseph passed the back of the cart, he veered off the road into the woods. Only then did he look back. His pursuer was far behind him, just barely visible. Joseph thought he had probably made good his escape, but he could not take any chances. He continued running through the woods.

When Joseph's pursuer returned to his comrades, the captain met him first. The captain looked at him sternly. "Armando, you idiot. You lost him. Friar Peter will not be pleased. He'll make you haul shit for a week. If you're lucky."

Armando bowed his head. "Yeah, I know. But he was too fast for me. Anyway, the friar should be pleased we got his friend."

He looked at Aaron, who was sitting on the ground, tied hand and foot.

Armando turned to the captain again and asked, "How's Carlo? Is he still alive? I don't see him here."

"Oh, he and Stefano are back there, down the road a bit. Bled a lot, but the wounds weren't too deep. We bandaged him. I think he'll be fine. That guy who passed you in the mule cart will take Carlo to Lucca. Then Stefano will join us, and we'll head back to Friar Peter with our prisoner."

The captain went over to Aaron. He untied Aaron's ankles but left Aaron's wrists tied behind his back. Aaron moved his legs. His feet were numb. He wiggled his toes.

Aaron looked at the ground. He closed his eyes and prayed silently: *God, please guard my sister Rachel and my good friend Joseph. Protect them. Do not let these men find them. And give me strength, that I may not say anything to endanger them. Give me courage to resist, no matter what my captors do to me, and make me worthy of the holy men, my ancestors who served you as priests in the Temple in Jerusalem. I am your faithful servant Aaron.*

The captain stood over him. "Get up. On your feet, Jew!"

Aaron opened his eyes and rose with difficulty. His legs were stiff, and sensation was just beginning to return to his feet. His wrists hurt terribly, and he tried to reposition them, to no avail. He staggered forward.

The captain slipped a rope around Aaron's neck and gave the other end of the rope to Armando. Armando stood in front of Aaron and looked him up and down. "On a leash, just like a dog."

Armando said, "Here comes Stefano now."

The captain drew his sword and prodded Aaron's back. "Walk, Jew!"

The men continued walking with their captive northward on the road for about half a mile when they encountered a horse-drawn cart traveling southward. The driver, a priest, waved to them.

"Salve, Padre," the captain called out to the priest.

"Buon giorno," the priest said cheerily. "May the Lord bless all his worthy children." But the priest was not looking at the captain. He was looking intently at Aaron.

"Thank you, Father," said the captain.

Aaron looked up at the priest and recognized him. It was Father John. Aaron started to smile, but the priest immediately turned away, and Aaron realized his mistake. He thought no one other than the priest had noticed.

"I see you have a prisoner," said Father John, continuing in Italian. "If I may ask, is he a dangerous criminal?"

"Yes," said the captain. "He's wanted for murder." He jerked the rope tied to Aaron's throat. Aaron gasped and made a gurgling sound.

Father John made the sign of the cross and said, "I see. May the Lord have mercy on his soul."

The priest made as if to leave, but after a moment he asked, "Was he alone, or did he have an accomplice?"

"In fact, he had two accomplices, a boy and a girl; but unfortunately they got away. They, too, are very dangerous. If you see them, will you notify us immediately?"

"I'm always eager to aid the cause of justice. Where may I find you?"

"We're heading north. At the crossroad, turn right and go east. That's the road to Florence. We'll be a few miles down the road, with Friar Peter."

"Then good day, sir." Father John tipped his hat, flicked his horse's reins, and continued southward.

CHAPTER 22

A chill wind blew. Friar Peter stood by the roadside, a staff in his right hand, his cowl pulled over his head, his black robe billowing in the wind. His face was a mask of fury.

"You dolts! How could you let those other two get away? Don't you know this one is just a follower? No, captain, don't try to put all the blame on your man Armando. He's to blame, no doubt about it. But you're all to blame. And you especially, captain. It was your responsibility to capture him."

"Yes, Friar Peter, I know. I make no excuses, and I beg your forgiveness. But there were only four of us, and one of us was wounded."

"Then, after you tied up this fugitive, you should have pursued the girl. Through her, you'd find the third one also. Have you no brains?"

"Again, Friar Peter, I sincerely beg your forgiveness. But perhaps we can use this prisoner to our advantage."

"Yes, indeed." Friar Peter sat down on the edge of a wagon and thought. He did not want to let the captain know that, despite the failure to capture Joseph and Rachel, he was generally pleased. After all, he had not really thought to find any of the three fugitives, at least not yet. It was certainly a stroke of good fortune that his men had encountered them and succeeded in capturing even one. And, of course, the captain was quite right: Aaron should be useful.

Friar Peter smiled benignly. "Alright, captain. I forgive you this time, all of you. But don't slip up again."

The captain bowed his head. "Thank you, Friar Peter. It won't happen again."

Friar Peter stood up and walked slowly to Aaron, who was sitting on the ground, his wrists and ankles bound. Friar Peter prodded Aaron's chest with his staff. "Will you tell us where your friends are heading?"

Aaron continued sitting immobile, stone-faced.

Friar Peter crouched down and looked deep into Aaron's eyes. "You do not wish to betray your friends? Is that it?"

Peter shook his head. He stood up and looked down at Aaron. He circled Aaron slowly and came back around to face him. Aaron did not look up at Friar Peter but stared vacuously straight ahead.

"Look at me when I speak to you."

Aaron turned his face upwards.

"So you seem to have a sense of honor, do you? You won't betray your friends. I'm surprised a Jew would feel that way. You had no such qualms when you betrayed our Lord. It is a small matter for a Jew to do such things, isn't it? So tell me, Aaron, where are your friends going? Surely you must know."

Aaron remained silent, but his gaze did not waver from Peter's face, and Friar Peter did not fail to note the deep contempt in Aaron's eyes.

The friar stepped back. He turned to the captain and said, "Stand him up, strip him to the waist, and bind his wrists to a horizontal pole above his head."

When Aaron had been stripped and bound as Friar Peter had commanded, Peter again walked slowly up to Aaron. He stood by Aaron's side and asked, "Do you know the nature of the treasure you are seeking? Did your good friend tell you, or are you following him blindly like a sheep? Do you know what he will do when he finds it? Does even he know himself?"

Aaron continued looking straight ahead, saying nothing.

Friar Peter's voice turned pleasant, amiable, comforting. "You can spare yourself a lot of pain. Tell me all I ask. I will help you find what you are seeking. I have certain powers, and once we have found it, I will know how to use it. I will know this better than will your friend, who is just groping in the dark; and I will know how to use its power to the fullest. Speak to me, Aaron." He bent down, his lips almost touching Aaron's ear, and whispered, "Deep inside, you want to tell me. Yes, you really do. So speak, and do not hide a thing."

Aaron shivered as the cold wind blew over his bare chest. But he still remained silent.

Friar Peter moved away from Aaron. He turned to the captain. "Alright," he said. "Whip him till he talks."

Aaron closed his eyes. He must not give in. He must not betray his sister and his best friend. He must remain true – true to his family, true to his friend, true to his people, true to Joseph's mission, and true to his own priestly heritage. His ancestors had served in the Holy Temple in Jerusalem, and moreover, his family was descended from the last High Priest before the Babylonian exile. As such, Aaron knew his own importance in the fulfillment of Joseph's mission, for when the Temple stood, only the High Priest was permitted to don the breastplate, and only he could use its power. Aaron strengthened his resolved and braced himself for whatever may befall him.

The whip struck with fury on Aaron's naked flesh. Aaron twitched, but he did not cry out. He tensed his muscles and braced himself for the next assault.

The whip seared his back again, with still greater force. Aaron squeezed his eyelids tighter, and colored lights danced before his vision. He must shut out the world. He thought of Rachel. He thought of Joseph. He thought of his parents. He imagined himself in Camryn, in a world of peace, in a world of his imagination, in a world that might have been.

Again the whip struck, and Aaron cried out in pain. He gasped for air.

"Tell us your comrades' destination. Speak now, and the pain will stop." It was Peter's voice. It was soft and silky, tempting

Aaron. But Aaron knew it was the voice of hatred, the voice of malice and of death. He tried to close his mind to it, tried to shut off all sensation.

Again he felt the whip. He almost cried out but managed to hold back. He must not give the friar satisfaction. He must resist with all his being.

The whipping continued for several minutes more, but Aaron did not give in. He felt his trousers being lowered. Vaguely, he heard the friar's voice again, but he did not discern the friar's words.

Behind him, he heard a man shout, and pain erupted through his buttocks. Other voices all around him cheered. Again excruciating pain coursed through his buttocks, this time radiating down his thighs. He heard the sound of laughter all around him.

He braced himself for the next blow. Again a man shouted behind him, and again he felt a searing pain. He felt something dripping down his thighs. He knew it was his blood.

He must not yield. He must not speak. He must not betray his sister and his friend. He remembered the Biblical admonition: A bearer of tales reveals a secret; but a faithful spirit conceals a matter. It all depends on spirit. It all depends on fortitude of spirit, and, whatever comes, he must be faithful.

His head was light. Once more, the pain seized him, encompassing his entire being in its grip. His breathing was more rapid now. He felt his skin burning as though with a fever, and yet he shivered. He was trembling all over.

The friar's voice again. A disembodied voice, wordless.

Aaron willed the friar's voice away. In his mind, he recited to himself the priestly blessing that he and his father – and all his ancestors through the centuries – had intoned so many times on holidays when they blessed the congregation: *May the Lord bless you and protect you; may the Lord's face shine upon you and be gracious to you; may the Lord turn His face toward you and grant you peace.* But this time, it was himself to whom he gave the blessing. He paused a moment, and in his mind he said, *Amen.*

The beating stopped. He heard shouts and taunts and raucous laughter. For a moment, Friar Peter appeared before him, smiling. Aaron closed his eyes. The friar issued a command, and Aaron felt himself being pushed down on his knees. Two men seized his arms, pinning him down, his face pressed to the ground, his buttocks up in the air.

Without warning, something struck him hard on his buttocks and thighs, and a terrible, excruciating pain enveloped him. This pain was different from before: more intense, perhaps a stick or club, or at the very least a different type of whip; but certainly wielded by a different person, a man of far superior strength and cruelty.

Another blow descended on his buttocks, and Aaron cried out. He tried not to think of the pain. He imagined himself serving as a priest in the Holy Temple in Jerusalem in the time of the prophets nearly two thousand years ago. He saw himself wearing priestly robes, his arms raised to heaven, blessing the throng that gathered in the Temple courtyard. And, as before, he repeated the words of priestly blessing: *May the Lord bless you and protect you; may the Lord's face shine upon you and be gracious to you; may the Lord turn His face toward you and grant you peace.* But again he felt an object strike him, and pain once more enveloped him.

Again he heard the shouting and the laughter of the friar's men. He heard the friar's disembodied voice echoing through his mind.

He floated on the verge of consciousness. Through a fog, he heard his own voice speak. "Southwards. South, past Naples, to Salerno. Then eastward to Otranto."

He felt his wrists being released. He heard the friar's voice again. He felt himself falling. Then all was silence.

"What should we do with him when he regains consciousness? Do you want to question him some more?" The captain glanced at Aaron, who was lying on the ground some ten paces away, still unconscious.

"No," said Friar Peter.

"Do you believe him?"

Friar Peter looked at Aaron's unconscious form sprawled on the ground before him. "I'm not sure. He sounded believable, did he not? And yet ... ."

"Then let's interrogate him again and be more certain."

"No," said Friar Peter. "He's a stubborn one. I doubt we'll get more reliable answers from him the next time. And besides, I don't think he can bear any more beating. We'll keep him prisoner for maybe two or three days more, to see that his wounds are healing. Then release him. Or better yet, let him think he escaped. Follow him, and he will unwittingly lead us to his friends."

CHAPTER 23

Late summer, 1178

I t was now thirty days since Judith's death, and it was at
least ten days since Friar Peter had heard anyone speak of
her. Her death apparently had been attributed to accidental
drowning, and that was that. He had even heard occasional
news of other insignificant events from Judith's village, but the
drowned girl was no longer a topic of conversation. The case
apparently was closed.

He was now many miles away, staying at another inn after
a successful day preaching to an enthusiastic throng. Contented
with a job well done, he looked forward to a restful, peaceful
night. He smiled to himself and turned over in his bed. Sleep
and dreams overtook him quickly.

He was in a forest. The trees grew close together, and their
branches were thick with leaves, obscuring much of the sun's light.
In the distance he saw a clearing, and he walked in that direction.
He heard the sound of running water. The scene seemed familiar,
but he couldn't remember why. He went onward, towards the
clearing, towards the running water.

He emerged from the forest. The sun was shining. A girl
knelt beside a stream, washing clothes.

Her face was turned away from him, and yet something about
her stirred him: the sheen of her dark hair in the sunlight, the
curve of her body beneath her garment, the rhythmic swaying of
her body as she washed her clothes.

She looked up, and he recognized her. It was Judith.

He advanced towards her. She rose and took him by his hand. She stroked his cheek. She kissed him gently on the lips.

Vaguely, he thought, *This is not how it happened.* But Judith kissed him again – this time more amorously – and he pushed the thought aside.

He drew her close and wrapped his arms around her body. She moaned sensuously and caressed his inner thighs.

He reached for her bosom, but she pulled away.

Had he done something wrong? Did she no longer desire him? He held his hands out to her, but she withdrew again.

She held her right hand up, signaling him to wait. She began to sing, her voice angelic, enveloping him in its delicate beauty.

Peter felt a throbbing in his loins. He took a step forward, but again she signaled him to wait. His member was erect. He needed to approach, to hold her in his arms, to feel the warmth of her body pressed against his chest, to feel the swell of her bosom and the beating of her heart. He needed to possess her. And yet he stood still, obeying her silent command.

She continued singing. Her voice ebbed and flowed. Slowly she danced to the tune of her song, her body undulating to the melody.

Her arms embraced her torso, her hands caressing her own breasts through her garment. She smiled at Peter, an erotic smile.

Her hands moved downwards, caressing her belly, her hips, and finally her thighs. Her dance continued, but her eyes never left Peter's face.

She smiled again, and Peter began to advance. But once again she signaled him to stay.

Her hands went to the hem of her dress. She pulled it upwards, revealing her nakedness. Slowly she pulled it higher, over her head. She flung the dress aside.

She walked toward Peter. She was completely naked. Her cheeks were flushed. Her nipples stood erect.

She undressed Peter quickly. Kneeling on the ground before him, she stroked his thighs and took his member in her mouth.

She pulled him down to the ground and sat astride him. Peter looked up at her, marveling at her radiant beauty.

She caressed his chest, his arms, his face. She bent down, and he closed his eyes as her lips met his.

When their lips parted, he opened his eyes again and looked at her. Her face had changed. She was no longer Judith but a woman still more beautiful, with bright eyes and long red, flowing hair. Softly, she spoke his name. She lay beside him, stroking his body gently.

He pulled her closer, and she kissed him. Again she sat astride him, and he entered her. She was very moist inside. He closed his eyes again, and his body resonated to her rhythm.

She cried out in ecstasy just as he reached climax.

He opened his eyes. He looked at her.

Her face again transformed before his eyes. Her eyes burned like fire, and her features became masculine, hard, commanding.

Peter cried out and tried to extricate himself, but the apparition sat astride him, pinning him to the ground. The apparition's face was terrible to look upon, and his gaze bored into Peter. Peter tried to look away but couldn't.

The apparition stood, his foot on Peter's chest. His face and upper body were clothed in flame. He pointed at Peter, and he laughed.

"Who are you?" Peter asked, his voice trembling.

"I am a messenger," the apparition answered.

"Whose messenger? And what do you want from me?"

"I am sent to exact retribution, to hurl you down to Hell. My master is calling you."

"No, no. There must be some mistake. I am a man of God. I am Peter the Pious."

"You are a murderer, not a man of God."

The apparition rose and pulled Peter to his feet. But Peter got down on his knees. "Please. I beg your mercy. Allow me to repent.

Judith was not human. She was a Jewess, a demon in human form. Only a demon could have tempted me as Judith did."

"No!" the apparition shouted. "She was no demon. And you are a murderer."

Peter looked up at the apparition, forcing himself to look upon his terrible visage and his burning gaze. But before Peter's eyes, the apparition transformed again. Its features softened, becoming feminine again. Its eyes again became sensuous, erotic. No longer was it clothed in flame. No longer was it terrible to look upon.

The red-haired seductress stood again before him, completely naked. And he was still on his knees, looking up at her.

"Rise, Peter," the red-haired woman commanded, and Peter rose on shaky feet.

"Who are you? And what will you do with me?"

"I am Lilith, Queen of Demons, consort of the Lord of Darkness. I have decided to let you live, that you may serve me."

"No, this cannot be! I am a man of God."

"You are not. Your soul is evil, and you have made your choice already. By committing rape and murder you have chosen to serve the Other Side."

"Can I not repent?"

"It is now too late for that. Throughout your life, you have been a man of hatred and of latent violence. Although you thought yourself to be a man of God, your soul seethed with evil. Even after you committed murder, the door to repentance was not yet fully shut. You had ample opportunity to examine your soul and to repent your sins. But you chose instead to stay your course. Tonight you consummated your choice by taking me, and thus you have committed yourself to serve the Lord of Darkness. While you live, I will give you certain powers, and with those powers, you will realize your greatest dreams. But when you die, Satan will claim your soul."

The apparition vanished, and Peter awoke. He sat up in bed. He looked around the room. There was no sign of Lilith, but

Peter was drenched in sweat. Had she really been there? Had she given Peter any special powers? Or was it just a dream?

Peter thought he knew the answer.

He collapsed on the bed. "What have I done?" he whispered.

He looked up at the rafters in the ceiling. It was still night, and the room was dark, but he could see a faint glow and a shimmering in the air above him. He smiled.

CHAPTER 24

Present time – late November 1190

When Father John estimated that he was far enough away from the men-at-arms, he slowed his horse and began to sing in English:

A lord there was who sought a knave;
A Jewish knave he sought.
He searched the country with his men,
But they found naught.

The lord will search until he finds
The Jewish knave, the Jewish lad.
Pity any Jew he finds,
Whether he be good or bad.

As he rode by, Father John scanned the road and the trees beyond, looking for signs of life. After about a half hour, something off the road caught his eye. It was just a fleeting glimpse of motion in the distance, but it was enough. He stopped his horse and waited.

A minute passed, and then another. Father John began to sing his song again.

When Joseph finally was convinced that he had eluded his pursuer, he looked around to get his bearings. He was sure the road was somewhere to his right, and he estimated the distance by which his path must have diverged from the road. He thought of the direction in which Rachel had run when she ducked into the forest during her escape. He had run in an arc cutting first northeast and then southwards. He calculated that if he were to continue along that arc, he would soon intersect Rachel's path, provided that she had not changed her course after entering the forest. Fortunately, Rachel had stayed her course, and thus it wasn't long before they met again.

Rachel came running towards him and fell into his arms. She held him tightly and pressed her face against his shoulder, sobbing.

"Rachel, what are you doing? What if somebody should see us here like this?"

"Don't talk nonsense. There's nobody here to see. Thank God I found you, Joseph. I was so scared. I thought I had lost you."

Joseph held her close. He kissed her head. "I'm here. You found me, Rachel."

She looked up into his eyes. "What would I have done if I had lost you? All alone in the world. Where would I have gone?" She pressed her face against his shoulder again and held him with all her might.

He heard the fervor in her voice. He felt the passion in her embrace. He wasn't certain what to make of it. *Is it just relief at finding me? Am I just her anchor to her familiar world? Or is this something more?*

Still she held him tightly, sobbing gently, her whole body pressed against him. He felt the swell of her breasts against his chest.

Could she be falling in love with me? He must not let that happen. But he was at a loss to think what he could do to stop it. And, to make matters worse, he felt something stirring within himself as well.

Cautiously, he drew away slightly, but Rachel clung to him, pulling him close again, and pressed her face against his shoulder. Joseph caressed her hair and kissed her gently.

He felt ashamed of himself for his feelings toward Rachel. He felt it was a betrayal of Sarah's memory, a betrayal of Aaron's friendship, a betrayal of Rachel's vulnerable state.

He thought of Sarah, imagined her alive again, standing before him, her face radiant as she caught sight of him. But that image quickly faded and was replaced by Sarah standing on the pyre, flames engulfing her. She was screaming, but the roaring of the fire drowned out her words.

He closed his eyes and opened them again. He shook his head. Sarah's image and the burning pyre faded from his mind.

I must not think of Sarah. Not now. It is too recent. It hurts too much. And I can't let myself wallow in sorrow. I must live in the present or I am lost. Later, there will be time to mourn.

He looked down at Rachel. She was no longer crying, and she seemed much calmer now. Gently he stroked her hair. "It's alright, Rachel," he said. "We're together again. Now let's find your brother and try to rescue him."

They walked back towards the road, then followed it northwards but staying off the road, well within the woods, trying to move as noiselessly as possible. Several minutes passed. Neither of them spoke, but whenever Joseph glanced at Rachel, he saw her gaze was fixed upon him, never wavering.

She smiled, and he averted his gaze.

Abruptly, Joseph stopped in his tracks and signaled Rachel to do likewise. "Do you hear that?" he whispered.

She nodded.

They crept closer, watching the road through the trees.

Again Joseph stopped. He pointed. "Look, Rachel," he whispered. "I think it's a priest. And he's singing in English."

"Something about Jews, I think. What can it mean, Joseph?"

Slowly and cautiously, Joseph moved closer to the road, and Rachel followed.

The priest stopped singing. He looked in their direction.

Joseph quickly lay down flat on the forest floor. "Get down!" Joseph whispered to Rachel. "I think he's seen something. He knows we're here."

The priest began to sing again.

Joseph looked at Rachel. "Look, Rachel! It's Father John."

"Are you sure?"

"I think so. But what's he doing here? Let's get a closer look."

The priest finished his song. Again he looked in their direction. Joseph and Rachel froze in place.

"You may come out now," said Father John softly. "There is no one else around."

Joseph was unsure what to do. He signaled Rachel not to move. He watched the priest.

Father John turned his eyes away and looked straight ahead down the road. In a low voice, he said, "Perhaps you're right. Stay in the woods. Don't let me see you. That way, if I am asked, I can truthfully deny having seen you. They have your friend, and they are taking him to Friar Peter. I will take this road south, but you go north. At the crossroads, turn right and go east, towards Florence. Friar Peter's camp should be a few miles down that road. May God be with you."

He tipped his hat and flicked his horse's reins.

The sun was close to setting when Joseph and Rachel arrived at Friar Peter's camp. Even before the camp came into view, they faintly heard the voice of someone screaming in the distance.

Rachel tensed. She looked at Joseph. Her voice was just a whisper, but it pierced Joseph's heart. "That was Aaron. I am sure it was. What are they doing to him?"

Another scream.

Rachel seized Joseph's arm and held it in a vice-like grip. He put his other arm around her. She was trembling.

"Come," he said. "We must get closer. But be very quiet, and keep down."

Slowly, they crept through the forest, coming as close as they dared. In the distance, they saw a body lying sprawled on the ground face down, naked. From their position, crouching low amidst the undergrowth, it was difficult to see details. But this much they could see: it was a male, and his back and buttocks were bloody. Friar Peter and several other men stood around the body talking, but Joseph didn't dare get closer, and at this distance the wind swallowed most of their words.

Rachel tugged at Joseph's sleeve. "It's Aaron, isn't it? Is he breathing? I can't tell from here." A tear ran down her cheek, and Joseph gently brushed the tear away.

"Yes, I think it is Aaron," he whispered in her ear. "And I thought I saw his chest rising. Now be quiet, and listen."

"No." It was Friar Peter's voice.

"... believe ...?"

Friar Peter's voice again: "... He sounded ... ? And yet..."

"... interrogate him ... ."

"No." Friar Peter again. "... stubborn ... answers ... next time ... Keep him prisoner. ... Then release him ... Let ... think he escaped. Follow him ..."

Joseph's face lit up. "Did you hear that, Rachel?"

"Only part. I still don't get it."

"Don't you see? They're letting him go."

"Why? Did he tell them where we're going?"

"I don't know. But it doesn't matter. They will follow him, expecting him to lead them to us. So we can't meet up with him. Not until they stop following him."

"But they won't stop, until he leads them to us. How will we ever be able to meet up with Aaron again without falling into their hands?"

Joseph put his arm around her. "Don't worry, Rachel. I'll think of something. Meanwhile, he knows where we are going, and he will meet us there. We just have to reach Bari and speak to Rabbi Tuviah before Aaron gets there. Now come. We have no time to lose."

Rachel turned and looked into Joseph's eyes. Her face was just inches from his. She looked to be on the verge of tears again, but her voice was steady. "We can't just leave him here," she said. "Please. We must do something. At least let's stay and watch until they let him go."

He held her gaze for a long time, marveling at the intensity of her deep blue eyes – a pleading insecurity intermingled with a sense of strength and force of will radiating from them.

"Please, Joseph. We cannot leave him here like this."

He drew her closer until their cheeks touched. He whispered in her ear. "I know. It hurts to leave him here. I feel the same way, Rachel. He is like a brother to me too. But there is nothing we can do, and we must reach Bari well before them. Besides, it may be days before they let him go. We can't linger here, or we will be discovered."

Gently, he turned her head and guided her deeper into the forest, away from the road, away from Friar Peter's camp, away from Aaron.

CHAPTER 25

Cardinal Bobone's door opened, and the secretary entered. The cardinal, who was standing by his desk, turned toward the door and nodded in acknowledgement.

"Your Eminence. Commander Silvio of the Knights Templar, emissary of the Templar Council in the Holy Land, is here to see you at your request."

"Yes, Marco. Please show him in."

Marco opened the door wider, and in strode a tall man dressed in a long white tunic emblazoned with a large red cross. On his broad shoulders was a white cape, also emblazoned with a large red cross. He walked up to Cardinal Bobone, bowed briskly, and kissed the cardinal's ring.

As the secretary left and closed the door behind him, Cardinal Bobone took his seat behind the desk and motioned his visitor to sit. "I greatly appreciate your taking the time to see me, Commander," said the cardinal. "I appreciate the great importance that your mission must be for the Templar Council, and I would not have taken your precious time except for a matter of equally grave importance."

The commander smiled broadly. "Your brother Ursus is very persuasive, Your Eminence. He caught me just as I emerged from my audience with His Holiness. I told Ursus that I must leave quickly for the Holy Land, but he insisted that I come with him. I heard the urgency in his voice, and I could not deny him that request."

The cardinal smiled. *Yes, I knew I could depend on my brother to bring the Commander here to me.*

Cardinal Bobone leaned forward. Almost in a whisper, he said: "So tell me, Commander. Was your mission successful? Did you obtain from His Holiness what you had sought?"

Silvio shifted in his chair. He began to speak but quickly checked himself. He cleared his throat.

"It's alright, Commander. You may speak freely. Yes, I know, your dealings with His Holiness today were secret. Don't worry. I will not reveal your secret to anyone. So tell me, Commander: did His Holiness approve your new Order, and did he approve the Templars' new plan of succession?"

"His Holiness and I discussed many matters relating to the Holy Land and to our mission of safeguarding Christian pilgrims."

The Templar's face showed no expression, no surprise. But Cardinal Bobone thought he saw something in the commander's eye, a mark of recognition that told him all he needed.

"I see. You discussed Christian pilgrims to the Holy Land."

The Templar nodded.

"And the mission of the Templars."

The Templar nodded again.

"And did His Holiness give his blessing to your new charter, your 'Order,' as you Templars refer to it?"

Silvio didn't answer, but Cardinal Bobone said, "Yes, I thought so. It is now a year since your Grand Master Gerard died in battle, but His Holiness would not permit you to appoint a new Grand Master until your charter was revised and issues relating to ensuring the future safety of the Grand Master were resolved. I am certain that His Holiness realizes the crucial role the Knights of the Temple play in the Holy Land, not only in safeguarding Christian pilgrims. I expect His Holiness is almost as eager as the Templar Council to approve your new charter, so that you may appoint a new Grand Master."

"How —"

"How do I know this? It is elementary deduction, my dear commander. And I am sure that others have deduced it also. But what about your Templar Council's plan for the succession? No doubt you presented the Council's view with great aplomb. Gerard was indeed a great leader, and very brave. But he placed himself at too high a risk, and he suffered the consequences. The Grand Master must never again place himself in such danger of capture by the infidel, or of being killed in battle. A new approach is needed. And what better way to introduce your new approach than to appoint as Grand Master a man with fresh ideas, untainted by years of training in the Templar ways of old? So tell me, Commander, what did His Holiness think of taking a man just recently made a Knight of the Temple and elevating him to the rank of Grand Master?"

"How could you know this?" Silvio blurted out, and the cardinal discerned how immediately the Commander regretted his outburst.

Cardinal Bobone smiled. "Ah, Commander, I have my ways."

Cardinal Bobone leaned back in his chair and studied the Templar for a while in silence. At length, he said, "Commander, I understand you are originally from Bari. Is it your intention to pass through Bari on your way back to the Holy Land?"

"I have not determined that yet. I intend to go by the fastest route available. I have no time to lose."

"Then I suggest you go by way of Bari. Yes, I see your hesitation. You don't want to be distracted by family who will want you to linger with them. But as it happens, Bari is the fastest route, and if you go that way, you will fulfill a holy purpose. Tell me, Commander: what is your opinion of Jews?"

The Templar looked perplexed. "Of Jews? I do not understand, Your Eminence."

"It is a simple question. I just want to know your opinion of Jews. What is their role in this world? Are they good? Are they evil? Do you find them repulsive? Are they to be despised? Pitied? Shunned? Punished?"

"It is indeed a simple question, but not one with a simple answer, Your Eminence."

The cardinal nodded but said nothing. He continued to eye the Templar inquisitively. A few moments again passed in silence. Finally, the cardinal said, "Please continue."

"Of course their souls are tainted, because they have not accepted our Lord, but many a Christian's soul is fouled by sin as well. We are all sinners to a greater or lesser extent. I despise no one."

"You do not, then, subscribe to the popular belief that the Jews are agents of the Devil? That belief, as I am sure you are aware, is widespread in all of Christendom."

The Templar laughed. "That is mere superstition, Your Eminence. Only the gullible subscribe to that belief."

"Including many friars, many well-respected priests, and even cardinals. Oh, and many Templars as well."

"Yes, Your Eminence, I know. Even a cardinal can be gulled, I fear. I hope my words have not offended."

Cardinal Bobone waved his hand dismissively. "No, Commander. You have not offended yet. But tell me, do you not believe in Satan? Do you not believe the Prince of Darkness commands a vast retinue of forces that do his bidding, spreading evil in the world, fighting against the will of God?"

"Of course I do, Your Eminence. Who could doubt the power of Satan? Certainly not anyone who has been in battle and seen the thrill of killing written on the faces of men. I have seen great evil done, both in battle and in life. But I do not believe the Jews are Satan's agents."

Cardinal Bobone smiled broadly. "That is good, Commander. That is very good."

"Have I passed your test?"

"Indeed you have, so far. But I have one more requirement, Commander. You must trust me completely."

The Templar was about to speak, but Cardinal Bobone held up his hand. "No, Commander. Do not agree so quickly. What I am about to tell you may seem very strange to you, and my interpretation of events may fly in the face of everything you have been taught. Even His Holiness has grave doubts about my views. But before I confide in you, before I tell you what I would have you do, I must know that I have your trust. It is not an easy thing I ask of you. Consider well before you answer."

The Templar did not hesitate. Immediately, he answered, "I have considered well, Your Eminence. I have no doubt. I put my trust in you."

"Oh? Have you, then, no doubts? How can that be, when you do not yet know what I have to tell you and to ask of you? Some of what I mean to tell you, I have already mentioned to His Holiness; and, as I told you earlier, His Holiness has his doubts. Does not that give you pause, Commander? Does that not make you doubt me?"

"No. I know your reputation as a man of God. But above all, I know your brother Ursus. I have known him well since my childhood, and I have full trust in him. I see in you the same sincerity and goodness that I have always seen in him. I therefore put my full trust in you, Your Eminence."

A faint smile flickered across the cardinal's lips. "Very well," he said. "You have just enlisted in God's army in a great battle against the forces of darkness. Yes, I know you already consider yourself to be a soldier in such an army and in such a war: you are, after all, a knight of the Order of Solomon's Temple. But the Templars fight against a human enemy whose forces are plainly visible. The battle of which I speak is quite another matter, Commander, and it will often not be easy to distinguish friend from foe."

"How, then, will I fight this battle, not knowing who is my enemy? And how can I wage such a battle at all? Will there not be conflict with my duties to the Templar Council?"

"I do not anticipate any such conflict. But if there is a conflict, you will have to grapple with it on your own and find a way to steer between your two duties. You have sworn an oath to the Knights Templar, and I do not take that lightly. But make no mistake: the battle in which I have now enlisted you is of utmost importance to Christendom and to the world. Last night a visitor came to me and spoke of things that have not happened yet but will happen soon. He appeared in human form, but there was a certain aura radiating from him, and I am convinced he was no human being but a messenger from heaven. He spoke of Satanic forces that are brewing in the world and hinted at a great battle between good and evil that is coming soon."

"Where will this battle take place, Your Eminence?"

"He did not say explicitly, but he gave me hints and left it for me to figure out. After his departure, I was given a sign that confirmed what my visitor had led me to believe: the war has already begun, and the next battle will occur in Bari. Do not be fooled by appearances, for evil may be dressed in holy garb. It is my strong suspicion that Satan's chief agent is none other than a friar, an itinerant preacher named Friar Peter. Have you heard of him, Commander?"

"I don't believe so. But I have been away in the Holy Land for a long time."

"Friar Peter is a man of great charisma, who stirs men's souls with his fiery words. He is popularly known as Peter the Pious, and he is thought to be a man of great holiness. I have not met him in person, but I have good reason to believe that it is hatred and malice and not piety that motivates him. He bears particular animosity against the Jews, and in several villages and towns he has instigated violence against them. When you encounter Friar Peter, as I know you will in Bari, use your intuition. You will know in your heart where justice truly lies. I give you my blessing, that your heart will know to distinguish good from evil."

"Then I must return to the Holy Land by way of Bari. But when I encounter Friar Peter, if my intuition confirms your impression that he is evil, what must I do?"

"I do not have the answer to that question, Commander. But you will know. My visitor told me that only few have the power to thwart the spread of Satan's tentacles, and one such combatant is now on his way to Bari. I do not know this man's identity, and, like Friar Peter, he may be other than what he seems. As it happens, he, like you, is bound for the Holy Land. Guard him well. Do not allow any harm to come to him, and aid him in any way you can. That is the mission on which I send you. Swear to me that you will be faithful to that mission, and that you will speak of that mission to no one else. The fate of the world may depend upon it."

"I swear it on my life, Your Eminence, and on my honor as a Knight of the Temple of Solomon."

Cardinal Bobone smiled and said, "That is all that I can ask. Again, I give you my blessing. Fair thee well, Commander Silvio."

CHAPTER 26

A road northeast of Rome
December 1190

After departing from Cardinal Bobone, Matthew visited the tombs of Saint Peter and Saint Paul in Rome, and each of those visits uplifted his soul. He lingered in Rome a few more days, returning to each of the two shrines again and feeling on his second visit the same spiritual elevation that he had felt the first time. But he knew he could not stay in Rome any longer: he had to complete the pilgrimage on which the cardinal had sent him. And so, reluctantly, he packed his few belongings in a sack and started on his way to Venice. It would be a long hike, and the weather was getting worse, but Matthew was prepared, and he felt that nothing could deter him from his purpose.

It was now three days since he had left Rome, but still the spirits of the saints continued to motivate him. He hummed a melody that he had known since childhood, a melody he had learned at church in Camryn. How he had loved that church, and its pastor with his mellifluous voice and golden words, words of peace and love. Little had he known then how things would later turn out in Camryn.

Now he felt cheated, his most precious memories stolen from him. The priest whom he had so admired in his childhood was the very man who introduced Friar Peter to his parish and endorsed the friar's platform of hate and murder. How could his pastor – that gentle soul whom he had known since childhood –

not perceive the evil in Friar Peter's words? How could his priest have listened to the friar's words and not denounced them? In his mind's eye, he saw his village priest listening attentively as Friar Peter spoke, his head nodding in approval as Peter stirred the men of Camryn to violence. And even his own father had joined the mob and participated in their murderous rampage. Matthew shuddered at the memory. Only his mother's memory remained untainted. In his heart, he knew his mother would not have approved of her husband's actions, and he fondly remembered his mother's voice – her spirit – blessing him as he fled his home in the aftermath of the massacre. A tear trickled down his cheek, and he wiped it away. There were so many sins for which he needed to atone: the sins of his father, the sins of his village priest, the sins of the entire village of Camryn. And, he knew, he was not blameless either. What a monumental task! But his visit with Cardinal Bobone and his pilgrimage to the tombs of Saint Peter and Saint Paul had rejuvenated him, given him the strength to continue. He quickened his pace.

He walked for many hours, with only an occasional stop to rest. Now and then, a passerby in a mule-drawn wagon would stop and ask whether he wanted to ride, but Matthew declined all the offers. It was his duty to walk: that was part of his penance. And besides, he needed the solitude.

In the late afternoon, he came upon a roadside inn and decided to lodge there for the night. The common room was dimly lit and fairly crowded. As Matthew entered, a hooded man in a darkened corner looked up and took notice. The hooded man turned to one of the three other men sitting at his table and said, "Hey, William. Look over there. I know that young man who just came in."

"Yeah, ye're right, Friar Peter. I remember him too. And he's a long way from home, isn't he? Camryn, if I remember aright?"

"Yes, Camryn. This is no coincidence. It was meant to be. Follow him, and see which room he takes."

"Yes, Friar Peter."

The man rose and sauntered across the common room, stopping a few feet from where Matthew stood talking to the proprietor. Matthew paid, picked up his sack, and headed upstairs to his room. The man waited three seconds and followed him upstairs.

Matthew found his room and opened the door. The man came up behind him, smiling broadly.

""I heard ye talking downstairs. Ye're from England, aren't ye? Name's William. Pleased to meet ye, son. And what may be yer name?"

"My name is Matthew, Sir."

"Matthew. That's a nice name. Ye're a long way from home, aren't ye? What brings ye to these parts?"

Matthew stood by the door but didn't enter his room. "I'm on pilgrimage," he said. "Now, please excuse me, Sir. I don't mean to be rude, but I have had a long day, and I must rest."

"Certainly, Matthew. I wish ye a pleasant night." William bowed with a flourish, smiled, and slowly shuffled away down the hall. Matthew stood by the open door, lingering in the hallway, his eyes still following William. William reached the steps but did not descend. Instead, he turned and looked again at Matthew. Matthew turned away from William and took a step into his room, but he got no further. Two men seized him from behind and pinned him against the wall. One of the men held his hand tightly over Matthew's mouth, while the other man bound Matthew's wrists behind him. They dragged him to the bed and shoved him down.

The man whose hand was over Matthew's mouth said, "I'm going to take my hand off now. Keep still. Shout out just once, and you're dead." He moved his hand away. Matthew looked up at him but remained silent.

"That's a good boy, Matthew. Keep lying there. Don't give us any trouble, and ye'll be alright." It was William's voice speaking.

Matthew heard another set of footsteps entering the room. A shiver went up his spine, and a feeling of dread as he listened to the footsteps approaching him.

"I hear you are from England. What is your name, my son?" He couldn't see the speaker's face. But he knew it was Friar Peter. Matthew would recognize that voice anywhere.

"You may answer now," Friar Peter said.

"Yes. I am from England. My name is Matthew."

"Very good. From which town do you come, Matthew?"

"It's a small village of no consequence, Sir, on the edge of Sherwood Forest."

The Friar chuckled and said, "There is no such thing as a village that has no consequence. Every town and village has consequence, my son. What is the name of your village?"

"Camryn, Sir. The name is Camryn."

"Ah, I see."

The friar looked steadily at Matthew. Several seconds passed in silence. Matthew looked away.

Friar Peter smiled a wry smile. "You can't look me in the eye, can you? That's a bad sign. It would seem you have something to hide." The friar paused. Matthew looked at the friar but still said nothing.

Friar Peter continued: "You are a long way from home, are you not?"

"Yes."

Friar Peter smiled benevolently. "Would you care to tell me why?"

"I am on pilgrimage."

"And what may be the reason for your pilgrimage?"

"I have many sins for which I want to atone."

"Such as?"

Matthew looked away again.

"I see. I didn't think you would answer me. But there is no need to tell me. I think I know."

Matthew turned his head toward Peter, and his eyes met Peter's cold gaze. A feeling of revulsion rose up within him as he looked in Peter's eyes, but he forced himself not to look away again.

"Yes," said Peter. "I know your pilgrimage has something to do with the events at Camryn these nine months past. But tell me, Matthew, will your pilgrimage take you to the Holy Land? Surely you can answer that much."

"Yes," said Matthew. "I am bound for the Holy Land."

Peter smiled again. He looked deep into Matthew's eyes, and, leaning forward, he said in a conspiratorial tone: "Tell me, my son: do you know a Jewish boy named Joseph? I believe this Joseph lived in Camryn also."

Matthew felt a pang of sadness pierce his heart, and he struggled to maintain his composure. He said nothing, but he continued looking into the friar's eyes.

"Yes, I thought you knew him. Perhaps he was even a friend of yours?"

Matthew was certain his gaze had not wavered, nor had his face expressed any emotion. How, then, could Friar Peter know that Joseph was his friend? Could the friar read his mind? A twinge of fear tugged at Matthew's consciousness, but Matthew suppressed his fear and held the friar's gaze.

"That is very good, Matthew. You no longer look away. You look me in the eyes. You have nothing to hide. Keep looking into my eyes; look deep, and let your tension melt away."

The friar's face was placid now. His voice was soft and droning. "Concentrate on my pupils. Look into them; and as you do so, you will see there is nothing to fear, nothing to hide from me. You are becoming more relaxed, more and more relaxed with every breath you take. That's right. Continue breathing slowly, and let the relaxation spread throughout your body. All your muscles are relaxing. Your arms, your legs, your face are all relaxed. Your eyes are getting heavy, and you can hardly keep them open."

Somehow, the friar's voice was soothing now. As if by magic, Matthew's feeling of revulsion was forgotten. He continued looking in the friar's eyes.

The friar's voice droned on, a little faster now. "More and more relaxed. With every breath you take, you are more and more relaxed. Look deeply in my eyes. Look into my pupils, and see the darkness there. It calls to you. Your eyelids now are very heavy. You can hardly keep them open. Just let them close. Let your eyelids close."

Matthew closed his eyes. His mind was in a fog, and through the fog he heard the friar's voice. The friar told him that his arms were light as feathers, and Matthew felt his right hand rise. The friar told him that his arm was heavy once again, and Matthew felt his arm descend. At the friar's suggestion, he felt himself in another time, in another place. Time and space themselves had been suspended, and he was as though transported to another world, a world where there was neither fear nor tension, nor even any will to resist the friar's wishes.

"Soon I will tell you to open your eyes; but when you do so, you will not wake up. When you open your eyes at my command, the spell will deepen and you will see only what I tell you to see. Now I will count to three. At each count, you will take a deep breath, and the spell will deepen further. At the count of three, I will tell you to open your eyes, and you will do so. One."

Matthew took a deep breath. He felt his body and his mind relaxing further, becoming more detached from the here and now. "Two."

Another breath. The fog deepened further.

"Three." The friar's voice echoed in Matthew's mind, coming to him as through a long tunnel.

"Open your eyes."

Matthew opened his eyes.

"That is very good. Now look up. Do you see your friend Joseph? He is here with us. He is there, in front of you. Do you see him now?"

Matthew looked through the fog. An image appeared before him, and it was coming towards him. He recognized the face.

"Yes. I see him."

"That is good. Joseph is turning away from you. Look closely as he turns his back. See the long red tail emerging from his back. Do you see the tail?"

Matthew looked again. Joseph was still coming towards him. "No," said Matthew.

"What is Joseph doing?"

"He is still coming towards me."

"Alright. That is very good. But soon he will turn around, and then you will see the tail that is normally not visible to men. Take a deep breath, and then another. Feel yourself relaxing further. Feel yourself in a state of calmness, absolutely calm and placid. You want to see what I have to show you. You want to know. You no longer wish to be deluded. You want to see the truth, and I will open your eyes, so that you may see it fully. You will not resist at all. Look again. Look at Joseph. See him as he really is. What do you see?"

Joseph continued to advance towards Matthew. Matthew took a breath, and then another. Slowly, Joseph turned and walked away.

"I see him turning."

"Do you see the tail?"

"No."

"At my command, you will close your eyes again. You will still see Joseph, even when your eyes are closed. I will count to five, and you will take a slow, deep breath with every count. Now close your eyes, Matthew."

Matthew closed his eyes.

"Do you still see your friend Joseph?"

"Yes."

"That is good," said Friar Peter. "That is very good. Now I will count ... . One."

Matthew took a breath.

"With each breath you will feel more and more relaxed. More and more relaxed. More and more relaxed. Two. Slowly, breath again."

Matthew took another slow breath.

"That is very good. Three. You are feeling very good. You are completely free: free of trouble, free of desire, free of will. You want to see what I have to show you. You no longer wish to resist. You want to do what I ask of you. It is what you yourself want. You desire it. Four. As you take another breath, you will know that you desire all I ask of you. It is your will to do so, Matthew. It is your great, sincere desire. Because what I have to show you will help to free you from the burden of the sin that weighs upon you. You know this in your heart. Five. You will take another breath, and you will be still more relaxed. Your mind is completely at ease, completely open to what I have to show you. Now you may open your eyes again."

Matthew opened his eyes. The fog had lifted. Joseph now stood before him, still more vivid than before. His back was partially turned toward Matthew.

"What do you see, Matthew? Has Joseph turned his back? Is his face away from you?"

"Yes."

"What more do you see?"

Slowly, Joseph continued turning. He walked away. Slowly, a tail emerged from between his buttocks, protruding through his trousers, a short tail at first, but it grew as Joseph continued to walk away.

"Now I see the tail. It is growing longer. It is long and pointed."

"What color is the tail?"

"Red. The tail is red as blood."

"Yes, Matthew. It is a demon's tail."

Matthew watched as Joseph continued walking away, his tail swishing behind him. "Come back!" Matthew cried out.

"He will return soon enough, Matthew. Watch him closely as he returns. When he faces you, you will see his horns. Watch."

Joseph turned and walked again towards Matthew. As he advanced, two horns grew from his temples. Startled, Matthew shouted out, "NO!"

"Do not be afraid, Matthew. He cannot hurt you. But now you see him as he really is, as he always has been, his true nature concealed from human eyes, hidden even from his friends. He is a demon in disguise. See him advancing towards you. Now you see him more clearly, do you not?"

"Yes."

"When I command you, you will close your eyes, and Joseph will disappear. But you will not forget his true nature as you have just seen it now – his true nature that he has hidden from you all these years. Take one last look, Matthew, and fix the image in your mind. Look at Joseph as he really is. He is a demon, not a human being. Do you see that now?"

"Yes."

"That is very good, Matthew. You may close your eyes. Do you still see Joseph?"

"No."

"That is good. Soon I will bring you out of this spell. And when I do, you will not forget what you have seen of Joseph's nature. You will remember him as he really is: a demon, not a human being. Do you agree?"

"Yes."

"That is very good, Matthew. Very good indeed. Now tell me, Matthew: what think you of demons? Are they good, or are they evil?"

"Evil."

"And would you do everything in your power to fight against a demon?"

"Yes. Of course."

"Even if the demon pretended to be your friend?"

"Yes."

"And what of Joseph? Is he your enemy or your friend?"

Matthew hesitated momentarily. "He was my friend."

"Yes, he was, Matthew. He said he was. But what is Joseph in truth?"

"In truth, he is a demon."

"Although he appeared to be your friend?"

"Yes."

"Remember that, Matthew. Do not forget. He is in truth a demon, and not your friend at all. In truth, he never was your friend."

"Yes."

"Now tell me again: is Joseph your friend?"

"No."

"What is he then?"

Matthew hesitated. In a whisper, he answered: "My enemy."

"Tell me again what Joseph is to you."

"Joseph is my enemy." Matthew's voice was louder now, and the hesitation was gone.

"Again, Matthew. Say it once again."

"Joseph is my enemy."

"And will you do everything in your power to oppose him?"

"Yes."

"Would you even kill him if it came to that?"

"Yes."

"Say it again. Are your certain?"

"Yes, I would kill him if it came to that."

"Then say it once again. Say it a third time, and use his name."

"I would kill Joseph if it came to that."

"Because?"

"Because he is my enemy."

"And why is that, Matthew?"

"Because he is not human but a demon."

"That is very good, Matthew. Do not forget. Soon, I will bring you out of the spell. You will not remember that we had this conversation, but you will remember vividly that Joseph is a demon. You will not remember that I have instructed you about this, but you will know in your heart that Joseph was a false friend. You will know he is in fact your enemy. You will do all in your power to oppose him. You will know you want to kill him, because he is a demon in disguise."

"Yes."

"That is very good, Matthew. When you awake from the spell, you will not remember our conversation, but you will know Joseph's true nature as something you have discovered on your own. And you will oppose him just as you have said."

"Yes, I will."

"Do you pledge to do this? Do I have your solemn word?"

"Yes," said Matthew.

Friar Peter said, "That is very good. You will be a soldier in the war against demonic forces in the world. Therefore, you are to change your course. You are not to go to Venice as you had planned. My men will equip you with a suit of chainmail and a sword. Go south to Sicily, and join King Richard's army in Messina. Join King Richard's army, and train with them. In due time, they will embark for the Holy Land, and you will go with them. Do you understand?"

"Yes. I will go with King Richard's army to the Holy Land."

"Do I have your solemn word on it?"

"Yes. I swear it."

"Then I will now bring you out of the spell. You will remember nothing of the oaths that you have sworn, and nothing of our conversation. But you will think of all these things as your very own ideas. And you will do them with conviction, just as you have sworn to do."

"Yes."

"Now I will count to ten. With each count, you will feel more and more yourself. One. At the count of ten, you will open your eyes. You will be very relaxed, but fully awake. You will remember nothing of our conversation. Shortly after I leave this room, you will fall asleep, and you will dream. When you awake from that sleep, you will not remember that we ever met tonight, but you will know in your heart what you have seen of Joseph's true demonic nature. Two. And, above all, you will do all the things that you have pledged to do, but you will think of them all as your very own ideas. Three."

As Friar Peter continued counting, Matthew felt himself arousing. His eyes fluttered but did not open yet. He knew he had just been dreaming something, but the dream had faded into nothingness, and only a wisp of its existence still remained. He tried to hold onto that gossamer thread, to no avail.

"Nine."

Peter's voice echoed in his head. He stirred again.

"Ten."

He opened his eyes. Friar Peter sat placidly, smiling at him. "I hope you had a pleasant dream," he said.

Matthew sat up. "I think so. Really, I don't know. I can't remember what I dreamt. Was I asleep for long?"

"Not long, Matthew. Now sleep again. You need to rest. You have a long journey ahead of you."

And with that, Friar Peter left the room and closed the door behind him.

PART IV

Nine entered Eden while still alive: Enoch,
the Messiah, Elijah . . . .

Yalkut Shim'oni on Genesis, ch 5, ¶48

CHAPTER 27

Bari, Italy
January 1191

The old man sat behind his desk and stroked his beard. He looked at Joseph, then at Rachel, and again at Joseph. "I see," he said. "That is a very interesting story. Am I to infer that you know where this emerald may be?"

"Yes," said Joseph. "I do."

"But you do not yet know the location of the breastplate, and you are hoping I can tell you how to use the emerald and how to find the breastplate."

"That is correct."

"And what makes you think that I can help, or that I would help you even if I could?"

"As I told you, Simone in Lucca told us to seek your help."

The old man paused a moment, apparently weighing his response. Then he said: "Yes, I knew Simone many years ago, and I still correspond with him from time to time. Simone is a good man, and very learned. Very learned indeed. But not in the mysteries of the Torah."

"That is exactly why he could not answer us and why he suggested that we travel to Bari to seek you out. He said that if anybody in Italy could answer me, it would be Rabbi Tuviah."

"Perhaps. But tell me, Joseph, how, in your estimation, would a man as learned as Simone not have the slightest information about such an important matter, a matter on which the fate of the Jewish people, and perhaps the fate of the entire world, may depend?"

"As you indicated, the matter of what happened to the High Priest's breastplate is a mystery, a secret known only to very few."

"That is correct. And why, in your opinion, have those entrusted with the information chosen to keep it secret for so long?"

"In the wrong hands, the breastplate could be misused."

"That is also correct, Joseph. Only those who are worthy may be told the secret. Are you worthy?" He looked at Joseph. Then, turning to Rachel, he repeated: "Are you worthy?"

Without hesitation, Rachel said, "If anybody is worthy, Joseph is. Joseph is a descendent of King David."

Tuviah nodded. "So you say. But how do I know this to be true? Besides, that in itself will not suffice. Surely there are many alive today who are descendants of the Judean royal family, but not all of those are worthy."

"What do you want us to tell you? What evidence will satisfy you?"

Rabbi Tuviah leaned back in his chair and said, "Ah, that is the question, isn't it? I believe there are things you haven't told me regarding your quest. You must be more open, more forthcoming."

Joseph said, "When we were in Simone's house, he told us that the less he knew, the better. Are you not also afraid to know too much about us, as Simone was?"

Rabbi Tuviah laughed, but it was a mirthless laugh, and his face remained composed and serious. "Afraid? No, I am not afraid. You have already told me enough to put my life at risk, if your friar is indeed pursuing you as you have said he is. I think a little more information will not add significantly to my risk. So why don't you start by telling me how you came to know as much as you do know about this emerald?"

Joseph hesitated. He wasn't sure just how much to reveal to Rabbi Tuviah. He looked at Rachel questioningly. She looked momentarily at Rabbi Tuviah and turned again toward Joseph. Almost imperceptibly, she nodded.

Joseph turned toward Rabbi Tuviah and said: "The existence of the emerald, how it came to be separated from the remainder of the High Priest's breastplate, and the emerald's current location were a tradition handed down in my family from father to son. Last Passover, my father apparently decided that I had come of age, and he was going to reveal to me the secret of the emerald, but he was killed that night, before he had a chance to do so. After we escaped from Camryn, we encountered Friar Peter's men again at a roadside inn, and, as I have told you, a stranger saved us. When we were clear of Friar Peter's men, the stranger told me the story of the emerald and what my father had intended."

Rabbi Tuviah shook his head. "Do you really expect me to believe such a far-fetched tale?"

"It is the truth."

"Perhaps," said Rabbi Tuviah. "But does it not strike you as strange that a man whom you had never met before, who was neither part of your family nor even a close friend, would know your father's intentions and would know this deeply-hidden secret that your father wouldn't even tell his son until he deemed him worthy? Or is there still something more that you are hiding from me? I repeat: if you want my help, you will have to be more open with me."

Joseph looked at Rachel. A faint smile crossed her lips.

Joseph turned again to Rabbi Tuviah and said, "He was not a stranger, although I didn't know it at the time. Later, when I thought about it, I realized I had seen him years before, and he had been to our home. He came and went mysteriously, and I have reason to believe he knew my father very well, although I don't know the nature of their relationship."

"Can you describe him for me? Do you know his name?"

"He was tall, with a white beard but a youthful-looking face. In fact, he seemed not to age at all, since he looked no older than

I remember him several years before. He had green, penetrating eyes. He wore a light-gray hooded cloak, and he walked with a walking stick, but he really didn't need the walking stick at all. Months later, he appeared again in Chateau Blanc to rescue me a second time from Friar Peter. When he confronted Peter at Chateau Blanc, he moved with a speed such as I have never seen even in much younger men."

"His name?"

"His name is Enoch."

At the mention of the name, Rabbi Tuviah was visibly perturbed. His eyes widened, and his hands shook. With trembling voice, Rabbi Tuviah repeated, "Enoch."

For a long time, Rabbi Tuviah said nothing. He looked at Joseph, appearing to study him carefully. Joseph met the rabbi's gaze and tried not to look away, although he felt a bit uncomfortable. Then, after a short interval, the rabbi's face seemed to relax, and his eyes became more inviting. Joseph wondered why Rabbi Tuviah's demeanor had changed so radically at the mention of Enoch's name.

Rachel said: "When Joseph mentioned Enoch, you seemed to recognize the name. What do you know of Enoch, Rabbi Tuviah? Have you met him?"

Rabbi Tuviah didn't answer immediately. He looked away and appeared to be deep in thought. When he finally spoke, his voice seemed distant. "Yes. In fact I have met Enoch, but not for many years. I was in my twenties when I saw him first and had just recently begun to learn the mysteries of Torah. One night, I was alone in the house of learning, all the other students having gone to sleep already, when unexpectedly a man such as the one you described appeared. He was old, with a white beard, and his eyes were green and penetrating. He sat down next to me, and we conversed a while. He taught me various esoteric matters on a wide range of topics, the depth of which I had never heard from anybody else, as though to demonstrate his erudition so that I should trust him and put faith in what he would tell me next. Finally, he said, 'Be sure to learn about the High Priest's breastplate and what became of it after the Holy Temple was destroyed and the Babylonians conquered Jerusalem. Devote yourself to the study of that matter, and learn all there is to know about it. Some day, a youth will come to you requesting your assistance, and you will need that knowledge to impart to him.' I knew that Enoch's prophecy would be fulfilled, but I never imagined it would take this long."

Joseph asked, "What happened after Enoch told you this? Didn't you ask for further explanation? Did he say anything more?"

"No, nothing more. Strangely, right after he told me these things, I fell asleep immediately and did not awaken for a long time. When I awoke, he was gone. After that night, I intensified my study of the mysteries of Torah. Of course, I did not confine my studies to the history of the High Priest's breastplate, but that subject became my special interest. Periodically, I prayed that Enoch would return again. But I never saw him again for many years."

"Then you did see him again?"

The rabbi fell silent. He looked vacuously into space and fidgeted with his hands. Presently, he rose, signaled Joseph and Rachel to remain in their seats, and went into the adjoining room. When he returned, he was carrying food and drink. He placed cakes and ale before his guests and, with a broad smile, bade them eat and drink; he placed a tankard of ale on his own desk. Then he sat again behind his desk, tented his hands, and continued speaking:

"I saw him briefly, somewhat over twelve years ago. I remember that, because it was three months after my wife died. I was sitting right here, where I am sitting now. It was well past midnight, and I could hardly keep my eyes open. And yet, I kept on studying, to drown my sorrow, and because I could not face going to bed alone. I think I had dozed off once or twice, but I shook myself awake, and there, where you are sitting, was a hooded man. He pulled his hood back, and immediately I recognized him. It was Enoch. Decades had passed since I had seen him last, but he did not appear any older than before. His green eyes looked at me intently, and he said, 'Have you learned what I told you to learn? I hope you are well prepared. It has begun.'

"I looked at him, perplexed, and said, 'I do not understand.' And he repeated, 'It has begun.'

"As Enoch sat before me, the placid features of his face hardened. His eyes burned with an intensity such as I had never seen before, and I saw unspeakable power in his gaze. He opened his mouth again, and I will never forget the words he said: 'Satan's forces have begun to march. Lilith, the consort of the Lord of Darkness, has ensnared a human and bestowed upon him fearsome powers. Even before, that man was evil; even before, that man was dangerous. But now, the man has Satan's consort herself to do his bidding, and he is a hundred-fold more dangerous than previously. A chain of events has been put in motion, and none can stop it, except for one; but even he will be powerless to thwart the march of Satan's forces if Satan's new recruit should find and gain control of the High Priest's breastplate. Tuviah, be prepared.'

"I wanted to ask him more, but he raised his hand, and I kept silent. Although now I felt wide awake, jolted into wakefulness by the strange experience, suddenly a great weariness overcame me, and I dozed again. I couldn't have been asleep for more than a few seconds, but when I awoke, Enoch was gone, and I never saw him again.

"After Enoch's second appearance, I intensified my studies further. I read all I could about the breastplate, but some of the most crucial facts remained shrouded in mystery, despite all my efforts. With apprehension, I awaited your coming, hoping against hope that my knowledge would be sufficient.

"Early in my studies, I discovered that shortly before the Babylonians conquered Jerusalem, the prophet Jeremiah hid certain holy objects, and among those objects was the breastplate. The breastplate has immense power, which can be used for good or for ill, but it has no power at all unless all twelve stones are set within it. Once all twelve stones are in the breastplate, any righteous person may use some measure of its power for good, but only a member of the priestly class can use that power to the fullest. When the breastplate is used for evil, however, it is quite a different matter. A man imbued with evil, and touched by Satan's or by Lilith's touch, can use the power for evil without restriction, providing only that all twelve stones are set within it. Jeremiah feared that someday the breastplate may fall into the wrong hands, and therefore he removed one stone, which he would give to a chosen member of the royal family, to be passed down through the generations until, in a time of greatest danger, only through the power of the breastplate could the danger be averted. I never determined for certain which was the stone that Jeremiah removed, but I suspected that it was the emerald, the stone of the tribe of Judah."

Joseph shifted in his seat. "Where did Jeremiah hide the breastplate? Were you able to determine that?"

Rabbi Tuviah smiled and said, "Patience, Joseph, patience. I will tell you all I know about your stone and about the breastplate. I was just coming to your question." He took a sip from his tankard of ale, replaced it on his desk, and continued:

"Where did Jeremiah hide the breastplate and the other holy objects that he removed from the Temple before Jerusalem was conquered? There are many theories. Some say he brought them to Mount Nebo, across the Jordan River. On that mountain, Moses was buried, and no man knows the location of his grave. Others say that Jeremiah sent the Ark of the Covenant to Egypt, perhaps with the breastplate and other objects from the Temple; and maybe Egypt was only a stop along the way to Nubia. I have examined all the theories and weighed their merits. Unfortunately, I cannot give you a definite answer, nor, I think, can anyone alive today. But, in my opinion, the High Priest's breastplate is hidden somewhere in Jerusalem or in the Judean Mountains. The Ark and other objects were probably sent elsewhere – Egypt, Nubia, or someplace else perhaps – but, I am convinced, the breastplate remained in the Holy Land, where its power can be used to its full extent.

"You see, only in the Holy Land can the stones of the breastplate manifest their full power, and the breastplate's power is greatest in Jerusalem itself. Thus, if the breastplate is intended to be used in time of greatest need, it makes sense that its hiding place be in the vicinity of Jerusalem."

Rabbi Tuviah paused briefly and stroked his beard, deep in thought. Finally, he said: "One additional thing: the breastplate's power, even in the Holy Land, waxes and wanes with the phases of the moon and with the seasons of the year. It peaks each month when the moon is full, but the one day on which the stones manifest their greatest power is on the day of the full moon preceding the Jewish New Year. This year, that will occur in the early morning hours of 5th September by the secular calendar."

Joseph thought back to his discussion with Enoch in the cave, just after Enoch gave him the emerald. Enoch, too, had mentioned that the stone would reach its greatest power when the moon is full. *Yes,* Joseph thought; *even in England, far away from the Holy Land, the emerald had glowed brightly, showing its power. And that was only a small taste of its true potential.* He couldn't even imagine what power it must have in the Holy Land itself.

"I see a mark of recognition on your face," said Rabbi Tuviah. "Something I said must have resonated with facts that are known to you already. Perhaps something Enoch told you. That is good."

"Yes," Joseph agreed. "It is. But how did Enoch know these things? He is not a descendant of King David, is he? Is he a prophet? Is he a sorcerer? Or something else entirely?" Joseph shuddered.

Rabbi Tuviah answered: "No, he is neither prophet nor sorcerer. As you must know, the last prophet was Malachi, and after him there is no prophecy until the Messiah comes. As for sorcery, that also is not likely. Enoch is a force for good and not for evil. I choose your third alternative: he is something else entirely."

"What do you mean by that?"

"In truth, I do not know. I only met him twice, and both times only briefly. Even so, I had the feeling that I was talking to someone extraordinary, someone with special powers, and your tale only serves to reinforce my feeling. He is a man of special powers, a keeper of mysteries, and apparently the guardian of the emerald. Oh, it was your father who actually had the emerald in his possession, and his father before him; but I surmise that Enoch was somehow always watching from a distance. Apparently, your father knew him and trusted him. He gave the stone to Enoch before he died, did he not?"

"So Enoch said."

"And there is every reason to believe that it was so."

"But what is he? How old is he, and how long has he been the guardian of the stone?"

"I do not know," said Rabbi Tuviah. "I could only speculate, but I would rather not. Besides, knowing who Enoch is will not help you in your mission. Your role is to find the High Priest's breastplate and to insert your stone among the others, so that the breastplate's power will be manifest."

"But you haven't told me where to find the breastplate. Saying it is in the Holy Land, or even in Jerusalem or the Judean Mountains is not sufficient. How will I find it? And what will I do with it once I have inserted the emerald? How will I use its power, and to what purpose will I use it?"

"As I mentioned, only a member of the priestly class can wield the breastplate's power to the fullest. You, being a descendant of the tribe of Judah, obviously do not qualify as such."

"But I am of a priestly family," Rachel blurted out. "And my brother Aaron certainly would qualify."

"Yes," said Rabbi Tuviah. "But where is he?"

"I do not know for sure," said Joseph. "But he is close, and I know he will soon re-join us. I feel it in my heart."

"That is good Joseph, and I sincerely hope you are correct. When you find him, keep him close, for you will need his aid when you find the High Priest's breastplate. Unfortunately, I cannot tell you any more about the location of its hiding place. I do not have all the answers. But this I know: time is short, and you must find the breastplate by the full moon preceding the Jewish New Year if you are to succeed."

Joseph shifted in his seat again. "The task seems impossible. How can I possibly know where to look?"

Rabbi Tuviah seemed about to speak, but for a moment he said nothing. He looked at Rachel, then at Joseph. For several seconds, he held Joseph's gaze. Almost in a whisper, he asked, "Have you ever made contact with the spiritual world?"

Joseph thought of warnings he had often heard spoken about the dangers of delving into the mysterious world of the spirit. It was not for the faint of heart, nor could it be done with impunity except by the learned and the very righteous. In a tremulous voice, he answered, "Of course not. How could I dare to do so?"

"You will have to dare!" Rabbi Tuviah exclaimed. "It is the only way that you can find the answers that you seek. The key to using the emerald, and indeed the High Priest's breastplate, is through the spiritual world. You will have to learn to make contact with that world before you can even hope to defeat Friar Peter. But you must be careful. There are two sides to the world of spirit: the side of holiness, and the Other Side – the *Sitra Achara*. I have no doubt that Friar Peter has made contact with the Other Side, and thus he will defeat you if you do not bring an equal force to bear.

"The spiritual world – the world above, as it is also called – is a world parallel to our physical world, and all men enter it when they die. But only few can enter that world during life, and then return to our physical world again. Therefore, purify your soul. Pray. Meditate. Turn your vision inwards, see into your soul; and, in so doing, learn to enter the world of spirit. Yes, you will need to do more than just make contact with that world and view it from the outside. Indeed, you must learn to merge your soul with the spiritual world and enter it. Then, and only then, will you succeed, for only through the spiritual world will you be able to obtain the power that you will need if you are to defeat your enemy, and only through the spiritual world will you be able to pinpoint the location of the object that you seek. I have said enough. Now, let me see the stone."

Joseph again exchanged a fleeting glance with Rachel. Slowly, his right hand reached under his cloak and extracted a pouch. He rose, and took a step towards Rabbi Tuviah. He gazed into Rabbi Tuviah's eyes for several seconds. Finally, hesitatingly, he inverted the pouch, and the emerald dropped out into his left hand. He extended his hand, and Rabbi Tuviah took the stone.

The rabbi turned the stone in his hand, examining every facet. Slowly, he rose and went to the door. He opened the door halfway to let in more light, but he did not go outside. He examined the emerald again in the sunlight, turning it over and over in his hand. His attention was focused on the stone, and thus he did not notice a man hiding outside in the shadows at the corner of his house. At length, Rabbi Tuviah closed the door, as the man in the shadows slunk away.

Rabbi Tuviah handed the emerald to Joseph and returned to his seat. "The stone is not authentic," he said.

"What?" Joseph rose from his chair. "It cannot be."

Rabbi Tuviah shook his head, apparently dismayed. "Oh, it is an authentic emerald. Do not mistake my meaning. It is a beautiful stone, and undoubtedly worth a fortune. But it is not the emerald of the High Priest's breastplate."

"How can you know that?"

"Sit down, and I will tell you."

Joseph sat down.

"You see, each stone of the breastplate had the name of one of the twelve tribes of Israel engraved upon it. The emerald should be engraved with the name of Judah, but your stone has no engraving. Perhaps this is a decoy stone, and the true emerald lies hidden somewhere."

"No!" said Joseph. "It cannot be. I feel it in my heart. And Enoch's words confirm it. I cannot explain the absence of an engraving on the stone, but I know it is the authentic gemstone of the breastplate."

Rabbi Tuviah thought a moment. "In that case, perhaps I am wrong and you are correct. I have told you what I know about the stone, about the breastplate. But, of course, there are many things unknown to me. I have nothing more to add."

"Isn't there anything further you can tell me? Is there anybody else who might be able to give me further information?"

Rabbi Tuviah appeared sympathetic. "Indeed there may be," he said. "But I do not know who. Also, there is little time to waste. I sincerely wish you well. Use the knowledge I have given you. Learn to contact the spiritual world. Then you will defeat your enemy. I give you my blessing."

For a long time, Joseph sat silently, digesting all that Rabbi Tuviah had just told him. Echoes of his conversation with Old Mab months ago in Sherwood Forest came back to him. She, too, had mentioned the world of spirit, and he had doubted her then. Vividly he remembered her words: "Someday you will have to enter that world. Otherwise you will not defeat your enemy." And now, Rabbi Tuviah confirmed what Old Mab had said, using almost identical words.

Joseph looked at Rachel. Their eyes met, and, though not a word was spoken, he could tell that she, too, had thought of Old Mab's words. He turned his eyes to Rabbi Tuviah.

"Something is troubling both of you, I see," said Rabbi Tuviah. "Do not be afraid. Speak your mind."

Joseph stole a fleeting glance at Rachel, and, in a shaking voice, he said: "You mentioned that I will need to enter the spiritual world if I am to succeed, and that merely making contact with that world and viewing it from the outside will not suffice. But I do not even know how to make the first approach to that world. I do not even know how to view it from the outside. How, then, can I hope to enter it? I will need your help. Will you help me?"

Rabbi Tuviah smiled and said, "I was just waiting for you to ask. Yes, of course I will help you, as far as I am able. Lately there have been great storms at sea, and I think no ships will be departing Bari at least for several weeks. That should give sufficient time for me to teach you how to purify your soul and how to enter a meditative state. If you apply yourself and learn well, you will be able to see visions of the world of spirit: visions of what was, what is, and what may be in the future – what may be, and not necessarily what will be. But know that all you will see while in a state of meditation is but a vision, a view of that world from the outside, and that is as far as I can take you. In order for your soul actually to enter the spiritual world, you will have to use the emerald, but I know not how. You will have to find the way yourself."

Rachel looked at Rabbi Tuviah and said: "Joseph will have to purify his soul before he can contact the spiritual world. But Friar Peter is a wicked man, and yet you think he has made contact with that world. How did he do it?"

Rabbi Tuviah smiled and said, "That is a very good question, Rachel. But remember what I said before: the world of spirit has two sides – the side of holiness and the Other Side. Just as only a pure soul may enter the side of holiness, only a soul immersed in evil may enter from the Other Side, and even then, only with the help of Satan or Lilith. Friar Peter would have entered through the Other Side. But the two sides are connected, and having entered through the Other Side, the friar will be able to infiltrate the world of holiness as well. Therefore, Joseph, you will need to be aware of this and be very careful."

Rabbi Tuviah rose from his seat and said, "I think we have covered a lot today, and it is quite enough for one day. Think over what I have told you. Return tomorrow, and I will begin instructing you."

Joseph and Rachel walked slowly away from Rabbi Tuviah's house. Rachel said, "I was disappointed. I thought he would be able to tell us more. What will we do now?"

Softly, Joseph said, "Rachel, do not fear. We will find it, somehow. Now we know the breastplate is in the Holy Land."

"No, we don't. That was just his theory."

"Yes, it was. But it was a theory strongly held. And when he said it, something resonated within me. It had the ring of truth, and I am certain he is right. We will go to the Holy Land — the land of our ancestors, the land of our destiny — and we will find it there."

She turned to him, her eyes pleading.

"Do not look at me like that, Rachel. I need you to be strong. Please be strong, for me, as you have been till now. I will do as Rabbi Tuviah said. I will pray, and I will meditate. I will learn to contact the spiritual world, and through it I will discover the location of the breastplate. Have faith, Rachel. With your help, I will succeed. Together we will succeed. We must not fail. We cannot fail."

Rachel turned from Joseph and looked down the street. In the distance, something caught her eye. "Is that Aaron?" she asked.

"It can't be. He, and Peter's men, must be at least two days behind us."

Rachel strained to see. "No, Joseph, it is Aaron. Even without seeing his face, even from this distance I can tell. I would know my brother anywhere." She turned to Joseph, and softly she asked, "What shall we do?"

Joseph whispered, "I must have underestimated their speed. No doubt that is Aaron, and that must mean that Peter's men also are in Bari, close behind him. Go back to Tuviah's house. You will be safe there. I will go on ahead and shadow Aaron. Perhaps I can get a jump on his pursuers."

Rachel opened her mouth to answer, but Joseph took her by the arm and said, "No, Rachel, you cannot come with me. Go back to Rabbi Tuviah quickly. There is no time."

When Rachel was out of sight, Joseph hurried to follow Aaron. Aaron was just a speck in the distance now, walking southwards. The sun was low on the western horizon, casting long shadows on the ground. Joseph slunk around the streets, keeping his head down and trying to stay in the shadows as much as possible. Soon, he spotted four men following Aaron: one man a short distance behind Aaron, another farther back, and a pair of men still farther away. Joseph fell in behind the pair, being careful to keep his distance from the men.

He continued to follow for several minutes. The men never turned around, and Joseph was beginning to gain confidence. The road veered slightly to the right, and Joseph followed the men in that direction. Suddenly, he noticed that something had changed: there were only three men following Aaron now. One of the two men closer to Aaron was missing. Joseph looked about, but there was no sign of the fourth man.

Something is wrong. Perhaps they know I'm here. Again, he looked about in all directions.

Nothing.

He tried to tell himself that he was reading too much into the fourth man's disappearance, but alarm bells kept on ringing in his head. And yet, the three men ahead of him continued onwards, following Aaron as before, apparently oblivious of Joseph's presence.

They continued walking for a few more minutes. The men's pace slowed, and they were closer to Aaron than they had been previously, but otherwise the situation seemed unchanged, and Joseph started to regain his confidence.

The sun was about to set, and the western sky was a fiery red. At an intersection, the men turned left. The shadows now were long, and the sun was behind them. Joseph had to fall back farther, so that his shadow would not attract the men's attention.

Joseph knew they couldn't go in that direction very far, because soon they would be by the sea. Again, he began to feel uneasy.

Suddenly, the two men ahead of him came to a halt. They turned around and started walking quickly towards Joseph. Their swords were drawn.

Joseph turned around and ran, away from the two armed men. The sun was in his eyes, and at first he did not notice another group of men advancing towards him, but presently three men came into view, and a fourth man behind them. Joseph halted. He realized he was trapped. He squinted at the three men in front of him and looked beyond them at the solitary figure coming up behind them. It was a black-garbed friar, his hood pulled over his head. The friar's face was hardly visible, but his gait and his demeanor were unmistakable to Joseph: it was Friar Peter.

Peter's men formed a ring around Joseph. There were now six men, all with drawn swords. Friar Peter stepped into the circle and approached Joseph.

"We meet again," he said.

Joseph said nothing, but glared at Friar Peter with loathing.

Friar Peter took another step towards Joseph. "Is this any way to greet an old friend?" he asked.

Joseph did not answer, but continued to hold Friar Peter's gaze. *Yes*, he thought, *I see the power in Friar Peter's gaze – an evil power. It is quite different from Enoch's penetrating gaze.* He wondered which of the two men was stronger, and he hoped he knew the answer.

"You realize there is no escape."

Joseph still said nothing.

Friar Peter stretched out his left hand. When Joseph made no response, Friar Peter said, "The emerald."

Joseph glanced at Peter's outstretched hand, then looked him in the eye again. He folded his arms in front of his chest.

"The emerald," Friar Peter repeated calmly. "Give it to me. One of my men saw you at the rabbi's house and overheard your conversation. I know you have it. If you refuse to hand it over, my men will take it from you by force. The choice is yours, but I will have it either way."

"Why do you want the stone?" asked Joseph. "It is useless to you. Or have you become a common thief, and you want the emerald for its monetary value?"

Peter looked perplexed, and Joseph realized that the friar believed there might be something behind Joseph's question.

"Useless?" said Peter. "Why would you say that?"

Joseph thrust his face forward and spat out his answer: "Because, I have been assured, it is not the authentic emerald of the breastplate, but a decoy stone."

Friar Peter fell silent, visibly taken aback; but quickly he recovered his composure and said, "Give me the stone anyway. Let me be the judge of that."

Joseph wavered, uncertain what to do. He looked around him at the six armed men. He looked at Peter's face and again at Peter's hand. The hand was again outstretched, beckoning.

I cannot give the emerald to this wicked man. How can I allow such a man as this to even touch the stone? Joseph made his decision. He shook his head.

Friar Peter nodded to his men and stepped out of the circle. Slowly, cautiously, the six men advanced towards Joseph, closing the circle. Joseph stood immobile, his face turned to heaven. He closed his eyes and prayed silently. Fear had left him. He was numb inside. He waited for the inevitable.

The sun had set already, and the redness of the sky was slowly fading. A sea breeze was blowing from the east, carrying the sound of marching footsteps.

In the distance, a voice called out: "Halt. Do not lay your hands on him."

Joseph's eyes snapped open.

Friar Peter's men stopped short but didn't look around. They kept their eyes fixed on Joseph, their swords still poised to strike. Friar Peter looked east, then west, then north and south. Confusion and dismay were evident on his face.

Joseph looked in the direction of the voice and saw three men advancing, dressed in long white tunics, each emblazoned with a large red cross. Chainmail covered their heads, their arms and legs, and each man held a long sword in his hand. Behind them, a tall man sat astride a warhorse. He too was clad in chainmail and a long white tunic like his men, but on his shoulders he wore a white cape emblazoned with a large red cross. Joseph recognized the men as Templar knights, and the man on horseback was apparently their commander.

Joseph looked around in each direction, and from each direction he saw more Templar knights advancing. They formed an outer circle around Friar Peter and his men, a circle of six Templar knights in all.

In a stern, authoritative voice, the man on horseback said, "I am Commander Silvio of the Knights Templar. I command you to sheath your swords. Release your prisoner, and withdraw immediately. He is under my protection."

The friar's six men sheathed their swords but did not immediately disperse. They looked at Friar Peter, but the friar made no move. Commander Silvio nudged his horse towards Peter. He drew his sword and pointed it at Peter's chest. "Furthermore," he said, "you and all your men must immediately leave Bari. You will not preach in Bari, and you will not incite a massacre as you have done in other places. Leave immediately. Do not return, for the Jewish community of Bari is under my protection."

CHAPTER 28

P eter opened his eyes and looked about. Outside, the sun had already set, and only a few candles illuminated the inside of the church. But even in the dim light, Peter could see that the church was empty but for him. Slowly, he rose from his knees and walked out into the street.

How long had he been in the church? He was uncertain. Surely, at least an hour; perhaps two. He had prayed to God for enlightenment, for wisdom, and atonement for his sins. He had pledged himself anew to Jesus. He had poured out his anguished soul. But, he felt, his words had been swallowed up in a great abyss, never reaching heavenward. God was not listening to him.

He knew his soul was tainted. He knew his sin was great. He knew what Lilith had told him years ago: for him, there was no turning back. But how could this be? Where was God's mercy? Were the gates of repentance really closed to him?

Slowly, he walked along the darkened streets of this village whose name he didn't even know, trying to find direction for his life. Indeed, he knew he had a reputation as a holy man, and people came from far and wide to hear him preach. And yet, things had not worked out as he had hoped. He had not achieved great power, and his preaching, though popular with the masses, had little impact on the prelates of the Church or on the course of world events. In short, the greatness that Lilith had led him to believe awaited him had not materialized.

It was now eleven years since Lilith had first appeared to him, and she had come to him again only three times since; but her last visit was six years ago. In those six years, he had called to her and summoned her innumerable times, and he had even called upon her consort – the Lord Samael – to answer him. But all his calls and summonses were met with silence. Eventually he had begun to wonder whether his encounters with Lilith had been illusions, mere figments of his imagination. And yet, ever since that day eleven years ago, he knew he was possessed of certain extraordinary powers. He knew he had never had those powers previously, and how would he explain them if Lilith's visitations had been mere illusion?

No, Lilith's visits must have been real. But, in that case, why was she silent for so long? Why was she avoiding him? A great void filled his soul. He felt rejected both by Heaven and by the Satanic realm.

Soon, he arrived at the inn where he would spend the night. He went straight to his room and stumbled into bed. He fell asleep almost immediately.

He was lying in a sun-lit field, the tall grass kissing his bare flesh. He opened his eyes and saw a naked woman approaching from a distance. She had dark, flowing hair, and her breasts were round and full. Peter sat up and squinted in the sunlight, trying to make out the woman's face.

The scene shifted, and the woman now sat beside him. He looked up into her radiant face. He recognized her: it was Judith. Judith, the demon he had killed eleven years ago.

Fear overcame him, and he turned away. But Judith took his head in both her hands. She raised his face, looked him in the eyes, and kissed him on his lips. She caressed his face, his hair, his chest. She kissed him on his lips again, more vehemently than before. "Do not be afraid," she said, and Peter's fear melted away immediately.

She sat astride him, smiling. He closed his eyes and smelled her fragrance. He felt her hands caressing him.

He felt her body pressed against him, and he entered her. Waves of pleasure enveloped him to his core, and he cried out to her, calling her name again and again. And yet again.

"Open your eyes," she commanded.

He opened his eyes and looked at her again. Her face had changed, and she was still more beautiful than before. Her eyes were bright, her lips were full and sensuous, and she had long red, flowing hair. She was no longer Judith.

He recognized her.

"Lilith!"

"Yes, Peter. It is I. And the time is near. It has begun."

"What has begun? I do not understand." After so long awaiting her arrival, now that Lilith was here, fear overcame him. He could not explain it. He looked at her face and trembled.

Lilith rose and stood before him. She was no longer naked, but clothed in a flowing gown of red and black. Her beauty was stunning, and she was awesome to behold. He tried to look away, but she held his gaze.

In her gaze, he felt the radiance of her power. Her presence thrilled him, exhilarated him, elevated him as did nothing else in his experience save for what he had felt on Lilith's previous visits. Only this time, his exhilaration was even more intense, and he was drawn to her still more strongly than he ever had been drawn to her before.

He looked deep into her eyes, and suddenly he realized why God had refused to hear his prayers: deep in his soul, he knew that repentance and return to God was not his destiny, not what he truly wanted. It was Lilith, not Jesus, whose approval his soul desired. It was always Lilith whom he had sought to serve. It had been thus all his life, ever since his first encounter with

Lilith, but now he felt her power more strongly than he ever had before. His desire was to serve Lilith with all his heart.

She looked at him, as though reading his thoughts. A faint smile crept across the corners of her lips. Her gaze burned into Peter's soul.

"Prepare yourself, Peter. The time has come. In three days hence, King Henry will be dead, and his son Richard will be king. Exactly two months from today, Richard will be crowned, and you must be present at the coronation."

Peter gasped. "Where will the coronation be?" he asked.

"At Westminster Abbey. A great throng will gather outside, and you will be among them. You will speak to the people. You will speak to their hearts. You will stir them to action."

"What shall I say to them? What action must they take?"

"Outside the abbey, many leaders of the Jews will be gathered, hoping to bring their petitions before the new king, hoping to gain the new king's favor. But you will convince the throng that the Jews are enemies of the king. You will convince the multitude that a royal order has been given to attack the Jews and kill them. You will incite a riot and a massacre outside the abbey."

Friar Peter could hardly contain his excitement. "Yes," he said, "I will do as you command."

"That is very good," said Lilith. "But that is just a beginning to your journey."

"I do not understand. What journey? What is my destination?"

Lilith smiled. "You are going to the Holy Land," she said; "for only there can you attain the power to which you aspire. But first, you must journey to the Mountains of Darkness. Arise. Get dressed. I will take you there."

Outside, the moon had risen, but clouds obscured the moon's face, and a thick fog was moving in. Lilith took Friar Peter's hand and led him through the darkened streets and out of the village. When Peter could no longer see the village, Lilith stopped abruptly.

"We wait here," she said.

"For whom or for what are we waiting?" Peter asked.

"Be silent. Wait, and you shall see."

For a long time, Peter waited. He looked about, but he saw nothing. Fear began to grow within him. He felt he had to run away, but Lilith held him tightly by the hand. He was her prisoner.

"Turn northwards!" she commanded, and Peter obeyed.

"Now close your eyes, and concentrate on the darkness. Concentrate on the sensation of my hand against your flesh. Concentrate on joining with me to the darkness of the world, to the darkness of the soul, to the realm of Samael, the Lord of Darkness."

Peter felt her hand. He felt the warmth of her flesh radiating into his own blood. She held him tightly; gradually the warmth receded, and her hand became as cold as ice. Her coldness radiated into him, coursing through his body, transporting him. He felt as though he were flying.

"Open your eyes, and look down," she said.

He looked down and saw only darkness below, a darkness more profound than any he had ever seen before.

"Now lift your eyes; look up," she said.

He looked up and saw a great shadow descending towards him from the north. Again, fear overcame him, and he wanted to run away, but there was no solid ground under his feet, and only Lilith's firm grip on his hand held him in place, preventing him from falling into the awesome, terrifying darkness beneath his feet. The descending shadow grew, and its shape gradually took form: a great eagle with a wingspan like the boughs of a mighty tree.

In the sky beyond the eagle, Peter saw two pillars approaching from the distance – a pillar of fire and a pillar of swirling cloud. The eagle hovered in the murky air, and the two pillars came to rest just behind the eagle's tail. The eagle dipped its head, and Peter saw there were two leaves in the eagle's beak.

"Take the leaves!" Lilith commanded, releasing Peter's hand. He tried to grasp her hand again, certain that otherwise he would fall and be swallowed by the ocean of darkness underneath his feet. But Lilith's hand was out of reach. Timidly, he took a step forward, keeping his eyes fixed on the eagle in front of him, afraid to look down. He took another step forward and extended his hand.

Trembling, Peter took the two leaves from the eagle's beak, holding one leaf in his left hand and the other in his right. In Peter's hands, the leaves grew and changed their shapes, transforming into two demonic faces. The demons laughed a terrifying laugh, and spoke in unison: "Come, Peter. To the Mountains of Darkness. Come to us. We are awaiting you."

The demons' faces vanished, and when Peter looked again, he saw only leaves in his two hands. The eagle took both leaves from Peter's hands and held them in its beak.

The eagle now was hovering over the two pillars – the roaring fire under its right wing, the swirling cloud under its left. The eagle dipped its head again and hovered downwards.

"Mount his back!" Lilith commanded, and Peter – terrified though he was – obeyed.

Peter looked to Lilith with pleading eyes. He held out his hand to her, but she shook her head. She sat astride the eagle's left wing and, in a deep, sonorous voice that resonated through Peter's body, she commanded:

"Fly, eagle. To the Mountains of Darkness, fly!"

The eagle's great wings rose and fell, and Peter felt the rush of air as the eagle cut through the darkness at terrifying speed. Peter held on as tightly as he could, afraid of falling into the great abyss below. In the distance, a faint halo of light glimmered on the horizon, but otherwise all was darkness. Now and then, he glanced at Lilith riding on the eagle's wing. Her wraith-like form, just barely visible, ascended and descended in a dizzying rhythm as the eagle beat its wings, but Lilith sat astride the wing, never wavering, and Peter turned his eyes away.

How long the eagle flew, Peter could not say for certain. How far the eagle flew, he also could not say; but he surmised it must be many hundreds of miles – perhaps a thousand miles or more, if distance, time, or space even had a meaning or existed in this other world, which clearly was not the world of his experience. Finally, the eagle descended into the great abyss below, and all at once, in the distance Peter discerned the shapes of mountains.

"The Mountains of Darkness," said Lilith, as the eagle descended, landing near an ancient olive tree. Lilith jumped off the eagle's wing and signaled Peter to dismount as well. Seated before them near the olive tree were the two demons whose faces Peter had seen previously in the leaves, but in real life they were far more frightening.

Peter gasped and turned his face away. He retched but managed to control his gorge. Slowly, he turned to look at them again.

Their faces were identical, and Peter could not tell them apart. They were hideously ugly, humanoid and yet goat-like simultaneously, with elongated snouts, pointed ears, and horns on their heads. Their eyes were red, burning like fiery coals.

"Take the two leaves from the eagle's beak," said Lilith, "and present them to these two spirits, one leaf to each."

Peter took the leaves and walked slowly, uncertainly, towards the demons, his arms outstretched, each trembling hand bearing his offering to one of the demons. His legs were shaking, and he almost tripped a few times. Both demons sat immobile, their gaze fixed on Friar Peter.

Peter took a step closer, and then another step. He feared the demons thought of him as prey, waiting to pounce upon him when he was close enough. But he suppressed his fear. He took another step.

The demon to his left took the proffered leaf and said, "I am Aza."

The demon to his right took the other leaf and said, "And I am Azael."

Then both demons said in unison: "Peter the Pious, why have you come to the Mountains of Darkness? Humans do not often come to seek our counsel. In fact, no human has come to us since King Solomon many centuries ago. So tell us, Peter the Pious: why have you come to the Mountains of Darkness to seek our help? And why should we give aid to one such as you?"

For a moment, Peter was at a loss to answer them. Indeed, he had never before heard of Aza and Azael, and he had not even heard of the Mountains of Darkness until tonight, when Lilith told him he must journey hither. He fumbled for an answer, but Lilith interjected:

"Friar Peter long ago pledged himself to serve me, and the time has come. He is now embarking on a journey to wrest the reins of the world from the earthly forces subject to the realm of holiness. I have given him great Powers, but those powers have not yet reached their fullest, nor can they reach their fullest without your help. Speak, then, and tell my faithful servant how he must proceed."

Aza looked at Peter. Aza leaped into the air, and his eyes flashed sparks of fire. His body hung in mid-air, defying natural law.

"Her faithful servant are you?" Aza asked. "Her faithful servant truly? I must hear you say it. Speak!"

Peter looked up at Aza, fighting terror. "Yes. I am truly Lilith's faithful servant, committed to her for all eternity."

Azael slowly rose from the ground, and his face hung just above Friar Peter, his foul breath assaulting Peter's senses. "And are you, then, the servant of the Lord of Darkness also?" asked Azael, his eyes flashing sparks of fire.

Peter winced. He felt his head become light, and he thought that he would faint. But he quickly gathered his strength and looked at Azael. "Indeed I am," he said.

Aza spoke again: "What are you prepared to do to prove your faithfulness? What sins will you commit? Will you murder?"

"I have done so already," Peter answered firmly. "And rape, as well. You may ask Lilith. She will tell you what I have done."

"No need to ask Lilith," said Aza. "We know as well as she."

And Azael said, "We wanted to hear it from your own mouth. We wanted to hear you say it without a quaver in your voice. We wanted to hear you say it firmly, with conviction, and with pride. And so you have. We have nothing more to ask of you. We will help you now."

Both demons descended and sat on the ground beneath the olive tree. Aza spoke again: "Lilith is right. The powers that she gave you are but a seed, a germ that only by your efforts and your actions can grow, mature, and fructify. Your full power can be attained only in the Holy Land, only in Jerusalem. Therefore, it is to Jerusalem that you must journey."

"But the Saracens hold Jerusalem. Their sultan, Saladin, conquered Jerusalem two years ago, and no Christian may set foot there any more. If I went to Jerusalem, they would kill me on sight."

"Indeed?" said Azael, his eyes once more flashing fire. "Are you again a Christian? I thought you served the Lord of Darkness."

"Yes, of course I do. But my point is, I am not a Saracen, not a follower of Mohammed. To them, I am a Christian. They will not let me enter."

"Then you must find a way," said Aza. "Did not Lilith give you Powers? Use them! Lilith has bestowed upon you all you need to achieve your destiny, but you must find your way to use her gift. Only thus can victory be achieved."

Peter looked away. He turned his eyes to Lilith, but she said nothing, her face expressionless. He looked down at the ground, thinking of how to respond.

Aza broke the silence. "A man, a boy, an ancient relic."

Peter looked up at Aza. "What are you saying? What do you mean?"

"A man, a boy, an ancient relic. Think Peter! What do I mean?" Azael continued:

> "A man, a Jew, secrets of old;
> A priestly garment, threads of gold;
> A priestly garment four and three
> For Peter's power these hold the key.
> A boy, his son, with powers hidden.
> We say no more; all else forbidden."

Peter looked away. He turned to Lilith, but she just shook her head. He turned to Aza, but his mocking smile taunted Friar Peter. He looked up beyond the mountains, but there was only darkness.

He gazed into the darkness, tried to penetrate its mystery. He closed his eyes and opened them again. He looked at the mountains and saw the rocky crags. He saw the darkening clouds billowing above the mountain peaks. He saw a looming tabernacle nestled beneath the clouds, its foundation planted in the air, its walls and pillars clothed in mystery. And from within the tabernacle, he heard the singing voice of angels.

He turned to Azael and said, "The ancient relic is an object worn by the high priest in the Temple in Jerusalem. A golden garment; four and three, you said. The high priest's breastplate was made of interwoven threads of linen and gold, with twelve gemstones set upon it in four rows of three. The high priest used the breastplate to commune with God."

"Very good!" said Azael, jumping up and perching on a branch of the olive tree. Ominous dark clouds descended, almost touching Peter's head, and lightning flashed above. From all directions, Peter heard the sound of thunder rumbling, getting louder, to an almost deafening crescendo. Peter crouched, cowering before the onslaught, his hands clasped above his head.

The demon raised his hands. The clouds dissolved abruptly. The lightning stopped, and all was silent. Azael spoke: "You must seek out the High Priest's breastplate. You must find it, and you must put it on. For only with the breastplate will your powers grow to their full potential. Only then will you attain the power to achieve your ends and rule the world. The breastplate had tremendous power, but not if any part of it was missing. Originally, twelve gemstones were set in the breastplate. Twelve stones. But only eleven now remain. Only eleven, Peter. Only eleven now remain."

"And," said Aza, "with only eleven stones, the breastplate has no power. None at all."

Azael dropped to the ground and continued: "It is said the Prophet Jeremiah removed one stone before he hid the breastplate, in order to insure against the breastplate's falling into evil hands. He hid the twelfth stone in a separate location. The prophet no longer had either the breastplate or the missing stone when Jerusalem fell to the Babylonians shortly after. Therefore, both must be hidden somewhere in the environs of Jerusalem, but we cannot tell you more."

"But which stone is it?" Peter asked. "Is it the diamond, the ruby, or the emerald? Or perhaps the sapphire, or some other stone?"

"We do not know," said Aza. "When the prophet Jeremiah hid the breastplate, a divine cloud surrounded him, shielding his location and his activities from our view. The breastplate is hidden somewhere in Jerusalem or its environs, and you will have to find it; but we can help you no further."

Azael began to laugh, a mighty, thunderous laugh that shook the ground beneath the friar's feet. Friar Peter startled, his whole body quaked, and an involuntary scream of terror escaped his lips.

Azael spoke: "Friar Peter, you have guessed the ancient relic, and now you know what you must do to reach the full measure of your power. But you will not achieve it unless you solve the remaining elements of our riddle. Tell us, Friar Peter: what of the man and the boy?"

Peter stood in thought, pondering the question. Several minutes passed in silence.

Peter looked at Azael and said: "The man with ancient secrets and the boy, his son, with powers hidden. Who are they? What are these powers? Does this boy have the power to thwart my objective? And where are they? Are they in England? How will I find them?"

"There are no more clues, Peter," said Aza. "Focus! Lilith gave you special powers. Use them! Find your enemies, and kill them!"

"That is all we have to tell you, Peter," said Azael. "Now fare thee well. The rest is up to you."

Peter was about to speak again. He turned to Aza, but Aza was no longer there. He turned to Azael, but he had vanished also. Only Lilith remained, and, a short distance away, the eagle stood immobile, waiting.

"Come, Peter," Lilith said. "It is time to go."

Of the return trip, Peter remembered little. He remembered only dismounting at the journey's end, and Lilith leading him to his inn. He stumbled up the stairs, got into bed, and slept a troubled sleep. He dreamt of eagles and of demons, of angels and of ancient temple priests, of Lilith and of Satan, of Heaven and of Hell. And he himself stood between, dressed in royal raiment, the ruler of the earth.

CHAPTER 29

J oseph, Aaron, and Rachel sat at a table in a darkened corner of the inn. Before them on the table there were various cakes, and each of them had a tankard of ale. Joseph kept his eyes on the front door as he silently sipped his ale. After a while, the front door opened, and Joseph let out a sigh of relief.

"There he is. Finally," Joseph said.

Slowly, Silvio wended his way through the press of the crowd and came to sit at Joseph's table.

"What's the news, Silvio?" Joseph asked.

"Not good. The weather is still bad. The storms at sea have not abated, and reports of another shipwreck have arrived."

"Where?"

"That ship was out of Venice. It was caught in a squall five days from port. This is the third shipwreck since we arrived in Bari a month ago. And that's with few ships daring to brave the weather."

Joseph looked at his three companions and said, "How long will this continue? We have wasted one month already." He looked accusingly at Silvio. "When will there be a ship to the Holy Land?"

Silvio shook his head. "I do not know. The port of Bari is closed. No captain is willing to brave the weather now, especially on such a long journey. My guess is that it will be next month at the earliest before we embark. I know your mission is urgent, but the delay cannot be helped."

Joseph snapped back, "How can you know the urgency? You don't know what my mission is."

"Of course I am aware of that," said Silvio, his voice calm. "And I know it is a secret the details of which you may not reveal to me. But you have told me enough that I sense its great importance. And even if you hadn't told me anything, I have sworn an oath to the holy man who sent me to Bari as your protector. I am sworn to stay by you and to do all in my power to assist you in your quest. I am your man, unquestioningly. Do not forget that."

Silvio's words stung at Joseph. *I have been unfair to him,* he thought. *Surely the weather isn't his fault.* "I am very sorry," he said.

He wondered who the holy man could be. Was he a Jew or a Christian? Surely a Christian, for it is doubtful that a Templar would consider a Jew to be a holy man whose dictates he must obey. But if a Christian, how did this holy man know anything at all of Joseph's quest, and how did he even know of Joseph's existence? He was tempted to ask the holy man's identity but decided against it.

Silvio nodded. "That is quite alright," he said. "I understand, and your apology is accepted. Now, my friends, I have things to do, and the three of you must have much to discuss among yourselves." He rose and walked towards the front door.

When Silvio had left, Rachel turned to Joseph and said, "The delay in finding passage was not a waste of time. You have had many more meetings with Rabbi Tuviah, and he has taught you much about the spiritual world and how you might approach it through contemplation and meditation. How is it going?"

Joseph looked down at the table. "I really can't say for sure. What he taught me is very interesting, and I have been able to deepen my meditative state progressively by degrees. I have entered what Tuviah calls a trance-like state by concentrating on a Biblical verse, and I have seen lights and colors flash before me, as he told me to expect. I have looked intently into the flame of a flickering candle and have seen the aura that surrounds the flame. But still, I have not made true contact with the spiritual world itself. All I have seen are merely glimpses of something far beyond my ken. It is as though I am in an ante-room waiting to be admitted to a second ante-room, but the door is locked, and all that I can see is the little that is visible through the keyhole."

Rachel smiled warmly and said, "Rabbi Tuviah told you that the road is long and difficult. It takes much self-training. You have only recently begun. Do not despair."

He stretched out his hand, taking Rachel's hand in his, and the warmth of her hand somehow invigorated him. "I know," he said. "Thank you, Rachel. But there is so little time. And meanwhile, Friar Peter surely isn't idle." He turned to Aaron and said, "Aaron, Friar Peter spoke to you while you were held captive. Perhaps you also had occasion to overhear his men. Did you learn anything about his plans?"

In a subdued tone, Aaron said, "I am sorry, Joseph. I was too afraid for my life, and in too much pain. I did not learn anything that might be of use to us. In fact, I thought I misled them when I told them you were going to Otranto, but it seems they never took the bait. When I escaped, I suspected they would follow me, but later I thought I had slipped away from them. And I knew I had to go to Bari. Otherwise, how would I ever find you again? Unwittingly I led them to you." His gaze turned from Joseph to Rachel. Finally, he looked down at the table and fell silent.

Joseph said, "That's alright, Aaron. Don't feel bad. You did your best in a bad situation, and you were right to come to Bari to find us. Despite Friar Peter's best efforts, we are still here, unharmed. Rachel is correct: we must not despair if we are to succeed."

The weather at sea remained stormy all through the winter, and thus it was not until 25th March 1191 that Joseph, Aaron, and Rachel, in the company of Silvio, boarded a ship bound for the Holy Land. It was a sunny day, and the weather forecast was propitious, but under the most favorable conditions it would be a month-long voyage to the Holy Land. Nineteen days out of Bari, the sky turned dark, a great wind swept over the surface of the water, and mighty swells pummeled the ship.

Joseph went to his cabin and prayed to God to spare the ship. When he had finished praying, he still felt the need for something more. He sat down, closed his eyes, and rested his hands on his lap. Trying with all his will to ignore the swaying of the ship, suppressing the fear that prodded at him each time the vessel yawed beneath his feet, in a tremulous whisper he began to recite a psalm. It was not the usual text that previously he had used in meditation, but he deemed it appropriate to his current situation: "A Psalm of David; from the depths I call to you, O Lord."

Concentrating hard, he recited the entire psalm twice, and then repeated the first verse again and again, and yet again. As his body rocked to and fro with the movement of the ship, he felt his limbs relaxing, and his mind became suspended in a dream-like state. He saw colored lights dancing at the periphery of his vision, and a feeling of calm enveloped him.

As Joseph continued to recite the verse, the vision shifted. The colored lights vanished and were replaced by a wall of water shimmering before him. It was not the sea or any other water of the world of his experience, but something wholly different – an insubstantial vision of another world.

Joseph continued to focus his attention, and presently the waters parted slowly, revealing the heavens shimmering in the distance. As Joseph passed beyond the water, the heavens stood out in vivid colors: blue and red and white. There was a turbulence in the heavens. The colors flew together, mixing and parting once again. Flashes of lightning streaked across his vision. Dark clouds gathered, and the heavens seemed to open as the awesome sound of distant thunder echoed through the void. Joseph tried to open his eyes but found he couldn't do so.

The heavens parted like a curtain being pulled away, and beyond the curtain a massive dark cloud loomed, approaching rapidly. The dark cloud churned and billowed before Joseph's eyes, a whirlwind contained within the midst of its terrifying maw.

The dark cloud came still closer, threatening to engulf him. Joseph wanted to flee, but he found he could not move. He was transfixed, staring into the whirling wind within the cloud. Suddenly, the center of the whirlwind darkened further, and a fire appeared within it. The fire grew, and Joseph felt the heat emanating from the swirling flames. For a moment, he thought of Sarah on the pyre, screaming in her final agony. But that thought flew away as the heat diminished, and he saw beyond the flames.

The flames vanished, but a reflection of them lingered as an aura surrounding the dark cloud. In the center of the cloud, the air shimmered, and a misty mountain was visible within. Joseph felt himself flying through the mist, approaching rapidly. The image of the mountain became more distinct, and the mist slowly dispersed. The dark cloud, no longer surrounding the image of the mountain, now congealed and stood upon the mountainside, pulsing, throbbing, breathing, seemingly alive.

Slowly, the throbbing cloud began to grow again. Appendages emerged from it on either side, growing longer, while Joseph watched the transformation in fearful fascination. The cloud trembled. It expanded and contracted. Yet another appendage grew out of its uppermost region, and now Joseph saw the cloud had taken the shape of a man – a black-cloaked man wearing a dark hood. Joseph recognized the face: it was Friar Peter. And on the friar's chest, Joseph saw the high priest's breastplate, the emerald set within it, among the other stones.

As Joseph watched in horror, Friar Peter's body grew, emitting an ominous dark light that slowly expanded and enveloped all other light. The friar raised his hand, and the earth shook before him. The friar spread his arms, and Joseph heard a rumbling, terrifying sound that echoed from the bowels of the earth. Graves opened, and horrible faceless creatures rose from the open graves, an army of ghouls, snakes, and giant lizards.

Across the valley, on the next mountain, Joseph saw Jerusalem enveloped in white light. Peter's army of wraiths and monsters marched on air across the valley, their numbers growing as they advanced.

They reached the holy city. They climbed the walls with ease. They overwhelmed the city, and the streets of Jerusalem were drenched in blood.

In Joseph's vision, Peter's army quickly spread out from Jerusalem to the valley and the hills beyond. Their numbers grew as they spread farther outwards, a mighty army marching with Friar Peter in the lead, across the land, across the sea, marching to conquer the entire world.

"No! No! This cannot be!" Joseph opened his eyes. He looked around. The vision was gone. He was alone in the cabin. And yet, he continued screaming. "No, it cannot be! It must not be! I will not let it happen."

The cabin door flew open, and Joseph nearly lunged, ready to strike out at whatever demon or apparition was about to enter. But it was Rachel.

"What happened, Joseph? I heard you screaming." She ran to him, apparently undaunted by his bellicose demeanor, and threw her arms around him. "Are you alright?"

"Yes, Rachel. I am fine. It was just a bad dream." But Joseph knew it had not been just a dream. He knew this was his first encounter with the spiritual world. He regretted he could not hold the vision longer and perhaps learn something that would help him find the breastplate. But at least this was a start. Trembling, he took Rachel's hand in his. He smiled.

When Joseph had calmed down, he realized the ship was no longer shaking violently, and no longer did he hear the howling of the wind. He and Rachel went up on deck. The sky was beginning to clear. The sea was choppy, but the waves were no longer violent.

"Thank God," he said.

The remainder of their voyage was uneventful, and they disembarked at Tyre, on the coast of Lebanon, on a warm and sunny day in May 1191.

CHAPTER 30

Rome, Italy
30th March 1191

encio Savelli, *camerarius* of the Holy See, watched the red-robed cardinals filing into the conclave chamber to resume their deliberations after inconclusive sessions on the previous days. He counted the cardinals. So far, there were only thirty one. He would wait another few minutes for the last three cardinals to arrive before closing the doors and allowing the conclave to resume. He thought back over the last five days, which had passed as though in a fog.

The day of 25th March had begun uneventfully. After a troubled sleep, Cencio had arisen early that morning, somewhat earlier than usual. On completing his morning rituals, he was just about to sit down to eat when he was interrupted by a commotion outside his door, and a priest called to him urgently. He must go immediately and attend to the Holy Father.

Cencio recalled his entrance into the Holy Father's chambers, where the pope lay in his bed, apparently asleep. With trepidation, Cencio approached the inert figure of his friend and mentor, Paolo Scolari, known to all the world as Pope Clement III. As he approached the Holy Father's bed, Cencio thought back to the day, just four years ago, when Paolo was elected pope. As Cencio thought about that day, he recalled that Paolo had been absent from the conclave because of illness – perhaps a portent of a relatively short reign as pope, although admittedly longer than those of his two predecessors.

Cencio stood over the bed, momentarily indecisive, momentarily afraid to do what ritual prescribed he had to do. He looked upon the chiseled features of the pontiff. Gently, he touched the pontiff's well-groomed white beard. He put his fingers on the pontiff's neck. He felt for a pulse. There was none. He held a mirror up before the pontiff's nostrils. The mirror showed no evidence of moisture on its surface.

Cencio inserted his hand into his own robe and extracted a small silver hammer. With the hammer, he struck the Holy Father three times gently on his head, and with each strike of the hammer he declared, "Paule, dormisne?" But Paolo did not answer, nor was he in fact asleep.

As Chamberlain of the Holy See, it was Cencio's duty to pronounce the pontiff dead. Slowly, mournfully, he rose and said, "The pope is dead." And with that statement, he, Cencio Savelli, became nominally the head of the Roman Church until the election and installation of a new pope.

He took the pontiff's hand in his, and from the dead pope's finger he removed the Ring of the Fisherman.

As he stood now at the doors of the conclave chamber, it was hard for Cencio to believe that only five days had elapsed since his friend Paolo's death. It seemed as though a lifetime had passed since then. He stood silently and watched as the last three cardinals filed into the chamber, took their oaths to obey the rules of the conclave, and found their seats around the table. Cencio shook himself out of his reverie. He stepped outside the conclave chamber, took the handles of the double doors in his hands, and swung them closed.

Cardinal Konrad von Wittelsbach, Dean of the College of Cardinals, sat at the head of the long table and scanned the assembled cardinals. He cleared his throat and said, "My friends, over the last few days, we have been through several ballots and several rancorous disputes, but no candidate has managed to win a majority vote. Does anyone here wish to propose a compromise candidate, one who will be acceptable to all factions among us? Think carefully, speak your mind, and may the Holy Spirit guide your choice."

After a short silence, Cardinal Gregorio Crescenzi spoke up. "May it please this holy conclave, I wish to nominate a man who is known for both his wisdom and erudition and his great piety. He has been a cardinal these forty-seven years and has won the respect of all of us. I think he is a candidate upon whom all of us should agree. I speak of Cardinal Giacinto Bobone."

Yes, thought the dean. *A wise choice, not only for the reasons mentioned. Giacinto is a very old man, and his reign likely will be short.*

Cardinal Albino and Cardinal Ottaviano – both unsuccessful candidates for election on previous ballots – looked pleased at Gregorio's proposal of Cardinal Giacinto, as did many of the other cardinals. But, the dean noted with dismay, near the end of the long table, Lotario, one of the younger cardinals, shifted in his seat, his expression sullen. Thinking back, the dean recalled several rancorous doctrinal disputes that Cardinal Lotario had had with Cardinal Giacinto in recent months, despite Lotario's relatively young age and his as-yet short tenure as a cardinal; and he wondered whether Lotario would soon initiate or join in an attack on the proposed candidate. For several seconds, all were silent. The dean kept his eyes on Cardinal Lotario, waiting expectantly; but Cardinal Lotario made no move to speak. Yes, the dean understood: Lotario hoped some day to be elected pope. But at this time, he knew he had no chance, and he did not want to say anything now that would embitter other cardinals against him and thus hurt his chances of being chosen in the next papal election several years hence. Meanwhile, Lotario would keep his temper in check and bide his time. A wise decision indeed.

Ottaviano di Paoli, Cardinal-Bishop of Ostia and Velletri, rose from his seat and addressed the dean. "May it please the Dean, and may it please this holy conclave, I wish to speak in support of Cardinal Gregorio's proposal. Cardinal Giacinto is a good and pious man, who has served the Church well and with distinction for many years. He is an astute politician, but at the same time he is a man whose every action is guided by a love of God and a desire to serve the cause of truth and justice. In my view, no one is more qualified to be elected to the papacy than he. Giacinto is not just a compromise but an exemplary candidate who should be the choice of all."

As Cardinal Ottaviano took his seat, Cardinal Albino raised his hand, smiling. The dean was about to acknowledge Cardinal Albino when another cardinal caught his attention. It was Cardinal Guillaume de Champagne, Archbishop of Reims. He had his hand up, his face strained, and apparently eager to speak his mind. The dean turned to him and nodded.

Cardinal Guillaume rose, and his gaze swept the room. "No!" he exclaimed. His voice was loud, and his tone was vehement. "Cardinal Giacinto is the wrong man. His head is full of subversive ideas that would turn the Church on its head. You cannot elect this man as pope."

The dean looked at Cardinal Guillaume silently. The other cardinals turned their attention to the dean, waiting to see how he would respond. No one spoke.

At length, the dean said calmly, "Cardinal Guillaume, please explain yourself. Has not Cardinal Giacinto served the Church faithfully for many years? And certainly you cannot deny his piety."

Cardinal Guillaume looked around the room, then turned his gaze again to the dean. "I do not deny his efforts these many years on behalf of the Church, nor do I deny his skill in diplomacy and his expertise in many important matters of state. I think it safe to say that Cardinal Giacinto's diplomatic skill is not at all in dispute. Nor would I dispute his apparent piety. But his theology is a different matter entirely."

There was an audible gasp from several of the older cardinals.

"Please continue," said the Dean as calmly as he was able.

Cardinal Guillaume now turned his gaze to Cardinal Giacinto, pointed his finger, and said, "He is a disciple of Abelard, whose heresies are well known throughout France. Did not Abelard leave multiple questions of dogma open for discussion, leaving the world open to freethinkers who would undermine the authority of the Holy Church? Did not Abelard advocate the use of reason in matters of faith, again undermining the unquestioned authority of the Holy Church? Cardinal Giacinto, despite his pious demeanor, endorses many of Abelard's heretical ideas. And was not Abelard, in his Colloquy, critical of the Holy Church's position on the Jews? What is Cardinal Giacinto's position on that matter? By all indications, in this matter also he is in agreement with Abelard, contrary to the affirmed position of the church. Lastly, please consider that, despite his age, Cardinal Giacinto is only a Cardinal Deacon, never having been ordained as priest. And while that in itself does not disqualify him from being elected to the papacy, nevertheless it should serve to give us pause. Taken together with all the other points that I have made, I do not think that Cardinal Giacinto deserves to be considered in the least."

As Cardinal Guillaume sat down, there was an undertone of whispers. To the dean's left, several cardinals appeared to be angered by the attack on Cardinal Giacinto, while only few seemed to agree with Cardinal Guillaume.

From the other side of the table, the dean heard someone mutter, "Yes, Giacinto is a Jew-lover, isn't he?" The dean turned in that direction, but he could not identify the speaker. He looked toward the end of the table and noted that young cardinal Lotario was expressionless, studiously guarding his tongue.

The dean recognized Cardinal Albino, who strongly endorsed his friend Giacinto as a pious, holy man who deserved more than anyone else to be elected pope. Several other cardinals affirmed that position, while only two of the older cardinals spoke against electing Cardinal Giacinto and proposed alternative candidates. Finally, the dean said, "There seem to be no further opinions on the matter. Therefore, if there is no objection, I will now put the matter to a vote."

The dean nodded to the Secretary of the College of Cardinals, who then began distributing the ballots. The dean said, "Before you vote, I remind you all of your oath to abide by the rules of the conclave. Vote for the man whom you deem to be most qualified."

When the cardinals had finished writing their choices on the ballots, the Secretary called the name of each cardinal in turn. As each cardinal was called, he came forward and deposited his ballot in the ballot box in the front of the room. When all the cardinals had been called and had cast their ballots, the secretary opened the box and tallied the votes. Giacinto Bobone was elected by a narrow margin.

Two weeks later, on Holy Saturday, 13th April 1191, Cardinal Giacinto Bobone was ordained as priest, and on the following day, Easter Sunday, he was crowned Bishop of Rome, taking the name Pope Celestine III.

CHAPTER 31

T he sun was shining brightly on this day after Easter, and a great crowd was gathered in the town square to hear Peter the Pious preach. The friar's speech had been greatly anticipated, and people of all classes had turned out to hear the holy friar: nobles and courtesans, priests and laity, merchants and vagabonds. And they were not disappointed.

Friar Peter stood on an elevated platform, dressed as usual in his black robe. His cowl was pulled back so that all could see his countenance. His powerful voice rose and fell, enveloping the crowd in its fervor. He raised his hands in benediction, his eyes turned upwards to the heavens. He had been speaking already for almost half an hour, but still the crowd stood in rapt attention, their eyes fixed on Peter's face, their bodies swaying to the cadence of his words.

In the midst of the crowd, a careful observer might have noticed three men who seemed different from the rest. Their manner of dress was Roman, and they had a military bearing although not clad in armor or in chainmail, and apparently unarmed apart from the short dirk or dagger that men commonly wore under their cloaks. Most notably, however, unlike everyone else, they were not mesmerized by Friar Peter's words. They appeared to be listening attentively, but periodically they turned to look around, whispering or signaling to each other before turning back again to listen to Friar Peter's words. They seemed just as interested in the reaction of the crowd as they were in the substance of the sermon. But Friar Peter was unlikely to have noticed those three men, buried as they were among the throng.

Friar Peter's gaze scanned the crowd. "My friends, it is now three weeks since the Holy Father passed away. Remember him. Remember how he battled against the forces of evil in the world. Remember how his words, as sharp as spears, were thrust against the infidel. Even now, our forces are amassing, preparing to do battle in the Holy Land, preparing to wrest Jerusalem from the Saracens' hands, and to drive the infidel from the holy city. But the forces of darkness do not rest, nor do they sleep. While the armies of the infidel battle against us here on earth, demonic forces strive against us both in heaven and on earth. They have struck at the very heart of Christendom. They have felled the leader of our armies. It is through the power of Satan himself that Pope Clement has been struck down."

He paused to let his words sink in. Briefly he scanned the crowd again. Then he continued: "But Satan cannot conquer. The true Church will not succumb. We have just celebrated the feast of resurrection; and like Christ himself, Christendom will rise again. Our brave warriors will not rest. Our armies go to fight the infidel in the Holy Land, and by the grace of God, they will succeed. But do not forget, my friends: it is not only in the Holy Land that Satan's agents may be found. No, my friends: make no mistake about it. Satan's forces may be found throughout the world. They are everywhere. Everywhere, I say! Even among you here in Brindisi."

A murmur rose up among the crowd. But Peter continued speaking, and the murmur quickly subsided, as all eyes turned back to look at Friar Peter.

"Yes, my friends. They are here in Brindisi as well, these agents of Satan. They live among you. They are merchants, traders, money lenders. You see them daily in the streets, and you speak to them. They have infiltrated your city, and they contaminate the very air you breath with their vile stench.

"Who are these agents of Satan, you may ask? They are the Jews, a people accursed for a thousand years, a nation condemned to wander this world on account of their rejection of our Lord. And yet they survive and even flourish, thanks to our mercy and compassion."

Again a murmur rose up among the crowd, but this time Peter paused to allow the frenzy of the crowd to build.

The three men in Roman garb turned to each other, and one of them spoke in whispered tones:

"It is just as Ursus said. We must return immediately and report to him."

"Wait, Guido," said another. "Let us hear the end of this. Then one of us will return, while the other two stay on."

Friar Peter raised his hands again. He appeared about to resume speaking. The crowd again became silent, listening. But before Peter managed to say another word, a tall man in long purple vestments pushed his way through the crowd and mounted the podium. He held up his right hand and announced in a stentorian voice:

"Hear me, people of Brindisi. We have just celebrated Easter, a feast day dedicated to holiness, a day celebrating the resurrection of Christ, a day embodying the spirit of peace and love, which Christ represents. As your bishop, I feel I must remind you of this lest you be lured into grievous sin. It is true the Jews have rejected Christ. But let me declare unequivocally: they are not Satan's agents, and it is not for us to punish them as though they were. Such matters are best left to God. The pope himself – whose blessed memory Friar Peter has invoked – has forbidden any violence against the Jews, sinners and infidels though they be. Therefore, the Jews of Brindisi are under my protection, and I forbid anyone to do them harm."

Friar Peter turned to the bishop, appearing unperturbed. "I yield to your authority," he said. "But surely it would be appropriate to exercise our displeasure at the Jews' rejection of our lord. Surely their rejection is a most shameful act, an act that merits a corresponding token of humiliation?" He turned to the crowd and spread his arms.

"Yes!" cried the throng. "Yes! Humiliate them."

"Surely," Friar Peter said, "the good bishop would not object to having the rabbi and the lay leader of the Jews of Brindisi paraded through the streets on their hands and knees, being made to kiss and lick the ground, and grunt like pigs, in token of their humiliation."

"Yes!" the people shouted, as the bishop shuffled off the podium. Friar Peter stood and scanned his audience, a broad smile on his face.

The three Romans pressed outwards from the throng. "I think we've heard enough," one of them said. "Guido, return to Rome immediately, and tell Ursus, while the two of us stay here in Brindisi to keep an eye on Friar Peter."

* * *

As these events were unfolding in Brindisi, about three hundred miles to the southwest a man dressed in chainmail with a long sword hanging at his side arrived in Messina and sought out the English camp. On entering the camp, however, he found it mostly empty. "Where is everybody?" he asked. "Where is King Richard's army?"

"They left five days ago," an old man said. "They've taken ship to the Holy Land."

The man in chainmail looked around. Of the remaining people in the camp, many were old or partially disabled men, and some were women, but there were also many younger men who appeared fit, and some were armed with swords.

"What are these men?" he asked, waving his left arm in an arc.

"Oh, these? There weren't enough ships for everyone. To boot, some needed to train a bit more. And some were ill when the ships embarked. Ne'er fear, though. They'll get their chance. Another ship or two will be leaving fer the Holy Land in about two weeks' time."

The old man looked the man in chainmail up and down. "Ye seem fit enough, though. Are ye fixin' to go with 'em?"

"Yes. Indeed I am, and I would be sorely disappointed if I arrived too late."

"Good. Then make yerself to home. Ye are from England, I take it?"

"Yes, from Camryn in Nottinghamshire. Name's Alfred. Alfred the blacksmith."

"And my name's Cedric, from Dover. Pleased te meet ye, Alfred. It's good te see a man like you, a blacksmith I mean, wanting te join the fight 'gainst the Saracen infidel. It'll help yer soul up in heaven, it will. Atone fer any sins ye have."

Alfred shook his head. "No, I'm not here for that, really, although I suppose 'twon't hurt to have some atonement."

"Then why'd ye want te leave yer home and journey all this way?"

Alfred paused a beat. He lowered his voice. "My son left me, and there's not much left to stay at home for."

The old man said nothing but just looked at Alfred and tilted his head.

Alfred cleared his throat. "Well, it's hard to explain really. My Matthew, he's a good boy, but he fell in with the wrong sort of friend." He looked down and cleared his throat again. "Y'see, he was friendly with this Jewish boy, and round about last Easter some Jews were killed in Camryn, and the rest o' them ran away. Matthew's friend was one of those who ran away. Next thing I know, Matthew was acting grumpy, wouldn't talk to me or my friends. And then he's gone. Just like that."

The old man said nothing but continued looking Alfred in the eye. Alfred met his gaze. "I mulled it over for a few weeks. I suppose I was hoping that Matthew would return, but he never did. I sold my place and bought myself some chainmail and a sword. So here I am."

The old man smiled, clapped Alfred on the shoulder, and led him into the mess hall. "Ye've come te the right place, Alfred. Make yerself at home."

* * *

A determined rider normally could have made the trip from Brindisi to Rome in three days on horseback, but the weather was bad, and thus it was four days later, on Friday the 19th of April, that Guido arrived in Rome. He immediately made his way to Ursus's home and reported on Friar Peter's activities in Brindisi. An hour later, Ursus, with Guido in tow, arrived at the papal offices. At first the chamberlain balked at letting Ursus interrupt the Holy Father's schedule, but finally he relented and allowed Ursus and Guido to enter.

Ursus genuflected, while Guido bowed low and kissed the Holy Father's ring.

Pope Celestine III sat down at his desk. He looked at Ursus. "You look troubled, my brother," he said.

"Yes, Giacinto. It is as bad as you thought. There was almost a massacre in Brindisi, and bloodshed was only prevented by the decisive action of the archbishop. I dread to think what would have happened otherwise. Guido here was witness to the friar's speech. I brought him with me so you can hear it directly from his mouth."

Guido recounted the details of Friar Peter's speech at Brindisi, and the subsequent interruption by the archbishop. Pope Celestine III sat at his desk and listened attentively, twice interrupting to ask a question. When Guido finished his tale, the pope rose from his seat and paced the floor. Ursus followed his brother with his eyes, trying to plumb his brother's thoughts and emotions. He saw the pathos in his brother's eyes; he saw the grave concern etched into his brother's visage; he saw a twinge of fear flit momentarily across his brother's lips.

In a subdued voice, as though to himself, the pope began to speak: "In Bari several weeks ago, Friar Peter's machinations were obstructed by the intervention of Commander Silvio. And now Friar Peter is in Brindisi, awaiting transport to the Holy Land. The friar is following the course predicted in my dream, and I can no longer doubt that the dream was sent to me through divine providence. It is true: the Great Deceiver, Satan, is working through the agency of this false friar."

The pope stopped his pacing and looked directly into Guido's eyes. "You must understand: it is not just the Jews whom Friar Peter threatens, but the underlying values upon which the Church itself is built. He seeks to contaminate us with hatred, malice, and wanton murder. Despite his apparent piety, despite his reputation, he is not a pious man at all. He is a demagogue who sways the hearts and minds of men, accruing followers everywhere he goes, a mighty army that he will use for his own purposes when the time is opportune. He must be stopped now, while there still is time.

"Guido, you must return to Brindisi immediately. By our order, you will arrest Friar Peter and bring him here. Ursus will provide as many armed men as you may need. Within the hour, we will provide you with four copies of a warrant for the friar's arrest. If, when you arrive in Brindisi, you learn that Friar Peter has already embarked for the Holy Land, you will dispatch one emissary to Joscius, Archbishop of Tyre, and a second emissary to King Conrad, ruler of Tyre, demanding Friar Peter's arrest and his immediate transport back to Rome. As insurance, you will dispatch two pairs of such emissaries on two separate ships, one ship from Brindisi and the other from Bari. Now hurry. And may the Lord be with you."

CHAPTER 32

May 1191

F riar Peter, flanked by his men-at-arms, stood on deck and watched as the ship approached the port. The sea was calm today, and the sun's rays shimmered on the waves. The fortress of Tyre loomed before him, and Peter squinted in the bright sunlight, trying in vain to see the soldiers who, he knew, must patrol the battlements.

Peter wiped his brow and said, "A welcome sight it is indeed, after these many weeks at sea."

"Yes," said one of his men. "But have we come in time, or have the fugitives escaped and are now far beyond our reach?"

"You worry too much, Martin," said Friar Peter. "Have faith. The good Lord will provide for our success. If the fugitives have been here and have left already, I have no doubt we will catch them yet."

Friar Peter reflected on the possibilities. He had boarded the ship at Brindisi four days after Easter, bound for Tyre. Tyre was about ninety miles too far north: he would have preferred a ship bound for a port closer to Jerusalem, since it seemed likely that Jerusalem was Joseph's ultimate destination. But it was now four years that the Saracen infidels held the ports of Acre, Jaffa, and Ascalon, as well as the city of Jerusalem itself. The Latin Kingdom of Jerusalem, therefore, was now a government in exile, based in Tyre, and Tyre was currently the closest available port to the Holy City. As things turned out, the sea was stormy, and the voyage had taken much longer than anticipated. Despite Friar Peter's confident tone when talking to his men, pangs of doubt gnawed at Peter. He wanted to have faith that the Lord of Darkness would see him through to victory. And yet, ...

He hoped that Joseph's ship had also been delayed by storms and that Joseph was therefore not far ahead of him. Perhaps, Peter speculated, Joseph's Templar friend even took him to Tyre; perhaps Joseph was still in Tyre, and they would soon meet. *Yes, Friar Peter thought, maybe he is here indeed.* And yet, that would be too fortuitous to expect. More likely, the Templar commander would have taken Joseph to the Templar stronghold of Tortosa, about fifty miles still farther north along the coast from Tyre – fifty miles still farther from Jerusalem.

The ship was now much closer to land, and Friar Peter could see men bustling about the pier. His eyes scanned the port, looking for any signs of trouble, looking for Templar knights; but he saw none.

His thoughts drifted to the Templar commander who had confronted him in Bari. Once again, he thought of the vexing question that had troubled him ever since that confrontation: why had a Templar commander been so intent on protecting the Jewish fugitives, and indeed all the Jews of Bari? To Peter's knowledge, the Templars were no more favorable to the Jews than were the majority of Christians. Was there, then, some mission unique to this particular commander, or did Commander Silvio's actions reflect a general Templar hostility to Friar Peter? Peter saw no reason to believe the latter possibility, but he could not be certain; and in any event, he always had mistrusted the Knights of Solomon's Temple. He therefore thought it best to keep his distance from the Templars.

When the ship had pulled into port, a crier stood at the pier and announced: "All ye who have arrived on this blessed day, in the name of King Conrad we welcome you to Tyre, seat of the Latin

Kingdom of Jerusalem. Know ye that the Kingdom is at war with the Saracen, and therefore as you disembark, by order of Conrad of Montferrat, ruler of Tyre and King of Jerusalem, you will state your business here. You will then submit to whatever questions the officer will ask of you. Only then will you be permitted entry into this fair city and to the protection of the fortress of Tyre."

The gangplank was lowered, and Friar Peter went ashore with a servant and his five men-at-arms. Peter walked the length of the pier and came to a halt before a man who stood immobile, holding a flag emblazoned with a large golden-yellow cross and four smaller golden crosses on a silver background – the flag of the Latin Kingdom of Jerusalem. An officer clad in chainmail stood beside the man bearing the flag. In his left hand, the officer held a staff of office; his right hand rested on the sword at his left hip.

"State your name, your place of origin, and your business!" said the officer.

"My name is Friar Peter. I hail from England, and I am here on urgent church business. I carry the blessings of the Holy Church and the word of our Lord, to stir the souls of the living and bring solace to the dead. I have also brought with me these men-at-arms in pursuit of a band of Jewish fugitives who have committed murder, sacrilege, and desecration of the dead."

"I see," said the officer. His tone of voice was skeptical, and his body language challenging. "And by whose authority do you pursue these matters?" he asked.

Friar Peter was put off by this officer's attitude and tone of voice. To Peter's dismay, the man was not at all in awe of Friar Peter and seemed never even to have heard of Peter the Pious before today. But Peter suppressed his outrage and answered as calmly as he could:

"My authority comes from the prior of the Newstead Priory in Nottinghamshire, and from the Sheriff of Nottingham, who eagerly awaits the capture of said band of murderers."

"Do you have a writ attesting to this authority?"

"Alas," said Peter. "We were attacked by brigands along the way, and I no longer have the writ." Of course, no such writ had ever existed, but Peter was confident the officer would not detect that he was lying.

"I see," said the officer again in a non-committal tone. He signaled a page to approach. The page hurried over, and the officer whispered something in the page's ear.

"Wait here!" the officer commanded Friar Peter, pointing to a spot off to his side, as the page scurried off towards a tower about two hundred paces distant. The officer turned his attention to the next man on line, while two men with spears barred the friar's way.

Friar Peter waited while the officer interrogated five more passengers before the page returned and whispered in the officer's ear. The page pointed to something in the distance and continued whispering. The officer nodded and sent the page away. He turned to Peter and said:

"Look beyond yon tower. You will see a priest coming toward us. When the priest arrives, you will go with him. Archbishop Joscius will receive you at his residence."

The archbishop, a middle-aged man of ruddy complexion and smiling countenance, was standing in his expansive sitting room perusing a document when Friar Peter entered. The archbishop looked up, spread his arms, and said:

"Welcome, Brother Peter. Welcome to the fair city of Tyre. I trust your voyage was uneventful."

"Your Grace, it is my privilege to stand before you. We had some rough seas, but by the grace of God, we have arrived."

"Come," said Archbishop Joscius as he led Friar Peter into an adjoining room adorned with brightly-colored tapestries along the walls, depicting knights in armor doing battle against the turbaned, scimitar-wielding Saracens. A long table stood in the center of the room. An ornately-decorated armchair stood at either end of the table, and nine chairs stood along each side. The archbishop put his hand on Friar Peter's shoulder and said, "I see you looking back toward where you left your men-at-arms. Do not fear for them. They will be well treated. Meanwhile, we will dine together, you and I, and you will tell me all the news from Rome."

The archbishop seated himself at the head of the table and motioned to Friar Peter to sit at the corner to his right. Three servants bustled over to them, bearing food and drink. The archbishop said a blessing and commenced to eat. He looked at Peter and said, "Now tell me, Friar Peter: how fares our newly-consecrated Holy Father? I understand he is a very old man."

"Yes. Indeed he is old – perhaps the oldest of the cardinals. May the Good Lord preserve his life for many years."

"Amen," said Archbishop Joscius. "But tell me, Friar Peter – for I really wish to hear your assessment – what changes, if any, do you think our new Holy Father will bring about?"

"I am afraid, Your Grace, I am not privy to the Holy Father's intentions."

"I see," said the archbishop, taking a draught of ale.

The next several minutes were spent in silence. The archbishop ate his meal, only occasionally glancing at Friar Peter. Peter also ate in silence, trying to mask his anxiety at the disquieting opening to their conversation. Why would Archbishop Joscius ask Peter for his assessment of the new pope's plans? And, moreover, what did the archbishop mean with his final pronouncement of "I see"? That was just how the officer on the pier had responded to Friar Peter.

The servants cleared the table, and three other servants entered, bearing trenchers filled with various pastries and more ale. When the servants left the room, the archbishop said:

"Now tell me of your preaching, Friar Peter. What is the substance of your message? To what holy purpose do you exhort your audience?"

"Your Grace, I preach about the influence of Satan and his minions in our midst. I preach of Good and Evil in the hearts of men. I exhort my listeners to extirpate the influence of Satan in the world, to expunge the forces of Evil that dwell among us, and thus to purify themselves and all of Christendom."

The archbishop smiled. "That is very noble of you, Friar Peter. And it gladdens my heart greatly to hear your words. Ridding the world of Satan's influence is certainly a holy mission, and I admire the fervor with which you speak of it. But, my good friar, I would that you be more specific: What, pray tell me, are those forces of Evil that you would have your listeners expunge? How will common folk identify Satan's minions, and how will they defeat them? Surely you do not expect your audience to know these matters on their own."

Friar Peter felt a favorable change in the archbishop's tone of voice, and he thought he sensed warmth in the archbishop's words. He began to relax a bit.

"Indeed, Your Grace, I do not expect my audience to divine my meaning or to recognize Satan's agents without my help. I help them to remove the veil before their eyes, to take away the curtain that obscures their vision. I have them look about them with open eyes, and thus notice things they have never seen before. Evil cannot hide forever from those who know to see the mark of Satan. I have my audience look upon their neighbors, recognizing signs of treachery, perfidy, blasphemy, and even sorcery."

The archbishop smiled and said, "I see, Friar Peter. You act as guide and sacred teacher to the masses."

"Thank you, Your Grace. You are very kind to say so."

"But now I would also know: what would you have the people do once they have identified these agents of the Evil One? What action should they take?"

"Why, they are to bring these agents of the Evil One to justice. They are to drive Satan's minions from their homes and expel them from our midst."

"But," said the archbishop, "I imagine it is not so simple as you make it sound. Surely these agents do not wish to leave their homes. Surely, Satan's agents are not defenseless. Surely, if the Evil One has sent them, they have certain powers to resist? How, then, should good Christians deal with that?"

Friar Peter looked at the tapestries on the wall. "Just as our valiant knights do in the Holy Land, Your Grace. When necessary, we fight the infidel by the sword. So, too, will we fight the armies of Satan in our midst: by the sword, Your Grace. By the sword."

"Indeed, indeed. But in the Holy Land, the enemy is easy to identify. The Saracens oppose us openly. Their garb is different, and their speech is different. They ride against our knights with sword and scimitar, and they even murder unarmed Christian pilgrims by the sword. Their dress, their speech, their actions all proclaim their nature. And if one were to capture a Saracen warrior, he would readily admit that he is a follower of his lord Mohammed, nor would he hide his hatred of the Christians. But the enemy of which you speak is different, is it not? What signs do you give your audience whereby they may recognize Satan's agents in their very midst?"

Friar Peter smiled and said, "They will know those enemies, Your Grace, in the same way that they know the Saracens. Their dress is different, and their speech as well. And, just like the Saracens, they blaspheme and heap scorn upon all that we hold sacred. The Saracens assault us from without, but the Jews have infiltrated our very towns and villages, and they assault us from within. If the Saracens are dangerous to Christendom, the Jews are ten times more so. Therefore they must also be defeated by the sword."

Archbishop Joscius eyed Friar Peter, and a chill ran up the friar's spine. No longer did he feel warmth in the archbishop's voice, and no longer was there a smile upon his lips. Suddenly, Friar Peter felt, the atmosphere had changed.

"Does the Holy Father approve of all that you have said?"

Almost in a whisper, Friar Peter answered: "As I told Your Grace before, I do not know the Holy Father's thoughts. Nor have I spoken with him directly. I expect, though, that he would be in full agreement."

"And what has given you that impression?"

"Ancient precedent, Your Grace. My words are not unique to me. I have not invented these ideas from the machinations of my mind alone. No, Your Grace. My words bear the holy imprint of the Church and the authority of long tradition, based as they are upon the sermons of Saint John Chrysostom."

"Be that as it may, Saint John Chrysostom lived eight centuries ago, and times have changed. As you well should know, the Church follows the teachings of St. Augustine of Hippo in this matter, and words inciting violence against the Jews do not have the approval of His Holiness."

Friar Peter made to reply, but the archbishop held up his hand, and Peter fell silent. Friar Peter's apprehension grew, but he kept his gaze fixed on the archbishop, intent to listen to every nuance of the archbishop's voice, to note each jot and tittle of his body language. The world and time itself seemed to stand still, suspended as it were, as Friar Peter waited to learn what Archbishop Joscius had in mind to do.

The archbishop drew a scroll out of his robes and said:

"It is with heavy heart that I must show you this missive. The scroll that I hold here in my hand arrived but a few days ago. It is addressed to King Conrad and to me. Its substance is clear, and our duties unequivocal, but I wanted to hear the words from your own mouth before I acted. Now hear me, Friar Peter."

He unfurled the scroll and held it up for Peter to see. "Friar Peter, commonly known as Peter the Pious. I have here a warrant for your arrest. By order of the Holy Father, Pope Celestine III, dated 15th April in the year of our Lord 1191, and by the authority of myself – Joscius, Archbishop of Tyre – and of

King Conrad, ruler of the Latin Kingdom of Jerusalem, I hereby declare you under arrest. Yield to our authority, and you will be sent back to Rome on the next ship out."

Peter felt a heavy hand placed on each shoulder. He looked around and saw a man in chainmail on either side of him, and two more men with drawn swords on either side of Archbishop Joscius.

Peter's initial impulse was not to yield and to use his powers against his assailants, but he quickly thought better of it. This was no time for a showdown with the authorities. If Joseph was indeed in the fortress, he might be alerted and soon escape. And, even if Joseph was not in Tyre, no purpose would be served by having a confrontation now. Later on, there would be opportunity enough for Friar Peter to escape.

Peter's cell was high up in one of the towers of the fortress. He estimated that the cell was approximately midway up the tower, but it was hard to tell for sure. There was a small porthole several feet above his head, which provided a small measure of ventilation, and through which some light penetrated into the darkness of the cell. The cell was square, approximately four paces on each side, with no furniture of any kind. In one corner, there was a pit in the floor, for excrement. This was to be his home until he could be extradited to Rome. Not a very pleasant home, but probably tolerable for the time he would have to spend here.

Friar Peter sat on the floor in the center of the cell and looked up at the porthole. Iron bars crisscrossed the opening, and Peter focused on the cross formed by the bars. He vacated his mind and began to sing in an undertone. He breathed slowly, in and out, in and out, his mind drifting with the melody of his song. Slowly, all his muscles relaxed. His vision blurred, and soon his eyelids drooped. He imagined himself descending a long flight of stairs, and he began to count his footsteps. With each step in his descent, he willed himself to become more relaxed, more detached from the here and now. Colored lights danced before his shuttered eyes. Lightning flashed, thunder roared, and a dark curtain shimmered in an eerie light that bathed it from below. Vaguely, he knew he still was sitting on the floor of his cell, and yet he felt his body moving, advancing slowly towards the shimmering curtain in his mind's eye, borne on wings of air, flying far away, no longer held within the confines of his prison cell. He had entered the spiritual world.

*   *   *

Joseph, Aaron, and Rachel disembarked with Commander Silvio at Tyre after a five-week voyage out of Bari. The storm at sea was now long behind them, but they were glad to be back on dry land again.

Ever since the Saracens' sweep through the Holy Land beginning four years ago, the Latin Kingdom of Jerusalem had been forced to relocate fifty miles north, to Tyre. But the Saracens controlled the surrounding territory, to the south and north and east. To the south of the Templar stronghold of Tortosa fifty miles north of Tyre, only the city of Tyre remained in Christian hands: a Christian island in a sea of Saracens. Even the city of Acre 24 miles south of Tyre, for many years the principal port of the Latin Kingdom of Jerusalem, was now in Saracen hands since four years ago. However, things were soon about to change.

The Frankish King Philip Augustus had just recently arrived in the Holy Land and joined the Frankish army besieging Acre. King Richard's army was on its way and due to arrive very soon; and the Templars, in anticipation were sending reinforcements to join King Richard's army. A contingent of Templar knights was currently in Tyre, preparing to sail south to Acre to join the siege, and a spirit of optimism was palpable in Tyre in anticipation that the port of Acre would soon be in Christian hands again.

On entering the fortress of Tyre, Commander Silvio brought them to the Templar compound, where they found themselves in a large courtyard. Silvio led them to the far end of the courtyard, where a small number of Templar knights – some in chainmail, some in white mantles emblazoned with large red crosses on their chests – scurried to and fro. There were also other armed men nearby, dressed in black tunics and black or brown mantles, and various unarmed men as well – some carrying loads on their backs, others leading horses to the stables. Silvio led Joseph, Aaron, and Rachel to a door adjoining the courtyard and delivered them into the care of another Templar knight named Bertrand, while Silvio himself hurried to report to his superiors the results of his secret mission to the pope. Bertrand showed Joseph and Aaron to their room, which they were to share, and Rachel to a separate room nearby.

Joseph and Aaron's room was sparsely furnished, with a double-decker bed and a small bedside table upon which there was a wash-basin. Another small table was in the center of the room, with a candle placed in the center of the table, and a single chair. There were no decorations.

"I hope your quarters are satisfactory," said Bertrand. "We Templars are a military order, as you know, and here at Tyre we are on the front lines. So you will understand and excuse the sparse conditions. But if there is anything you need, please let me know. I am at your service. Any friend of Silvio's is a friend of mine."

"Thank you," said Joseph. "You are very kind."

When Bertrand had left, Joseph whispered to Aaron, "I wonder how kind he would have been had he known that we are Jews."

Aaron smiled. "Not very, I surmise. And that goes for the majority of these Templars. It was prudent of Silvio to advise us to keep that a secret."

"Yes. I just wonder what makes Silvio so different, and so eager to do all in his power to give us aid. And can we really trust him?"

Aaron put his hand on Joseph's shoulder. "Do not fear," he said. "I feel the strength of his character and the kindness of his soul. I think, however, that he bears some secret within his bosom. You have felt that also, and that is what gives you pause. But I have faith in him. He is among the righteous of the gentiles. I feel it in my heart. He will not betray us."

There was a knock at the door, and Rachel entered. Excitement was evident in her face, and Joseph asked, "What is it, Rachel?"

Rachel smiled at Joseph and said, "We are very close now. I can feel it. It won't be long before we find the breastplate."

Aaron looked at Rachel and said, "Yes, I feel it also. We are getting closer. Much closer. Jerusalem is no longer across the sea; it's just a hundred miles away, and Joseph seems more confident than he has been for many days. Perhaps you've thought of something, Joseph. Perhaps you have discovered some new evidence to help us find the breastplate?"

Joseph looked at Aaron and smiled broadly. "Yes, I think I have. Actually, I found the evidence weeks ago, on board ship, in my one and only encounter with the spiritual world. When we set out to sea from Bari, we thought Jerusalem to be the most likely place wherein the breastplate lies. But that was just a theory, a theory about which I continued having many doubts.

"When I entered the world of spirit, I saw Jerusalem in my vision. But that same vision was also filled with many terrifying images, and those images distracted my attention, preventing me from realizing the full import of what I had seen there, in that world. After I reflected on my vision over many days, gradually, slowly, I became convinced that Rabbi Tuviah's hunch was right: Jerusalem is our destination, for that is where the breastplate lies. Now I am sure of it. It is no longer just a likely supposition. It is our destiny."

Aaron closed his eyes and covered them with his hand. After a few moments, he dropped his hand to his side, he opened his eyes and looked at Joseph. "That is very reassuring. But we need a more exact location. We need more information, and Rabbi Tuviah gave you the tools to find out more. I know that you have only entered the spiritual world that one time when we feared for our lives at sea. And I know that, despite your multiple attempts, you have not been able to enter that world again. But Joseph, you will need to enter the spiritual world once more, for only there will you be able to find the answer. I know that you can do it. Think again about what Rabbi Tuviah taught you. You will find a way."

Joseph sat down. For a long time, nobody spoke, while Joseph sat in thought. Finally, Joseph looked up at Aaron and said, "It's no use, Aaron, I can't think of anything. But knowing the exact location is only part of our problem. The Saracens hold Jerusalem, and their army controls all the roads that lead to it for miles around. If the breastplate is indeed there, how will we approach Jerusalem unseen?"

Aaron put his hand on Joseph's shoulder. "Have faith," he said. "We will find it. Rabbi Tuviah told us you will find your answers in the spiritual world, and I am confident you will discover not only the location of the breastplate but also how to reach it despite the Saracens."

Joseph stood up and paced the floor. "But how will I enter that world? I did it once, but I am at a loss to do so again, and time is running out."

Suddenly Rachel's face brightened, and she said, "A thought just occurred to me. I think I know how."

Joseph and Aaron turned to look at Rachel. "How?" they asked in unison.

"I have thought about it a long time – ever since our meeting with Rabbi Tuviah that first day we were in Bari. But it wasn't until now that I finally figured it out, and now it seems so obvious to me. Rabbi Tuviah spoke of the great power of the emerald and how its power grows in proximity to Jerusalem. Later, you met with Rabbi Tuviah again, and he taught you how to enter a trance-like state through repetition of a Biblical verse or while gazing into the aura of a flame. Inducing a trance-like state, however, was only a beginning, a training method to develop your abilities and prepare you for the final leap into the spiritual world."

"But I couldn't make that leap."

"I know. And yet, you did succeed that one time. You can do it again. We are now much closer to Jerusalem, and the power of the stone should be greatly magnified here. Use the emerald as you would have used a flame. Gaze into the emerald, and use its power to enter the spiritual world. I know you can."

Joseph shook his head. "I'm not so sure. Didn't Rabbi Tuviah also say the true emerald of the high priest's breastplate would have the name of a tribe inscribed on it? This stone has no inscription, and Tuviah therefore doubted it was the authentic stone. Initially, I dismissed Rabbi Tuviah's words; I was so convinced my stone must be authentic. But now, after thinking about it further, I'm not so certain. Rabbi Tuviah is a learned man and has spent many years studying this very matter. Why should I be so quick to dismiss his doubts?"

Rachel said, "Yes, he did have his doubts at first. But later he conceded that the stone may be authentic after all."

Joseph said, "Perhaps Rabbi Tuviah only said that to make us feel good, and I did, after all, say some things to make him reconsider his first conclusion that the stone was not authentic. Nevertheless, deep down I think Rabbi Tuviah stayed with his initial impression."

Rachel glared at Joseph. "But you are not Rabbi Tuviah. How can you have any doubt? That stone has been passed down in your family for many generations. And you, unlike Rabbi Tuviah, have seen the stone's unique qualities with your own eyes. Didn't Enoch show us its power shortly after our escape from Camryn? Do you doubt Enoch? I do not."

"You are right," Joseph conceded. "We can't doubt Enoch. I am sorry that I doubted, even for a moment; but the road ahead seems so uncertain, and sometimes doubts gnaw at my soul."

Rachel smiled. "Of course the road is difficult, and it is a natural response to doubt yourself. But that is why you have me, to set you right again."

"How can you be so sure that the emerald is the tool that I can use to enter the spiritual world?"

"I just know it deep inside me. The same way Aaron knew that Father John was kind; the same way Aaron knows that Silvio is a righteous man who can be trusted. I don't know how I know. But I have no doubt about it." She looked into Joseph's eyes. "You will just have to trust me."

Joseph smiled. "I do."

"Good," she said, and, taking Aaron's hand, she led her brother to the door. "We will leave you now to meditate. Remember: gaze into the emerald as you would into a flame when you induce a trance-like state."

When they had left the room, Joseph extracted the emerald from its purse and held it in his hand. A long candle burned in the center of the table. Joseph sat down and placed the emerald on the table, near the burning candle. He looked into the flickering flame and whispered a brief prayer. Then he moved the candle farther away and fixed his gaze upon the green stone in front of him.

He watched the reflection of the flame dancing in the facets of the emerald, focusing his attention on the reflections in the stone, blocking all else from his consciousness. He imagined himself plunging into the depths of the emerald's essence, immersed in its radiance, at one with its power. His breathing slowed, his muscles relaxed, and in a monotone he began to recite in Hebrew: "Blessed be the name of His glorious kingdom for ever and ever."

Again and again he repeated the verse, while concentrating on the purity of the emerald's hue. With each repetition, his muscles relaxed, and his consciousness drifted on a sea of colored lights, first green, then blue, and red. The colors whirled before his eyes, seeming to form a vortex within the stone. His eyelids became heavy. He could no longer keep them open. Slowly his eyes drooped shut, and yet he still saw the vortex of colors whirling before him, still more vivid than before.

He felt himself hurtling through the vortex, caught up in the maelstrom of color and light. Somehow, he knew his body still was sitting in the room, and yet he felt himself propelled through space and time, beyond the colored lights, into another realm. A wall of water appeared before him, shimmering, reflecting the light of a thousand stars. And yet there were no stars. The waters parted, revealing a dark cloud that billowed before him, expanding and contracting as though alive and breathing. Lightning flashed before his vision, and thunder echoed in his mind.

Within the cloud, a flame took shape, growing and swirling in the midst of the cloud. Slowly the cloud dissolved, consumed by the whirling fire. Joseph heard the roaring of the flames, he felt the heat surround him, and yet he felt no fear at all; only a sense of calm tranquility.

Soon the flames dissolved, and in their place, a curtain of luminous air shimmered before him. He drifted onwards into the curtain, and the curtain parted, revealing a mountainous, desolate terrain that shimmered in the misty morning light, stretching out for many miles. And Joseph was floating in the air, high above the desert floor.

Presently he felt his feet touch ground. He looked down. He was on a rocky mountainside, overlooking the desert to the east, toward the rising sun. He scanned the desert to the east and to the south, looking for familiar landmarks, but there were none.

He scanned the mountainside on which he stood, and in the distance a large gray, irregularly-shaped boulder caught his eye. He walked a short distance towards the boulder, negotiating the rocky terrain. Suddenly he stopped. He felt someone watching him. He looked around in all directions, but he saw nobody there. A strong wind gusted, nearly blowing him off his feet, but he pushed onward to the boulder, drawn forward by a mysterious force.

For several minutes he continued walking, glancing behind him now and then, his anxiety increasing with every step. He turned. A shadow caught his eye, moving quickly towards him. He ducked, and a rock hurtled past his head, barely missing. He tried to see where the rock had come from, but he was looking eastward, into the sun.

Again he sensed danger, and again he ducked. Another rock sped by his head. He dropped to the ground and rolled. Two more rocks struck the ground not far away from him, but he remained unharmed.

Again he saw a shadow, but this time it was the shadow of a man, dressed in a flowing black robe that billowed in the wind. The man's head was covered with a hood, but a sudden gust of wind blew the hood away, and Joseph saw the face illuminated in the morning sunlight. It was Friar Peter.

"You cannot have it. It is mine." Friar Peter's voice thundered, echoing through the mountainside. "It is mine to take, mine to have, mine to rule the world!"

Joseph stood up slowly, keeping his eyes on Friar Peter. "I don't know what you are talking about," he said.

"Do not toy with me!" Friar Peter bellowed. "You know my meaning very well. But you do not know where it is. I see it written on your face. No matter. When you are dead, I will find it. It is here, on this mountain somewhere."

He saw Friar Peter crouch and pick up another rock. He began to run.

Friar Peter's voice again echoed through the mountainside: "Where are you in the world below? You cannot escape me now. Perhaps here, in the world of spirit, you can run away, but in the real world down below, I will find you. I will track you down."

Friar Peter hurled the rock. It whistled through the air, aimed squarely at the middle of Joseph's back. Joseph dropped to the ground again, falling to his right. But his evasive action succeeded only partially. He felt a sudden searing pain in his left shoulder, as the rock grazed his skin. He screamed. Peter shouted out in triumph and picked up another rock. Joseph screamed again, and yet again.

The light dimmed. Dark, ominous clouds gathered overhead. The mountain dissolved from Joseph's vision, and a curtain covered the sky. Joseph screamed again. He opened his eyes. He shook his head and looked around. He was in his room in Tyre, a burning candle flickering before him, and the emerald sitting on the table where he had placed it earlier.

The door burst open, and Rachel ran in. "What happened, Joseph? You were screaming. Are you hurt?"

Joseph shook his head. He opened his mouth, but no words came out.

Rachel ran to him and put her arms around him. "What happened, Joseph? What did you see in the spiritual world?"

Again he tried to speak. He was breathing rapidly. In a croaking, shaking voice, he said, "I was on a mountain, near the desert, but I don't know where exactly. Friar Peter saw me. And he may have followed me. I'm not sure, but he may have just discovered where we are, here in Tyre."

Rachel held him tightly. Joseph winced.

"What is it, Joseph? Are you hurt?"

"My shoulder," Joseph said. He pushed away from Rachel and stripped off his tunic. And there, where the rock had hit him, was a large welt.

CHAPTER 33

Acre, The Holy Land
June 1191

Baha' al-Din Qaragush sat nervously on his ornate throne. It was now four months since Saladin had appointed him Governor of Acre, replacing the previous governor, whom Saladin had removed for incompetence. In these four months, Qaragush had strengthened the city's walls, fortified its towers, and deepened the dry moat surrounding the city. And yet, the situation in Acre had gone from bad to worse. The Christian army, undeterred after two long years of siege, was still camped outside the city walls, their catapults hurling great boulders into the heart of Acre both day and night; the city's food supplies were dwindling; and morale among the Muslim soldiers was at an all-time low.

Of course, the military stalemate was not his fault, but how was he to hold the city against a massive Christian assault? Just last night, his scouts informed him of an English fleet that was sailing southwards along the coast, twenty-five ships strong, under the command of the English king, may Allah grind his bones to dust. While King Richard, Qaragush thought, was not the royal equal of the Frankish king Philip, the Lionheart nevertheless was richer and commanded a greater force than did the Franks. Still, Acre's fortifications were strong, and resistance had not seemed futile until now, until this latest piece of news!

Governor Qaragush was dressed in a long white flowing robe, and on his head he wore an ornate white turban. His fingers were bedecked with golden, jeweled rings. He sat up straight on his throne. He knew he must give the appearance of authority, the appearance that all was under control, although he also knew that was far from the truth. He looked around the audience hall and saw the city officials and military commanders gathered before him, waiting with bated breath for confirmation of the terrible news, of which they had heard only disjointed rumors.

An emir entered the audience chamber and stood before the governor. The emir wore a golden-yellow, tight-fitting robe, and a long, curved sword hung at his left hip. He lowered his gaze slightly but did not bow, then looked up at the governor, his expression grave. "My lord," he said, "I bring you word of our supply ship."

The governor heard the emir's words as through a fog. He already knew that the great supply ship was presumed lost, with its seven hundred chosen warriors, its large supplies of food, of weapons, incendiary liquid, and two hundred deadly snakes to be released among the Christian camp. The trip from Tyre to Acre was short, and the seas were calm. The ship should have arrived in Acre yesterday. He braced himself for the emir's next words.

"The ship, indeed, is lost at sea, rammed and sunk by the English fleet. Our men fought bravely, but they were outnumbered. Only one man survived."

At the other end of the audience hall, the two great wooden doors swung open, and two soldiers entered, supporting a pale and haggard man dressed in a blood-stained robe, walking with great difficulty between the soldiers.

The haggard man approached the throne, waved the two soldiers away, and bowed his head. "Your excellency," he said, "I am Ahmed, a sailor on our supply ship out of Beirut. Just a few hours out of port, we spied a Christian fleet sailing toward us at great speed. Seeing we could not outrun them, we pretended to be a Frankish ship, but the Christians were not fooled. They attacked, and a great battled ensued."

The man paused, breathing hard. His body swayed, and he looked as though he was about to faint. The two soldiers caught him. A third soldier quickly brought a chair, and the man sat down.

"Take your time," said Qaragush, although in truth he was eager for the man to hurry up and tell his tale.

The man slumped over but stayed in his seat, breathing hard. At length, his breathing became more steady. He raised his head and looked at Qaragush. In a low, quavering voice, he continued:

"Our men fought bravely. Several times, the Christians tried to board us, but we beat them back, shooting flaming arrows and hurling poisonous snakes onto their ships. When the English king, may Allah curse his bones, saw that boarding us would fail, his ships retreated temporarily. His fleet formed a ring around us so we could not escape, but they stayed out of range. This continued for several minutes. Then the great ship of the English king began advancing, gathering speed as it approached. We saw it coming and knew what they intended, but their ship was too fast, and we were unable to evade it. They rammed us below the water line and sank our ship. They took no prisoners except for me, but killed our men as they tried to swim away. Only I survived. They let me live, to tell my tale."

The man again was breathing heavily, and the blood stain between his legs was spreading. Qaragush looked at the spreading stain and said, "Ahmed, what have they done to you?"

Ahmed opened his mouth, apparently about to speak, but no words came out. Instead, he swooned and fell to the floor. The two soldiers lifted Ahmed, one by the shoulders and the other by the legs, and carried him out. A third soldier bowed to Qaragush and said, "Your excellency, he's been castrated. The Christian dogs who did this deed also put his severed genitals in a bag, and Ahmed brought them with him."

*   *   *

Matthew looked up at the sky. The moon was low on the horizon and soon would set. It was a waning crescent now, just a sliver of a moon, providing little light. He lifted the bundle of wood that lay on the ground before him, slung it over his shoulders, and entered the earthen tunnel. As he plodded through the tunnel, he thought back over the past two weeks since landing at Acre and joining the Christian forces besieging the city. The English fleet had landed uneventfully, unchallenged by the Muslim defending forces. The Frankish army was camped to the east, and King Richard chose to billet his army to the north of the city, in a vast, sprawling camp meant to intimidate the citizens of Acre.

King Richard had wanted to dig tunnels to undermine the city's walls, but his fleet had landed just past the full moon, and the night sky was not dark enough in the first few days following his arrival. Besides, Richard's first priority was to build two new trebuchets − catapults of a new, advanced design − that would hurl much larger boulders, and hurl them deeper into Acre, than even the mightiest of the seven Frankish catapults could do. Matthew had been put on the team assigned to build the two new trebuchets and to transport from the ships to the English camp the massive boulders they had brought with them from Sicily and Cyprus.

When the catapults and boulders were ready, Matthew had been re-deployed. In the last few days, English sappers dug tunnels under the city walls and extended them. On several occasions, the Muslim defenders attempted to interfere; but each time, they were beaten back, and thus the sappers continued their work relatively unimpeded. The far end of Matthew's tunnel was now beneath the north tower of Acre's wall − the Cursed Tower, as the English called it. The sappers were still widening the tunnel's end, and as the tunnel widened further, more wood would be required.

Matthew walked with his load almost to the end of the tunnel, a few paces from where several men were still digging. He dropped his load and unbound the logs. Carefully, he positioned the larger logs standing vertically to support the ceiling. The smaller logs he placed around the support beams at the far end of the tunnel. In a few days, the tunnel would be finished and fully packed with wood. Then the sappers would set the wooden beams afire, and, they hoped, the Cursed Tower would collapse under its own weight. Matthew finished placing his logs. He saluted the foreman, turned around, and started back to bring more wood.

It took longer than Matthew had expected for his team to finish the tunnel and pack it with wood. On several occasions, the city's defenders sallied forth and attacked the besieging Christian forces. Just two days ago, a section of Acre's northeast city wall had collapsed, and the Frankish army had attempted to scale the ruined wall, but Acre's defenders drove them back. Following the Frankish retreat from the city walls, the Muslim army that was camped to the south had then attempted a full-scale attack on the Christian camp, but the English archers and crossbowmen managed to repulse the Muslim force. It was now four weeks since King Richard's fleet had arrived at Acre, and finally the northern tunnel was ready to be set afire.

It was night, shortly before dawn. Matthew crept forward on his belly and approached the tunnel entrance. Silently, his accompanying archers spread out. Another man inched up to Matthew and handed him a torch. Matthew entered the tunnel, lit the torch, and advanced a short distance. He touched the flaming torch to the kindling wood on the tunnel floor and waited just long enough to see the kindling wood ignite. He threw the torch; he turned, and ran.

Deep in the tunnel, the fire raged, and Matthew felt the heat behind him. He exited the tunnel and looked back, but only momentarily. He turned away again and ran, his comrades with him. When he reached the outskirts of the English camp, he turned back and watched.

For a long time, Matthew watched the city walls expectantly, and nothing seemed to happen. But as the sun began to rise, he saw the walls of Acre swaying and the battlements begin to tremble. The swaying and the trembling increased gradually, until at length the walls of Acre groaned, and, with a resounding crash, the northern tower toppled to the ground, and a several-yard stretch of the adjoining wall collapsed upon itself.

A cheer rose up from the English camp, and thereupon the entire English army surged forward like a great wave at sea, rushing towards the breach in the city wall. Matthew seized a battle axe and ran, joining the surge.

Matthew heard a whistling sound overhead, and a commander shouted, "Down!"

Matthew dropped to the ground. Behind him, he heard a mighty crash, and men were screaming in agony. He knew it was a boulder flung from a catapult within the city. The cries of his dying and wounded comrades tore at his heart, but he did not look back. Quickly, he rose and again ran forward, together with the mass of men, driven forward by a battle frenzy.

He screamed a battle cry, in unison with a hundred other men. Together they swarmed over the scattered rubble that had been the city's wall, but the massive stones were still piled high, making their way difficult, and a cloud of arrows darkened the sky above them. The city's defenders cheered as their arrows felled dozens of the English infantry. Again a barrage of arrows filled the sky, and Matthew raised his shield above him, deflecting two arrows.

Again the English infantry surged forward, trying to mount the fallen wall. Matthew braced for another barrage of arrows, but none came. Instead, a wall of Muslim infantry advanced before them, their curved swords drawn, moving in unison as though they were a single living being. As one, they shouted something in the Saracen tongue, raising their swords above their heads, and running at the Christian soldiers.

Matthew clambered over a large rectangular stone and jumped to the ground. A great curved scimitar whistled through the air, and Matthew parried quickly with his shield. Matthew swung his battle axe, but his adversary was faster, thrusting at Matthew with his sword. Matthew dropped to the ground and rolled away. His enemy pursued him. Matthew tried to rise, but the Muslim warrior's boot connected with his ribs, and Matthew caught his breath, momentarily immobilized by pain.

He saw his adversary's sword swooping towards him. He raised his shield to block the sword thrust, and his enemy kicked Matthew's shield away. But the kick threw his enemy off balance momentarily. Matthew saw his opportunity and swung his battle axe, striking his adversary's legs. The axe sliced through muscle and bone, and the Saracen warrior fell to the ground with a blood-curdling scream. Matthew jumped to his feet and swung the axe again, cleaving his enemy's skull.

No sooner did Matthew catch his breath than he saw two turbaned warriors racing towards him, brandishing their scimitars and crying a shrill battle cry in the Saracen tongue. They spread out, one to his right and one to his left. Matthew decided that the man to his left, though closer to him, was somewhat slower. He shifted to his left and raised his shield to block the warrior's thrust. He spun around and swung his axe, striking the man in his mid-section.

The other man came at him rapidly, but Matthew was prepared. He parried with his shield and swung his battle axe. His adversary parried with his shield, and spun around, his sword raised for a cut to Matthew's neck. Again, Matthew parried with his own shield, but his reprieve was brief. His adversary lunged at him, nicking Matthew's left arm, drawing blood. Matthew stepped away, but his adversary was moving faster now, thrusting, parrying, and cutting, all the while advancing, pushing Matthew back.

Matthew clambered back over the large rectangular stone, almost falling, just barely warding off another blow from his adversary's sword. Bravely, he continued fighting, but he knew how this must end. The Saracen was gaining on him, weakening him for the final fatal thrust.

Suddenly, his adversary stopped. His eyes widened. He dropped his shield and scimitar. He grasped his throat, uttering a gurgling sound as he fell to the ground, an arrow through his neck.

Matthew turned. An English archer stood beyond the fallen wall. The archer waved to Matthew, signaling him to retreat. In the distance, Matthew heard a bugle from the English camp.

He turned the other way again, looking back at Acre. A band of Saracen warriors were coming towards him once more. He looked around and saw his comrades were retreating. A hail of English arrows whizzed overhead, and several of the Saracens fell. The bugle sounded once again, and Matthew ran, as fast as his legs would carry him, back to the English camp.

For the next two nights, rumors circulated in the English camp that Acre was about to surrender, but still the city hung on stubbornly. Despite undermining the city's walls, the Christian army had not been able to penetrate the breach. They had made three attempts to do so, but each time the Saracen defenders had driven them back. A large Saracen army was poised to the south of the Christian camps, and Christian scouts had to keep a close watch both on the city itself and on the Saracen army to the south. But none of the defending Muslim forces within the city had sallied forth to attack the English forces, nor had the sultan's army to the south attempted a frontal attack on the Christian camps, having been thwarted decisively in a previous attempt several days before. Both sides waited.

As little success as the Muslim army had in frontal attack, they did have a certain measure of success in raiding the Christian camps. As they had been doing even before the crumbling of Acre's walls, each night, Muslim warriors crept into the midst of the Christian forces – sometimes into the Frankish camp and sometimes the English – and carried off pots and pans, spears and shields, and often Christian soldiers whom they took as prisoners.

Not being able to enter the city, the Christian forces intensified their bombardment. The catapults worked day and night, hurling boulders and the carcasses of horses slain in battle; and Matthew was assigned to a team that manned a catapult. Finally, Matthew's shift was finished for the night, and he lay down for some badly-needed sleep.

Despite his weariness, Matthew slept fitfully, dreaming of battles past and future. Somewhat after midnight, he suddenly awoke, uneasy, his senses alert to danger. He looked around him. The man to his right was lying peacefully, his sword on the ground at his side. The man to his left also seemed quietly asleep. Matthew turned over, closed his eyes, and tried to fall asleep again.

He heard a muffled sound. He opened his eyes but saw nothing unusual. He propped himself up on his left elbow and reached for his sword with his right hand.

The sword was not there.

He sat up hurriedly and was about to shout a warning. But out of the darkness, he heard a voice behind him, whispered in his ear, and a fleshy hand clamped down on his open mouth.

"Do not move. Do not resist, or you will die," the heavily-accented voice behind him said.

A gag was placed in his mouth, his wrists and ankles were bound, and he felt himself lifted off the ground. His captors placed him in a sack, which one of his captors slung over his shoulder, carrying him away.

At first his captors went on foot, sometimes walking, sometimes running, and Matthew marveled at how long the man who carried him could go without the slightest bit of rest. After perhaps half an hour, Matthew was taken out of the sack, and, still bound hand and foot, he was placed in a cart along with two other

Christian captives. Now his captors broke their silence and spoke among themselves in Arabic. Matthew strained to hear, but he had learned only a few words of the Saracen language, and he was unable to understand anything of substance. The conversation was brief, and soon his Muslim captors once again fell silent.

The cart rolled onwards, swaying as it went, rocking Matthew gently, until at last he fell asleep. When he awoke, the first glimmer of light had appeared in the eastern sky, and he found himself in the midst of the Muslim camp.

PART V

CHAPTER 34

12ᵗʰ July 1191
Saladin's camp, south of Acre

The emir entered the tent briskly and came to a halt in front of the turbaned man seated at the far end of the large tent. The emir did not bow, but he lowered his head slightly, passing his right hand quickly over his forehead, his lips, and his heart.

"Your Majesty," he said. "A pigeon has arrived from Acre. I bring you the message that the pigeon carried."

His Majesty, Sultan Salah ad-Din Yusuf ibn Ayyub, better known to the Christian world as Saladin, was sitting on a low, ornate, cushioned platform, his legs crossed before him, his forearms resting on his knees. He wore a bright, golden-orange robe, the sleeves billowing around his arms. His greying beard was neatly trimmed. His face was serious but betrayed no emotion. On his head, he wore a brown, unadorned turban. A short, curved dagger hung in a jeweled scabbard at the sultan's left hip. Several turbaned men sat in front of him to either side.

Saladin fixed his gaze on the emir. "Very well," he said. "Read the message."

The emir unrolled a small parchment and read: "Your Majesty, conditions have worsened. Acre can hold out no longer. By the time this message reaches you, we will have surrendered the city. May Allah be merciful. Signed, Baha' al-Din Qaragush, Governor of Acre."

Saladin stretched out his hand, and the emir gave him the parchment. The sultan read it to himself, quickly scanning the words, his face betraying no emotion. He looked up, and, to no one in particular, in a low, steady voice, he said, "Without my permission. Qaragush was to hold the city. Just a few more days. My army is growing daily. Very soon we would have had the strength to attack the Christian camp. Just a few more days. That was all we needed."

He looked at the emir and gave a very slight nod of his head, a signal of dismissal. The emir again bent his head slightly and passed his hand over his forehead and lips. He turned and walked briskly out of the tent.

When the emir had left, Saladin turned and addressed the first of the three men sitting to his right: "Al-Adil my brother, what do you advise?"

Al-Adil shook his head. "Your Majesty," he said, "we must not react in haste. We must learn more. Then we will act. If the infidel has razed the city and taken no prisoners, we must attack their camp as soon as our numbers are sufficient – in a day or two at most. If, as seems more likely, they have spared the city, we may then negotiate an exchange of prisoners."

Saladin nodded. "Yes, my brother. That is what I think exactly. Select seven infidel prisoners for special treatment. Give them a tour of our camp. Show them everything. Let them see our might. Impress them. Treat them as honored guests, and not as prisoners. But guard them well. When the time comes, we will send them back to the Christian camp as an offering of peace."

"Yes, my brother. It will be done." Al-Adil stood and walked briskly out of the tent.

The Christian prisoners were confined in several large cages, ten prisoners to a cage. In Matthew's cage, there were three Franks and seven Englishmen including Matthew. One of the Englishmen stood up and pointed to the tall Saracen warrior who was making his way in their direction accompanied by several other Saracen soldiers, apparently inspecting the prisoners. "That's Al-Adil, the Sultan's brother. What's he doing here, I wonder?"

"We'll know soon enough, I wager," said another English prisoner. "He's coming this way."

Matthew stood up and pressed his face against the bars to get a better look. Al-Adil stopped several feet from Matthew and spoke in a commanding voice, in the Saracen tongue. His interpreter looked at Matthew, and, in heavily-accented English, said, "His Excellency asks you, Infidel, why did you look at him with such apparent interest just now?"

Matthew bowed from the waist. "Your general, the sultan's brother, is famed and feared. I was trying to get a better look at him."

Al-Adil again spoke in Arabic, and the interpreter translated: "Does he, then, meet your expectations? And do you also see the light of Allah's blessings when you look upon his face?"

Matthew looked into Al-Adil's eyes and held his gaze for several seconds. "Yes," he said. "Indeed I do."

The interpreter looked surprised. "Indeed? Do you not think His Excellency an infidel?"

"I do not judge other men," said Matthew. "The righteous and the evil man, God alone will judge. It is not for me to say. But yes, I do see the fervor in his eyes. Truly, the Lord's grace has shone upon him."

The interpreter conveyed Matthew's words, and Al-Adil smiled. He looked at Matthew and conferred with his interpreter. At last, the interpreter said, "That was a noble speech. But, His Excellency wonders, was it spoken from the heart, or were those merely empty words meant to ingratiate yourself before your captors? Surely these are not words that you would utter if you were free and in the Christian camp."

"No, indeed they aren't. I do not speak all that is in my mind, even when I am among my own people. I know when I must hold my tongue. But when I speak, I do not lie. My words were truly spoken, from my heart."

At a signal from Al-Adil, a soldier unlocked the cage and led Matthew out. Another soldier motioned to Matthew to go with him, while the first soldier locked the cage again, leaving the other nine Christian prisoners inside.

The translator turned to Matthew and said, "His Excellency Al-Adil wishes to show you around our camp. After that, you will dine with him tonight as our honored guest. He wishes to discourse with you and to get to know you better. But for now, please wait here with these soldiers. His Excellency will return very soon."

The translator turned and walked briskly away, following Al-Adil to one of the other cages, leaving Matthew in the company of only two soldiers, each of whom stood stiffly at attention, his hand poised over the short, curved sword that hung in its scabbard at his hip. Despite the talk of his being an honored guest, Matthew had no doubt what would happen if he tried to escape.

Several minutes passed, and another Christian was brought to stand with Matthew, and after several more minutes there was yet another. When the seventh Christian was brought over, Al-Adil joined them, and, smiling graciously, he signaled the seven men to follow him.

The seven Christians were escorted through the entire length and breadth of the Muslim camp. They were shown the infantry and the cavalry troops, the scimitar-wielders and the crossbowmen, and Matthew marveled that Al-Adil would show an enemy such detail of the Saracen troop strength. But, on second thought, perhaps that was the entire point: that they should see their enemy's strength and be afraid.

The tour concluded with a demonstration of the Saracens' fine horses. Al-Adil waved his hand spaciously, and there was obvious pride in the tone of his voice. The interpreter said, "You see before you the most beautiful horses, the strongest and fastest horses that were ever bred. These horses are the pride of our cavalry, and when they ride into battle, the horse and its rider are as one. Watch!"

Al-Adil clapped his hands, and two riders in flowing white robes mounted their horses. At a signal from Al-Adil, they began to gallop in opposite directions. When they were almost out of sight, both riders wheeled around in unison, although neither rider could see the other before they turned around. Both riders galloped back and came to a halt simultaneously in front of Al-Adil.

"And that," said Al-Adil, "is how our soldiers ride. You will find no better horses or horsemen in all the world."

That night, they dined with Al-Adil in his tent, and on the following night they dined with him again. On the second night, Al-Adil said, "It has been our pleasure to show you our camp. You are our honored guests."

Matthew said, "You call us guests, not prisoners. Do you mean that we are free to leave?"

Al-Adil laughed. "Yes. Indeed you will soon be free to leave. But not yet. The time will come. And when it does, you will return and tell your king what you have seen here. Let him know he cannot conquer us. Our strength grows daily, as more warriors join us from the south. All you English, Franks, and Teutons are aliens and invaders in our land. This land belongs to us – to us alone – and through us it is kept holy. But you Christians contaminate the land. You are a sickness in our midst, and sooner or later, by the grace of Allah, we will expel you."

When Al-Adil's words had been translated, Matthew asked, "Why do you fight us? Why can Christian pilgrims not go to Jerusalem and Bethlehem to pray at our holy shrines? We are not invaders as you claim. Christians have lived in Jerusalem and in the Holy Land for a thousand years. But your Saracen warriors attacked and murdered Christian pilgrims, and it is now a hundred years since the pope declared a holy war to safeguard Christian shrines and protect our pilgrims journeying to Jerusalem and Bethlehem. Why do you deny us this right?"

When the translator had finished translating, Al-Adil looked into Matthew's eyes. For several seconds he held Matthew's gaze. He looked him up and down. A faint smile crossed Al-Adil's lips. "I see the light in your eyes," he said. "I hear the fervor in your voice. I see the confidence and the earnestness in your demeanor. Certainly you are brave to speak such words as you have spoken, especially before me, the Sultan's brother. And yet, you are an infidel. You are all infidels. You speak of shrines, where you would worship your tripartite God." He waved his hand dismissively. "Hah! That is foolishness. God does not have three parts, three aspects, or however you may choose to phrase it. Your view of God is wrong. It is sacrilege! God is one, indivisible. There is no god but Allah, and Mohammed is his prophet. Allah has given us this land, and no infidel army will take it from us. Our sultan, Salah ad-Din, is the sword of Allah. You cannot defeat him. You have taken Acre. You may even succeed in winning other battles. But in the end, you will not conquer. You will tell your king what you have seen here. May your king have the wisdom to heed my warning."

* * *

Friar Peter sat in his dark cell, his legs crossed in front of him, his hands resting on his knees. His eyes stared blankly into space, focused on an existence beyond the world of substance, his consciousness drifting through a higher world. Images floated before his vision, flickering into view and fading quickly. He felt himself flying through space and time. Mountains and valleys passed before him; saints and sinners, Christians, Saracens, and Jews. He saw the high priest's breastplate floating in the air, eleven stones glimmering among its golden threads. Far from the breastplate, hovering in the air at the edge of his vision, he saw the twelfth stone, its pure green facets reflecting the light of the setting sun. He saw Joseph suddenly appear, as though materializing out of nowhere. Joseph seized the stone. Peter saw himself lunge at Joseph, but Joseph stepped aside, and a vast gulf opened up between them.

The image faded, and all was dark again, as dark as the darkest night, with neither moon nor stars. In the distance there was laughter. Somebody was laughing at him. He looked around, but nobody was there.

"Where are you, Joseph?" Friar Peter called. "Are you in Tyre? You cannot hide from me. Wherever you may be, I will seek you out and find you. I will take the stone, and I will find the breastplate."

But the laughter didn't stop. It got still louder. Was it a man or woman laughing? He could not tell for certain.

"Lilith, come to me. Assist me in my quest. You gave me powers. You said I am your servant. I call to you for help."

But Lilith did not answer. Friar Peter came out of his trance. The laughter stopped. Only the sound of his own rapid breathing did he hear. And in his heart, he knew Lilith would do nothing more to help him. She had given him powers. She had infused him with her spirit and the spirit of her master, the Lord of Darkness. Now it was up to him alone to use his powers. It was up to him alone to find his way and conquer.

CHAPTER 35

Early August 1191
Tyre

The chainmail-clad knight entered the hall, walked briskly to within several feet of King Conrad, bent his knee, and bowed. "Your Majesty, King of Tyre, and King of Jerusalem, it is good to see you return unharmed from Acre. I welcome you back to Tyre. I am your faithful servant."

The king stepped forward and placed his hand on the knight's shoulder. "Rise, my leal Commander Stephen. In my absence, you have indeed performed commendably. But, unfortunately, I must insist on one correction."

Commander Stephen got to his feet. He looked at Conrad questioningly, but he did not speak.

King Conrad sat down upon his ornately ornamented throne and motioned to the commander to sit likewise. He looked at Stephen and said, "No, Sir Stephen, it is not a knowing error that you have committed, but it is an error nonetheless, it seems. You see, as of a few days ago, I am no longer King of Jerusalem. Oh, I am still King of Tyre, and of Sidon and Beirut as well. But the French and English kings held a council at Acre and decided that henceforth, Guy of Lusignan, not I, will bear the title of King of the Latin Kingdom of Jerusalem."

Stephen shook his head. "How can that be?" he asked. "It was Guy who lost Jerusalem to the Saracens four years ago. It was Guy who surrendered the city and fled in shame. And it is you, not he, whom all the troops acclaim as worthy successor to the throne. How can they award the title to that man? Is this decision final?"

"No," said Conrad. "Not officially. But it might as well be. The council was not able to reach a final conclusion, and the decision was only tentative, but there is little chance of altering the judgement. What further evidence can we bring in my support? King Philip argued for me at the council, but the English king now has the upper hand, and King Richard after all is Guy's overlord. So it is no surprise that the council gave the title to Guy, despite his ignominious past."

Commander Stephen smiled and said, "I think there is a way you might convince the council to change its mind, but there is a risk."

King Conrad half rose from his seat. "Out with it!" he roared. "Don't keep it to yourself. We will take any reasonable risk to gain the kingdom."

"What if you were to lead an assault on Jerusalem and take the city back from the Saracens? Would not that force King Richard to concede the crown to you?"

"Yes, but it is preposterous," said Conrad. "How could we hope to conquer Jerusalem on our own? King Richard's army is ten times the size of ours, and he is joined by the Templars and the Hospitallers. If he can't conquer Jerusalem, what chance do we have?"

"There is a way, Your Majesty. But, as I said, there is a risk. Have you ever heard of Peter the Pious?"

"What are you offering me – a man of God? It is an army that we need, not a man of God."

Commander Stephen shook his head. "Friar Peter is no ordinary man of God. Truly, he first made his reputation as an itinerant preacher, but he is much more than that. It is rumored he has special Powers, which he possesses by virtue of his great piety. He can will the wind to blow and the rain to fall. He can cause clouds to gather and the sky to darken. Thunder and lightning are at his beck and call. And with but a look, he can cause an infidel to fall down dead before his very feet. Many have witnessed Friar Peter's performance of such acts in England and in France. He is now in Tyre, and with his assistance you can hope to conquer."

King Conrad thought for a moment. "You spoke of a risk," he said. "What is that risk?"

"Friar Peter is widely revered as a holy man. Nevertheless, for reasons not known to me, the new pope has called for his immediate arrest. The writ arrived from Rome while you were at war in Acre. It was addressed both to you and to Archbishop Joscius, and the archbishop has executed the warrant in his own name and in yours. Friar Peter is currently incarcerated in the tower, awaiting extradition to Rome."

"I see. That is indeed a complication. But how long has Friar Peter been incarcerated, and how much longer before we have to ship him back to Rome?"

Commander Stephen smiled and said, "Ah, there's our opportunity. You see, the friar has been incarcerated here since May. But no sooner was he arrested than a second missive came from Rome, instructing us to hold him here for now, indefinitely. It seems the Holy Father fears that Friar Peter would have too much support in Rome, and it is more politic for Peter to remain in jail in Tyre until the Holy Father sees fit to have him extradited. I doubt that Friar Peter will be leaving us any time soon."

"One more question, Sir Stephen. If this Friar Peter has such powers as you ascribe to him, why has he not broken out of jail?"

"Your Majesty, I cannot answer that. But if Your Majesty deem it worth the risk, you may have Friar Peter brought here. Question him yourself, and gauge his response."

"We thank you, Commander. But a decision such as this must not be made in haste. We will consider your suggestion. You may leave us now."

*   *   *

At first, King Conrad resolved to drop the matter and not to question Friar Peter. Trying to conquer Jerusalem with his small army seemed a fool's errand, doomed to ignominious failure, even with the friar's help, and thus he resolved to let the matter rest. Certainly, he had much more pressing matters to attend – affairs of state that had lain dormant while he was off fighting at Acre. But a glimmer of hope kept prodding at his heart. Perhaps the idea was not so crazy after all; perhaps, with Friar Peter's help, he could attack Jerusalem and prevail. Perhaps the Lord had sent him this opportunity to regain the title he had lost to Guy de Lusignan – ruler of the Latin Kingdom of Jerusalem. Finally, after days of soul-searching deliberation, after days of oblique questions posed to Archbishop Joscius regarding the pope's intentions about Friar Peter, King Conrad arrived at a decision.

On the following morning, Friar Peter was led in chains into King Conrad's presence. The king was sitting on his throne. Several feet to the king's right, Commander Stephen stood immobile, a longsword at his side, and his right hand resting on the hilt of his sword. Two soldiers held Friar Peter by his arms.

A third soldier stepped forward and bowed to the king. "Your Majesty, we bring you the prisoner, Friar Peter, as commanded."

"Thank you," said King Conrad. "The three of you may leave us now, and close the door behind you. You will stand guard outside the door. Commander Stephen will suffice to guard our person."

The three soldiers bowed and left the hall. Friar Peter remained standing before the king.

King Conrad's arms rested upon the armrests of his throne. His fists were clenched. His face was taught. He looked the friar up and down but did not speak. The friar met King Conrad's gaze, his face expressionless.

The king leaned forward slightly. "We hear that you have certain powers."

Friar Peter did not answer. He was not certain to what end the king intended to lead this conversation. Peter resolved to wait and see the king's direction before committing himself to any response.

"Have you nothing to say to that?"

"That is a matter of opinion and conjecture, if it please Your Majesty."

"Then you deny it?"

"I neither confirm nor deny. Every man has certain powers, some in lesser measure, some in greater. The magnitude of my powers, as compared to other men, is a matter of opinion, and not for me to judge."

"It is said that you can influence the elements – that you can cause the wind to blow and the rain to fall; and it is said that you can kill your enemies by force of will alone. What say you to that?"

"I am a man of God, Your Majesty. I do not murder, nor am I a sorcerer."

"Then you deny you have such powers as we described?"

"I do not deny that men have said such things about me. I do not deny that I have great power of persuasion. I do not deny that I have spurred many men to action through my words. But, perhaps, my followers exaggerate my powers somewhat."

The king turned to Commander Stephen and said:

"What think you, Commander? Does he or does he not have special powers beyond the ordinary?"

Commander Stephen did not turn to look at his king. He kept his eyes firmly fixed on Friar Peter, his right hand resting on his sword. "I think," he said, "we cannot yet be sure. The prisoner is being cautious in his answers."

"Cautious or not," said King Conrad, turning to look again at Friar Peter, "if he will not admit to any special powers, he is of no use to us. And the fact that he has not made use of his powers to break out of jail suggests that he does not in fact have any special powers at all."

"May I speak, Your Majesty?" Friar Peter asked.

"Indeed you may," said the king. "If you have anything of note to add to what you have already told us."

"I do, Your Majesty. First I wish to say, I hope Your Majesty will not think ill of me for engaging in certain mystical pursuits. Certainly such activities are not forbidden, and, in fact are commonplace among certain men of the cloth."

"Yes, among monks and hermits; but not so commonplace among itinerant preachers."

"Indeed, Your Majesty. And yet, my point is that it is no sin to pursue such matters. It is through my learning of such matters that I have acquired certain skills. But I hasten to add that those skills are for use against the infidel, against the enemies of God. They are not to be used against the God-fearing men who hold me prisoner here."

"Then do you now admit to having such powers over the elements of nature as we described before? Do not be afraid to speak the truth. We are not accusing you of sorcery, nor of murder."

Peter still was hesitant to answer in the affirmative. And yet, he felt somehow it would be to his advantage to admit to having such Powers. "Your Majesty," he said, "perhaps my followers have exaggerated, as I said; but I do not deny that I have certain powers over the forces of nature, powers that I may use – indeed have used on certain occasions – against the enemies of God."

"In that case, Friar Peter, we would command your assistance in a certain matter."

Ah, now we come to the crux of this interrogation. "If what you ask is within my power, I am at Your Majesty's service for the glorification of the Lord. But you have not yet told me what it is you ask of me, so I cannot say whether it is within my power."

The king again leaned forward. "What was your purpose in taking ship to the Holy Land?"

"I am in pursuit of three Jewish youths who have committed murder in England. One of the three has certain demonic powers, which only I can overcome. Thus it is my duty to bring these murderers to justice."

"Then you deny that your purpose was to escape arrest at the Holy Father's command?"

"Indeed I do deny it. I was in pursuit of the murderers for many months, long before incurring the Holy Father's displeasure. In fact, when I arranged for passage to the Holy Land, I was unaware of the Holy Father's warrant for my arrest."

King Conrad leaned back again on his throne. "I see," he said. "But what say you to using your powers to fight the Saracens? Could you do that?"

Now we are getting still closer to his motive. "That would be a worthy cause indeed, and it may be in my power, although that was not my purpose in coming hither. If I may ask, what specifically would His Majesty have me do against the Saracens?"

King Conrad paused, and his eyes bored into Friar Peter. He turned his gaze momentarily toward Commander Stephen, then gazed again into the friar's eyes. "We would have you help us conquer Jerusalem."

Friar Peter tried to hide his surprise. His gaze did not waver, his lips did not quiver, nor did he even blink. But the enormity of the king's objective was daunting, yet thrilling all the same. Peter drew a breath and said, "It would be my honor to assist in such a holy enterprise. But, Your Majesty, a city cannot be conquered by force of will alone, even using such powers as I possess. An army will be needed – a mighty army. How many men does the English king command?"

King Conrad rose from his seat. "You mistake our meaning, Friar Peter. It is not Richard's army that we mean you to assist, but our own. Now that King Richard has conquered Acre, he is bound to march his army southward down the coast to Jaffa, and from there, eventually inland to Jerusalem. But it will be many weeks before that happens. It is our intention to march our army from Tyre to Jerusalem and, with your assistance, to take that city from the Saracens.

"The question is not how many men do we command. That is our concern, not yours. Our question to you is simply this: do you have the power to strike fear in the hearts of the Saracen, to unleash the elements of nature against our enemies, to wield the forces of heaven and earth on our behalf? Or are the stories of your powers a fabrication or a gross exaggeration? Speak!"

"Your Majesty, I have never attempted to use my powers in the way that you suggest, but I will do my best."

King Conrad took a step closer to Friar Peter and pointed a finger at the friar. "It was not a suggestion, Friar Peter. We do not suggest. We command! You will assist us in the conquest of Jerusalem."

"Yes, of course," said Friar Peter. "I am at your service. But there is precious little I can do while incarcerated in the tower. And what will become of the holy mission that brought me to this land?"

The king shook his fist in Peter's face. "Do not think to toy with us," he growled. "You will remain imprisoned in the tower until such time as we see fit to mobilize our army. And even then, you will remain under guard and closely watched, until you have given us Jerusalem. Once Jerusalem is ours, you will be free to pursue your 'holy mission.' Not before."

"So be it," said Friar Peter. "I had no intention of toying with Your Majesty, nor would I ever dare to do so. But the murderers whom I seek are here in Tyre at this moment, and it would seem an awful shame to allow such an opportunity to pass. Therefore, Your Grace, I would beg your kind assistance at this time."

King Conrad eyed the friar suspiciously. "How would you know their whereabouts, imprisoned as you have been in the tower these many weeks?"

"I have seen them in my visions; I have tracked them in my dreams. They are here in Tyre now, but they will not be here long. And, Your Majesty, while I mean no disrespect nor insubordination, I submit to you most humbly that my soul would be much more at peace and my mind therefore more focused on the task you have assigned to me if the three fugitives whom I seek were captured and safely incarcerated."

"Very well. We will assist you now. Call it a *quid pro quo*. After you are returned to your cell, within the hour we will send you the Master of the Guard. Give him the names of these fugitives, and tell him where they may be found. They will be arrested and brought to you in the tower. In return, you will obey our every command and deliver Jerusalem into our hands."

* * *

Joseph, Aaron, and Rachel were sitting at the table in Joseph's room conversing when Commander Silvio burst in, accompanied by three servant brothers clad in long brown robes, each carrying in his arms a set of neatly folded clothes.

Silvio looked distraught. His tone was pressured and abrupt. His gaze darted from Joseph to Aaron to Rachel, and back again to Joseph. "Quickly, rise," he commanded. "And change into these garments. You must depart immediately."

Two of the servant brothers placed two pairs of boots at the foot of Joseph's bed and laid out two identical sets of clothing on the bed: two suits of chainmail, circular metal helmet, black tunic, gloves, and black mantle with a large red cross emblazoned on the chest. The third servant brother continued standing at the door, a similar set of garments in his hands.

Joseph rose and stared at the chainmail, tunics, gloves, and mantles on his bed. He looked at Silvio questioningly, but he did not speak.

"I know you are not pleased to dress thus, as Templar sergeants, with the cross displayed prominently on your garments, but it is

298

the only way. Our informer at the palace has sent urgent word that King Conrad has issued a warrant for your arrest. The king's men-at-arms will soon arrive, and they must not find you here. Fortuitously, we have a ship at the harbor, fully equipped and preparing to sail to Acre. As soon as you are suitably attired, one of our sergeants will take you to the ship. Disguised as Templar sergeants, I expect you will not be questioned. You will board the ship and soon be out of Conrad's reach. I will join you in Acre in a few days' time."

Joseph and Aaron went over to the bed and began to don the garments. The third servant brother beckoned to Rachel. "Come with me," he said. "I will place your uniform in your room."

Rachel looked at the garments in the sergeant brother's hands and hesitated.

"Yes," said Silvio. "You must also be dressed as a sergeant brother. It is the only way. Appearing as a woman would arouse suspicion. As you well know, we Templars have considered the company of women to be a dangerous thing, and we have no women in our ranks. You will put up your hair and hide it under the chainmail and casque. The chainmail headdress will cover your face sufficiently that the absence of a beard should not be noticed. Now hurry, before the king's men arrive."

*   *   *

The knight dismounted just outside the gate and signaled his five men-at-arms to do likewise. He walked up to the gate, leading his horse behind him. Two black-clad guards with large red crosses emblazoned on their mantles stood at attention on the other side of the gate's vertical iron bars, each with spear in hand. The knight standing outside the gate waved at one of the guards a writ of parchment bearing the king's seal, and with an air of authority, he proclaimed: "By order of King Conrad, Lord of Tyre, we demand entry into your compound. Raise the gate!"

The Templar guard stood unperturbed. "State your name and the purpose of your entry."

"I am Sir Edmund of the King's Guard, and I am here to execute this warrant for the arrest of three fugitives."

"The Order of the Temple of Solomon does not harbor fugitives from the king's justice. We are not aware of any fugitives in our midst."

The knight began to lose his patience, but he reined in his temper and said, "Sergeant, I am certain the Knights Templar would not knowingly harbor such; and yet, we have reports that the three fugitives we seek are indeed – perhaps unwittingly – in your midst. By order of King Conrad, I demand entry to execute this warrant." Again, he waved the warrant demonstratively in the guard's face.

The guard glanced at the warrant cursorily. He looked at the king's seal, but Sir Edmund doubted that he actually read the text of the warrant, which did not surprise Sir Edmund in the least, since he assumed the man was probably illiterate. The guard signaled to another man inside, out of sight, and slowly the gate began to rise. As Sir Edmund and his men-at-arms began to enter, several servants emerged from within the compound and swarmed around them.

A third guard emerged from inside the compound and hurried over to the king's men. "Leave your horses here. The servants will take care of them," he said. "Remove your helmets and carry them in your hands. Follow me. I will escort you inside the commandery."

The guard led them down a short hallway to an inner gate, in front of which they had to wait until the gate was raised, a process that Sir Edmund thought was excruciatingly slow. When that was finally accomplished, the guard led the king's men along winding passageways until they came to a sudden stop in a large hall deep inside the Templar compound. Before them stood a tall man with a stern face and neatly-trimmed beard, bedecked in a white mantle adorned with a large red cross. His gloved right hand rested on the hilt of a sword slung from his left hip. "I am Hugo, Commander of the Templar stronghold in the City of Tyre. I bid you welcome. I am given to understand that you seek a group of fugitives from the king's justice. We are not aware of any fugitives among us, but we are eager to assist the king in pursuit of justice in any way we can. Please describe these fugitives for us."

Sir Edmund nodded slightly. "I thank you for your most gracious welcome, Commander Hugo. I am Sir Edmund of the King's Guard, and I have come to execute this writ, signed in the king's own hand." He unfurled the writ and waved it in front of the commander's face.

When Commander Hugo had examined the writ to his satisfaction, the knight continued: "Said fugitives are three Jewish youths – two male and one female – who have committed heinous crimes both in England and across the channel. They recently arrived in Tyre, in May or June, and we have information that they are still here among you."

"Indeed, we have a number of youths staying here as guests. But I cannot say I know of any Jewish youths among them."

"Be that as it may. Perhaps they did not identify themselves as Jews, but we have reliable information that they are here. By order of King Conrad, I bid you take us to them."

At a signal from Commander Hugo, a second man in a white mantle with a large red cross entered by a side door together with two squires clad in ankle boots, black breeches, and unadorned black tunics.

"This man," said Hugo, indicating the newly-arrived man in the white mantle, "is Silvio, Commander of Knights of the Temple of Solomon. He is recently come from Rome, and he arrived in Tyre during the period you have indicated, in the company of certain guests. I am sure that Commander Silvio will be most helpful to you. I will leave you now in his care. Good day, Sir Edmund, and may God be with you."

When Commander Hugo had left the hall, Silvio turned to Sir Edmund and asked, "I understand you are seeking a band of fugitives. Pray tell, what is the nature of their crimes?"

"They are murderers, Commander Silvio. They murdered a soldier of God in cold blood and are wanted for that and other heinous crimes. They are three Jewish youths, agents of the Devil – two male, one female. If you have any knowledge of their whereabouts, by order of King Conrad, I bid you take us to them."

"Indeed," said Commander Silvio, "I did arrive in Tyre in the company of three youths – two male, one female. But I cannot say that they were Jews, nor was their behavior or their demeanor strange in any way that would make us think they were agents of the Devil. In fact, a man of high repute in Rome did vouch for them, and thus I have no doubts about their good character."

"Nevertheless," said Sir Edmund, "I demand you take us to them, and let me be the judge of that."

Commander Silvio smiled and said, "Very well. I will take you to their rooms."

He turned and signaled the king's men to follow him. Without a word, he led them down several cloistered hallways. Sir Edmund thought they were going in circles, but just as he was about to remark on that thought, Commander Silvio halted in front of a wooden door and knocked. When there was no answer after two knocks, Silvio opened the door.

"Here is where the two boys were staying, but as you may see, it is uninhabited."

"Where are they? Are you playing games with us?"

Silvio shook his head. "Oh, no, of course not. I brought you here, as you requested. This is the room where the two males were staying. But, you see, the three youths were due to depart today, and now I see they must have left already. Unless, of, course, they are now in the room of the female guest, to help her with her belongings. Come. I will take you to her room."

Silvio turned and, without waiting for an answer from Sir Edmund, he strode briskly several paces down the hall and knocked on another door. After but a moment's pause, he opened the door and entered.

"I am sorry," Silvio said. "This room is empty also. All three youths must have left already."

"How long ago, and by what route?"

"That is difficult to say. But it could not have been too long ago. As you may know, a Templar ship is now at port, due to sail today. Our three guests will be on that ship. If you hurry, you still may catch them before they sail. But, if I may add, I sincerely doubt they are agents of the Devil, nor is there any evidence that they are criminals. They are merely three youths on pilgrimage to the Holy Land."

*　　*　　*

The four mounted men came to a halt at a checkpoint. All four were identically garbed – Templar sergeants clad in chainmail from head to foot, round metal helmets, black tunics, and black mantles with large red crosses on their chests. One of the sergeants – a great bear of a man – dismounted and walked up to a guard at the checkpoint. He tipped his helmet courteously and said:

"I am Sergeant Brother Eugene of the Order of the Temple. Myself and three more brother sergeants, here to board the Templar ship."

The guard looked at him suspiciously. "I was not told of any more passengers. The ship is almost set to sail."

"I know. We just received our urgent orders, and a runner was dispatched to the ship to wait for us." He unfurled a parchment and presented it to the guard. "Here is our bill of lading."

The guard waved the document away. "Alright, alright. It seems to be in order. Have your men dismount. Present your writ to the guard at the end of the pier, and you may board the ship."

At a signal from Sergeant Brother Eugene, the other sergeant brothers dismounted and led their horses down the long pier to the waiting ship.

"Not so fast," Sergeant Eugene whispered to the other sergeants. "You appear too anxious. You must not raise their suspicions. We are almost there."

Three guards stood at the far end of the pier, blocking the gangplank. As the four Templar sergeants drew closer, the three guards conferred among themselves, and one of the guards pointed to the sergeants, shaking his head.

"Sergeant Eugene," one of the other sergeants whispered, seeming eager to say something. But Eugene raised his hand for silence, and the one who had attempted to whisper said nothing more.

Sergeant Eugene strode up to the guards, leading his mount behind him, and handed his parchment to the guard who had pointed at them. "Four more passengers to board the ship," he said.

The guard took the parchment but did not look at it. He pointed at one of the sergeants. "You, sergeant. Come here, and let me see you closer."

When the indicated sergeant had advanced, the guard eyed him suspiciously and said, "You look rather young, sergeant. What is your name, and how old are you?"

Before the youthful-looking sergeant could answer, Sergeant Eugene interjected: "Please excuse Sergeant Brother Roland. He cannot answer you. He has taken a vow of silence until we reach Acre. Therefore I must speak for him."

"A vow of silence, eh? A sinner, what? What has he done? Is it murder, thievery, or lechery perhaps?" The guard came still closer and looked into the sergeant's eyes. "Yeah. Look at those eyes. Blue as the sky, and lecherous as hell is deep."

The three guards laughed merrily at the jape. The first guard turned to his men and asked, "How old would you say he is? Fifteen? Sixteen? Hardly old enough to be a sergeant, isn't he?"

He turned to Sergeant Eugene and looked at him accusingly. "So, tell me, sergeant: how old is your comrade here? The one who lost his tongue."

Sergeant Eugene stepped forward. He stood just two feet from the guard and towered over him. "Brother Sergeant Roland is much older than he appears. Behind that youthful face is a brother of great piety and holiness, and not at all a lecher or a sinner of any form."

Sergeant Eugene backed off a step and continued: "Our urgent orders, coming directly from Commander Hugo, are to board this ship bound for Acre, and we are not to speak of the nature of our mission to any man outside our Order. Good Sir, I bid you, by the grace of God, do not question us further, and do not hinder our sacred mission. If you value your soul's salvation and your place in Heaven, you will not delay us further."

He took one more step back, looked at his three comrades, and began to lead his horse forward, to the gangplank. The first guard stood by silently and let them pass. The other two guards stood aside. When the four sergeants were on board, the ship's crew scurried about, raising the gangplank and untying the lines.

As the four sergeant brothers went below-deck and the ship pulled away from the pier, the blue-eyed sergeant brother whispered, "Thank you, Brother Eugene."

But Sergeant Brother Eugene looked around, making sure that no one was in earshot. Then he turned to the blue-eyed sergeant in a reprimanding tone and said, "Have you forgotten your vow of silence, Brother Roland? You must maintain your silence until we disembark at Acre. Only once we are in Acre will it be safe for Roland to vanish and Rachel to emerge from her male cocoon."

CHAPTER 36

19ᵗʰ August 1191
Saladin's camp

l-Adil sat on the floor, his legs crossed in front of him. He dipped his bread in a bowl and raised it to his mouth, casually popping it in without it touching his lips. His eyes scanned the seven Christian men as he chewed his bread in silence.

Matthew also dipped his bread and raised it to his mouth, mimicking his host. It was now more than a month since the first time he had eaten with Al-Adil in his tent, but this was only the fourth time. On other nights, he and the other six Christians had taken their evening meal in the tents of various emirs, each night in a different emir's tent. Somehow, Al-Adil's mood seemed different tonight, and Matthew wondered what was afoot. He did not have to wonder very long.

Al-Adil swallowed. He looked again at the seven Christian captives and said, "The time has come. Tomorrow, shortly after dawn, you seven will be leaving us. I should tell you that your king demanded payment of a large amount of coin as ransom for the lives of the men and women of Acre. An exorbitant amount, I would say. Unfortunately, we were unable to raise the required amount in time for his deadline, and as a token of our good faith we have sent word that we will release seven Christian prisoners tomorrow. In return, the Lionheart has graciously said he will release seven distinguished men of Acre who were captured when the city surrendered last month."

When Al-Adil's words had been translated into English, Matthew smiled a wry smile. *Ah, he admits we are prisoners and not guests. Of course, we had no doubt of that, but it is good to hear him say it.*

It was just a thought. Matthew had not spoken, but he was sure that Al-Adil understood his meaning.

A wan smile crossed Al-Adil's lips. He looked into Matthew's eyes, nodded, and said in halting, heavily accented English, "Yes, that is correct."

Al-Adil tore off another piece of bread and dipped it. While looking at Matthew, he raised his bread to his mouth and chewed slowly. Finally, he spoke again in his own language: "I trust you will report that you have been well treated in our camp, and that we are civilized people, not the savages that your people imagine us to be."

Yes, thought Matthew when the translator had conveyed Al-Adil's message, *and no doubt, although he hasn't said it now, he wants us also to tell of the military prowess of his troops and of the advanced catapults that he has shown us. Else he would not have shown us these things at all.*

Al-Adil again looked at Matthew and said, "Your face betrays some hidden thought. Could it be that you have found fault in our hospitality, or is it something else that gives you pause?"

"No, Your Excellency," answered Matthew. "I do not have any such thoughts. I only wondered at how our superiors will take our report and what will be the final outcome of this prisoner exchange."

Al-Adil smiled again. "Well spoken," he said. "You would make a fine diplomat."

The night passed uneventfully. On the following morning, Matthew and the other six Christians who were to be released were aroused before dawn. After a hasty breakfast, they were marched out of the Saracen camp under guard. They were loaded onto a horse-drawn wagon and driven several miles over rocky terrain until they were within sight of the Christian camp but still far out of bowshot.

A Saracen warrior carrying a white flag of truce rode ahead. When he was almost in range of the Christian archers, he stopped and signaled to the wagon driver. Matthew and his six comrades were told to get off the wagon and walk. The mounted Saracen then called out in a stentorian voice:

"His Majesty, Sultan Salah ad-Din Yusuf ibn Ayyub, is merciful. As a token of his good will and of his future intentions to pay the sum agreed upon, the sultan is releasing seven Christian prisoners."

The rider turned and galloped back, and the wagon driver also turned back to the Saracen camp. Matthew and his six comrades walked towards the Christian camp, at first at a brisk pace, but the distance was great. When it was apparent to them that the Saracens had left and that they were free indeed, they slowed their pace.

Several minutes passed. The ruined walls of Acre were now clearly visible. Matthew saw a group of Christian knights on horseback heading southwards, in his direction. They had apparently come from Acre but were already well south of the city walls, and a small group of Saracens were on foot in front of them. The knights soon came to a halt, and the Saracen men continued walking southwards. Matthew counted them. There were seven Saracens, to match the number of Christians that the Saracens had released.

Perhaps, he thought, *King Richard and the sultan will come to terms. Perhaps there will soon be peace.*

At that thought, his spirit rose. He looked up to heaven and gave thanks to God. He looked down to earth again, turning his gaze to his right, to the hill beyond the city to the east. And immediately his heart sank again.

He saw a long line of people – Saracen men, women, and children – trudging up the hill. He saw a row of mounted knights in chainmail riding on either side, herding their captives up the hill.

He froze in his tracks, dumbfounded, unwilling to believe what he was seeing, unwilling to see what he knew would happen next. And yet, he couldn't take his eyes away.

His six comrades were far ahead of him. One of them turned around and called to him. But he waved them on. "Go on," he said. "I will catch up."

They kept on walking. Now and then, one of them would turn to see whether Matthew followed, but Matthew remained standing in place, his face vacuous, his gaze fixed. Eventually they stopped looking back and just continued walking, towards the Christian camp.

Many minutes passed. The front of the line of captives reached the top of the hill, and their numbers swelled as the seemingly endless line of men, women, and children congregated there: at least two thousand, maybe three.

A phalanx of hundreds of mounted knights and footmen marched southwards out of the Christian camp, advancing slowly towards the Saracen army. A knight on horseback galloped forward, a line of twenty mounted archers arrayed to either side of him. The knight and his retinue came to a halt well beyond the range of Saracen bowmen. The knight raised his hand, and his voice rang out:

"Hear me, Saladin, sultan of the Saracens. Hear the word of Richard, King of England and conqueror of Acre. King Richard, in his mercy, has offered you the lives of the citizens of Acre in exchange for a ransom to which you have agreed. But you have broken your word. The deadline has passed, and you have failed to pay the ransom in the sum agreed upon. Instead of coin, you have offered us seven Christian captives – seven of our brave men whom you shamefully abducted from our camp in the dead of night, not captured honorably in the heat of battle.

"As a token of our mercy, we also have released seven men, seven of the most distinguished men of Acre, including Qaragush, your governor. This is a fair exchange of prisoners.

"Nevertheless, you have failed to pay the first installment of the ransom. It is a full week now since the deadline passed, but your payment still is not forthcoming. You have failed to fulfill your solemn word and to abide by the terms to which you swore. That failure must be punished. You see before you, gathered on that hill, the men and women of Acre, and their children. Look upon them. Look upon them well. They number close to three thousand. These are the people whom you have failed to ransom. May their blood be on your conscience."

The knight and his retinue of archers turned abruptly and galloped northwards, to the safety of the Christian camp. Seconds passed, but nothing happened. Matthew watched, holding his breath, his heart in his throat, his vision blurred by a mist of incipient tears. He glanced behind him at the Saracen camp, now far away. Vaguely, he saw the forms of men, some on foot and some on horseback, but no one moved. They all seemed riveted in place, just as Matthew was, watching helplessly as the English knights high up on the hill began to slash and stab with sword and spear, and English archers loosed their arrows and their crossbows into the throng of Muslim captives. Cries and screams rang out, but the slaughter did not stop.

Even at this distance, Matthew heard the screams of women and the cries of children. He closed his eyes, but the vision would not go away. In the distance, a woman screamed, her shrill voice reverberating in his skull. Had he really heard the scream, or was it only in his mind? He wasn't sure. Again Matthew heard the scream, and he thought he was back in Camryn. He heard the voice of Joseph's mother as she was dying, killed by his own father's hand. He heard the terror-filled screams of Joseph's little sister as she was caught and butchered by one of his father's friends. He saw his father as he emerged from Joseph's home, his hands covered in blood. He opened his eyes again, if only to dispel the memories and the phantasms of Camryn, but what he saw before him on the hill-top was just as horrifying. Still the slaughter on the hill continued. Tears filled Matthew's eyes. He fell to his knees, turned his face to heaven, closed his eyes, and prayed: "Oh merciful God, have pity on these your children."

For several minutes he remained motionless, kneeling on the ground, his face upturned. Slowly he rose and opened his eyes again. He looked upon the hill, but still the slaughter continued. Matthew turned and ran, away from the Saracens, away from the English, away from the slaughter and the terror he had witnessed. He ran and ran, not caring where, just so he would be away, far away from Acre.

After a long while, he stopped. He could run no farther. He had to rest. He looked around him. There was nobody in sight. He listened for the sound of battle, but there was only silence. For a moment, he thought of going north, back to the English camp. But now he was a deserter, and only danger would await him there. And due south of Acre along the coast the Muslim army waited. Matthew turned inland. He would keep to that direction for a few miles, then turn southwards toward the forest of Arsuf. There, he thought, he should be able to find a place to hide.

CHAPTER 37

21ˢᵗ to 23ʳᵈ August 1191

F riar Peter sat in his cell and looked up at the barred porthole high above. The night was dark and moonless – perfect conditions for what he had planned.

Peter had waited expectantly for several days after his encounter with King Conrad. Each day, he awoke hopeful that Joseph would be brought to him, and each day he went to sleep disappointed. Of course, he could not directly ask the guards for news of the outside world and hope to get an answer, but the guards did talk to each other during change of shift, and Peter knew to listen at the door at such times. And today, amidst the murmurs and the whispers of the guards that faintly filtered through the wooden door, Peter was able to catch a wisp of news about the fugitives he sought. He managed to hear only snatches of the guards' conversation, but it was enough.

Apparently, King Conrad was in a foul mood these past few days. As the guards told it, the king had dispatched men to arrest certain fugitives and bring them here to the tower, but those fugitives had already fled the city on a Templar ship bound for Acre and were now out of Conrad's reach. Their escape had occurred at least a week ago, and Friar Peter cursed his ill fortune. There was only one guard – Edward by name – from whom Peter could get information freely, but that guard had been temporarily reassigned these past ten days. Fortunately, Edward was returning later today, and Peter would be ready for him.

When Peter was first imprisoned in the tower, he had not yet
known Joseph's whereabouts, and thus he had thought it better
to remain imprisoned here, where he could employ Edward as
a conduit for news, rather than flee and become a target of pursuit.
And shortly after he had determined that Joseph was in Tyre, the
king had offered Peter what seemed a golden opportunity: not
only had the king agreed to arrest Joseph and bring him here,
but Peter's side of the bargain would play right into Peter's hand,
because he would be able to use King Conrad's army to help him
conquer Jerusalem from the Saracens. Now, however, everything
had changed. King Conrad would be unable to keep his side of
the bargain, and Peter saw that it availed him naught to remain
imprisoned here in Tyre. Joseph was getting closer to his final
goal, and Peter must catch up to him. Tonight, on Edward's
shift, Peter would escape.

*   *   *

Joseph sat fidgeting. He raised his head and looked at his two
companions sitting across the table. He looked into Rachel's eyes
and held her gaze for a long time, silently. Never before had
he looked into Rachel's eyes like this. He remembered another
girl, so long ago. Sarah. It seemed as though it was in another
world, in a different life. But that world, that life, that joy, was
gone now, just as surely as the world he had known in Camryn
was also gone, and Joseph knew he must not dwell upon the
past too much, for in that direction lay despondency and self-
destruction. He continued looking into Rachel's eyes. He sensed
a steadfast strength there, and a calming force that spoke to the
inner reaches of his soul.

She smiled a mischievous smile and said, "What do you see in
my eyes? Have you found your answer there?"

Joseph continued holding Rachel's gaze, but he did not return
her smile. "This is serious, Rachel. No, I have not found my
answer in your eyes, although I wish I had. Here we are in Acre,

still miles away from Jerusalem, and we do not even know for certain whether Jerusalem is our final destination. The full moon is on the morning of 5th September, and that is only two weeks away. We can wait no longer. But what can we do? How will we know where to go? And if Jerusalem is indeed our destination, how will we get by the Saracen army to reach our goal?"

Aaron said, "As I see it, there is only one way. Rabbi Tuviah told you that only in the world of spirit will you find the answers that you seek. So, despite your qualms, despite the risks, that is where you have to go."

Joseph's face was drawn. He looked at Aaron, and, in a whispered voice he said, "But what will I do once I have entered that world? And how will I avoid another encounter with Friar Peter? Remember what happened the last time. I just barely escaped with my life. If I must enter that world again, I must have a clear plan. Else it is not worth the risk."

Aaron looked down at the table, dejected. "Yes, I see," he said.

But Rachel looked again into Joseph's eyes. She took his hand in hers and said, "You will find a way. Do not fear."

Joseph began to draw his hand away, but Rachel held him tightly. "You are not alone," she said.

"Do you intend to go with me?"

"You know I can't. I would, but I don't know how. I do not have that skill. However, Peter is not the only one besides yourself who knows how to enter the world of spirit. There is Enoch."

"Enoch? If he could help me, he would have done so already. He knows much more than he would tell us. That was very clear to me. But he intends for me to find the way myself. He has given me all the help that he is going to give. He will help no further."

Rachel squeezed his hand. She smiled, and said, "Yes, I suppose that is correct. But I just had a thought: there is one other, Joseph."

"If you know, do not hide it. Tell me, who?"

"Think, Joseph. It was no coincidence that we met Old Mab in Sherwood Forest. Enoch sent her to us, and she has Powers. Even Friar Peter withdrew before her power. And she told you that someday you would have to enter the spiritual world if you were to defeat Friar Peter. She knew, even then. Enter the world of spirit, and summon her. She said she is your friend. She will help you, I am certain."

Joseph's face lit up. He squeezed Rachel's hand and smiled. "Yes, Rachel. I will try."

When Aaron and Rachel had left the room, Joseph placed a candle in the center of the table. He took out the emerald and placed it on the table next to the candle. As he had done before, he whispered a brief prayer, then gazed into the greenness of the emerald, watching the reflection of the candle flame flickering in the facets of the stone. As before, he repeated to himself: "Blessed be the name of His glorious kingdom for ever and ever." He repeated the words many times, again and again, and yet again; and all the while concentrating his attention on the flickering reflections in the stone, willing his mind to travel beyond the confines of space and time and thus to enter into another world. Soon, he was caught within a vortex of colored lights; his head felt light, and his eyes began to close. He had entered the world of spirit.

"Old Mab," he called. "I am here. Come to me. I need your help."

He waited, but he heard no response.

He felt himself floating, soaring high above the clouds. He hurtled through the air at unimaginable speed. His head spun; his vision blurred. For a long while, he saw only a cloudless, sunless, shimmering blue void spread out before him, until at length he started to descend; his speed began to slow. He saw the earth below, spread out before him, green as emerald.

He felt himself descending further. A forest sprawled below, the leafy branches of the trees turned upwards, heavenwards, beckoning. Down he went, into the thickest of the forest. His feet touched the ground. He looked around, trying to get his bearings. The forest seemed familiar. He was sure it was Sherwood Forest, and yet it was different from the way he remembered it.

In the distance, a mist hovered over the ground, and in the center of the mist, a human form. Slowly, the mist advanced towards Joseph, coming to a halt a few feet away. The human form turned toward Joseph, but the face was hidden behind a hood.

Momentarily, Joseph cringed inwardly. Was it Friar Peter? *No, it can't be Friar Peter. Not here. Not in Sherwood Forest.* He braced himself and advanced a step towards the apparition.

The apparition raised its hands and drew its hood back. It looked at Joseph. It advanced, walking out of the mist.

It was not Friar Peter after all. It was a woman, and as she came still closer, Joseph recognized her face.

"Old Mab!"

"None other. You called me, and I came. Or rather, I brought you here to me."

"But why here? Why did you bring me to Sherwood Forest?"

"You know the answer to that yourself, do you not? Yes, I see you do. In the world of spirit and of dreams and apparitions, Friar Peter can follow you. He can track you down. And he has powers that you yourself do not possess. But here, in Sherwood Forest, his powers cannot touch you. You saw this many months ago. Old Mab is one with the soul of Sherwood Forest, and in this forest Friar Peter can do naught against my will. You are safe with me."

Joseph relaxed somewhat. "Yes, that is good. But do you think you can help me?"

Old Mab eyed Joseph for a moment. "Yes," she said. "I can."

Joseph was surprised. "You don't need to ask with what I need your help?"

"Old Mab knows many things. No, you do not need to tell me. I know already. And your request for my help was no surprise either. Enoch told me to expect it. Come, walk with me, and I will tell you what I can."

She took Joseph's hand and led him deeper into the forest, into the mist that had covered her before. For several minutes they walked in silence through the mist, which grew thicker with every step they took, rising from the forest floor, enveloping them. Joseph was bursting to ask Old Mab to speak, but he knew she wouldn't say a word until she was ready, and so he held his tongue.

At length, Old Mab stopped walking. She turned to look at Joseph and asked, "Have you ever heard of The Cave of the Mysteries?"

*   *   *

Friar Peter sat in his cell, waiting. He knew the daily routine. A guard came twice a day to give him food and drink: once at noontime, and once when it got dark. Peter calculated it was almost time for the guard to come to his door for the evening meal. The guard would open the little hatch in the bottom of the door and call to Peter to slip his tray through. Then the guard would put bread and water on the tray and slip it through the hatch again, without a word. But today, Peter decided, the routine would change.

Several minutes passed. Friar Peter heard the muffled sound of footsteps. The hatch opened, and a voice called, "Your tray."

Peter got up slowly. He put his tray on his side of the hatch but did not push it through.

"The tray!" the guard said. "I've no time for games."

Peter pushed the tray forward slightly. He spoke in a whisper, but his voice projected through the hatch, its intensity and vehemence enveloping the space beyond the door. "Night comes. Darkness cloaks the earth. Breathe the darkness in. Take the tray, and sink into the twilight. Let the mists of nighttime overcome you."

He pushed his tray all the way through the hatch, and the guard took it. Peter smiled, knowingly. When Peter had first been brought to the dungeon many weeks ago, just before he was put in his cell, he had hypnotized the guard, and he had planted the phrase in the guard's mind: "Breathe the darkness in." Thereafter, any time that Peter spoke that phrase, the guard would immediately fall into a trance again. After that initial time, Peter had hypnotized the guard several times more before tonight. He knew the guard was now hypnotized, but he needed to deepen the trance. Peter continued:

"As you took the tray from me, the dark has taken you. Yield to the power of the night. Relax. Feel a great calmness overtake you. Your eyes are still closed, but when you open them, you will be even more relaxed, more focused, and you will follow my suggestions. Now open your eyes and gaze into the darkness."

Peter sat again and listened. He heard the guard's breathing, slow and steady. Peter smiled again.

"Guard, what is your name?"

The guard's answer wafted across the door, a voice like gossamer thread. "Edward. My name is Edward."

"Very good, Edward. Put the bread and water on the tray, and push it back across the hatch. Then get your keys, and unlock the door. Do you understand?"

"Yes, I do."

Slowly, the tray was pushed across the hatch, with a loaf of bread and a flagon filled with water.

Peter heard the guard's footsteps walking away. A minute passed. Peter waited. Another minute passed, and Peter began to grow anxious. But soon, he heard the guard returning. He heard a key inserted in the door. He heard the turning of the key and the creaking of the door upon its rusty hinges. A faint light entered Peter's cell.

"That is very good, Edward. Now step back, and leave the key in the door. You will remember nothing of this. Nothing. Do you understand?"

"Yes, I do. I understand."

Friar Peter stepped through the doorway. He closed the door behind him and turned the key. He handed the key to Edward, and Edward took it in his hand.

"When I am gone, you will go about your business normally. You will remember only that you passed me the tray of bread and water through the hatch. You will not remember that I spoke to you, nor will you remember opening my door, and you will not remember that I left my cell."

The guard nodded. "Yes," he said.

"Now tell me, Edward, is there a ship in port preparing to embark for Acre? But not a Templar ship, mind you."

Edward nodded dreamily. "Yes, of course. There are always ships bound for Acre. One will leave tomorrow at dawn."

That is excellent, thought Peter. *I can stow aboard the ship tonight. If Joseph is still in Acre, well and good. And if not, at least I will have narrowed the distance between us.*

"One last question, Edward: how can I leave this fortress unobserved? The last time we spoke, you told me of a secret passageway leading to the outside beyond the fortress walls. Can you take me to it?"

"Yes. Come this way."

Edward led him through a dark tunnel. He unlocked a door and opened it. Pointing into the darkness beyond, Edward said: "Count exactly fifty paces, and turn left. There will be a ladder propped against the wall. Climb up the ladder. It's only a short way up. Open the hatch above, and you will be out. Just be sure to close the hatch again, and cover it with dirt and rocks."

"Thank you, Edward. Lock the passage door behind you, and return to your post. When you do so, you will come out of the trance, and all will seem normal. You will forget that you opened the door. You will forget that I left. You will forget this conversation. You will remember only that you pushed my tray across the hatch and that I took it. To your knowledge, I never left my cell."

"Yes," he said as he closed the door, leaving Friar Peter in darkness.

* * *

Joseph raced down the corridor, his feet pounding heavily on the stone floor, his footsteps echoing from the vaulted ceiling. Aaron and Rachel ran after him, but they had trouble keeping up. Abruptly, Joseph came to a halt in front of a large wooden door. He knocked but did not wait for a response. He opened the door and entered.

"Silvio, I must talk to you, immediately."

Silvio, who had been seated at a table talking to a fellow Templar, stood up. "What is it, Joseph?"

Joseph looked at Silvio, his gaze intense, his facial muscles taught. Silvio quickly dismissed the Templar knight and gestured to Joseph, Aaron, and Rachel to sit down.

When all present had seated themselves around the table, Silvio asked, "What is so urgent, Joseph?"

"There is no time to lose," Joseph said. He looked at Silvio, took a deep breath, and asked, "What do you know about The Cave of the Mysteries?"

Silvio thought a moment. "The Cave of the Mysteries. Yes, I have heard that name before, but not for many years. Ancient relics were found there once, but I know little else about the cave."

"Do you know where it is?"

Silvio paused again and said, "Yes. It's somewhere in the Judean hills."

"Could you take me there?"

Silvio smiled and said, "That would be very difficult. First, because I do not know the exact location; and second, because the entire region is held by Saladin's army. To what purpose do you ask me this?"

Joseph looked into Silvio's eyes, he took a deep breath, and said, "I know it is behind enemy lines. I am fully aware of the danger. But I must go there. Immediately. Who can take me there?"

"I will accompany you part of the way," Silvio said without hesitation. "But I have other urgent duties, and I needs must leave you once I deem it safe enough for you to proceed without me. Anyway, my knowledge of the terrain is insufficient. Someone else must be your guide. Only very few know the exact location of The Cave of the Mysteries, but fortunately, I believe there is at least one man here in Acre who could take you there. His name is Brother Raymond."

Joseph cocked his head and pursed his lips. "A friar?" he asked.

"A monk, but it's alright, Joseph. Don't worry. Brother Raymond is not like Friar Peter. He is one of us. He is my good friend, and you can put your trust in him."

"How soon can we leave?"

"Tomorrow at the earliest," said Silvio. "It's late today already, and I doubt the ship could be equipped tomorrow in the early morning. Perhaps by noon or thereabouts we could be underway. The ship can take us near the coast a few miles north of Jaffa, and we would arrive tomorrow afternoon; but there are Saracen patrols, and it would be too dangerous for a ship to approach the shore in daylight. We would have to stay out to sea beyond their vision and, under cover of darkness, drop a small landing craft into the sea for us to row to shore. If we make landfall undetected, and the enemy doesn't capture us, we will immediately head inland, to the Judean hills. But tell me, Joseph: once you find this Cave of the Mysteries, what is the next step? Do you know your ultimate destination?"

"Jerusalem."

"Yes, but where? Jerusalem is no small place, and it's swarming with Saracens. You must have your destination clearly in mind, or it is folly to undertake such an enterprise. So tell me, Joseph, do you know exactly where you are going?"

Joseph looked down at the table. His voice dropped to a whisper. "I will know when I get there," he said.

Silvio pounded on the table and said, "That's not good enough. It's much too dangerous. I am Commander of Knights of the Order of the Temple. As you well know, a Templar knight would ordinarily not be helping you, much less do your every bidding. But I have been commanded by a holy man of great authority to assist you in any way I can, and I have done so to the best of my ability. I have kept your secrets, and I have done your bidding. But I will not undertake to lead you on a suicidal quest. I will not participate in a mission of sheer folly. If you know something more than you have told me, say it now. Otherwise I say it is a fool's errand. Speak!"

Joseph swallowed hard. He hesitated momentarily. Then he blurted out: "Old Mab told me that The Cave of the Mysteries leads into a secret tunnel deep in the Judean hills. I am to follow that tunnel through the mountains. It will take me to Jerusalem, near the foot of Mount Scopus. That is my ultimate destination."

"But where on Mount Scopus?" Silvio asked. "Do you know the exact location?"

Joseph looked at Silvio. "No," he said. "Not yet. But very soon, I will."

Joseph turned his gaze to Aaron, and continued: "Mab told me I must enter the spiritual world again tonight, before we depart. Then, she assured me, I will know exactly where to go."

Joseph looked again at Silvio and said, "Take me to Brother Raymond."

Rachel stood up. "No, Joseph. You are not going to Jerusalem without me."

Joseph shook his head.

"I insist."

"And I," said Aaron, also standing up.

Joseph shook his head again. "Too large a party will attract attention. It's much too dangerous."

Aaron said, "We've come this far with you. You cannot leave us behind now. Besides, you know you need us. You know that only a member of the priestly class may wear the breastplate."

"And what of Rachel? Why must she go?"

Aaron looked at Joseph and smiled. "You know you need her with you too, Joseph. At least as much as you need me. Perhaps much more."

*   *   *

The sun had just set a short while ago, and Matthew was finishing his hastily-eaten supper. He looked around to make sure nobody was nearby. He listened to the rustling of the trees and the chirping of the birds, trying to distinguish any sounds of human beings lurking in the background but hoping there were none. Not far away, he thought he heard faint footsteps. He looked in that direction, his heart pounding within his chest, but it was only a coney scuttling through the underbrush. He waited several more minutes, until it was almost completely dark. Finally, he deemed it safe. He gathered his few belongings and kicked dirt, twigs, and leaves over the remaining traces of his campsite. It was time to find a new location to spend the night. He walked deeper into the forest.

Tonight would be the third night since his arrival in Arsuf Forest, and he was beginning to adapt. The first days after his escape had been difficult; but fortunately, before the first night fell, he had come upon a Christian corpse, a man in chainmail, recently killed. Matthew stripped the corpse and took his chainmail, sword, and scabbard.

He wondered that the Saracens had not stripped the corpse before his arrival, but shortly Matthew noticed two Saracen warriors lying slain not far away. The Christian had probably inflicted mortal wounds upon his attackers before he died, and no other warriors had been nearby to see. The two Saracen corpses still had their scimitars, one lying a short distance from the Saracen's outstretched arm, the second scimitar clutched tightly in the other corpse's grip. Matthew left the scimitars alone, but he took both of their curved daggers. Just when he was about to leave, he saw a crossbow hidden in the grass, and several crossbow quarrels scattered on the ground. Not far away, he also found a quiver with a few additional quarrels. He looked up to heaven and blessed the Lord for watching over him.

Despite his good fortune that first day, he knew he was still in constant peril. Several times, Saracen scouts passed by and almost saw him; and once, on the day after his release from Saladin's camp, a band of three mounted Saracens did see him from a distance, but Matthew quickly took cover behind a boulder and was just able to get off a crossbow shot. The quarrel struck one Saracen in the chest, and the other two galloped away. Matthew retrieved his crossbow quarrel and took the dead Saracen's mount. After that, the going was much easier, although food was still scarce. However, when he finally reached Arsuf Forest, he found there were rabbits and coneys aplenty, and, thanks to his crossbow, he was never at a loss for food. He just needed to be careful to avoid any encounters with Saracen warriors who might happen by. Fortunately, he encountered Saracens in the forest only once, but they didn't see him, and they passed uneventfully. Nevertheless, he continued to keep his guard up, and, after that close encounter he thought it best to abandon his horse, in order to be less conspicuous. He encountered no more Saracens, however.

After about an hour of walking, Matthew found a suitable spot for a new campsite where he would spend the night. He put his quiver on the ground, lay down, rested his head on the quiver, and closed his eyes. He quickly fell asleep.

But it was not a peaceful sleep. In the distance, Mattthew kept hearing voices – screams of dying women and children, battle cries of men, and the thundering of horses' hooves. He heard the keening of the wind blowing through the forest, and the voices of demons flitting through the midnight mists. In his dreams, he saw demonic forms and faces floating in the air above, calling to him, taunting him, beckoning. He tossed and turned but did not awake.

The scene shifted, and Matthew stood in a dark and dingy cell, illuminated only by a distant, eerie light that filtered through a barred window high above. In the near-darkness, he could just make out a hooded human form sitting in the corner of the cell. Matthew cringed as the figure rose and advanced towards him.

"Do not be afraid," the figure said. He pulled back his cowl, and Matthew saw his face. It was Friar Peter.

"Where am I?" Matthew asked.

"Your body is still asleep in Arsuf Forest, but I have summoned you here so we can talk."

"Where is 'here'?"

"It is no matter," said Friar Peter. "You will not be here long, nor am I here now in body. In fact, I left this cell two nights ago, but it is a convenient place for us to talk, so I sent my apparition here to speak with you."

"Why did you summon me, and how did you bring me?"

"Why, and how? Those are two good questions, Matthew. First, I will address the second question. I want you to remember that I have Powers. I brought you to this place so that you will always remember and will not forget my powers. Neither of us is here in the flesh, but I have transported your spirit here. Now, as to your question of why: you have been in the Holy Land for many weeks already, and I fear you have forgotten your purpose."

"I came to the Holy Land to expiate my sins. I undertook a pilgrimage to purify my soul. That is my purpose."

"No!" Friar Peter exclaimed. His tone was firm, and Matthew thought he detected an overtone of restrained anger. "That was your purpose before you met me. And it is still your purpose, in a sense. But your road to purification now involves another goal as well. You must find your erstwhile friend Joseph and his companions. Remember what I showed you when we spoke last. Remember that Joseph is not as he appears to be. Do you remember, Matthew?"

"Yes, I remember."

Friar Peter smiled, and his tone became amiable again. "Yes," he said. "That is very good. Now tell me, Matthew, what do you remember? What is Joseph's true nature?"

"He is a demon in disguise. For years, he played my friend and lured me into sinful thoughts. He is evil, and I must bring his evil to an end."

"Yes, Matthew. And how will you do that? How will you bring the demon Joseph's evil to an end?"

Matthew hesitated.

Friar Peter asked again, "How will you bring Joseph's evil to an end? Say it. Do not hesitate. Speak!"

In a quivering, whispered voice, Matthew answered, "I will kill him."

"Say it again, louder, and with more conviction."

"I will kill him." This time, Matthew's voice was louder and did not quiver.

Friar Peter smiled. "And yet again. Say it a third time."

"I will kill him. I will kill the demon."

"That is very good. But thus far, you have made no effort to find Joseph. You have whiled away your time, first in the siege of Acre, then camping out in the forest of Arsuf. Of course, your lack of direction is not entirely your fault. You do not know where to search for Joseph. And that is why I have summoned you here."

"You know where Joseph is?"

"Not exactly. But I do know where he is going, and I know the company he keeps. His destination is somewhere in the vicinity of Jerusalem, and he is in the company of a Templar knight, a commander by the name of Silvio."

"But Jerusalem is held by the Saracens. How will he, or I, approach Jerusalem?"

"It will be dangerous, infiltrating behind enemy lines. But it is necessary, and you must find a way."

"Is he there already?"

"No, but he will be soon."

"When?"

"I do not know for certain, Matthew, but I suspect it will be no later than the next full moon."

"But that is only days away."

"Twelve nights, to be exact. Joseph will need to be in Jerusalem twelve nights hence, or at latest on the morning following. And that is why you need to hurry. Let me be your guide. We will speak again in dreams and visions of the night, and I will lead you to him."

Friar Peter vanished, and Matthew found himself walking on a mountain, the wind gusting in his face, his vision cast over a vast expanse of desert. Again, the scene shifted, and Matthew was walking in the forest. Behind him, the morning sun shone through the trees. In the distance, from both north and south, he heard the sounds of horses' hooves and the shouts of men, approaching rapidly. Matthew took cover behind a boulder and watched.

To the right, a phalanx of mounted Templar knights appeared, their faces hidden behind their helms, the sunlight reflecting off their drawn swords, their large red crosses emblazoned on the whiteness of the tunics that covered their chainmail. To the left, a wall of turbaned, mounted Saracens emerged from among the trees, their scimitars raised above their heads, poised to strike their foes; and at their head, mounted on a pure white steed, rode their commander, al-Adil.

Matthew braced himself, awaiting the clash of the two armies, but the scene shifted again, and he was back on the mountain, the wind in his face. Behind him was a cave, and before him lay the desert. The sun was overhead, its heat beating down upon his head. A strong gust of wind almost blew him off his feet.

From high above, he heard a keening sound. At first, he thought it was the wind, but even when the wind abated, the keening kept increasing. Matthew looked up and saw dark forms hurtling through the shimmering air. Demonic faces glowered at him as they whisked by above his head. A dark cloud passed before his eyes; and in the midst of the dark cloud, a whirlwind roared. The demons rode the whirlwind, spinning round and round, faster and faster, and their terrible piercing screams echoed in his ears. He dropped to his knees and crossed himself. He bowed his head and closed his eyes in silent prayer. Then all became dark, and there was silence.

Matthew woke up. He was still in Arsuf Forest, and dawn was just breaking. He sat up and looked around. A light breeze blew, but otherwise all was still. There were no armies, and no demons. He was all alone. Still, his hands were trembling, and his chest was throbbing. Slowly, he rose and gathered his belongings. He slung his crossbow quiver over his shoulder and covered his campsite with dirt and leaves. It was time to go. There was no time to waste. He must reach Jerusalem before the next full moon.

CHAPTER 38

24ᵗʰ to 26ᵗʰ August 1191

t was midnight. Silvio leaned over the ship's railing and looked eastward. The sky was clear, but it was a moonless night, the faint sliver of a moon having set shortly after nightfall. In the dark, the ship had come a little closer to the shore, but they were now as close as a large ship could dare approach. He knew they could not be much more than a mile from land, but in the darkness all he could see was water, and that was just as well. If all went as planned, they would reach the shore without detection.

A brown-cloaked monk came on deck and approached Silvio.

Silvio turned from the railing. He returned the monk's salute and whispered, "Is everything prepared, Brother Raymond?"

"As ready as it's going to be."

Silvio signaled to Joseph. "It is time," he whispered.

A small boat was suspended just above the surface of the ship's deck, and a sailor was sitting in the boat at the far end. Joseph, Aaron, and Rachel climbed into the boat. Silvio and Brother Raymond climbed in after them and took their seats. Four sailors worked the winch and slowly lowered the boat into the water. The pulleys squeaked each time the boat descended slightly, and Joseph's heart sank with every squeak and squeal the pulleys made, afraid the sound would be audible to the Saracens on shore. After many minutes, the boat finally slipped into the water, and Joseph breathed a sigh of relief. He looked about, trying to discern whether there was any activity on shore, but he could see nothing. He closed his eyes and said a prayer to himself.

Silvio and Brother Raymond detached the boat's tether and pushed away from the mother ship. The sailors on the ship waved to them and made the sign of the cross. Silvio and Brother Raymond waved back at the sailors, took up the oars, and began to row.

Silently they rowed, and the only sounds that Joseph heard were the gentle dipping of the oars into the water and the lapping of the waves against the boat. After at least an hour, Joseph saw a flickering light in the distance, and then another light. He pointed at the lights, but Silvio quickly pushed Joseph's hand down.

"Do not point," Silvio whispered. "They may notice you. Those are torches. Saracen torches. We are not far from shore."

Silvio and Brother Raymond stopped rowing. They put fingers to their lips, and, saying nothing more, they waited. Many minutes passed in silence, watching the shore intently, waiting for the lights to move away again. The wait was nerve-racking, sickening, and Joseph could hardly bear it any longer. *Do they know we're here? They are waiting for us on the shore, waiting for us to land. They must be. Why else would they not have moved in all this time?* He stretched out his arm and took Rachel's hand in his. Her palm was sweaty, but her grip was firm. In the darkness he saw her smile at him, and her smile gave him courage.

They sat still, waiting for the enemy to leave. And yet, the flickering torches lingered at the shore, seemingly taunting them. After perhaps a half hour more, they heard the sounds of horses' hooves, and the lights disappeared. They waited for about a half hour longer before they began to row again.

They made landfall with trepidation, expecting to be attacked at any moment, but all was quiet on the shore, and no enemy was in sight. They went ashore, each carrying a backpack laden with provisions. The sailor who had come with them remained in the boat. He waved farewell to them and silently began to row away, returning to the mother ship and leaving Joseph and his comrades on the shore. Quickly, Silvio led them inland, into Arsuf Forest.

Once in the forest, they slowed their pace; but even in the forest, Silvio still did not consider them out of danger, and he insisted that they continue farther inland, deeper into the forest. It was only when dawn began to break that Silvio deemed it best to stop and make camp. By good fortune, the terrain had turned craggy in this small part of the forest, and Silvio was able to choose a strategic spot for the campsite. Not daring to light a fire, silently they ate the cold food they had brought with them in their backpacks: dried figs and dates, and salted fish. Then they lay down to sleep, while Silvio took the first watch.

It was late afternoon before they all awoke. When they had finished eating supper, Silvio said, "I must leave you now, as we agreed."

Rachel took the Templar's hand in hers. "Couldn't you stay with us just one more night? I would feel much safer."

"Yes, I know, Rachel. But I have already stayed with you longer than I should have. My orders were to head north as soon as we arrived in Arsuf Forest and to join King Richard's army, which is marching south along the coast from Acre to Jaffa. It is a near certainty that the Saracens will attack King Richard long before he reaches Jaffa, and I must join the Templar force that is marching with him as his vanguard. But do not fear. Brother Raymond is a man of many talents, and the bearer of many secrets. Besides his great piety, his scholarship, and his good cheer, Brother Raymond has served us well on many occasions as a scout. Not only does he know the location of the cave you seek, but he also knows of many hidden paths through the forest and through the Judean hills. He will lead you safely to The Cave of the Mysteries, and God will be with you to keep you safe. Farewell, until we meet again."

Silvio took up his backpack, raised his hand in valediction, turned northwards, and began to walk briskly away. He did not look back.

When Silvio was out of sight, Rachel picked up her backpack and said, "Let's go."

But Brother Raymond sat down and signaled the others to do likewise. "It is not safe yet. We wait until the sun has set and the sky begins to darken. Meanwhile, sit, relax, and save your strength. You will need it. We will maintain a rapid pace all night, and we will not make camp again until close to dawn. We will make only four stops to rest along the way tonight, and only for a few minutes each. Tomorrow the road will become more difficult, as the terrain becomes more mountainous. If we can maintain the pace I have in mind, we should reach The Cave of the Mysteries in five days' time. That will be on the 31st of August, and I will leave you then. Once in the cave, you will be safe from attack by Saracens, but your trek through the cave will be long and arduous, and it will take you four days to reach the far end. That should be before dawn on 4th September.

"After emerging in the open, in about a half hour Mount Scopus will come into view across the valley. But you must travel only by night to avoid detection, and you will not have time to cross the valley and ascend Mount Scopus while it is still dark. Therefore, you will have to wait until the evening of the 4th, and even then there will be danger, because on that night the moon is almost full, and there is great danger you will be seen. But nothing can be done for that."

Joseph said, "That gives us no time to spare. What if we should be attacked before we reach the cave, or what if we lose our way and take a wrong turn inside the cave?"

"You are quite correct," said Brother Raymond. "There is very little room for error. You will simply have to pray and put your trust in God, as you must in any case."

CHAPTER 39

31ˢᵗ August to 4ᵗʰ September 1191

The march to The Cave of the Mysteries was difficult, as Brother Raymond had warned. The terrain became mountainous and rocky, and they made slower progress than Joseph had hoped. Nevertheless, Brother Raymond was of good cheer and kept reassuring Joseph that they were making good time. Joseph had his doubts about that, but – to his surprise – on 31st August, shortly before dawn, Brother Raymond halted them as they came around the bend of a mountain pass. He pointed up the southwestern face of the mountain and said, "There it is. The Cave of the Mysteries."

Joseph squinted, looking upwards at the indicated spot. The night was dark, the moon having set already several hours before, and thus it was very difficult to discern any landmarks. "Where is it? I don't see any cave," he said.

"Nor I," Aaron and Rachel said in unison.

"Yes," said the monk. "It is well hidden, and difficult to find even by day. In fact, you will not see it until we are right on top of it. We should be there in a half hour at the most. But hurry. I want to reach the cave by dawn."

They accelerated their pace, climbing in silence, and in less than half an hour they arrived, just as the faintest glimmer of light appeared over the mountains to the east. They entered the cave and walked about twenty paces in darkness. Their path curved, and soon they could no longer see the mouth of the cave. Only then did Brother Raymond stop and light a torch.

They walked onwards in silence, deeper into the cave. After several minutes, they found themselves in a large cavern with a high ceiling. Bats hung upside down from the ceiling, and an occasional bat flew down and passed them, high above their heads. Rachel startled and, crouching down, covered her head with both her hands. But Brother Raymond smiled at her and said, "Do not fear. They will not harm us, nor will they approach."

Crags protruded from the floor in several places. The monk looked around briefly, headed towards one of the crags, and started climbing. When he had reached a ledge in the rock, he turned and signaled the others to follow him up.

When Joseph reached the ledge, Brother Raymond pointed to the rock wall and said, "Look here, Joseph. Do you see the crack in the wall? Lean against it. Put your shoulder to it, and push hard."

Joseph did as he was told, and the rock slowly rolled back, revealing a tunnel opening into a vast expanse of cave beyond.

"Well, here we are," said the monk. "From this point on, the way is clear. Now I must leave you, as we agreed. My orders, as you know, were to bring you to the cave and to return in all haste. I trust you know the way? Repeat it for me, Joseph, exactly as I taught you."

"At the first fork, we are to take the leftward path. After that, we are always to take the right fork when the path splits in two, the middle path when it divides in three."

"That is correct, Joseph. Now God-speed, and may you reach your goal successfully. I give you my blessing."

Rachel looked into the darkness of the tunnel. She turned around again, looked at the monk, and said, "I thank you for your blessing, Brother Raymond, and I am certain it will help us."

Brother Raymond smiled at Rachel. He stepped back two paces and said, "Enter the tunnel now, and may God be with you. As soon as all of you have entered, pull the rock back into its place to hide the entrance."

Brother Raymond handed the torch to Joseph, lit another torch, and headed back. Joseph, Aaron, and Rachel entered the tunnel and pulled the rock into its original position, closing the tunnel entrance.

"Now, at least, we're safe from attack by Saracens," said Joseph. Rachel laughed nervously and took his hand.

* * *

While Joseph, Aaron, and Rachel were trekking through The Cave of the Mysteries, the Christian army was camped along the Mediterranean coast, at the River of Death. It was the wee hours of the morning of 3rd September, and the camp was just beginning to awaken, but Alfred and several other early risers were already finishing their breakfast.

Alfred looked westward, toward the sea, toward his home far away beyond the water. He thought of his home, thought of the friends he had left behind in Camryn, thought of his long-dead wife and of his only son who had gone astray and disappointed him. For a long time, he looked down at the ground. He sighed, and looked up again, at his new companions.

One man looked at Alfred and said, "Don't look so glum. Just a short while, and we'll start to march again. 'Tis pity ye missed the assault on Acre. 'Twas a beauty of a battle! What ye've seen so far since we started marching south from Acre is child's play. No serious battles. Marching is necessary, but such a bore, and it makes for blisters on yer feet. But the Saracens can't let us get to Jaffa, and we're getting close now. So they'll likely attack us very soon: a few days at the most. Then ye'll get yer first real taste o' battle, Alfred. "

"Yeah, and not a moment too soon for me. As you say, it's too bad I didn't arrive at Acre until after the city was captured, but I did get there in time to see its citizens marched up the hill and slaughtered. That was a joy to see. Serves 'em right, I say. Reminded me of my last days at home, when we killed off all the

Jews in Camryn. Saracens and Jews, they're all alike, all infidels and enemies of Christ, all agents o' the Devil, all fit to be killed."

"I agree. That's clear to any Christian, isn't it?"

Alfred closed his eyes a moment. He shook his head and said, "Yes, it should be, to any Christian but my good-for-nothing son."

"What happened to yer son, Alfred?"

"I don't know. I tried to bring him up proper. I tried to teach him right from wrong. Took him to church, and taught him to always bless the Lord before he eat. But he went off and made friends with Jews. Those Jews must have cast a spell on Matthew, 'cause right after we killed all the Jews of Camryn and thought we'd rid ourselves of those sons of Satan, Matthew had the gall to call us murderers. He left in anger, and I never saw him again."

"And that's why you took up the cross?"

"Aye. I had to atone for Matthew's sins: his lack of faith, his lack of knowing good from evil, and not to mention his disrespect for his father. It must have been my fault I didn't teach him well enough to stay away from Jews, to know that they are sons of Satan and will lead him into sin and to eternal punishment. After he left, I waited a few days, hoping he'd return, but he never did. I hope he came to his senses finally, but I have my doubts he ever did or ever will. So here I am, ready to fight the Saracens and atone for Matthew's errant ways. That river over there on the edge of our camp? I like its name: River of Death. For death is what I hope to see, and death is what I hope to give our enemies. Death to the Saracens. Death to all the enemies of Christ. God wills it." He stood up, drew his sword and held it up, pointing heavenwards.

His comrades stood up and drew their swords as well. "God wills it!" they echoed after him.

The march southward from The River of Death began shortly after dawn and proceeded uneventfully at first. As the Christian army had done since leaving Acre, they kept close to the shore, with the coastline within sight, to the army's right flank. But not long after they had crossed the river, the lay of the land forced Richard to guide his army inland, and as the Christian army wheeled around, the Saracens attacked in force.

A row of mounted Saracen archers darted forward, shooting their arrows from horseback at a full gallop, then wheeling around and retreating as another row of mounted archers galloped forward. Alfred knelt upon the ground and raised his shield above his head to protect himself from the steady rain of arrows. Wave after wave of Saracen bowmen loosed their arrows against the English host, their exultant battle cries almost drowning out the screams of dying men, and Alfred thought it would never end. The man to Alfred's right fell silently to the ground, an arrow through his neck, and four arrows bounced off Alfred's shield. In the distance, he heard the neighing of horses, the shouts of soldiers, and the clash of arms, but he dared not look up from under his shield for fear of being pierced by a Saracen arrow.

After several minutes, and several more arrows bouncing off his shield, the rain of arrows stopped. Alfred got up just as a wave of English footmen surged past him, advancing to meet the enemy in battle. Alfred raised his sword and shouted a battle cry as he lunged forward, joining his comrades-in-arms.

The Saracen cavalry came charging from the left, driving into the Christian flank of infantry. The riders cut down all before them, slashing left and right with their scimitars, and the Christian infantry scattered before them. But Alfred stood his ground and waited until a Saracen rider was almost upon him. Just as the rider was about to run him through, Alfred quickly feinted to his right, spun around, and slashed at the rider's right leg. The Saracen wheeled his horse about and charged at Alfred again, but Alfred saw that the Saracen's leg was bleeding badly, and the rider was not as nimble as before. Alfred dropped to the ground and rolled. The rider turned his horse around again and charged. Alfred waited until the horse was almost upon him before spinning away and coming back again, slashing at the horse's exposed flank. The horse pitched forward, and the Saracen rider was thrown forcefully to the ground. In an instant, Alfred was upon him. The fallen Saracen was still alive but dazed. Alfred raised his sword with both his hands, looked into his enemy's eyes, and, with a loud battle cry, he thrust the sword downward, into the Saracen's heart.

But Alfred's elation at his victory was fleeting. No sooner had he extracted his sword from the dead Saracen's chest than an arrow caught Alfred in his flank. He fell to the ground writhing in pain, as the battle passed over him. He tried to take a deep breath, but breathing was excruciating. He tried to put his hand on the wound, but he felt only the chainmail and the Saracen arrow protruding from it. His hand was moist and sticky, and he knew his blood was oozing through his suit of mail. In a fog, he heard his comrades surging forward, shouting a victorious battle cry, beating Saladin's forces back, and despite his pain, he smiled. After that, he remembered nothing more.

*   *   *

The tunnel widened, and Joseph raised his torch, shifting it from side to side as he gazed into the void, trying to take in the vast expanse of cavern that stretched before him. After many hours along a difficult, downward-sloping path, it was hard to believe they were finally here. The flame of Joseph's torch flickered, causing Rachel and Aaron's shadows to dance along the cavern walls. An occasional bat flew overhead but did not come close to them. Joseph raised his hand, signaling a halt.

"There it is: the great craggy hall under the mountain, just as Brother Raymond described it, and here is where he said that we may stop to rest for several hours, until the evening. If Brother Raymond's calculation is correct, it should now be close to mid-morning on 3rd September. With God's help, we will emerge on schedule and find the High Priest's breastplate on Mount Scopus.

But Friar Peter, no doubt, has not been idle either. I expect we will encounter him again; and I pray to God that when we do, we will have the wherewithal to thwart his evil plans, despite whatever powers the Other Side has conferred upon him."

Rachel put both her hands on Joseph's shoulders. "Do not fear," she said. "God is with us, and He has sent us Enoch to guide us. At every step of our way, providence has intervened, first through Enoch, then through Old Mab, Father John, Commander Silvio, and even Brother Raymond. See this cavern, just as he described it. One more night's travel, and we will reach the end of the tunnel. Then we will emerge in sight of Mount Scopus. As you said, today is 3rd September. I am certain we are right on schedule. The full moon is two days off, and we are almost there. We will conquer."

*　　*　　*

Matthew stopped and looked around. This would be a good strategic spot to make camp. He had been walking all night, and he was now very close to his final destination. Soon it would be dawn, and it was time to rest. He ate a hasty meal and looked around once more to make sure there were no Saracens in sight. When he had satisfied himself that he was quite alone, he lay down on the ground and quickly fell asleep. And, as on each night since Friar Peter had first appeared to him in a dream in Arsuf Forest, a maelstrom of dark clouds, fire, and demonic faces whirled around before him.

"Matthew!" The voice called to him from the distance, and Matthew recognized the voice immediately. It was Friar Peter.

"Yes, Friar Peter. I am here. But where are you?"

"On the mountain, waiting for you."

"Where on the mountain? I looked around before I went to sleep, but I saw no one here."

"And indeed I am not there, Matthew. I am on Mount Scopus, awaiting your arrival."

"You are there already? Today is only 4th September. Are you there in body, or just in spirit?"

Friar Peter laughed. "Body, spirit, it is all the same. I am here on the mountain, preparing, searching."

"I do not understand. Preparing and searching for what?"

"Why, preparing for your friend Joseph's arrival, of course. And searching for the object that calls him to this mountain."

"Joseph is no longer my friend."

"Yes," said Friar Peter emphatically. "And do not forget that. I felt your resolve wavering last morning."

"No, Friar Peter. My resolve has never wavered ever since you showed me the truth. Joseph is a demon, sent to trap my soul and lead me into sinful ways. You opened my eyes to his true nature. I am no longer deluded."

"Then what was the agitation I detected in your spirit on the morning of the 3rd?"

"Indeed I do not know myself. It was mid-morning, and suddenly I felt a shudder, as though something terrible had happened. I felt a pain in my side, as though I had been stabbed. I caught my breath. The world spun around me, and I felt that I may swoon. It lasted but a moment."

"Ah," said Friar Peter, and Matthew saw a faint smile trace itself across the friar's lips.

"What is it, Friar Peter? Tell me. What made me shudder, catch my breath, and almost swoon? You know. I see it written on your face."

"In truth, I do not know. That was the very question I asked you, if you remember. Now sleep. Do not forget your purpose. Joseph is your mortal enemy, and you must confront him. I await you soon upon this mountain."

Matthew was about to retort, but he could not remember what he had been about to say. His vision blurred, and he found himself again in a dreamless sleep.

*   *   *

The path through the mountain curved sharply to the right, then to the left, and inclined steeply upwards.

"This is it," Joseph said. "We are about to emerge at the far end of the tunnel. We go another hundred paces and put out our torch, lest the Saracens see us when we emerge from the cave."

Aaron said, "I can't see the outside world yet."

"It should still be night," said Joseph. "But I can tell we are approaching the end, because things are exactly as Brother Raymond described them."

Joseph led them forward, counting the paces. The way continued sloping upwards for the first eighty paces and then leveled off. After yet another ten paces, Joseph held up his hand and said, "Smell the air. It's fresh. And I can hear the wind blowing in the distance. Put out your torch now, and advance in silence. Speak only in a whisper, if you must speak at all."

Slowly, silently they advanced in darkness, their hands caressing the stone wall of the cave, their feet searching for the path. After twenty more paces, the stars appeared, and shortly they discerned a light in the distance – undoubtedly a Saracen campfire on the mountain opposite, beyond the valley.

Joseph turned back and re-entered the cave, signaling Aaron and Rachel to follow him back inside. When the outside world was again no longer visible, Joseph said, "It must be shortly before dawn on 4th September. Mount Scopus should be around the bend and just across the valley, but, as Brother Raymond told us, there is insufficient time for us to cross while it is still dark. So let us eat now, and go to sleep. We rest here until darkness falls again tonight. Before dawn tomorrow morning – 5th September – we should reach our destination as the moon becomes full, and Friar Peter will await us there; I have no doubt of it. I must go on and face my enemy, but I cannot force you to put yourselves in danger. Now is your last chance to return."

Aaron and Rachel said in unison, "No, Joseph. We will go with you."

"Then may God be with us, and may our quest succeed."

CHAPTER 40

The black-cloaked monk walked slowly through the rows of wounded. He stopped beside each wounded man, inspecting him briefly for signs of life. Now and then, he looked up at the sky, trying to assess the time. He estimated it was now close to midnight. Far away, he heard a jackal's wail, and he shuddered. He strained to gaze into the distance, half-hoping to catch a glimpse of the beast whose cry had pierced the night; but he saw nothing there, and somehow that calmed his nerves.

As he approached the next wounded man, he smelled the all-too-familiar stench of putrefaction even before he got close. He steeled himself and moved closer. The man groaned.

"It's so cold," the man whispered almost inaudibly. "I'm freezing. Please cover me."

The monk looked down. The man was shivering despite the torrid summer air. The monk put his hand on the man's forehead. It was very hot and sweaty.

The wounded man looked up at the monk, with tears in his eyes. "Cover me, Matthew," he said.

The monk reached across the man's body, fumbling to find the blanket that had fallen off, and drawing it gently over the man's shoulders.

"Thank you, Matthew." The man continued trembling, but his eyes glazed over, and his head lolled to the side.

The monk paused a moment longer to verify that the man was still breathing. He crossed himself and said, "Sleep now, Alfred, and may The Lord bless you."

Hastily, the monk went to the end of the row of wounded men and towards a tent a short distance away. At the entrance to the tent, a knight stood guard, his coat of mail covered with a black tunic emblazoned with a large, eight-pointed white cross. The guard's chainmail-clad right hand rested on the hilt of a sword that hung at his left hip. The monk saluted the guard and entered the tent. After a few minutes, he emerged with another man, also dressed in black but wearing neither mail nor sword. Silently, quickly, the monk led the other man to Alfred.

Alfred opened his eyes as they approached. "Are you back already, Matthew? It's so good to see you. Is it almost light?"

The monk turned to the other man and said in a whisper, "He's been calling me Matthew ever since this morning. I think that may be his son's name. The fever has made him delirious."

The monk took a deep breath before gently lifting the blanket off Alfred's flank. Carefully, he peeled back the blood-stained bandages that covered Alfred's wound. Looking again at the other man, he said, "What do you think, doctor?"

The doctor bent over Alfred. He probed the wound with a blunt instrument, and Alfred screamed in pain.

The doctor wiped the instrument on Alfred's blanket and gently covered him again. He stood up and walked away a short distance, signaling the monk to follow him. "It is difficult to see the extent of the putrefaction in the dark of night, but the stench is worse than ever, and he has weakened greatly since last I saw him. I have already cauterized his wound thrice, yet it still festers, and his body burns with fever. Perhaps another poultice. I will have to re-examine his wound when it is light, but I fear there is not much left for me to do, and precious little time for me to do it. He is fading rapidly, and I doubt he will survive the morrow."

*　　*　　*

Matthew stopped to rest. He had been walking since shortly after sunset. According to his calculation, he had traversed the valley more quickly than anticipated, and his ascent of Mount Scopus was going smoothly, at least as quickly as planned. It was still shortly before midnight on 4th September, and he should have no trouble reaching his destination long before dawn of the 5th. He felt he deserved this rest. And yet, the voice within his head seemed agitated, insistent, prodding him onwards.

"You must not rest for very long. I am waiting for you on the mountain, Matthew, and there is much to do."

Matthew looked around, although he knew there was no one nearby to be seen. "Where are you, Friar Peter?" he asked.

"At the appointed place, not far from the summit."

"And where is Joseph? Has he reached the mountain yet?"

"Yes, Matthew. He and his friends are on Mount Scopus also, somewhat ahead of you but traveling along a different path. You will not meet up with Joseph yet, not until the morning."

"Am I in danger of encountering any Saracens on this mountain?"

"Not tonight, Matthew. There is a small contingent of Saracens not far away, but they will not see you."

"How can you know this? How can you be sure?"

"Matthew, Matthew," said the voice inside his head. "Do you not know my powers yet? Do you not trust my powers?"

"Yes, Friar Peter, I know you have great powers. But we are now in the Saracens' stronghold. You cannot defeat an entire army all by yourself. Else, you would hardly need my help against Joseph and his friends."

"You underestimate me, Matthew. And, I think, you also underestimate your erstwhile friend. He is a demon of great power – much more powerful than you imagine. But, in fact I do not have to defeat an entire Saracen army. Look around you. Do you see any signs of a large Saracen force? As I told you, there is only a small contingent here, and I have taken care of them. The rest of the Saracen army has withdrawn, as Saladin commanded, and is marching towards the coast to join with Saladin in battle against the Christian forces. Those Saracens that remain are all confined within the walls of Jerusalem. So you see, Matthew, you are safe enough from Saracens. Now rise, and do not dally any longer. We too have a battle to fight, and I await you here."

* * *

They had been climbing all night, and Joseph estimated it was very close to dawn. He looked up at the western sky. The full moon shone brightly down on them, illuminating the mountainside with its silvery light. He cast his eyes up the mountain, searching. Aaron and Rachel were a few paces behind him, and he paused to let them catch up.

Rachel said, "It can't be far from here. We must be close to the summit already."

"Yes," said Joseph. "Not very far at all. But the summit is still not visible, and it will take at least a half hour, perhaps an hour longer to reach it. Let's go up to yonder boulder. We should reach it in no more than five minutes, and then we will take a short rest."

They continued climbing, and it took somewhat longer than expected before they reached the boulder. Dawn was breaking in the east, and the sky was beginning to get brighter, but the sun had not yet risen, and the full moon was still visible low in the western sky. Joseph stopped to scan the terrain once more.

"What is it, Joseph?" Rachel asked. "Do you see something?"

Joseph pointed. "That boulder up ahead. Its color and its shape are unusual – somewhat out of place. It's a different type of rock from all the others on the mountain. And it looks very familiar, as though I have seen it before."

Slowly, Joseph approached the strange boulder. He put his hands on its rough surface and closed his eyes, thinking, trying to remember when and where he had seen this place before. After a few seconds, he opened his eyes and turned around, scanning the mountainside and the distant landscape. To the east and south, the desert sprawled beyond the mountain, seemingly endless. A gust of wind nearly blew him off his feet, and he put a hand on the boulder to steady himself.

"I've got it!"

"What is it, Joseph?" Rachel grasped Joseph's tunic. "Is this the place?"

"Yes, Rachel. I think it is. I know where I have seen this boulder and this landscape. It was in my vision in the world of spirit. I saw it all that evening, at the Templar stronghold, when I used the emerald to enter the spiritual world. I was transported here, to this very place. It is no coincidence. I recognize the boulder. I recognize the mountain. This must be the place."

Joseph darted to his left, skirting the boulder, stumbling on the rocky ground. At the far edge of the boulder, the ground sloped sharply downward for a distance of several feet, and Joseph descended carefully. He paused to catch his breath, standing with his back to the boulder. Before him, the ground sloped steeply upward again. He started to ascend, but Rachel tugged at his sleeve.

"Look, Joseph. Over there." Excitedly, she bolted to the right, pulling Joseph with her.

"What is it, Rachel? Where are you taking me?"

Rachel pointed upwards and to her right. "There. Don't you see it? There's a crevice in the rocks." She let go of Joseph's sleeve and scrambled upwards as quickly as she could among the slippery rocks, steadying herself with both her hands.

Soon she reached the crevice. She paused only momentarily before plunging into the darkness beyond, Joseph and Aaron following close behind her. Only a small amount of daylight filtered in, but even in the dim light it was evident to Joseph that they were in the entrance of a large cave. He reached into his backpack and extracted a torch and a pair of flints. In his excitement, he fumbled with the flints a few times before succeeding in lighting the torch, but when the torch was finally lit, Joseph was pleased to see his own excitement reflected in both Aaron's and Rachel's faces.

They went deeper into the cave, Aaron now leading the way. Joseph said nothing but was content to follow, somehow believing that a certain spirit of otherworldly origin was animating Aaron, guiding him. Aaron scrambled up a ledge, snaking his way among the rocks. Joseph and Rachel followed.

Aaron stopped abruptly, pointing to a depression in the rocks. "Quick. Shine the light over here."

Joseph tipped the torch downwards, illuminating the spot where Aaron indicated. And there, wedged in between the rocks, was a small metallic chest.

"I think this may be it." Aaron's voice trembled. "Give me the torch, Joseph. It is most fitting that you be the one to take the object from its resting place."

Joseph gave Aaron the torch and lay down on his belly, reaching down into the crevice. The metal chest had a handle on either side, and Joseph grasped the two handles in both his hands. But the chest was heavy and wedged in tightly among the rocks, and he was only able to wiggle it slightly.

Joseph looked up at Aaron and said, "Give the torch to Rachel. Get down and help me lift it. I don't think I can do it by myself."

Aaron lay on his stomach and grasped one handle of the metal chest, while Joseph held the other. He and Joseph pulled together, but still the chest was not dislodged completely. It did, however, move a little.

Joseph said, "Let's rock it back and forth."

And so they did. With each rocking motion, the chest moved slightly, and after ten times they finally were able to lift the chest up out of its rocky bed. They put it down on the ledge and stood up, looking down at the metal lid. Joseph brushed sand off the lid, revealing an engraved design: two hands spread in priestly blessing, the second finger of each hand joined to the third finger, and the fourth finger joined to the fifth, with a space between the middle finger and the fourth.

Joseph looked at Aaron and said, "The breastplate is a priestly vestment. If the breastplate is indeed inside, it is not for me to open the chest."

But Aaron shook his head. "No, Joseph. You are not correct. The task is yours. It always has been. And did not Enoch designate you for this mission? I am just a vessel. Now lift the lid, and open the chest."

Without a further word, Joseph bent down and grasped the lid in both his hands. He looked up at Aaron, and then at Rachel. "What if the breastplate is not here?"

Solemnly, fervently, Rachel said, "It is, Joseph. I have no doubt of it. And in the depths of your heart, I know you know it also. Now lift the lid."

Still looking at Rachel, without looking down, Joseph raised the lid, and only when he saw the smile on Rachel's face did he look down into the metal chest.

Rachel lowered the torch closer for better illumination. "Look at it," she said. "Neatly folded, lying peacefully in its chest as though it had been placed there only yesterday."

Joseph reached down and held the breastplate in his hands, caressing its golden threads. He unfolded it and held it vertical. "It is two thousand years old, yet it shows no sign of age at all."

"Yes, it's beautiful," Rachel said.

But Aaron only stared at the breastplate in awe, saying not a word.

Rachel pointed into the metal chest. "Look. There are two golden chains. Aaron, take the chains and attach them to the breastplate, so the breastplate can be worn suspended from the shoulders."

Aaron slowly took the two chains and went over to Joseph. The two upper corners of the breastplate were equipped with small gold rings, and Aaron threaded the golden chains through the rings.

Joseph held the breastplate suspended by the two chains and ran his hand over it, gently touching each of the eleven stones. There were four rows of gemstones, three to each row, each stone held in place by a thin gold clasp; but the rightmost stone in the second row was missing, and Joseph's finger came to rest over that spot.

"That's where the emerald should be," Rachel said. "Take out your stone, and insert it there."

"No," said Joseph. "Not here in the cave. Do you remember when Enoch first showed us the power of the emerald? He first took us out into the moonlight. Let us go out of this cave, and then I will insert the emerald."

Aaron shook his head and said, "Enoch only needed to take us out of the cave so he could demonstrate how the stone would glow in moonlight, not because it was improper to look at the stone in the cave."

But Joseph answered, "No, Aaron, Enoch did not need to take us outside. If you remember, the moon was not full then, and the stone would not have glowed in moonlight, but Enoch willed it to glow. Today the moon is full. We must go outside, and only then insert the stone into its proper place. But hurry. There is not much time until the moon will set."

When they reached the cave entrance, Joseph signaled to Rachel to extinguish the torch. They left the cave and climbed back up beside the boulder that obscured the entrance to the cave. Joseph looked at the sky. In the east, the sun had not yet risen, and the full moon was still visible to the west; it had not yet set.

Joseph smiled broadly and pointed to the moon. "There. Do you see it? Now we are ready."

Aaron quickly placed the closed chest on the ground, and Joseph spread out the breastplate on the metal chest.

"Look!" said Rachel, pointing. "Look at the stones. Something is missing. Do you not see?"

Aaron looked perplexed. "I see nothing missing. They number eleven, just as they should. And Joseph's emerald will make twelve."

"No," she said. "Not their number. The names. Shouldn't each stone have the name of one of the twelve tribes engraved upon it? But look: there is no engraving on any of the stones. What can it mean?"

Instead of answering, Joseph reached under his tunic and produced a pouch. Untying the fastening strap, he inverted the pouch, emptying the emerald onto his palm, and in one fluid motion he inserted the stone into its appointed place, while fastening it to the breastplate with its golden clasp.

No sooner had Joseph inserted the emerald in its place than the image of a lion rampant flashed before his eyes, but only for a moment before it vanished.

Joseph startled. His head snapped back, and his hands suddenly withdrew from the breastplate as though he had been burnt.

"What is it?" Rachel shouted, grasping Joseph by his shoulders. "Are you hurt?"

"No," said Joseph, but his voice was barely audible.

Aaron and Rachel seemed not to have seen the evanescent image. Joseph looked around him, and all seemed normal once again. He looked down at the breastplate. He tried to speak but couldn't. In amazement, he pointed at the breastplate.

The twelve stones flickered, emitting an eerie light that pulsated as though it were a beating heart. The colors of the twelve stones danced before them, and the interplay of colors emanating from the stones held them enthralled. Gradually the light intensified, and faint markings emerged on the surface of each stone. With each pulsation of the light, the markings on the stones became more clear: ancient Hebrew letters engraved where previously only a smooth surface had been evident; and on the emerald, five Hebrew letters were inscribed, spelling the name "Judah."

CHAPTER 41

When the light emitted by the stones stopped pulsating, Joseph turned to Aaron and said, "I think it is time. Put it on."

Aaron took a few steps forward. His right hand reached out but did not quite touch the breastplate. His hand trembled. He looked at the breastplate; he looked at Joseph. Slowly he withdrew his hand.

"I can't," he said, his voice cracking. "I am not worthy. Only a high priest may don the breastplate." He took a step backwards, away from the breastplate of woven golden threads and its twelve softly glowing stones. Trembling, he steadied himself against the boulder.

"Yes," said Joseph; "in ancient times that was so. But times have changed. There is no high priest now. There hasn't been one in many centuries. And yet, the prophet Jeremiah hid the breastplate for a purpose, knowing that in future days there would be no high priest, and no Temple in which the high priest would serve. It is no coincidence that you, my friend, are here with me today. Just as it was my task to be the bearer of the stone of the tribe of Judah, you also have a role to play if we are to thwart Friar Peter's machinations and to save the world from Satan's grasp. So fortify yourself, Aaron, and don the breastplate. That is your task and no one else's."

Aaron again took a step towards the breastplate, and he stretched out his hands, first the right and then the left. He grasped the golden breastplate, lifting it slowly from its resting place on the lid of the metal chest. He swallowed hard and closed his eyes.

"Come on," Rachel said. "Put it on."

Aaron opened his eyes. Slowly, he raised the breastplate and began to slip his arms through the two gold chains, first his right arm, then his left. The breastplate hung loosely from Aaron's shoulders, and Aaron reached behind to fasten it. The full moon hung low in the western sky, and Aaron turned slightly, to face the moon. Immediately, the stones of the breastplate glowed more brightly – first the emerald, and then the other stones. Their light waxed and waned, pulsating like the beating of a heart.

"DO NOT MOVE!" The voice echoed among the rocks, and Aaron froze in place, the breastplate still unfastened, hanging loosely from his shoulders.

Joseph's eyes scanned the rocks, searching for the source of the voice. He did not have to search long. A dark-robed, hooded figure shot out from behind the boulder beyond Aaron, hurtling towards Aaron.

"DROP THE BREASTPLATE!" the intruder shouted, as he lunged forward.

Aaron tried to run, but the intruder was too fast for him. Before Aaron had gone three steps, the dark-robed man caught Aaron's right arm and twisted it, while uttering an animalistic roar. Aaron tried to twist away, but the man seized Aaron by the neck and threw him to the ground. Aaron tried to rise, but the intruder pounced on him and, with both his hands, smashed Aaron's head upon a rock. Aaron lay motionless on the ground, blood trickling from his scalp, while the intruder ripped the breastplate off Aaron's shoulders and quickly began to put the breastplate on himself. Rachel darted forward, screaming.

The intruder began to rise, but Joseph was now upon him. With his left hand, Joseph seized the intruder's garment, while Joseph's right fist smashed into the man's jaw. The intruder's hood fell away, and Joseph instantly recognized his adversary: it was Friar Peter.

Friar Peter shouted a battle cry. His hands closed around Joseph's neck and squeezed.

Joseph clung to Friar Peter's shoulder. He drew his right arm back and buried his fist in Peter's belly. Peter gasped, relaxed his grip on Joseph's neck, and Joseph threw his adversary to the ground, pinning him on his back.

While Joseph was struggling with Friar Peter, Rachel took her brother's face in her hands. "Aaron, speak to me. Please, Aaron. Speak!" But Aaron did not move, nor did he speak. Rachel turned her brother's head. She looked at Aaron's smashed-in skull; she looked at the blood-stained ground. She threw herself down over Aaron's body; she kissed him gently on his face and cried, tears streaming down her reddened cheeks.

How much time elapsed, she was not sure. It could not have been very long – perhaps only seconds. Through her cries and tears, as though from another world, Joseph's voice resounded in her ears, forcing her back to reality. Did he really call, or did she just imagine it? She was not certain.

Again she heard his voice, more urgent now: "Rachel, get up. Quick! Take the breastplate."

With all her strength, she willed herself to rise. She turned away from Aaron and ran to Joseph's side. Joseph was still atop the friar, struggling to keep him pinned in place.

The breastplate's left chain was slung over Friar Peter's left shoulder, and the other chain was held tightly in Peter's right hand. Friar Peter began to move his right shoulder downwards, and his left hand swung upwards at Joseph. But Joseph anticipated the move and slammed the friar's arm down against a rock. Friar Peter uttered only a grunt, but he was obviously in great pain from Joseph's blow, and he made no further move to raise his arm.

Rachel bent down, wiped her bloody hands upon the ground, and grasped the breastplate in both her hands, trying to wrest it from Friar Peter's grip. Friar Peter tried to hold on, but Joseph hammered his fist into the friar's nose, and the breastplate began to slip out of Friar Peter's hands. Rachel pulled hard on both the breastplate's chains, and Peter lost his grip. But at the last instant, Peter's right hand closed over the emerald; and, as Rachel pulled the breastplate away, Peter opened the clasp that held the emerald in place. His fingers closed around the stone as Rachel, with all her might, wrenched the breastplate from his grasp.

Joseph, realizing that Peter now had the emerald, tried to pry the friar's fingers open, but Friar Peter's fingers wouldn't budge.

Friar Peter, still pinned to the ground under Joseph's weight, smiled a wicked smile. He looked up at Joseph. He opened his mouth and uttered a shrill scream. "O wind, I summon you. Do my bidding. Fight my battle."

The wind struck with fury at Joseph's back. It lashed out at him, throwing him off his balance. Friar Peter immediately rose, shaking Joseph off him.

Rachel, slinging the breastplate over her left arm, ran to the metal chest that still lay beside the boulder near the entrance to the cave. Without stopping, she grasped the metal chest in both her hands and continued into the cave, dragging the chest along the ground. It was very heavy, and she was amazed that she could move it at all, but somehow she found the strength and managed to drag it back into the cave, just beyond the entrance.

Peter started to follow Rachel, but Joseph blocked his path to the cave. For a moment, they stood facing each other. Joseph's back was to the cave, slightly off to his left. Friar Peter tried to rush around Joseph's left flank, but Joseph's hand shot out, arresting Peter in his path.

Friar Peter threw himself at Joseph, but as he did so, the earth beneath his feet began to tremble. Joseph was thrown backwards, and Friar Peter fell to his side.

As Joseph and Peter both got up again, the ground continued shaking, more violently now, and a crevice opened up between them, cutting off Peter's access to the cave. Friar Peter attempted to leap at Joseph across the crevice, but the swaying of the earth threw Peter again off balance, and he nearly fell backwards.

The crevice in the ground continued to enlarge, and soon it was too wide and too deep for either Joseph or Peter to traverse. Friar Peter glowered at Joseph across the gap.

Suddenly, something about Friar Peter's expression caught Joseph's eye, and Joseph spun around to look behind him to his right. In the distance, a man appeared, running over the rocky ground towards Joseph.

The man continued running forward. He drew his sword and shouted, "I have you now. You will not escape, you demon."

All at once, Joseph recognized the voice, and he could hardly believe it. "Matthew! It is Joseph. Your friend. Don't you know me? Sheath your sword."

Matthew continued running towards Joseph. He did not put down his sword. "You are not my friend!" he shouted. "You are a demon sent by Satan to deceive me and to draw me into sin."

"No, Matthew. I am not a demon. Who has told you such a lie? And how could you believe it? Are you possessed?"

Momentarily, Matthew stopped. His sword arm drooped slightly. He looked at Joseph and at Friar Peter.

Matthew was now almost within striking distance, and Friar Peter called out to him:

"Matthew, strike! Do not allow this demon to deceive you any longer. Strike. Put an end to his evil, and redeem your soul."

Matthew again brandished his sword above his head and advanced towards Joseph.

*　　*　　*

Miles away, a different black-cloaked man knelt on the ground, his right hand clasped in the hand of another man lying beside him.

The supine man drew a breath with difficulty. In a voice barely audible, he said, "Please don't leave me, Matthew. I need you badly. Do not leave me. You are my only hope."

The black-cloaked monk tightened his grip on the other man's hand. "It's alright, Alfred. I am here with you."

Alfred tried to speak again, but the words caught in his throat, and he gasped for breath.

"Rest now, Alfred," the monk said. "You do not need to talk."

Alfred strained to raise himself but couldn't. "No," he said. "I must speak. I must beg your forgiveness, Matthew, before I die."

"Yes," said the monk, "I forgive you if you have sinned against me."

Alfred smiled a feeble smile. "I will kiss your mother for you when I see her."

The monk felt Alfred's grip relax. He let go of Alfred's hand, and it fell limply at his side. He looked at Alfred's chest and verified that Alfred was not breathing. He felt Alfred's neck and verified that there was no pulse. He closed Alfred's eyes. He stood up and crossed himself, and slowly walked away as the sun was rising in the east.

*　　*　　*

Matthew looked at Joseph. Hatred for the demon who pretended to be his friend coursed through his very being. He raised his sword, prepared to strike.

From across the jagged fissure in the ground before him, he heard Friar Peter's strident shout: "Strike, Matthew! Cut him down."

But just as Friar Peter called for him to strike, in the distance he heard another voice. He felt a new sensation, a feeling of serenity, of peace, redemption, and release.

He listened, trying to discern what the second voice was saying. It was a female voice, but very faint and very far away. He strained to hear her words, and all at once it struck him: it was his mother's voice.

"What is it, mother?" he heard himself say within his mind.

Again he heard his mother's voice, this time more distinctly. "Matthew, my son. Your soul has been released."

"Released from what?"

"From the bonds of evil. Your father has just died, and with his death, your soul is free. Use your eyes, and use your heart. Listen to your heart, Matthew. It speaks the truth."

Matthew looked at Joseph. He raised his sword again, prepared to strike, but something tugged at his heartstrings, and he hesitated.

Joseph said nothing but looked deep into Matthew's eyes. As though from far away, Matthew heard the friar's voice again, calling for him to strike. But Matthew did not strike. He turned away from Joseph and ran full-speed towards the crevasse.

With a mighty leap, Matthew bounded across the gap, just barely landing on the other side. He pounced on Friar Peter and stabbed at him. But Peter dodged, and Matthew's sword only wounded him in his flank.

Peter squirmed away from Matthew, his right arm raised, and hit Matthew in the face with the emerald. Matthew reeled, stunned momentarily, and Friar Peter staggered away.

Matthew quickly recovered. He lunged at Friar Peter, his sword raised.

Friar Peter slunk away, trying to escape. But a great wind blew at Peter's back and threw him to the ground, as another tremor of the earth ensued, throwing Matthew backwards, away from Friar Peter.

The wind increased its fury, and the tremor of the earth increased. Matthew, unable to advance, merely raised his sword and shouted into the wind:

"It is you who are the demon, Friar Peter. You, not Joseph, are my true enemy. You must die."

As the moon prepared to set and the sun rose in the east, sunlight glinted from Matthew's sword, and the sword appeared to be aflame. Friar Peter began to rise again. He held up his right hand, and the sun's rays reflected off the emerald in his palm.

"You cannot kill me, Matthew. You cannot overcome my power."

Again the wind increased. Again the earth shook. Peter fell to the ground, sprawled on the rocks.

A crack opened under Friar Peter's feet. He screamed and slithered backwards like a crab, trying desperately to prevent himself from falling into the crack. The gap widened. Rocks began to fall from somewhere up above, and one rock struck Friar Peter on his shoulder.

He bellowed in pain. His right hand opened as he grabbed for a handhold to prevent his fall into the earth's maw, and the emerald rolled out of his grasp. He reached for it, but it rolled away into the crack, disappearing deep into the earth.

"No!" Friar Peter screamed. He tried to rise again, but once again the earth shook under him, throwing him to the ground. Another jagged crack opened up beneath him, and he struggled to hold on, but the tremor grew in force, and he lost his grip. The crack beneath his body widened further, and Friar Peter's body tumbled headlong into the earth.

Rachel ran out of the cave just as Peter lost his grip on the emerald. Joseph looked up and saw that rocks were falling from somewhere up the mountain.

"Hurry, Rachel!" he called out. "Get away from the cave."

Rachel ran to Joseph, reaching him as a deluge of rocks fell from above, covering the mouth of the cave. She threw her arms around Joseph, and he held her close, comforting her. He could feel the beating of her heart, and he felt the rapid rise and fall of her chest pressed against him. But, he noted, she did not cry.

Joseph heard Friar Peter's voice screaming "No!" He saw the black-cloaked body fall into the earth. He heard the friar calling: "Help me."

But there was no help. For no sooner did Joseph hear the friar's call for help than the earth shook one more time, rumbling from its depths, and the gaping, jagged crack closed again, swallowing Friar Peter without a trace.

Gradually, the wind diminished. The trembling of the earth ceased, and all was quiet once again. Matthew sheathed his sword.

Rachel released Joseph, and Matthew ran to him, embracing Joseph. "I almost killed you, Joseph," he said.

"But you could not do it," said Joseph.

"I would have. Really. How can I ever atone for that?"

Joseph held Matthew close and said, "You do not need to, Matthew. You were possessed. It's over now, and all is forgiven."

"No, no. All is not forgiven. You do not understand."

Joseph held Matthew by both his shoulders and shook him gently. "Matthew, I said that I forgive you. You were possessed. Friar Peter had Powers, and you could not help yourself."

Matthew pulled away from Joseph. He sat down on the ground and held his head between his hands.

"No, Joseph. My soul was weak, and I have sinned. I went on pilgrimage to atone for my sin, but my atonement was not yet finished. It was my sin that gave Peter power over me."

Joseph sat on the ground beside Matthew. "What sin did you have, Matthew? What are you talking about?"

Matthew hesitated. He shook his head and swallowed. "Do you remember that terrible day in Camryn, just before I left you at the edge of Sherwood Forest? I told you then that I must atone for my father's sin, and for my own."

"Yes, of course I remember. But I did not understand what sin you had, and I still do not."

"I know," said Matthew. "How could you understand? But I have lived in shame since then, hardly daring to speak of it even to myself. My sin haunted me for many months. It made me weak, unable to resist the friar's power."

Joseph again seized Matthew's shoulders. "Out with it already! Tell me what it is. What sin do you have that haunts you so?"

Again Matthew hesitated. He looked into Joseph's eyes, and into Rachel's. He bent his head and said, "I could have prevented all of this."

Joseph said nothing. He let go of Matthew's shoulders. Matthew lifted his head, and Joseph looked into Matthew's eyes.

"Yes," said Matthew. "All of this could have been prevented. Your father's murder, and your mother's. The massacre. My father's sin, and Camryn's. We could still be living there now, in peace. You see, I knew the massacre would happen, but I refused to believe. I did nothing to stop it."

"How could you have known, Matthew? How could you have prevented it?"

"I knew, and I did nothing. A certain man of our long acquaintance happened by my father's smithy just one day before, to fix his horse's shoes. I overheard him tell my father tales of Friar Peter and how the friar would soon rid Camryn of all its Jews. He told my father about the massacre at York the week before, and said the massacre at Camryn would be still greater in ferocity if not in numbers of dead. But I knew that man, and I knew he was a liar. In short, I did not believe him. Had I not dismissed his words, I could have warned the Jews of Camryn. I could have warned the rabbi. I could have warned the priest. Perhaps, at least, I could have saved your family. But I did nothing."

Joseph shook his head and said, "No, Matthew. You are mistaken. There is nothing you could have done. Did you think the priest, the rabbi, or anyone would have believed your tale? They would have disbelieved for the same reason that you did. And even if the priest had believed you, what would he have done? I know it is against your nature to think ill of any man, especially a priest; but open your eyes, Matthew. He was at least as prone as any man in Camryn to think of us as devil's spawn. It may not have been in his nature to incite men to riot and to murder, nor would he himself participate in such vile acts. But make no mistake: to him, Friar Peter was a holy man, and he would have done nothing to oppose the friar's exhortations. There was nothing you could have done to prevent the massacre."

"What about you, Joseph? Wouldn't you have believed me? Perhaps I could have told you and saved your family."

"No, Matthew. You would have told me of your reservations and your doubts, and thus it is unlikely you could have convinced my father or my mother. Besides, Matthew, there is much you do not know. After our escape from Camryn, Friar Peter continued to pursue us, and he almost captured us, but for the intervention of a man named Enoch, a man my father trusted and whom I remembered seeing at our house years ago. Enoch told us it was no coincidence that Friar Peter had come to Camryn. It was the emerald that brought him to our village, and it was the emerald that he was seeking.

"Enoch told me about Friar Peter's powers, and said that I alone in all the world could stop him. Friar Peter would pursue me forever, until one of us was dead. I did not believe Enoch. I escaped to Lyon, and later to Lucca and to Bari, but Friar Peter followed us. You see, Matthew, there was nothing you could have done to save the Jews of Camryn or to save my family. Friar Peter was on a mission to kill all the Jews in Christendom. Indeed, Friar Peter was an agent of Satan, endowed with certain Powers, and there was nothing you could have done to stop him. Before he died, my father perhaps had the power to stop Friar Peter, and thus Friar Peter was determined to kill him and all his family. You are guiltless, Matthew, and you saved my life. You will always be my friend."

Matthew closed his eyes and thought. He opened them again and said, "Thank you, Joseph. I will consider what you said, and I will pray."

Matthew slowly rose and looked around. "Come," he said. "Let us bury Aaron. Then we shall go home."

EPILOGUE

Sixteen years later

Joseph closed the door as the last of his guests departed. He turned to Rachel and asked, "Are they all in bed?"

"Yes," she said. "All four of them."

"Even Benjamin?"

"Even Benjamin."

There was a knock at the door, and Rachel said, "Who could that be at this hour?"

From across the door, a voice said, "It's Matthew. I've come to congratulate you on your son Benjamin's bar-mitzvah."

Joseph threw the door open. The large man in priestly purple garb stood there but made no move to enter. "Have they all left?" he asked. "Is it alright to enter?"

Joseph embraced the priest warmly and said, "Of course, Matthew. You are always welcome here. But you should have come earlier to celebrate with us."

"No," said Matthew as he entered and closed the door behind him. "I did not think it proper for a priest to be present at your celebration. Your friends might be uneasy. So I waited until all had left."

Joseph punched Matthew's shoulder playfully. "That's my thoughtful Matthew, my very foolish friend. All our friends know of our long friendship and would not think you out of place at all."

He motioned to Matthew to sit, and Rachel brought food and drink.

When all three had taken seats, Matthew looked at Joseph and Rachel and said, "It's so good to celebrate with you like this, just the three of us together, like olden days. If only Aaron could have lived to be with us. And to think I almost killed you, Joseph."

"No," said Rachel. "You would not have killed your friend."

Matthew shook his head. "Of course I would have. Peter had convinced me that Joseph was a demon. I no longer considered him my friend. Only my mother's voice, coming to me as I was about to strike, released me from the friar's spell."

Rachel looked deep into Matthew's eyes and said, "Yes, Matthew, I know you believe that, and it has weighed upon your soul these many years. I know otherwise, and I have wanted – tried – to tell you, but you refuse to talk about the subject."

Matthew looked down at the floor. His hand began to move toward Rachel, but he drew it back. In a whisper, he said, "It hurt too much to speak about it. How did I let Friar Peter delude me so? How could I let it happen?"

Joseph put his hand on Matthew's shoulder. "You must not torment yourself any longer over what you think occurred. Sixteen years have passed, and that is long enough. Your assumptions are mistaken, and it is high time the past be put to rest. Will you listen now to Rachel?"

Matthew looked up at Joseph but did not speak immediately. He turned to Rachel and held her gaze. "Yes," he said; "I will."

Rachel said, "I know you, Matthew. I know you better than you think. I know your goodness and the purity of your soul. I know the depth of your friendship for my husband, and I know how you saved his life that terrible day of the massacre in Camryn, when my family, and Joseph's parents, and Joseph's little brother and sister were slaughtered. I know of your quest to find atonement for your father's sins, and even for the sins of all your father's friends. But deep in my heart, I also know that you would not have killed your friend.

"I see you shake your head. You do not believe me, but I know my words are true. You think it was your mother who convinced you; you believe you heard your mother's voice calling to you. Perhaps it was your mother's voice, but it was really your own conscience speaking to you in your mother's voice. Peter had great powers, no doubt bestowed on him by the forces of the Other Side. Do not blame yourself for your failure to resist his power. Peter was a master of control of people's will, a master of deception, a master of men's minds. Yes, he was able to influence your thinking and your reason. But your inner soul remained untouched. In the end, your inner nature conquered, overcoming all. It was your inner soul that spoke to you in your mother's voice. Believe me, Matthew. You could not have killed your friend. You didn't have it in you."

Matthew sat silently, looking from Rachel to Joseph. For a long time, he did not speak, and neither Rachel nor Joseph said another word.

At length, Matthew rose from his seat, bowed slightly toward Rachel, and said, "Thank you, Rachel. My soul is finally at rest." He opened the door and went out into the night.

When Matthew was gone and out of sight, Joseph closed the door. He put his arms around Rachel, held her close, and whispered in her ear, "I, too, thank you, Rachel. Only you could have convinced him. You have done well."

Suddenly, there was a knock at the door.

Rachel said, "Again? Who could that be? Yet another visitor at this late hour?"

""No," said Joseph, going to the door. "It must be Matthew returning. Perhaps he forgot something."

Joseph threw the door open. For a moment, fear gripped him as he looked at the grey-cloaked, hooded figure at the door. Memories of Friar Peter flitted through his consciousness, and he shuddered.

The hooded figure took a step forward and drew his hood back. Only then did Joseph recognize him. He smiled and led the man inside.

"Did you not recognize me?" the man asked. "It has been many years, but I would think you still would know me. My appearance has not changed much, I believe." His green eyes twinkled as he entered the house and took a seat.

"Of course I recognize you, Enoch," Joseph said. "But it has been so long, and I did not think to see you any more again."

"Indeed," said Enoch, "Chateau Blanc was very long ago. The years pass quickly, especially for one such as myself. But there was no need for me to return. You have done very well on your own. And so, I stayed away."

"I do not understand. You still could have come, if only to visit with us awhile and pass the time."

"Yes, I know. That is the way of the world, is it not? But, I think you know, I am not like other men."

"Yes," said Joseph. "You have not aged in all these years. You look the same as you looked then."

"No matter," Enoch said with a wave of his hand. "I have come to wish you well. I have come to congratulate you on Benjamin's bar-mitzvah."

Joseph's face lit up. "We thank you, Enoch, and we are most happy that you came. But, I think, that is not the only reason for your visit. Your words lead me to believe that somehow I have need of you."

Enoch smiled and nodded. "In fact, you do. I have come to give your son my blessing."

"Your blessing?"

"Yes, my blessing. And something else as well."

Just then, Benjamin ran into the room. "I can't sleep," he said.

"Come here," said Enoch. The boy hesitated only for a second, and ran across the room to Enoch.

Enoch put both his hands on the boy's head and said, "Benjamin, may the Lord bless you with His goodness and keep you from harm all the days of your life."

When Enoch removed his hands from the boy's head, Rachel said, "Now go back to bed, Benjamin."

"Can't I stay up a little longer?"

Enoch smiled and said, "Listen to your mother, Benjamin. I think you will be able to sleep now. But we will meet again someday. I promise you."

Benjamin gave his mother a kiss. He waved to Enoch. "Good night," he said, and ran back to his room.

When Benjamin had gone, Enoch rose from his seat and said, "He is a good boy, and again, I congratulate you. But now I, too, must go."

"Wait!" said Joseph. "Didn't you mention that you came for something else besides my son's bar-mitzvah?"

"Yes, I did."

Enoch reached into his robe and extracted a small pouch.

Joseph stared at the pouch. His mouth opened, but he couldn't speak the words he had in mind. His heart began to race as Enoch slowly opened the pouch.

Enoch tipped the pouch, and a green stone dropped into his other palm.

Joseph looked at Enoch questioningly.

"Yes, Joseph. That is your emerald. The same one that I gave you many years ago. Take it. It is yours."

"But," Joseph stammered, "is it really the same emerald that Friar Peter took from me? How could that be? The earth swallowed it with Peter."

"Yes, it did," said Enoch, handing it to Joseph. "But I retrieved it for you."

Enoch opened the front door, and, as he walked out into the night, he said, "Guard it well, Joseph, and give it to your son when it is time."

Joseph ran to the door. He looked outside. The moon was full, and the street was well illuminated in the bright moonlight, but there was nobody in sight.

THE END

HISTORICAL NOTE

Although Friar Peter is a fictional character, many of his speeches are based on documented attitudes of various medieval preachers. During the Middle Ages, anti-Semitism was rampant all over Europe, and the belief that Jews were agents of Satan, or that they were actual demons or offspring of demons, was prevalent. Itinerant preachers often stirred up the feelings of animosity against the Jews, sometimes resulting in pogroms in which all the Jews of a town or city were killed. While the massacre in Camryn is fictional, wholesale massacres of Jews did occur in Norwich, Lynn, and York during the period in question.

Many of the characters in the novel were actual historical figures, including Cardinal Giacinto Bobone (later Pope Celestine III) and his brother Ursus, King Conrad and Archbishop Joscius of Tyre, and all of the cardinals whose names are mentioned at the conclave that elected Cardinal Bobone as pope in 1191. Cencio Savelli, the chamberlain of the Holy See (and who himself later became Pope Honorius III, in the year 1216), is also a historical figure, and I have given his title as *camerarius*, which was prevalent at that time, in preference to the later appellation *camerlengo*. Finally, of the Saracens named in this novel, Saladin, al-Adil, and Baha' al-Din Qaragush (the governor of Acre) were also historical figures.

The siege and the Crusaders' conquest of Acre, and King Richard's subsequent massacre of the inhabitants of Acre, are historical events, as are the sinking of the Saracen supply ship described in Chapter 33, and the release of one mutilated Saracen sailor to report the sinking to the governor of Acre. I have tried to depict those events faithfully.

King Richard's march from Acre to Jaffa commenced on 22 August 1191. The clash with Saladin's forces on 3 September 1191, south of the River of Death, as described in Chapter 39, is a fictional account of a skirmish that occurred in the course of the march. The Battle of Arsuf, which took place on 7 September 1191, is not described in this novel.

The search for the Mark of Satan using a long needle, as described in this novel, was a practice that was used as evidence of sorcery during a somewhat later historical period. Although I know of no evidence that the method was employed during the 12th century, I have taken the liberty of having Friar Peter use it in the course of Sarah's trial for sorcery.

The Kingdom of France during the 12th century occupied only a small portion of what we now call France. Nevertheless, for convenience I use the term "France" to refer to the entire territory that is called France today.

ACKNOWLEDGEMENT

I want to thank my wife Madeline for her advice and encouragement, and in editing the manuscript. This book would not have been written without her. I love her and appreciate her more than I can express in words, and I am most fortunate to spend my life with her.

Made in the USA
Middletown, DE
23 August 2021